About the Author

Faraday Rose lives in Mid Devon where she can usually be found roaming the hills with her two lurchers. She has a background in psychology and is fascinated by people. In both her life and writing, she disregards stereotypes and preconceived ideas, instead delving into the complexities which make us so vulnerably and beautifully human.

This is a work of fiction. Names, characters, businesses, places, events and incidents are either the products of the author's imagination or used in a fictitious manner. Any resemblance to actual persons, living or dead, or actual events is purely coincidental.

THE TIES THAT BIND

FARADAY ROSE

THE TIES THAT BIND

Vanguard Press

VANGUARD PAPERBACK

© Copyright 2023

Faraday Rose

The right of Faraday Rose to be identified as author of this work has been asserted by her in accordance with the Copyright, Designs and Patents Act 1988.

All Rights Reserved

No reproduction, copy or transmission of this publication may be made without written permission.
No paragraph of this publication may be reproduced, copied or transmitted save with the written permission of the publisher, or in accordance with the provisions of the Copyright Act 1956 (as amended).

Any person who commits any unauthorised act in relation to this publication may be liable to criminal prosecution and civil claims for damages.

A CIP catalogue record for this title is available from the British Library.

ISBN 978 1 80016 456 7

Vanguard Press is an imprint of
Pegasus Elliot Mackenzie Publishers Ltd.
www.pegasuspublishers.com

First Published in 2023

Vanguard Press
Sheraton House Castle Park
Cambridge England

Printed & Bound in Great Britain

Dedication

This is for you; you know who you are. Thank you for believing in me.

Part I
Kate

"Unless we learn to know ourselves
We run the danger of destroying ourselves."
   Ja A. Jahannes

One

The early morning sun was making its watery way through the kitchen window, passing through the branches of the blackthorn tree and casting a dappled light over the kitchen table. The tree was ripe with unpicked sloes, and it tapped its spindly fingers on the pane as though calling for attention. It had been one of those glorious autumn weekends where sunshine was all the more enjoyable because it was unexpected, like finding a bank note in an old pair of jeans always seems twice as valuable. But now it was Monday, Kate's least favourite day. Oliver was away with work again which meant she had to get the kids to school by eight in order to make her first appointment. Glancing at the time at the bottom of her screen she hit send on another email. *Shit.* It was seven forty-five and that wretched boy was still nowhere to be seen.

'Jack! If you don't get down here now, we're leaving without you,' Kate yelled up the stairs for what she vowed was the final time that morning. Returning to the kitchen she found a small figure waiting, a duffle coat buttoned to her chin, a piece of overdone toast clamped in her hand. Goodness knows how long she'd been standing that way. *She seems to have grown up without me,* Kate thought with a guilty pang.

'Do you have your ballet shoes, Lucy?' she asked, re-establishing her parental role as she closed down her laptop.

'It's maths club tonight, Mum, ballet's on Thursdays.' Lucy sighed in that way which made her seem alarmingly like a teenager already. 'Anyway, you said you'd pick me up straight from school tonight because we're going to Nando's for Jack's birthday, re-mem-ber?'

Kate watched Lucy roll her eyes as she felt her chest tighten; she'd completely forgotten about the arrangements for that evening when she'd booked her last appointment yesterday. *Oliver will just have to step up,* she thought grimly, whilst noting that this tightness in her chest, so disproportionate to the situation at hand, was occurring more frequently of late.

'Jack! For heaven's…' She left the yell unfinished as Jack appeared around the door.

'Yeah, happy birthday to me,' he grumbled as he took the cold piece of toast from beside the toaster and shrugged himself, one-armed, into his jacket. Kate looked at him, feeling her heart expand and her anger melt. Even on these grumpiest of days she still loved him so much it hurt. She stood on tiptoe to ruffle his deep red hair, the colour of autumn bracken and so different to the rest of the family. He flinched away from her in a way he never once would have, and her softened heart trembled in her tightening chest.

'Yes, happy birthday to you,' she said, laughing it off and giving him an elbow in the side. 'And if you'd bothered to get up, we could have had more of a celebration before school.'

'College, Mum, I'm at college now.' Jack remained stony and Kate felt her jaw clench.

'Whatever. You'll have to open your cards and things tonight; we have to leave *now*.' Making a mental note to text Oliver and insist he or his mum collect Lucy from school, Kate opened the front door, pressing the key fob of her Range Rover Sport parked across the driveway. She cast a fleeting glance at the envelope propped beside the microwave, set apart from the other cards and presents, and feeling a flutter of anxiety, she closed the door.

***

It was lunchtime. In fact, even that was pushing it at eleven fifty. Kate should have been on the way to her next appointment but had found herself drawn inexorably back to her front door, back to her kitchen, where she now stood gazing at the envelope on the worktop.

Her intention that morning had been to forget about the thing, but she'd succumbed once again to fears she felt powerless to quell. Her mother's voice haunted her with its dire warnings, '*This is a tricky time, Kate, don't let your guard down now. Kids Jack's age feel compelled to go digging around in the past and the last thing he needs at the moment is Annie and her wacky ideas, not with university on the doorstep. You have to be on top of it, Kate!*'

She picked up the card and held it in her cold hands. The scrawl looked untidy to her, like a child's, like the writer had never grown up properly and learnt how an adult might address a letter. The writing looked uncannily like Jack's, the Gs were the same. She gazed around the very modern, very clean kitchen and almost unconsciously flipped the envelope over to assess her mode of entry.

This was not the first letter or card or whatever to arrive, many had come over the years. She hadn't opened them all. They arrived at different times, under different circumstances and sometimes she was able to overcome the compulsion to check the contents, at others she was just as likely to destroy the whole bloody thing without even opening it. Some days, like today, she had a vague feeling that she was playing an old script, that this fear which plagued her was not her own; it felt like a parasite which had grown in her since childhood, fed and fondled by her mother, and more latterly, her desperate need to control the happenings around her. She stared about the kitchen again, as though searching for inspiration.

In her twenties she'd dreamt of having a kitchen like this: the island with the top-of-the-range Neff hob, the copper-bottomed pans hanging from the ceiling, the super-stylish brushed aluminium backsplash and black marble worktops, all set off by strategically placed spotlights. The family table cluttered with Lucy's drawings and craftwork; the American-style fridge complete with ice maker and water cooler; the modern wall art on stretched canvas. She'd worked so hard for this, it had the form of everything she'd hoped for and yet, in the pit of her stomach, she feared it lacked the substance. All this passed through her mind as she held the glued edge of the envelope over the quick-boil kettle and gently peeled it open.

It was a birthday card (of course) *Happy 18th to Someone Special*. She was hit with the usual gut punch of emotion which spread upwards to her chest and into her throat, finally leaving her cold. She was livid that Jack could be called *someone special* by the one who'd neglected him so. Why couldn't Annie just leave them alone? Why did she have to make things difficult? But at the same time was the nagging feeling that something else was lurking. Annie always had a way of making Kate doubt herself, like *she* was the one who'd got it wrong. It made her furious.

There wasn't much written in the card; a date scrawled in the top corner, *3rd October 2015*, then, *Dearest Jack, with loads of love, on your special day and always, Annie.* Kate was irritated by its blandness, yet the card would almost certainly be confiscated had it contained any hint of what she felt to be *emotional blackmail*. There was money; she counted it onto the shiny worktop. One hundred pounds. Nothing really, not when compared with what Jack would receive from the rest of the family. But enough for him to have to make contact, enough for Annie to be in his mind, if only for a moment, and those moments were rare nowadays.

Kate would never directly forbid Jack to contact his *biological mother*, as they called her. Nor had she explicitly refused Annie access to him, but she'd made it difficult and her displeasure at any burgeoning relationship had been obvious, even when she was doing her very best to conceal it, and she knew with Jack this was enough; she knew he valued her opinion and yearned for her approval more than anything else in the world. God how she'd tried not to abuse this privilege, yet she knew, on the dark days, on the days her wall of anger let her down, that she was no stranger to the art of emotional blackmail. If it wasn't okay with her then it wasn't okay with Jack. The guilty-sick feeling began to creep back in, and she quickly shuffled the card and notes into the envelope and placed it with the others.

***

The car seemed to take itself to her next appointment. Kate no longer noticed the cheerful sunlight playing on the dashboard and warming her forearms or the splendour of the trees in their autumn best. Her head was full of memories and the usual irritation that Annie had the power to penetrate her life and turn her day topsy-turvy, even now, all these years on. She gripped the steering wheel a little tighter and rolled the dial with her thumb causing Radio 2 to blare out more loudly, trying to drown out her thoughts. But her mind was like a filing cabinet which shot open against her will, an invisible hand selecting a file from the hundreds to choose from. This one was marked *Baby Jack, January 1997*. The memory felt like yesterday, its bitterness twisting her pretty face.

Annie had been living in Tiverton at the time, a rather grubby little town, Kate remembered thinking. There was no parking, so Kate had to leave the car several streets away and carry an enormous bundle of disposable nappies under one arm and a heavy Tesco carrier bag crammed with jars of baby food, wet wipes and nappy cream, in the other. The bag banged painfully against her knee and caused her cold fingers to throb as she made her way along the street. She'd felt guilty that it was a full three months since Annie and Jack had left hospital and this was her first visit. But it couldn't be helped, work had been nightmarishly busy, and weeks had simply run into each other, then it had been Christmas with all its attendant obligations.

Just as she thought her frozen fingers might drop off, she saw she'd arrived at number 12. It wasn't as bad as she'd anticipated; there was a bit of litter outside, but the street looked quite nice, and Annie had said there was a park nearby. Kate looked up at the red-brick terrace, there were four steps leading to the front door and a rather mangled looking black railing ran from top to bottom. The door was black, the paint was peeling, as was the paint around the windowsills. There was a blanket over the downstairs window, serving as a curtain, and a steady thump of bass came from within.

She rang buzzer 'A' and couldn't help her intake of breath when a half-naked man of about her age opened the door and gazed at her, bleary eyed. He had a crudely drawn tattoo of a broken heart on his lean, hairless chest. At first, she thought he was tanned but then decided he looked slightly grubby and more boy than man. He had a mop of very straight, dark blond hair which fell into his sleepy eyes. Kate concluded he was either mad or high to be wearing so little in the icy weather then, fearing her face must betray her distaste, said hastily, 'Oh, I'm sorry, I thought I pressed buzzer A.' She felt herself blush as she rearranged her grip on the nappies.

'You did.' He had a surprisingly soft and well-spoken voice. 'Annie's not able to come to the door. Come in,' he said, stepping back to admit her. The nappies began to slide out from under Kate's arm and he made a grab for them, smiling reassuringly. He had a full set of very white teeth. *Was this Annie's latest acquisition* Kate wondered anxiously. She knew it couldn't be Jack's father who was in prison for something drug-related. She shuddered as she thought of the poor baby within. The man-boy had lifted the package onto his head and now resembled a bizarre Mowgli caricature as he turned his tattooed back to her and sauntered down the dimly lit passage in his sawn-off jeans.

'This way,' he called in his public-schoolboy's voice.

There were letters, flyers and at least three Thomson directories littering the floor of the entrance. Kate navigated these and followed cautiously. There was a door to her left; this must belong to the blanketed-window flat; the pounding beat was a little louder from this side. To her right, a staircase went up to the flats above, the banister was of dark wood with peeling varnish. The carpet was an ill-defined mishmash of red, brown and black and her shoes made a little *shlup* each time she peeled them off the slightly sticky surface. There was an odd, musty, sweet smell in the thick air along with what Kate recognised to be the pungent tang of marijuana.

Mowgli kicked the door twice with his dirty, bare foot. *Probably with his toenail* Kate thought with a little shudder. The door was opened by another stranger, this one a woman, older than Kate, with dirty blonde hair and a hand-rolled cigarette in the corner of her mouth. She squinted against the smoke and nodded to Kate who hesitated, feeling outnumbered and overwhelmed.

'Comin' then?' the woman asked, having stepped back to let Mowgli and his cargo through.

Kate pulled herself together and smiled at the woman. 'Sorry, I wasn't expecting there to be so many people here!' she managed, catching herself wiping her feet and feeling ridiculous as she entered the uncarpeted hallway.

'Annie's in the kitchen, she won't be a mo,' said the blonde. 'I'm Sue. I'm a friend of Annie's. Come in the front room, little Jack's in 'ere.' She smiled a crinkly grin and beckoned Kate deeper into the flat, opening a door to a much lighter room with two large windows overlooking a steep bank of grass with more houses beyond. Kate crossed the threshold. There was a dirty, fawn-coloured carpet, overlapping in places, and an assortment of furniture: a crumbling sofa, chair and coffee table, all marked with cigarette burns, and a teak-coloured bookcase overflowing with books.

'And 'ere's little Jacky,' Sue crooned as she stooped to the side of the sofa, to a Moses basket Kate hadn't noticed before, and scooped the baby into her arms.

Kate couldn't get herself together at all. Who was this woman? Where was Annie and why wasn't she with Jack? Were this woman's hands even clean?

'Er… should you really be smoking around him?' Kate managed to find her voice. 'Sorry to sound like a nag,' she added with forced chuckle.

'Oh gawd, no, of course I shouldn't.' Sue responded by thrusting the baby in Kate's direction, who promptly dropped her carrier bag and took Jack into her arms.

'I wasn't smokin' with him before,' Sue said defensively, stubbing out the cigarette in the ashtray on the coffee table. 'He was sleeping in his basket, and I was smoking out the window, but I came out and opened the door dint I?' She smiled again, showing missing bottom teeth. 'Ee's a lovely fing innee?'

Kate looked down at the little form in her arms, already with a thick shock of dark red hair and the palest face, devoid of any kind of imperfection.

'Yes, he is,' she said as she found herself smiling warmly back.

'Come an' sit down look.' Sue gestured into the room. The chair looked moderately cleaner and firmer than the sofa, so Kate headed in that direction.

'Oop, wait!' Sue exclaimed and lurched over to pull a supersized beer can from down the side of the cushion. 'Don't want that shite all over yer jeans.' She looked around for a new home for the sticky can and decided on the coffee table, putting it down awkwardly so that it fell and dribbled the last of its contents onto the stained wood, then she shoved her hands deep into her pockets and sat on the sofa, looking rather self-conscious.

Kate managed another smile and perched on the edge of the chair, crooning to Jack and running her fingers gently through his hair. He was awake now and observing her with his alert blue eyes, eyes which would one day turn gold-green. He made grabbing motions towards her with his chubby fists and gurgled contentedly. Kate was enchanted.

'He's so big, I can't believe it!'

'Innee just! Has Annie up at all hours for his feeds.' Sue was rolling another cigarette and leaning against the wall by the open window. The yellowing net curtain had been tied in a knot.

'She's started him on formula now mind, so he's sleeping longer, ha and shittin' more!' Sue cackled and coughed as she lit the cigarette, blowing the smoke fastidiously out of the window. Kate swallowed down her grimace. She wished Sue wouldn't smoke at all but didn't like to belabour the point.

'Where *is* Annie?' she asked instead.

'Oh, just in the kitchen, she'll be out in a mo; she knew you was comin, frettin' she was.'

'Well, can't I just go and see her?' Kate asked, getting up.

'Er... best not. She asked me to tell you to wait in here.'

'But why?' Kate asked, starting to feel concerned. 'Is she okay? Who's that man? Is he, her boyfriend? Are they arguing or something?'

Annie's relationships were always turbulent.

But Sue laughed. 'Gav? Ha! Gav's bent as a nine-bob note. No, he's... 'elping her is all.'

Sue looked shifty.

'Well, I'm sorry but I'm going to see,' Kate said, putting Jack up to her shoulder as she crossed the room. Sue flapped behind her, pausing to put out her cigarette and giving Kate time to make it into the hall. She opened the first door she came to, which swung back to reveal a dark bedroom with no windows, just a vent high on the wall letting in a trickle of light, flecked with dancing dust particles. There was a discoloured mattress on the floor along with a crumpled duvet, and a cot in the corner with a mobile of winged horses and discs which caught the light from the open door. The walls were a pale, dirty blue, the ceiling nicotine yellow. It was a drab and soulless room and Kate felt another wave of anguish for the little child in her arms.

'It's this one,' Sue's voice broke through as she tapped gently on the next door. 'Annie?' Silence. 'Annie? I've got Kate 'ere. She wants to come in.'

'No, no! Go away Sue! I can't see her yet!' came Annie's cry from within. 'Take Jack to the park or something.'

Sue looked awkwardly back at Kate, 'Er... okay, we'll do that then.'

She held both palms skywards and shrugged as though there was nothing else for it, but Kate had had enough. She moved past Sue, who didn't attempt to stop her, and opened the door.

The room was lighter than she'd expected, again having a large window looking out onto the grassy bank. There was a family sized table pushed against the far wall and fitted units with dark wooden doors lined the other side of the room. The cream-and-brown chequered lino was dirty looking, like everything else.

Annie sat on the floor in the middle of the room wearing nothing but greying pants and bra; she was hugging her scrawny legs to her chest with her skinny, blotchy arms. Her skin looked as grey as her underwear. A Calor gas heater was close beside her, blaring its three bars in her direction and giving that side of her body a weird orange tinge. Her red hair looked greasy and lank and was held in an untidy knot by a large butterfly grip. She turned her freckled, elfin face to Kate who moved, trancelike into the room.

'Oh, Kate, Kate, please just give me one more minute, we're almost there!' she begged in a voice that sounded half excited, half fearful.

On closer inspection Kate could see Annie's feet were streaked with blood. There was blood on the floor around her; her thighs were spotted with blood and even the mounds of her small breasts appeared to have pinpricks of red and looked patchy and sore. Gav was hovering uncertainly with a syringe of bright mahogany liquid in this hand, his half-naked appearance finally explained by the sweltering heat of the room.

'What the fuck are you doing to her?' Kate cried aghast, torn between rushing to Annie's aid and shielding Jack from this horror.

'I didn't do this!' Gav said indignantly. 'She was like this when I got here, just before you did. I was about to sort her out when *you* arrived,' he added in a tone that suggested it was somehow Kate's fault.

'Please Kate.' Annie spoke again. 'Please just wait and I'll explain everything.' She turned to Gav. 'Just get on with it, please.'

Kate watched in stunned silence as Gav gripped the very top of Annie's arm and twisted slightly.

'You have a whopping vein right up here, you see?' he said in his honey voice. 'It's easy on you because you're so skinny.' He inserted the needle and drew back to produce a flush of deep red blood. To Kate it was like watching one of those episodes of *Casualty*, where she felt she really should look away from some gruesome surgical procedure but found her eyes were glued to the screen. Gav had now compressed the plunger and emptied the vial's contents into Annie's arm.

'Oh, thank you, thank you!' Annie was hugging him and clambering to her feet. 'There's gear on the table, just help yourself; you too, Sue,' she added to her friend who'd been hovering uncertainly by the door. 'Oh Kate! What a nightmare. Where's my baby?' And she took Jack into her bloody arms and cradled him there, then held him away from her body so she could look at him. Her face was a golden glow of love and Jack was wriggling ecstatically, his little arms and legs waving as he chattered and laughed and crowed with delight. Kate felt stunned, unable to process the disturbing parody playing out before her. Gav was now sitting at the kitchen table holding a lighter beneath a metal spoon. Sue was moving across the bloodied floor to join him.

'I've got myself in such a muddle,' Annie said finally. 'Here, hold him whilst I put some clothes on. Let's go into the lounge.'

She handed Jack to Kate. He was pressing his fist into his dribbly mouth and smiling goofily at her. Annie scooped jeans and a jumper from the floor, pulled the jumper over her thin frame and hopped into her jeans as she made her way to the lounge. Kate followed.

'Oh Kate, what a nightmare—'

'I thought you were clean?' Kate cut her off. 'Were you using whilst you were pregnant?'

'Of course not! How could you even think that?' Annie said in a wounded tone that utterly belied the reality of a few moments ago. She reached to take Jack back, but Kate found she didn't want to let go.

'Let me have him just a little longer,' she said reasonably. 'It's the first time I've seen him since he was born.' She bounced a delighted Jack on her knee. 'So, what the hell happened?'

'I just couldn't cope Kate; it was too hard.' Annie was sitting on the arm of the sofa, picking at the frayed strands of material, not meeting Kate's eyes.

'I came off my methadone 'script so I would be clean when I had him, so he wouldn't be addicted y'know? And I thought I'd be fine. I was fine, for ages!' She looked up with pleading eyes, 'But it was really hard Kate. We came back here, and the weather was awful, we couldn't go anywhere, I was lonely. The only people I know take drugs. They're good people!' Annie cut Kate off before she could interrupt. 'They've really helped me. Sue's brilliant with babies. No one made me use; I asked for it. I just couldn't get my head straight. I thought it would help…'

Annie looked desolate now; she desisted with the strands on the sofa and got up to pace the room. 'Before I knew it I was hooked again.' She stared out the window with a faraway look in her eyes. 'And then what could I do? I have to be well to look after him.' Her eyes softened as she looked at Jack. 'I keep trying to stop but then I get ill and cave in and use again. There's just never a good day to get clean with a baby to look after,' she said earnestly, the irony of the statement lost on her.

'You could have asked for help, Annie.' Kate finally found her voice. 'You're not alone in this. It's nonsense that the only people you know take drugs. You've got me. You've got those lovely people from the church you spent Christmas with, who got you your furniture—'

'Look I know I've fucked up, Kate, all right? Don't you think I know?' Annie cut in, with a spark of temper. 'I just couldn't believe it today, that you were coming and I'm like this again. And then I couldn't get a hit, butchering myself like that trying to get a vein.' She pulled her sleeves back revealing bloody streaks down both arms.

'I was so ill, and I can't take care of Jack when I'm like that. It's all a disaster.'

Annie was crying now; she looked wretched.

'Okay. Okay. We'll work it out,' Kate said consolingly, coming to stand at the window with Jack, who'd suddenly gone very quiet. 'Don't let Jack see you like this; they pick up on everything, you know.'

Annie took a shuddering breath and sniffed hard. 'I know,' she said, taking the baby to her; Kate didn't resist.

'So, can you get back on your script then?' Kate took a deep breath, realising she'd been holding it. 'At least to stop this madness. You must know you can't have this going on with Jack in the flat, Annie.' They stood side by side, looking out the window, Annie holding Jack so he could see too. It had started to rain, and the baby made grasping movements towards the rivulets of rainwater as they streamed down the window like tears.

'Raining again,' Annie sighed, closing the window and coming to sit on the sofa. Kate followed her and sat in the chair, leaning towards her, elbows on knees. She could see the effects of the heroin in Annie's glassy, hazel eyes, her pupils, infinitesimal pricks.

'I don't want to go back to the drugs project Kate, I'm worried they'll take Jack away.' She hugged the baby closer to her. 'I need to get clean, but I can't do it here. I've tried. Sue's tried to help but it's just too hard. I was wondering—' She gave that pleading look again. '—I was wondering if we could come and stay with you for a week or two?'

Two

The blast of a car horn ripped Kate's mind back to the present as a gesticulating white van driver undertook her in the inside lane. With a jolt she checked the satnav fearing she'd passed her exit as she daydreamed. *Waking nightmare more like,* she thought grimly as she gripped the wheel a little tighter and put her foot down to overtake a car up ahead.

She could remember that flat so vividly, she'd been there several times over the following couple of years, met its various inhabitants, seen it cleaned up and decorated, looking almost homely, then watched it decline again, just like Annie, as she inevitably lost her hold on things once more. Kate made an involuntary, 'huh', as she recalled her optimism when Annie had asked if she could stay. The whole thing had been a complete disaster from start to finish.

First, she'd had to convince Oliver that it was a good idea to let Annie come and detox in their home, then she'd taken ten days off work at a critical time in her career — Annie had assured her it wouldn't take longer than that.

They arrived on a rainy Sunday morning, Jack in his Moses basket, which surely couldn't have been a legal way to transport him in the battered green Volvo which brought them, driven by another of Annie's *friends*.

'I couldn't find his car seat,' Annie had mumbled evasively.

Along with the Moses basket she'd brought a rickety old pram and around half a dozen carrier bags overflowing with clothes, toys and official-looking letters. All this had been left on the pavement by the driver of the decrepit vehicle, a balding, greasy looking man of indeterminable age, who nodded and grunted and gave Annie a swift hug before chugging away in a haze of acrid exhaust fumes.

Together Annie and Oliver took everything up to the back bedroom whilst Kate occupied Jack and watched from the kitchen window. When Kate went up to the room a short while later it was obvious, by the dank, stale smell that was already creeping down the landing, that all of Annie and Jack's clothes, along with Jack's blankets and cloth toys, would need to be washed. Kate gritted her teeth and set about the task whilst Annie and Oliver played with Jack on the sofa. It hadn't taken Jack long to win over Ollie, Kate had thought fondly and loaded the washer with less umbrage.

On the first night, Annie got drunk on the strong white cider she'd brought with her. When Kate questioned her about it, Annie assured her it was the best way for her to get through the withdrawals. The sitting room now stank like a brewery as Jack gurgled contentedly on his playmat. Oliver had walked out, shaking his head and saying he was getting an early night. Later Kate had insisted on carrying Jack up the stairs lest Annie fall and injure them both.

At around four a.m., the wailing started. Kate couldn't be sure who wailed first, Annie or Jack, but pretty soon it was a cacophony of Jack's cries and Annie's moans. Jumping up, Kate had pulled on a robe and cast a quick glance at Oliver, seeking reassurance, only to see him roll over and put a pillow over his head in one irritable motion. On entering Annie's room, she found Jack still in his Moses basket, yelling, and Annie on the bed, the pillows and duvet strewn every which way. Annie was curled in a foetal position, facing the wall, her bony spine and long limbs giving her the look of an emaciated whippet as she gave another low moan.

Kate scooped the baby into her arms, and he ceased crying immediately.

'Annie!' she whispered urgently then wondered why she was whispering. Annie rolled over and clutched the mangled duvet closer to herself. She was wearing an oversized Snoopy tee shirt and looked about twelve.

'What's going on? Why are you moaning like that?' Kate could hear the short-tempered edge to her voice and added kindly, 'It's just, I think you're frightening Jack.' She bounced the baby a little in her arms and he stuck his fist in his mouth.

'He needs a feed. Oh, oh, oh!' Annie kicked out violently at the duvet and writhed around, causing Kate to step back in alarm.

'I can't do it Kate, I can't, I feel so fucking ill!'

'What, withdrawals? Already? Or is it all that cider?' Kate moved Jack to her hip and stooped to put the duvet back on the bed with her free hand. He was looking adorable in Peter Rabbit pyjamas and made a grab for a lock of her hair as she leant forwards.

She gently freed it from his grasp, as Annie spat at her. 'No, it's not the fucking cider. I'm sick. I'm rattling. I've had no gear since yesterday morning, have I? Oh!' She pulled the duvet up to her chin. 'I'm sorry, Kate, I'm sorry, but I only drank the cider to give myself more time. But it's full on now, it's full on.' She kicked out with her legs again. 'I can't be near him when I'm like this, Kate, I can't! Please, please, take him away!' Annie had rolled back to the wall and sobbed. Jack began to cry again.

'Okay, okay. I'll feed him and take him in with us.' Kate grabbed the handles of the Moses basket and began to back out of the room. 'Is there anything you need? What can I do for you?'

'Just go Kate, please just go,' Annie said to the wall.

'Okay. You have a bucket, loo roll, water, look? Annie?' Annie glanced over her shoulder and Kate nodded towards the jug of water and plastic beaker she had left when they came up to bed, anticipating Annie waking furry mouthed and hung-over. Annie said nothing and rolled back towards the wall.

'Right. Right. I'll just go then.'

Kate backed out of the door and pushed it closed with her free hip. Jack gazed up at her, he'd stopped crying now. After dropping the Moses basket outside her and Oliver's room she took him downstairs and prepared his bottle. It felt strangely familiar despite it being the first night feed of her life. She took baby and bottle back upstairs where it was warmer. Oliver no longer had his head under the pillow, he was lying on his back with his hands beneath his head, eyes open. He looked at her as she came in.

'Is this it for the next fortnight then?' he'd asked grumpily, propping himself up on his elbows, not trying to keep his voice down.

'Shh!' Kate moved some clothes from the bedside chair and sat back, leaning Jack against her as he mouthed enthusiastically at the teat of the bottle. 'I think the first three days are the worst. We did agree, Ollie. And anyway, it's not that much earlier than if I had an early start for work.' She looked down fondly at Jack and tilted the bottle a little higher.

'Yeah, and we just love those mornings too, don't we?' Oliver grumbled. Another wail sounded from down the hall and Oliver huffed and flumped over again, punching his pillow into a more comfortable shape and covering his head with his arm.

Kate sat quietly with Jack until he finished his bottle then put him to her shoulder to wind him. There was no getting away from it, this just felt *right*. She'd never thought of herself as maternal, and she wasn't quite sure if that's what this was. It was more specific to *this* little baby, to Jack, like it was her job to make sure he was all right, to protect him, like this was what she was always supposed to do but she'd only just remembered. He'd fallen asleep on her shoulder, and she laid him gently in the basket. 'We really should get a cot for him, just in case…' she said, to no one in particular.

***

The next three days had been hell on earth. Annie turned into some kind of creature that Kate had never met before. Spitting and snarling and swearing when anyone came near her. Pacing the floors at night, slamming doors and crashing about, running baths at three a.m. and switching on lights, raiding the drinks cabinet and throwing up all over the landing. Jack was sleeping in Kate and Oliver's room, but all the noise couldn't help but wake him and his wailing joined Annie's, promising to drive them all insane. Night after night found Kate trying to mollify Oliver, calm Annie and soothe baby Jack back to sleep.

Annie would have nothing to do with the baby, day or night, and flew into a fury when Kate suggested it. 'Can't you fucking understand? I can't be with him when I'm like this!' she'd screamed as Kate had tried again to bring the baby to her. 'It just confuses him! He's used to me cuddling him, loving him, I can't be *near* him! It's better he doesn't see me at all. Please. Please…' and she would dissolve into sobs. In calmer moments, she would apologise profusely and lament what a truly awful human being she was. Oliver left for work each morning grumbling about living in a madhouse.

Almost a week in and things began to settle down. Annie finally felt able to be around Jack and she, Kate and the baby were at the kitchen table eating pastries for breakfast (Annie had mentioned she had a penchant the night before, and as Annie hadn't eaten for a week, Kate had rushed out to the supermarket and found the tubes of semi-baked dough, ready for the morning). Now Annie sat rolling bits of pain aux raisin in her cracked fingers, her fingernails bitten to the quicks. Jack was cooing contentedly on her knee, bashing his little hands on the table, mesmerised by the dancing shadows of the blackthorn tree in the weak January sunlight.

'This,' Annie popped another ball of dough into her mouth, 'is the best breakfast I've ever had! You're such a star Kate.' She'd put a hand over Kate's and looked in her eyes with genuine admiration and gratitude, 'Thank you so, so much for doing this. I'm sorry I've been such a royal bitch.'

'It's nothing. It's fine.' Kate moved her hand and stood up. She felt tired and scratchy but most of all she felt agitated by the way Annie had so fluidly resumed care for Jack and how happy and relaxed the baby was in his mother's arms.

'I need to go into town today,' she said, flicking the kettle on. 'Why don't I take Jack with me so you can get some rest now you're feeling better?'

'Oh no, I couldn't possibly let him out of my sight now!' Annie had said, lifting Jack up to blow a raspberry on his cotton-clad tummy as the baby laughed delightedly. 'Not when I can finally hug him and squeeze him and gobble him all up,' she added to shrieks and cries of glee.

'Right,' Kate said, feeling irked and not really knowing why. 'Well, he'll need a change, why don't I do that before I go?' She put a mug of tea in front of Annie and made to take Jack.

'Oh no, it's fine Kate, honestly. I'll take him up now. I was thinking we might have a bath.'

'Is that safe?'

'Of course it is! Look, Kate, I'm so grateful, I can't tell you how grateful I am but I'm fine now, honest.' Annie had stood, resting Jack on her hip, Kate reached out and offered him her finger. 'I just want to make up for the time I missed out on. Another day or so and we'll be out of your hair, ha! You can have your life back and I bet Oliver will be pleased.'

She disappeared out of the room leaving Kate standing at the table, her finger still held out where Jack had been clasping it.

Kate had spent several hours in town; she sat in a café and made a call to her friend Sally, with whom she'd been firm friends since college. Sally sympathised, especially about having a *raving loony* in the house as she put it, but Kate found she couldn't quite articulate her feelings about Jack, and so skirted around the troubling thought she'd had, that things were better when Annie was shut away in the back room. She'd rung off feeling unresolved and instead wandered around the shops, lost in thoughts which didn't go anywhere and haemorrhaging her bank balance in Gap and Mothercare.

When she got back that evening she found Oliver, Annie and Jack in the living room and the smell of something good cooking in the kitchen.

'I went to the shops too,' Annie had said in explanation. 'I thought the least I could do was cook you guys a meal for putting up with us.' She was sitting on the floor with Jack lying on his back beside her and she reached over to jiggle his tummy.

'Jack's been no problem,' Kate said, coming into the room and putting a brightly coloured teething ring, one of her many purchases, into Jack's grasping hands.

'Ha, but I have,' Annie had said, without heat, as she got to her feet. 'I know I have, I'm sorry, but it's all over now.'

She kissed Kate on the cheek as she went past her and into the kitchen. Kate thought she had an odd look about her. Torn between seeing Jack and checking up on Annie she'd scooped the baby up and followed Annie into the kitchen. Annie had her back to her as she stirred a pot on the stove.

'Annie, look at me,' Kate said

'Mmmm, coconut curry, my absolute favourite!' Annie had said as she turned around, licking the spoon. The light wasn't great in the kitchen, it was five p.m. and almost dark outside but Kate could swear that Annie's eyes were lit up on more than good spirits.

'Have you taken something?' Kate asked in disbelief, moving in closer, jiggling Jack on her hip.

'What?' Annie sounded genuinely surprised. 'What?' She faltered a little under Kate's scrutiny. 'Of course not, no.' She turned back to the oven and busied herself putting the lid back on the pot.

'Annie...' Kate put her hand on Annie's shoulder and made to turn her around, but Annie wheeled about first.

'Just fuck off Kate, all right? Fuck off. Following me around, checking up on me, accusing me. I just wanted to make a nice meal for you to say thank you and you have to go and spoil it!'

'Annie...' But Annie had taken Jack and stalked out of the room. Kate heard her heading upstairs.

The next day Kate began to doubt herself; true Annie's eyes just didn't look right but in other respects she was being perfectly lovely, helping around the house and taking care of all of Jack's needs. On the third day after the argument, the ninth of Annie's stay, Oliver was asking when exactly she was going home. Kate was torn, she'd taken the rest of the week off and didn't want to say goodbye to Jack just yet, but something told her things hadn't gone to plan. The following night the wailing started again.

'Oh Kate, what have I done? I just wanted to take the edge off. I thought it would be okay!'

Annie was writhing and kicking out again. Jack was to be taken from her room; she couldn't bear to be near him.

'This stops now,' Oliver had said the moment Kate came in with the baby. 'She goes home tomorrow. I can't take any more of this, neither can you. If you want to do something for Jack, call social services.'

So the following day, Annie had left. She hadn't protested; she couldn't get away fast enough. She'd phoned her greasy Volvo driver and stuffed her and

Jack's things back into carrier bags. Kate felt stricken, exhausted, she suspected that Annie needed more drugs, and this was all she was thinking about. It had been such a waste of time.

'Here.' 'She handed Annie a new car seat as Annie went to lay Jack in the basket. 'It's safer.' It all felt so surreal.

'Thanks. Thanks for everything.'

And they were gone.

Kate didn't call social services, not on that occasion. Three weeks later Annie called to say she was back on a methadone 'script and a fortnight after that they met in the park near Annie's flat. Annie looked a little better, her hair was clean, and her gold-green eyes were brighter. Jack looked the picture of health. They'd joined a mother and baby group, Annie said, and were making new friends. It always amazed Kate how quickly Annie seemed to pull it together, and then just as quickly tear it all down again.

When the weather got worse, they met in cafes or Annie's flat, and in the summer, they fed the ducks on the canal and ate cake at the tearooms. It was never certain how Annie would be or whether she would turn up at all, but she always seemed to hold it together by the very edges, until the day when Kate finally persuaded her to let go and Jack moved in for good.

Kate allowed herself a moment's fantasy that that had been the end of it, that they never heard from Annie again and they lived happily ever after. She sighed.

She didn't see the queued traffic until it was too late. Though she stamped on the pedal with such force a lesser vehicle would have skewed, she smashed into the back of the dirty Luton lorry, burying the nose of the Range Rover into the concertina doors before being punched in the face by the airbag.

Three

'I think she's waking up.'

'Talk quietly Jack! We should let her sleep.'

Kate opened her eyes, they felt dry and scratchy, like someone had rubbed sand in them while she slept. She had a vague recollection of an ambulance and a noisy emergency room, of being moved somewhere quieter and the children arriving, then she must have dozed off. Everything looked painfully white and bright. She tried to move her head and found she couldn't. Panicking she tried again and realised she had a brace about her neck. Then she lurched sideways, and she threw up. Lucy snatched up a cardboard petri dish and caught a little of the yellow bile whilst the rest splattered the crisp white sheets and floor. It was then that Kate noticed Oliver as he stepped in from the corner he'd been occupying, holding a wodge of paper towels.

'Just lie back,' he said quietly, stooping to mop up the metallic smelling liquid. 'You've jarred yourself badly.'

No kidding, Kate thought as she gingerly felt her face. 'Water. Please.' She smiled weakly at Lucy who tried to offer her little sips from a beaker. 'I think I can manage that, hun.'

'We were so worried!' Lucy said fervently as she relinquished the cup, 'When you didn't pick me up from school, I thought you'd forgotten again.'

Kate felt a stab of irritation and winced at more than her headache.

Lucy just shrugged. 'Then Daddy arrived and said you'd had an accident. Were you on your phone again?' Lucy took the beaker and felt Kate's forehead in an absurdly grown-up gesture.

'Poor Jack missed out on Nando's, not that it matters of course.' She dampened a paper towel and attempted to apply it to Kate's brow.

Another little jibe. How can she be so like my mother and not yet ten years old? Kate made a grab for the paper towel, the sudden movement feeling like hot knives to the back of her head.

'I've forgotten to collect you once, Lucy, *once in your whole life*,' she muttered defensively, sitting a little more upright, though it made her want to vomit again, 'and, for your information, there was a tailback; I can't have been the only person to crash.'

'Actually, you were.' Oliver spoke again quietly. 'Unless you count the poor guy you crashed into. He's in here too, somewhere, although he's probably going home today.' Oliver stood up and binned the paper towels. 'They want to keep you in because of your *condition.*'

Oliver was going to blame her and belittle her, Kate thought furiously, when all she really needed was some kindness and support.

'What do you mean, my *condition*?' she asked irritably.

'Kids, go and get your mother some chocolate or something; she probably hasn't eaten all day.'

Kate noted how they left without argument, though Lucy looked as though she'd have liked to. If it had been she giving the order there would have been more resistance. Waves of self-pity threatened to engulf her. Then Oliver spoke and her mind snapped shut.

'You're pregnant, Kate,' he said, without preamble. The hot scratchy feeling in Kate's stomach suddenly became a flurry of trapped birds trying to escape from her chest. At first her mind remained resolutely shut as she stared at Oliver without comprehension, then it slowly began to grind into gear. How could this be? Surely God was not so cruel that the one time she and Oliver had made love in the last six months had resulted in a pregnancy?

'I thought you were on the pill?' he asked, whilst she registered the enormity of the situation. He spat the word "pill" with a little "puh", the only giveaway that he was feeling any tension at all.

'I was. I mean, I am,' she stuttered. 'I mean, sometimes I forget... let's face it Oliver it's hardly a requirement nowadays!'

Fear was making her defensive. 'But I'm absolutely sure I was taking it regularly back then, you know, when we...' *God, our sex life has become so remote I'm embarrassed just mentioning it.* 'I'm sure I was,' she finished lamely.

'And what about your period?' He appeared not to have been listening. 'Surely you must have noticed you missed your effing period?'

Restraint, restraint, why not just say "fuck" like the rest of us Oliver? But a sinking feeling told her that Oliver was right. How had she missed her period without noticing? What was going on with her lately? At the edges of her consciousness, she touched the white-hot tentacles of impending doom. Was she falling apart? Then she tore her mind away, she was being stupid, and anyway, she didn't have time to start navel gazing. She took a deep breath.

'Look, I've been stressed lately.' Kate felt the usual resistance to let her guard down and admit weakness. 'You know my job's more demanding than yours.' *That's why I earn twice as much as you,* she thought sourly. 'Lucy's playing me up constantly and I just don't know what's going on with Jack. It feels like he's slipping away from me...' And then she was crying, and he was holding her clumsily, like he always had, like emotionality and physical contact weren't written into his DNA. But she knew he was trying and that made her cry all the more.

'Please don't be angry with me, Ollie.' She caved in and let the tears flow. 'I'm trying so hard. It feels like I've been trying so hard for so long and I can't cope with you being against me too.' Kate surprised herself with the force of her anguish; she felt like a little girl.

'It's okay. We'll work it out. I'm not angry with you.' Oliver tried to pat her in a place that wouldn't cause greater discomfort. 'But you know we can't keep this baby, Kate. You know that, right?'

Kate felt numb, far away. She was remembering Lucy as a baby. God that had felt like hard work. The whole thing: being pregnant, getting fat, trying to keep working until the last week of pregnancy but finally being rushed to hospital with pre-eclampsia (of course she got the blame for that too, even though she was just trying to keep her full wage for as long as possible). Having a C-section was awful, she felt like she'd failed, she'd read so many negative articles during her pregnancy.

Then there was Lucy herself. Perhaps it was because she didn't have a natural birth, perhaps it was because Kate found breastfeeding just too painful; whatever the reason, she knew she didn't bond with this baby, that her crying irritated her, that as Lucy pulled herself upright at just ten months old, Kate was not overcome with pride but rather frustration at the sticky fingers, the upended wastepaper basket and crayon over the wall. Lucy was a precocious child, speaking and then learning to read incredibly young. She was always happy, always singing or telling stories. Kate knew she should be proud, but she couldn't help resenting her, as though somehow, they were in competition, vying for *best female in the household*, which felt like such a ridiculous, shameful thought that Kate hadn't shared it with anyone.

It was never like that with Jack. Jack had always been so easy. In some ways he'd been like a little old man in those first months, so self-reliant and quiet, a sad knowing in his eyes. But Jack hadn't been a baby when he came to live with them, she didn't have to carry him, birth him; he didn't take his first steps or make his first words in her care. It was difficult to remember that, he felt like such a part of her.

'Kate?' She came back to herself. 'Kate, I said we can't keep this baby, right?'

'I know Ollie, I don't want another baby.'

And they held each other, each lost in their own very private thoughts, until Lucy and Jack returned, and they all ate chocolate together as though they were on a night out at the cinema.

***

Hours later, as Kate lay staring at the ceiling, she remembered Annie's card. She wondered if Jack had opened it. She hadn't mentioned it to Oliver, not that she ever spoke to him about Annie much, he was so straightforward about everything and usually left her feeling foolish or melodramatic when she confessed her simmering rage or her confusion over the *right thing* to do. Because she really did want to do the right thing, didn't she? Wasn't she the good guy? The one who stepped up and took care of everything, the reliable, responsible one? It was exhausting.

The noise outside the room suggested the hospital was coming to life again. It was still dark outside. The silence had lasted maybe an hour, when the wailing of a patient on the ward finally subsided. Kate couldn't tell whether the wail belonged to a man or a woman. She guessed a woman. And now the poor thing was about to be woken again for blood pressure checks and morning medication. Kate hated hospitals, they reminded her of Annie.

She pulled off the sheets and gingerly swung herself upright. She was fed up with thinking about Annie. She moved over to the wash basin and took her first proper look in the mirror. Both her eyes were blackened down to her prominent cheekbones, her nose was swollen. *Christ,* she thought, *aren't airbags supposed to spare you the damage?* She gently sponged at her gluey eyes with a paper towel. Crying had made them worse for sure and she began to cry again at the thought; big fat tears squeezed themselves painfully from the corners of her bruised-plum eyes.

And now she had to face a termination. Even saying the word inwardly made her recoil. It just wasn't part of her agenda. The steady one, the achiever, the career mum who supported her family and still looked fabulous. She managed a dry little laugh at that and pulled a face in the mirror. They'd spoken with the doctor last night, that's how she'd wangled the private room, she reckoned. They must have taken one look at Oliver's face when he discovered her *condition* and decided the family was going to need some privacy. The doctor suggested taking more time to consider, but noting they were both adamant, arranged for it to happen before Kate left the hospital today.

Kate put her hand on her abdomen. 'I'm sorry little guy but this just isn't the time or place where you want to be born.'

She began to cry in earnest. She couldn't help it; she was remembering the day that Jack finally came to live with them. How different things had been then. Now *that* was a time and place to be born into. Had she been so different too? She certainly remembered it that way. She'd felt strong, invincible even. She'd had a plan. Already noticed by her superiors, she was on an almost certain trajectory to the top of her sales firm. Oliver was the perfect mate; stoic, predictable, dependable, if a little unimaginative and certainly underpaid in his work as a carpenter. But he was great at DIY, and they had high hopes for their run-down semi which they'd bought at a snip. Over the years they'd re-mortgaged to finance Kate's ideas, but it was always much cheaper because Oliver could do most of the work himself. It made it easier to bear that she would always be the main breadwinner. Their relationship was balanced, they were a team.

They covertly planned Jack's arrival for months. It was obvious that Annie was spiralling out of control and unable to care for a child, but it was a delicate matter; Annie wouldn't give up care for Jack easily, even if that care was highly erratic and haphazard. Kate had made some discreet enquiries and it seemed there was a consensus to keep children with their birth mother whenever possible, but surely it was becoming impossible?

Kate had Oliver decorate the nursery and spent a fortune kitting it out as the perfect haven for a two-year-old little boy. When she looked back now, Kate wondered if even back then, in her innermost, secret thoughts, she'd intended on keeping Jack. She didn't like to think so. After all, it was just a stopgap whilst Annie got her act together. One day Kate and Oliver would have children of their own, when the time was right with her work and their finances. No, she was just being of service, her motives were pure.

Then Annie went and landed herself in real trouble with the police. Of course, it had only been a matter of time. And Annie, in her typical arrogance, decided to make a run for it, taking Jack with her. Well, there was no way that could be allowed to happen. With a few phone calls and some quick thinking, Kate convinced Annie to change course. Though she would hate to do it, Kate had said, if Annie forced her hand, she would call the police and give them Annie's whereabouts and Annie would lose Jack anyway. Kate had strapped Jack into the already prepared car seat and whisked him away, leaving Annie inconsolable and incoherent, doing the only thing she seemed capable of doing in a crisis, taking more drugs.

So, Jack had arrived. It made Kate's heart ache to think of the pale little boy with his huge eyes and rosebud mouth. He'd been so uncomplaining, so quiet to begin with, unless Annie phoned and then he would start wailing and yelling for his mummy. It just wasn't right; it was like torturing the poor little thing. Kate realised early on that the only way Jack was going to settle was to stop Annie having contact altogether.

They couldn't have known, as they reacted hurriedly to Annie's plans to flee, the benefits of having Jack in their custody and Annie on the wrong side of the law. As time went on, Annie became increasingly entrenched in her life as a fugitive and her pleading calls became less frequent. Jack soon stopped mentioning

Mummy and settled into his new life, where he was adored by anyone who laid eyes on him, particularly once they heard his sorry tale. Other than a few drunken calls during the first twelve months, where Kate had needed to negotiate a signature for the residency order, they heard nothing from Annie. Another year went by without a word and every time Kate came across a newspaper article about a dead drug addict, she expected it to be Annie. That was until the phone call of course.

Four

Oliver picked Kate up from the hospital later that day. He hadn't been able to be there for the procedure and he seemed genuinely apologetic for that. It was a quiet journey home. At one point Oliver reached across and put his hand on her thigh and the unexpected intimacy made her cry again.

'God, I've got to get my shit together. I've got to get back to work tomorrow,' she said brushing impatiently at her battered face.

'Don't be ridiculous, you can't work like that. And you're not supposed to take that brace off for another ten days. Take some time for goodness' sake.' Oliver took his hand from her thigh to change gear; it left her feeling oddly bereft.

'I can't just take time off, Ollie,' she pressed on. 'I'll work from home; I can do most of it by phone and email, at least for the rest of this week, and I can't be falling apart every time someone says something kind to me.' She managed a watery smile. 'I just can't wait to get home, in my own space, you know. I'm sure I'll feel better when Jack's made me a cuppa and we're all sat down to *Bake Off*.' She pictured the familiar scene in her mind's eye and felt soothed. She put her hand on his thigh now, something she did more tentatively nowadays, because she couldn't bear the indifference he often displayed. 'Let's make an effort again, shall we? I really want to. I really need a home base at the moment.' *Don't cry again!*

'Jack's not in,' Oliver said as he indicated to turn onto their road. 'He's gone out with his mates for his birthday.'

'Gone out? But that wasn't arranged, was it? I thought Ali and Joe were coming to Centre Parcs with us at the weekend?'

'He's not with Ali and Joe, he said. He's with some new mates from college. He's eighteen now, Kate, you're going to have to start giving him a longer leash. There aren't many eighteen-year-olds who want to spend their birthday with their parents and little sister.' Oliver swung the car into the drive, and as he got out, he added in an undertone, 'And I don't think Jack does either.'

Kate pretended not to hear him. They'd been over this a thousand times since Jack became a teenager. Kate felt that he was too sensitive to be hanging around the streets of Exeter, playing arcade games and skateboarding. Oliver, having grown up in South London, felt that Exeter was the height of suburbia and not in the least bit threatening to a teenage boy. But Kate was not to be swayed and Jack was *her ward* (how many times had they rowed over that particular card). Jack, she said, was a geeky kind of boy and far happier playing computer games with Ali and Joe, who'd been his friends since his first day at nursery.

It still left her glowing when Kate remembered how Joe seemed to possess some kind of intuitive-toddler-superpower on that first day, and understanding that this quiet, shy little boy would need extra love and encouragement, put out his pudgy hand and said, 'It's all right Jack, I'll be your friend now.' Kate cuffed at her tears again; the nurse had warned she may be tearful, but this was ridiculous.

And besides being geeky, Jack adored his little sister. He'd always been brilliant with her, better than Kate herself. She was sure spending time with the family was what Jack preferred to do, even if he couldn't admit it to his friends. But when she'd used this line with Oliver recently, he'd retorted 'No, Kate. Jack prefers spending time with his friends even though he can't admit it to *you*.'

They went into the house in a silence full of unspoken things.

Oliver's mum, Jan, was sitting at the kitchen table with Lucy. Kate found herself appalled to realise that in her chagrin at Jack's abscondment she hadn't even considered who would be collecting Lucy and sitting with her after school.

'Hi, hun.' Kate collected herself, kissing the top of Lucy's head as she moved past to drop her bag on the island worktop.

'Hi Jan!' she also managed cheerily.

'Hi yerself,' Jan said, getting up from the table and giving Kate a gentle squeeze. 'What on earth have you been gettin' up to now?'

Kate sought out Oliver's eyes beyond Jan's shoulder, looking for reassurance that they would keep the termination to themselves. Oliver shook his head almost imperceptibly; Jan would be horrified at the thought of an abortion.

A small, stout woman with a heavily lined but kindly face, Jan had a crease for every sacrifice she'd made for her five children and wheelchair-bound husband, Ron, who'd been a telecoms' engineer until a freak accident lost him the use of his legs in the late nineties. Until the accident Jan had been a devoted housewife, bringing up five children almost single-handedly whilst Ron worked long hours, often staying away from home for several days at a time. When Ron came home for good, the youngest child was fourteen and Jan may have considered what else she would like to do with her life but found herself instead with a new, full-grown person to care for, and this one far more prone to rages and temper tantrums than any of her five children. Jan took up the mantle valiantly, though her children often berated their father for treating their mother so shoddily. Ron soon settled into a morose kind of acceptance and when grandchildren started coming along, Jan was in her element once again.

When Jack arrived, there were initial reservations among Oliver's family, but these soon melted away, along with their hearts, when Jack cracked a smile. Jan was surprised, but equally pleased, that Kate intended to return to work within a few days of Jack's arrival and asked if Jan would take on childcare duties, for a fee of course. On through the years Jan anticipated Kate and Oliver having children of their own yet it was a full six years before Lucy arrived and again Kate hoped (or expected?) Jan to take on the role as nanny. To a homemaker like Jan this made no sense at all, and she was far more reticent this time around.

Years passed and Kate's working hours became longer and more erratic, keeping her away from home for several days each month. Almost invariably it was Oliver who collected the children and Jan's opinion of Kate began to sour as she sensed her son's loneliness. When she questioned Oliver, he would become stony, always defending Kate; she was doing what she thought was right for the family, he said, and she worked bloody hard too. He didn't earn enough to support them, he said, so he did his bit in other ways. Jan knew this couldn't be his sole opinion on the matter, he could defend Kate all he liked but in recent months, Oliver had been doing less *stepping up*, as Kate called it, and expressed a clearer expectation that Kate should pitch in. It had put tremendous strain on the marriage, which was already on the rocks a year before when they sought out couples counselling. Whatever next.

Jan kept her opinions to herself; she saw no need for them to spend so much money on the house or have three overseas holidays a year or for Jack to have the latest computer and trainers every five minutes or for Lucy to have pony lessons, ballet lessons, swimming lessons *and* piano lessons. Good grief. A child needs love and attention and a mother to be there, those were the things that mattered. She thought these things, but she was careful not to say them. And she didn't say them now, as her thin lips set in a grim line over Kate's shoulder.

'Rushing to your next appointment, were you?' Jan took Kate's shoulders and held her at arm's length so as to scrutinise her. 'You look worn out,' she said kindly, curling a stray hair behind Kate's ear. The gesture caused Kate's eyes to well up again.

'I've just got a lot on my mind, Jan.' Kate could hear her defensive, curt tone. She shrugged out of Jan's grasp, feeling claustrophobic.

'Like what love? Tell us and we can help you!' Jan flicked the kettle on, pulled out a chair for Kate and sat back down next to Lucy.

Oh yes, Oliver's family with their unshakeable united front, Kate couldn't help thinking bitterly. Yet she knew they only wanted to help. She'd already had missed calls from two of Oliver's sisters, Karen and Fay. She liked them well enough and had even unbuttoned a little when things had really started to fall apart with Oliver last year, but she'd never been very good at talking about what was going on with her, what was *really* going on. She knew she avoided the deeper questions, the stuff that might lie festering beneath *the problems*. Problems were manageable, problems could be identified and fixed, this was a world she felt safe in.

She looked from Lucy, to Jan, to Oliver and felt utterly alone. Even at a problem-solving level, where would she begin? What was safe ground? The termination? The failing relationship? The increasing work stress? That she still couldn't seem to bond with Lucy? That she feared something was broken because of how her own mother parented her? She saw them now, her family, and felt as though she were on the wrong side of the glass, peering in but unable to enter. Jack was eighteen and she could feel him slipping away from her, her one certainty, the one person she thought would never leave her. *Had she really believed that?* And then there was Annie, always Annie.

'It's just work stuff,' she heard herself saying, vilifying herself as usual. 'I've got a terrible headache; I think I'll go and lie down.'

When she reached the cool bedroom, she felt like she was coming up for air. She took great gulps, putting her hand to her chest as though reassuring herself she was safe. What was going on with her? These people were her family, if anyone were on her side these people were and yet they felt like the panel of judges, biting back their disappointment after she'd showed such promise at earlier points in the competition. Had she made them this way? Did everything really come down to her performance? Maybe they did just want her to be okay? *Don't be ridiculous* her inner voice cut in, which sounded so much like her mother's, *just being okay doesn't cut it, that won't help you succeed; it won't pay university fees or provide a well-shaped life; it won't take care of you in old age.*

'Oh!' she surprised herself when she cried out loud, enfolding her aching head as though bracing for impact and curling onto the bed. She didn't have the energy to cry any more. She dozed fitfully, drifting in and out of half-waking dreams of car crashes, endless corridors, crying babies and used syringes. She heard Oliver putting Lucy to bed, she heard the landing creak and the door open a fraction but pretended to be asleep. She imagined him returning downstairs to Jan and talking hours into the night about her inefficiencies. Oh! Where was this coming from? It must have been the bump on the head. *It must have been the termination* said that caustic little voice.

She had a sudden awareness of something warm and wet seeping between her thighs and leapt up. The pale green yoga pants which Oliver had brought into the hospital were now deep red at the crotch, worse it had soaked through onto the light-coloured throw on the bed. She'd completely forgotten to change her pad when she got in. She grabbed up the throw and tossed it to the corner of the room, she would deal with it tomorrow. Then she peeled off her clothes where she stood, gingerly removed the neck brace and went to the ensuite shower. The water pummelled her shoulders and back, and despite the hour, she carefully tipped back her head and wetted her long blonde hair. The water was almost scalding, beating back unbidden fears. She looked down and watched the remnants of blood, now pink in the water, running in rivulets down her thighs and calves and swirling into the plug hole.

The best thing she could do was to forget this whole bloody mess, she thought grimly as she towelled her hair and wrapped it in a turban. Jack was back tomorrow, and they were going away for the weekend. She and Oliver seemed to be getting on okay and she would make an extra effort with Lucy. She picked up the soiled clothes as she stepped out of the bathroom, committing herself to pulling it back together.

'Time to forget this whole, bloody mess,' she said as she dumped the clothes on top of the bloodied throw, smiling at the irony.

Oliver came up an hour or so later and slid quietly into bed beside her.

'Okay?' he asked tentatively, feeling for her hand.

'Yes, I'm okay. It's going to be okay,' she said, surprised at the rush of comfort she felt as his hand folded around hers. 'I'm sorry about earlier,' she added.

'You've nothing to be sorry about. People just want to help you Kate,' he said, rolling to face her. Even in the palest light, cast by the streetlights through the smallest crack in the curtains, the closeness felt too much for her, as if, when he looked into her eyes, he may see something hidden there that she didn't know herself. She turned over and snuggled her back into him.

'I know,' she said.

It was three a.m. when she heard Jack's Golf growling in the driveway, and she finally fell asleep.

Five

Kate woke late the following day. The heavy slate-grey curtains had been closed more tightly so that the room was silky dark, punctuated only by the silhouettes of the chaise longue, vanity dresser and wardrobe. The daylight sliding in beneath the door and peeking around the edges of the curtains gave the time away, certainly later than six anyway, when Kate usually liked to rise. Throwing back the covers she found she ached all over and when she stood the room swayed alarmingly. She moved cautiously over to the dresser and sat on the stool to appraise her face in the mirror.

Her father had paid for the vanity dresser, as a wedding gift, though she hadn't wanted anything from him. They'd barely spoken since she was eight years old, but he'd heard through Granny O'Shea (her paternal grandmother) that she was getting married and had wanted to contribute something. As with everything else in her life, Kate had wrestled with the *right thing to do*, much to the confusion of Oliver's family who seemed to see things much more simply. Eventually she'd felt it would be gracious to accept a gift, but unfortunately, couldn't offer an invitation as it would be too distressing for the rest of the family. Granny O'Shea had pursed her lips at this but obviously relayed the message. When the funds arrived, Kate was overcome with guilt and said that yes, her father could come to the wedding ceremony but not the wedding breakfast or subsequent festivities and he was to arrive sober and as well turned out as he could manage.

She could still recall the feeling, as she turned to walk back down the aisle and saw her father at the farthest corner of the church, dressed in probably his only suit and looking a hundred years old. Their eyes had met, and his face had lit up in a gummy smile, but she'd whipped her eyes away at the rush of pity, grief and revulsion that threatened to overwhelm her. When she looked for him outside, he'd gone. Over and over, she'd relived that memory, wishing she'd managed just a small smile. He died a year later.

Kate gazed critically at her reflection. She knew she was a good-looking woman, but if anything, that just felt like more pressure, another performance to keep up. Well, she'd definitely zeroed today's score card. The bruising was worse, changing from yesterday's blackcurrant to a technicolour of blueberry, raspberry, lemon and lime. Her eyes were marginally less slit-like and at least weren't full of gunk, but she was nowhere near ready to see clients, via the internet or otherwise.

I'm a walking fruit salad, she conceded, sticking her tongue out at her reflection and moving off to find some slouchy clothes. She showered again for good measure, begrudgingly fitted her neck brace and headed downstairs.

The house was light, airy and quiet. She loved this house. Oliver and his brother had knocked out a couple of partition walls so that the downstairs hall was simply enormous, it housed a small sofa and a telephone cabinet, and the rest was glorious space, made better by the oversized Persian rug in palest pinks, blues and golds that seemed to magically absorb and utilise any accidental spill or muddy shoe print to make it look even more brilliant (admittedly some of the red wine spills looked slightly suspect). One turned right into the kitchen or left into the sitting room, which again had once been two rooms, knocked together and then extended out into the garden with huge bi-folding doors that made the decking and barbeque area, with optional awning, an extension of the living space.

The neighbourhood wasn't upmarket, the same house a few streets away would have almost doubled the value. Their road eventually backed onto a run-down housing estate, but there was rarely any trouble and they never had cause to venture down that way. Their immediate neighbours were *the right kind of people* as her mother would call them, and anyway, Kate was nothing if not a sticker. She knew some might say she feared change, but she'd stuck with her job for twenty years and it had served her very well; she'd stuck with her house for almost as long and was very satisfied with the results; she'd stuck with the same man for twenty-two years, and with all their ups and downs, they were working it out.

Her own childhood had been filled with inconsistencies, sudden rule changes, broken relationships and upheavals. She felt a fierce pride that she'd created this; she had what the textbooks would call a *secure base* for her children. She'd made this happen, fought for it from the ashes and provided a safe haven for Jack to fall into and be nourished and nurtured and adored.

She made herself a cup of strong coffee and went outside, sinking down on one of the rattan sofas and gazing out at the garden. It was a bit untidy, Oliver hadn't been out here for weeks, but it still looked wonderful for the time of year. Several of the shrubs were still flowering whilst the leaves of others were turning rust or blackish-red. Her favourite, the Cotinus, turning the exact colour of Jack's hair. The water feature was a succession of waterfalls which caught the late morning sunlight whilst the birds jostled for their turn to take their morning bath in the little pool at the bottom. There was a slight breeze, enough to cause Lucy's swing to move gently to and fro, just a few inches, as though the fairies were playing secret games. Kate closed her sore eyes.

She was wondering again whether Jack had opened Annie's card. It was all such a muddle. Though she hated to admit it, she was pleased and relieved that he wasn't showing any new signs of wanting to know Annie. She could hear her mother's voice, back when Jack turned thirteen. *'It's not over yet, Kate, you mark my words. Teenagers are renowned for throwing their toys out the pram. If you're not careful he'll be throwing it all in your face and telling you he wants to go and live with her.'* The very idea made Kate's insides retract. *'You have to play it carefully, allow enough rope so you're not blamed for making things difficult but don't go encouraging anything or making it easy. You'll thank me for it later. Jack has a full, healthy life with you, he doesn't need anybody else.'*

Over the years Kate had followed her mother's advice, not refusing contact, but just making it tricky. Jack had so many clubs and events that it was easy to say, *'Sorry not this weekend,'*, and *'Oh, not that one either,'* without feeling too guilty. Then there was the fact that Jack didn't want to see Annie anyway, they always had more fun things to do without her. Kate experienced a little squirm of discomfort, knowing that she bore at least some responsibility for making *Annie days* much more an obligation than a fun day out. But what was she supposed to do? She was just trying to do the right thing for Jack. Always, right from the very beginning, it was about protecting Jack.

Kate realised she was gripping the arm of the rattan sofa. She suddenly felt cold despite the unusual warmth of the day. It was always like this, each Christmas or birthday, whenever Annie pushed back into their lives, these memories would be waiting in the corners of her mind, waiting to remind her, demanding that she defend her actions. It was true that when Jack first came to stay, she'd wished Annie would just disappear and yes, when Annie did seemingly disappear, she'd allowed herself to believe it would stay that way forever, come to hope it. But who wouldn't?

She got to her feet and wandered down the garden. The grass really was quite long, it would need a cut before the rain came, they couldn't hope to have this sunshine for much longer. She made her way down the paved slabs to Lucy's play area, running her fingers through the spindly needles of the cypress trees which lined the fence. A red admiral butterfly fluttered past her, making it feel like summer, but it was not summer, it was October and soon it would be winter. She sat on the swing, which was far too small for her, her knees level with her chin, and looked back at the house. They hadn't had the extension back then, the day that Annie called. The hand of her mind was in the filing cabinet again, this time choosing *'The phone call, May 2002'*.

She was in her kitchen; it didn't look quite as it did today, but it was taking shape. There was no island, *and of course there was no Lucy*, she thought ruefully. Just

Jack. Just her beautiful, vibrant Jack, the personification of sunlight as he scrambled around the kitchen where the island now stood. Her face relaxed and broke into a smile as she recalled his freckled face and seemingly constant smile. She pushed with her feet and allowed the swing to rock a little. She remembered the house phone ringing, as it rarely did, and drying her hands on a tea towel to answer it, expecting a fraudster or cold caller, only to find it was Annie. She felt the breath leave her chest as it had all those years ago.

'My God, Annie, we thought you were dead! Where have you been?' And there it was, that maelstrom of emotion that only Annie could elicit, making her doubt herself, and whether she was a good person. Because over the past twelve months she'd come to believe that Annie *must* be dead, come to accept it... *come to hope it? No! I'm such a terrible person as that!* She'd squashed the thought down. From far away Annie was speaking.

'I got into some trouble Kate. Look, I don't have much money. Can I reverse the charges?'

'Of course... of course.' The line had gone dead. Kate's hand shook as she replaced the receiver. Annie was alive. She sounded so wretched. Poor Annie, what had happened to her? What would happen now? Would she want to see Jack? To *take* Jack? No, that just wasn't possible. And there it was again, that thought. *Why couldn't she have just stayed dead?* The phone was ringing.

'This is the operator. Annie is calling you; will you accept the charges?'

'Yes, yes.' Kate wiped her hands over her face, took a shuddering breath and pulled herself together. 'Yes.'

'Kate?'

'Annie, I'm here. What's happened? Are you okay?' Her voice sounded strangled as her mind whirred.

'Yes Kate, I'm fine. Look, I'm in a bit of bother here. My bag's been stolen, and I've got nowhere to stay. Could you wire me £200?' All this in a clipped, faraway tone.

Money, was that all? Money was easy.

'Two hundred? Yes, of course, yes.'

'Brilliant, thanks. I'll wait in this phone box.'

'Sure,' Kate realised she was speaking into a dead line. Like a sleepwalker she went through the well-worn routine of wiring Annie money through Western Union. Jack was still sitting in the middle of the kitchen with his brightly coloured trucks, he was such a good, self-reliant little boy. She felt a whoosh of anxiety as the phone began to ringing again.

'This is the operator—'

'Yes, yes, I'll accept the charges,' Kate cut in.

'Kate? I realised you didn't have the number. Did you do it?'

'Yes, it's done. Do you have a pen?' And she read out the code Annie would need to claim her money.

'Great. Got it. Thanks so much Kate, you're such a star. I don't know what I'd do without you. I'm sorry I'm such a fuck up, y'know…'

Annie was suddenly sounding far less wretched. Kate felt the first pricklings of anger.

'Where the hell are you, Annie?'

She was gone. Kate realised she'd been holding her breath for the entire call. Annie was alive. She was alive and she was back… somewhere. She hadn't even asked about Jack! Her whole body seemed to vibrate, in her head, down her arms, there was a ringing in her ears. She hadn't asked about Jack! But that was good, wasn't it? That meant they were safe, didn't it? Fury and relief swept through her. How could those two feelings co-exist? Trembling, she'd sunk to the floor and squeezed Jack tight. Delighted at the unexpected attention, Jack had hugged her back enthusiastically and she loved him more.

Six

Kate wandered back inside in search of more coffee. She heard movement in the kitchen, and expecting Jack, braced herself for whatever mood he might be in today. Instead, she found Jan at the sink with last night's *bloody mess*: the scrubbed yoga pants on the drainer and an excess of throw spilling over the side of the basin as she worked furiously at the offending area. Jan turned her head as Kate entered and smiled warmly. Kate saw smugness, superiority, matriarchy.

'Jan, you had no reason to do this!' She moved alongside the little woman to chivvy her away, but Jan kept hold of the cloth and planted her feet firmly.

'Now Kate, don't be ridiculous. I'm a woman, I've borne five nippers, you've no reason to be embarrassed.' All this whilst pushing firmly back against Kate's attempts to hip-shove her away from the sink. 'You're exhausted. I want to help. Please let me help.' The last in a tone so sincere that Kate relented. Of course, Jan only wanted to help, why did that always trigger her feelings of inadequacy? She moved over to the coffee maker and clicked a cartridge into place. With her back to the room and the noise of the machine she could only just hear Jan add, consolingly, 'It's no wonder, after an accident like that, you'd forget your monthly.'

'Yes,' Kate managed, as she took the earthenware mug back to the table. 'How come you're here today, Jan?' She wondered if that sounded rude and blushed a little as put her feet up on the chair next to her.

'I thought you migh' need some help is all, Kate. And I thought Lulu migh' need a ride to school.'

'No, it's Oliver's turn,' Kate replied automatically as she took her feet from the chair, deciding that wasn't comfortable at all. She flicked listlessly through a pile of magazines Lucy had been cutting up to make collages with Jan.

'Ollie left for work in the early hours,' Jan called from the laundry room, where she was now feeding the throw into the washer. 'He said you might forget, with the accident an' all,' she added as she appeared at the side door. 'Anyway, Jack took Lucy to school, he's got no classes this morning, so I was free to help around 'ere.'

Kate said nothing as she stared into her cup. She couldn't articulate, even to herself, why she found Oliver's mushrooming workload so disconcerting. It wasn't that he didn't work hard before, but he was never a *go-getter* as her mother would say. They had their balance: Kate was the grafter and the breadwinner; Oliver did childcare and DIY; it worked. Yet about twelve months ago he'd secured a contract in the Midlands. It started as a day or so a week but had crept up until, in recent months, it seemed to occupy most of his time. Increasingly he would travel up on a Sunday for an early start on Monday and only return before midweek if Kate were away and there was no one else to taxi Lucy to school and her various clubs and classes.

The new arrangements were a mixed bag; Oliver certainly seemed happier and more confident, he was more tactile and attentive when he was around and took on responsibility with more enthusiasm than the sullen, begrudging air he'd acquired in recent years. He'd finally agreed to attend couple's counselling, and somewhat irritatingly, seemed able to talk easily and coherently about the problems in their marriage and about his own, albeit very straightforward, feelings.

Kate liked to think that a lot of the behaviour change was down to the counselling, which she'd been suggesting for several years now and could therefore take some of the credit. But there was no getting away from the fact that Oliver just seemed happier being more grafter and less homemaker and it made Kate uneasy. Things had been difficult before and without doubt needed addressing, but they had a balance, they had their way of doing things which had served them very well.

Once Kate would have said the problems started after Lucy was born but it was during a counselling session that Oliver pointed out they'd decided to try for a baby because things had been going stale and her work always seemed to take precedence. Her work, Jack, Oliver; that was the pecking order. He was right of course but in Kate's eyes her work was *for* Jack, to give him the life he deserved. So, yes, the problems started before Lucy but now she had Lucy to think about too; her development, her education. All this cost money, and let's face it, Oliver's new work pattern didn't really impact the bank balance, once his accommodation and travel had been taken into account, they were barely better off for it, but all of a sudden Oliver was unavailable for that last minute pick-up or school run or to fetch the items that were missing from the Waitrose delivery. He seemed somehow less reliable, less safe, and despite the positive aspects of this new Oliver, Kate didn't like the change.

'It wasn't on the board,' she said finally, looking up to find Jan scrutinising her over her mug of tea.

'You wha' love?'

'Oliver leaving early, it wasn't on the board, he's down for drop-off and pick-up most of this week,' Kate said, getting up and crossing the kitchen to the large whiteboard which had been laboriously drawn up into many columns and rows dedicated to various commitments and whose responsibility it was to provide taxi services. Up until recently it also detailed the many nights each month that Kate was away for business, now Oliver's away dates were also inked in.

'Here, look.' Kate pointed at the little square with today's date. 'Oliver, Oliver…' She pointed to the following days. 'Oliver, Oliver, Oliver.'

'What's Dad not done now?' Jack smirked at Jan as he entered the kitchen. 'God, you look awful,' he added to Kate.

She glanced at the clock. 'That took a long time. What have you been doing since you dropped Lucy off?'

'Injecting drugs and stealing cars.' Jack moved past her and into the kitchen, straight to the biscuit tin. 'What life-changing event has Dad forgotten?' he asked again, taking four or five biscuits from the tin and making a little stack on the work surface.

'He was supposed to take Lucy to school,' Jan interjected. 'And don't be cheeky to your mother.'

'Yeah, all right,' Jack mumbled through a mouthful of biscuit. 'But I took her anyway, so what's the big deal?' A few crumbs escaped his mouth at the "buh" and the "'duh".' Kate only noticed because she was watching him so intently. What was happening to her family? Everyone seemed to be morphing around her, into people she didn't know or particularly like. Of course Jack had been a regular teenager in a lot of respects; slept more, talked less, but this nonchalant, insolent creature who didn't say please or thank you, in fact didn't say much unless it was sarcasm, and most worryingly, didn't appear to like her very much, seemed to have sprung into being at a time she couldn't seem to pinpoint.

'You've left it a little late to become a moody teenager, don't you think?' she said, attempting to recover some ground as she elbowed him away from the side and swept the crumbs into her hand.

'You've left it a little late to become domesticated,' he retorted. God he was quick. Just like Annie. *Annie.*

'Did you open all your cards whilst I was in hospital?' Kate asked, choosing to ignore the barbed comment.

'Yeah.'

Kate waited for more. 'And?' she prompted when more was not forthcoming.

'And what? I opened my cards.'

'And have you thanked everyone?'

Jack sucked through his teeth in an irritating gesture he'd recently acquired. 'Oh, for fuck's sake. Yes.'

Kate paused but decided to plough on. 'You've thanked everyone? Didn't you get a card from Annie? I recognised her handwriting,' she quickly added in explanation.

'Oh. Yeah. I did. And some money, a hundred quid.'

Nothing, no giveaways about how he might feel.

'Well, have you phoned her to say thank you?'

'No, and I'm not about to either.'

'Well, you should.'

Jack looked as though the biscuit in his mouth had turned sour.

'Why?' he said, his full lips curling into a grimace. 'Thank her for a measly hundred quid, what, does that make her mother of the year? And like *you* care anyway.'

Kate took him in, his spite and churlishness. Did she do this? Did she create this hostility? She heard a tiny, sinking *yes* before she batted it away. She took a breath.

'Jack, it's the right thing to do. Text if you must but you should say thank you.'

'You…' Jack picked up the last biscuit, 'are a complete weirdo.' He turned and stalked out of the kitchen as Kate looked to Jan.

'What's got into him?!' Kate asked, looking to the older woman to explain her new, alien child. 'Did any of yours go like this?' She took a biscuit from the tin and began breaking little bits from the edges, got halfway through and realised she didn't want it at all. 'He's never been like this,' she added fretfully as she binned the remaining biscuit.

'You should eat something,' Jan reproved, going to the fridge and examining the contents of its cavernous innards. 'Karl went a bit wacky for a while there, I think they call it *middle child syndrome* or summink.' She chuckled at the idea of such a thing, putting cheese and a wilted-looking lettuce on the side. 'And Deborah's never been right! Ha! But then she's the youngest and had to put up with her dad when he first 'ad the accident. Enough to turn anyone's 'ed. They've both come good though, Jack will too. Can I make you a sandwich, love?' And that was it. Years of childrearing, family dramas and sleepless nights wrapped up in a few short sentences. That was the Jones' way.

Karl, in Kate's opinion, was almost certainly alcoholic, and to her knowledge, had spent time in prison. He did have a job now, as a shopfitter, and seemed normal enough. He lived around the corner and stopped in on Jan for lunch most days. Deborah had a baby at seventeen, married another man at nineteen and was divorced by twenty. She was only two years younger than Oliver but only fully left home a year ago, a year after her own daughter left to start university. *Jan must be lonely in that big house now*, Kate found herself thinking, surprised it hadn't occurred to her before. When Deborah moved out it had been all about the new man, the first in over a decade, and Kate hadn't stopped to consider Jan; she didn't think Oliver had either.

'It must be lonely for you now Jan, with it just being you and Ron?' she said.

'Oh, Ron keeps me busy enough,' Jan replied easily. 'And there's Lucy of course, and Eddie's littluns.' Eddie was Karen's eldest, who already had two boys of his own. 'Karl comes in most days and even Ollie when he's around. But I prefer the nippers if I'm honest, maybe it's me mental age!' She chuckled again. Kate just looked at her. Was this woman an automaton? She seemed so contented. Her baseline of *okay* seemed so much lower than Kate's and certainly light years away from Kate's mother's. In fact, Kate had told her mother to cut it out on a number of occasions when she'd been making disparaging remarks about Oliver's family. Well, sometimes she had, anyway, other times she let her mother rattle on, it made Kate feel better about herself.

She thought she should probably call her mother now but wasn't quite ready. She felt a fleeting wave of loneliness that she didn't have a mother in whom she could confide wholeheartedly, confess her fears and doubts and receive support and consolation. That said, she told her mother almost everything, the external facts at least. In that way she was a bit like a loyal Labrador who returned again and again to its master, hopeful of praise and recognition, only to be beaten or chastised for taking too long or going about it the wrong way. Yet she returned because she always had.

Her internal world she kept hidden. She'd learnt that confessing her fears or failures to her mother left her open to doom-laden lectures, usually lasting well into the night, about the cost of *taking your eyes off the prize*. She understood this was really about her mother's fears, that she just wanted the best for Kate, but Kate learnt all the same not to add her own fears into the mix. So, in the retelling of her life story she cast herself as problem solver, the one holding it all together against the odds. Her mother liked that, and eventually Kate began to believe her own version, who wouldn't?

Only the strong cut it, only the strong survived. If she made a mistake, at work or in the family, she would rationalise and justify it away as somebody else's problem that she had to deal with, mistakes were so forbidden. But she'd been doing this for so long that her fears had begun to seep out, and having never been defined, handled or resolved, they were vague, unnamed, insidious things which she tried to shove back in a box named *Childhood, Annie, Oliver* or *Jack*. And, as time went on, she began to look at situations with a sense of doubt, was this somehow her fault? Was she the one who'd got it wrong even though she'd been trying so hard to get it right? She had begun to feel the sand shifting beneath her feet.

She declined Jan's second offer of a sandwich and headed back upstairs.

Seven

'Kate!' Jan's voice broke into Kate's troubled half-dreams. 'Kate, your mum's on the phone.' Jan stood hesitantly in the doorway as Kate pushed herself to sitting and blinked her sore eyes, 'Shall I ask her to call back?'

'No, no, I'm here,' Kate said, her mouth feeling sticky and foul. Jan proffered the phone then backed out of the room, quietly closing the door.

'Hi, Mum.' Kate tried to gather herself.

'Kate?' came her mother's clipped tone. 'I thought you were dead. Why haven't you called me?'

'I'm sorry, Mum, it's been a heck of a week, I had an accident in the car—'

'I haven't even spoken to Jack for his birthday!' So Jack hadn't thanked everyone. 'What do you mean, an accident?'

'I'm sorry, Mum, he told me he'd said thank you.' Kate winced and sat up a little straighter.

'Never mind that; you had an accident you say. When?'

'On Jack's birthday, that's why I haven't called. Everything's been crazy, they kept me in hospital overnight.'

'Oh Kate! You must be more careful. You can't afford to lose your job because you can't work. Are you working? What have they said about the car?'

Kate gritted her teeth. This was typical of her mother, no mention of her being in hospital or whether she was okay, no, just worried that she'd be unable to work, unable to perform.

'Work's fine, Mum. The car's insured. People have accidents, it's not like I've done it before. And no, I'm not working yet, I only got out of hospital yesterday… but I expect I'll be back to it tomorrow.'

She felt compelled to tag that onto the end, always hopeful for a stroke of approval.

'Well, that's good. You don't want to fall behind on your targets and lose commission.'

Kate sighed. 'Don't worry Mum, I won't.'

'So that must have ruined poor Jack's birthday. No wonder he forgot to call me.'

Kate heard the clicking of a lighter and her mother drawing on a cigarette. She imagined Jacqui's thin, painted lips puckering into little lines as she pulled deeply on the filter and experienced the familiar tightness in her chest.

'We didn't have much planned for the day, it being a school night. We're going to Centre Parcs this weekend.' Kate would kill for a cigarette, but she gave up when she was pregnant with Lucy and hadn't allowed herself a lapse since, she wasn't going to be one of those parents who sent their kids to school reeking of cigarette smoke. 'Ali and Joe are coming with us.'

'Oh, that will be nice for Jack, they're good boys those.' Jacqui said approvingly with a long exhale of smoke. 'Straight-A students, aren't they? It's good for him to have friends like that, might encourage him to work harder.'

Kate bristled, as she always did when her mother insinuated Jack could do better.

'He should be getting all As, himself, with a brain like that; much brighter than you were, Kate, you need to push him you know. 'It's no good just letting him drift.'

'Annie sent a card,' Kate heard herself saying, wanting to change the subject but also knowing that she was deliberately needling Jacqui and wondering, dully, what sadistic part of herself wanted to initiate the inevitable rant.

'Annie? Well, it's just a birthday card I suppose, but still…'

Here we go, Kate thought.

'You have to be careful Kate. These are very tricky times. Jack's about to take his A levels; you don't need Annie getting in his head with her namby-pamby, hippy-dippy nonsense. When did the card arrive?'

Without waiting for a response. 'I know you need to be cautious, but you must intercept those cards whenever you can and get rid. You hear? Get rid.' Jacqui breathed heavily into the phone.

'I told him he should phone to say thank you,' Kate said, following her twisted urge to be contrary. There was a long pause. Kate imagined Jacqui stubbing out her cigarette.

'Well, you must do what you think is right, Kate,' Jacqui finally managed, in a tone of sufferance, 'but the boy's future is in your hands and trust me, you'll regret it if you screw it up through carelessness.'

Kate felt the tightness in her chest reach a peak as a whoosh of fear rose up from her navel. Her mother knew just how to work her: her fear of failure, her fear of getting it wrong just because she didn't try hard enough for one instant.

'I just thought it was the right thing to do,' Kate said quietly, backfooted, as always. 'Anyway, you don't have to worry, Jack seems livid with her at the moment… in fact he seems livid with everyone.'

No, I'm not ready to talk to you about that, Kate caught herself.

'At least this way she can't say I've stopped him calling,' she said instead.

'Well, yes, I suppose. I'm sure you're doing your best, Kate,' in a tone that suggested she doubted that very much, 'the most important thing now is his education. He needs to perform well if he's going to make anything of his life. You have to push Kate, push.'

'Right.'

'And I suppose Oliver's been absent for all this?'

'No. Oliver was right here, he picked me up from hospital.'

Kate wondered vaguely how it would feel to tell Jacqui about the termination, about how wretched and lonely she felt, she knew she never would.

'Oh. I'm surprised he managed to drag himself away from his little Birmingham project.'

'He's working hard, Mum, he's trying to do the right thing,' Kate said, without enthusiasm.

'He's doing what suits himself you mean and earning peanuts to boot.'

Kate sighed. 'Probably. I don't have the energy for this now, Mum, sorry.'

Jacqui made her excuses then and ended the call; she had to get something from the chemist for the dreadful headaches which were plaguing her, she said. Kate put the phone on the bedside table. There was a little nerve flickering in her eyelid. She felt extraordinarily tired. She heaved herself upright and headed for the stairs. Perhaps she did need a sandwich after all.

She heard voices as she passed Jack's room, he must have left the telly on. She pushed the door open, thinking to switch it off.

'Oi! Don't just walk into my room!' Jack barked, leaping up, making Kate jump. The room smelt stale and airless.

'What are you still doing here, Jack? You've got classes this afternoon!' Kate said from the doorway. 'I was just coming to switch your telly off,' she added in defence.

'I'm not going to college today, all right? Just fuck off out of it.'

Jack began to push the door closed on her.

'But—'

'I said fuck off!' And the door closed.

Kate knew she should say more, knew she should challenge him, ground him, do something but she found she had nothing. She simply stood staring at the door for a few moments before returning to her bedroom and falling onto the bed. When she awoke it was well into the afternoon and the house was empty.

Eight

The following day Kate decided she needed to get back to work. Her boss had been amazing and suggested she take at least the week, but Kate had just started a new promotion with some of her national retailers and felt it was too crucial a time to be leaving them to it. Secretly, she didn't think she could bear one more minute with only her thoughts to occupy her.

Despite the bruising on her face, she set up a number of video calls and arranged for her courtesy car to be delivered so that she could get back on the road the following week. She spent forty minutes with her concealer and compact, trying to make her face look a little less garish. The neck brace had to go, no question, and as she shrugged herself into a dark blue Louis Vuitton blazer ready for her first online meeting, she felt a little of the usual determination creep back in.

'You've got this Kate Harper-Jones,' she said to the mirror, applying her usual coral-pink lipstick — not too drab, not too dazzling.

She'd decided to keep her maiden name when she married Oliver, for continuity with her clients, she'd said, but also because she couldn't help thinking *Kate*

Jones definitely bordered on the drab side. Harper-Jones had a very upmarket ring to it, even her mother said so.

Of course, Harper wasn't strictly her maiden name, it was her mother's maiden name. Jacqui's married name had been O'Shea, but she'd reverted to Harper following the divorce, when Kate was nine years old. Kate was allowed to change her name too and had used Harper ever since, despite Jacqui having two subsequent marriages before Kate turned eighteen. Kate found the name comforting, it was part of her history, old and unchanging, an anchor.

Kate had never known her maternal grandparents, unless one counted the dour weekly visits to her grandfather's care home before he died when Kate was seven. She could still remember the thunk of the ancient wall clock as it punctuated the silence, the sour smell of cabbage and urine, the grandfather never seeming pleased to see them, barking this or that but otherwise silent and stony-faced, her mother's crying and wringing of hands.

Kate knew her mother's relationship with her parents had been strained. Her grandmother, Jacqui's mother, had died when Jacqui was just nineteen and Mr Harper apparently blamed this largely on Jacqui's wayward behaviour. Though the Harpers had tried for more children, Jacqui was their only offspring and Mr Harper, disappointed not to have a son, had heaped expectation upon Jacqui. Having aced ten O levels at the local grammar, hopes were high for a place at Oxford or Cambridge but halfway through her A levels, Jacqui had met Kevin O'Shea, fallen in love and flunked out, pregnant, before taking a single exam. In Jacqui's retelling of the story, Kevin had done little less than bewitch her, charming her into bed and ruining her life forever. The marriage had lasted a little over nine years and only that long because Jacqui was determined to show her parents, she hadn't written her life off for nothing.

It became apparent very quickly that Kevin had a drink problem; he was absent a lot of the time and seldom held on to a job. He was never violent and was well liked in the community, *a loveable rogue* most would say, but eventually Jacqui found someone who could keep her in better style and Kevin got the boot for good. Jacqui was still young and very attractive, but she was bitter, she felt she'd been tricked out of the life she should have had and the thing she'd craved more than anything — the approval of her father — had been robbed from her. Without realising it she began to set her own expectations impossibly high, partly through fear but mostly to prove to herself that she wasn't alone in her failure, that other people failed to meet expectations too.

Kate gave her appearance a final appraisal and headed across the landing to the office. Today was going to be a good day. She took her first meeting with bright enthusiasm and charm; her clients, the CEOs of Dunelm, B&Q and Homebase were enthralled, telling her how brave and dedicated she was to be back at work. This was her drug; in this world, she felt fully in control, admired and approved of. She'd fought her way here by tooth and claw and had earned the right to rub shoulders with the bigwigs. By the end of the morning, she was feeling on form, the plates were spinning, and she was adrenalized. She fired off several emails in the afternoon and signed for her courtesy car, a very nice-looking Audi SUV. When Jan arrived with Lucy at around four o'clock, Kate was dancing around the kitchen to Steve Wright's afternoon show, butter knife in hand and a half-made sandwich on the worktop.

'Hooray!' Lucy cried, dropping her schoolbag and joining in a shimmy to the Scissor Sisters. 'Mum's feeling better!'

'Aw, I am Lulu!'

Kate hugged Lucy to her. Even before the accident and subsequent horrors, she'd really not been feeling herself. Perhaps it had been the drag of the unknown pregnancy? Anyway, she was feeling better now. The three of them danced and laughed as they prepared supper and Kate found she didn't even care too much when Jack came home and stomped up to his room without even saying hello.

It's just a phase, she said to herself and took Lucy's hands as an upbeat song blared out of the radio.

***

Oliver came home the following day and was also in good spirits. He'd brought a colouring book and a Pussycat Dolls CD for Lucy, the new Grand Theft Auto game for Jack and even a pot plant for Kate's office, to cheer her up, he said.

'All this extravagance,' Kate had joked. 'Anyone would think you've got a guilty conscience!'

Oliver kissed her on the cheek then moved past her, taking off his scarf and hanging it in the hall.

'Don't be stupid, Kate,' he said, as he came back into the kitchen, kissing the top of Lucy's head and going to the fridge for a beer. 'Of course I feel bad for being away so much. And I miss you,' he added, kissing her again. 'Where's Jack?'

'In his room, as always. I've told him he needs to pack because we're leaving early in the morning. Ali and Joe are being dropped off at nine.' Kate, in her renewed high spirits had done her best to ignore her sense of foreboding about the upcoming trip. Jack had shown no enthusiasm whatsoever, so different to a similar trip they'd had last year. He'd been increasingly surly all week and she was worried how it would be for Ali and Joe, being stuck with this new, taciturn Jack whilst she, Oliver and Lucy did their own thing. It felt like she was inviting them to spend the weekend with a wild creature who might be unresponsive and reticent one minute then suddenly lash out and attack the next. Kate tried broaching the subject with Jack but received nothing but snarls and grunts.

'I just don't know what's got into him lately,' Kate said, taking a casserole dish out of the oven and putting it on the table. She leant past Oliver to replace a tea towel then turned and called up the stairs, 'Jack! Supper's ready!' No response. 'Jack!'

'Little shit,' Oliver said good-humouredly. He'd been sitting on the worktop, and he hopped down saying, 'I'll go and get him.'

Kate felt a warm, comforting glow that Oliver was home, and they could present a united front.

'Wash your hands please, Lucy,' she said, as she put cutlery on the table. Lucy got up and obediently washed her hands; she was being so good lately, Kate thought fondly.

'Kate! Kate! Get up here now!' Oliver's urgent voice rang out from the landing. 'And call an ambulance!' Kate dropped the remaining cutlery and ran to the bottom of the stairs.

'An ambulance? No, Lucy, you go back in there please,' she added as Lucy appeared in the kitchen doorway. 'I'll be down in a minute.' She took the stairs two at a time. Oliver was in Jack's room, knelt beside the bed where an inert Jack was sprawled, white as death, his eyes rolling upwards. Oliver was shaking him and slapping his slack face.

'He's taken something,' Oliver turned and held up a small clear packet with the residue of a white powder within. 'Jack? Jack! What have you taken? Jack! Kate, just call an ambulance!'

Kate hesitated for a moment longer, watching aghast as Jack's eyes rolled again, then dashed to the bedroom to grab the phone.

'Lucy, I said no! Go and wait in your room,' she yelled to the stricken child who stood on the landing. 'Please, for me,' she added more gently as she dialled 999. 'Ambulance please... it's my son... we think he's taken something... eighteen.'

Kate's head was whirling, she rushed back into Jack's room where Oliver was now sitting on the bed, Jack half across his lap.

'No, we don't know... yes, he's breathing, I think! Oliver, is he breathing? Yes, he's breathing.'

Kate fought hysteria as Oliver slapped Jack's pale face again, suddenly Jack rolled sideways and vomited spectacularly over Oliver's knees and shoes, then he remained that way, motionless.

'He's just been sick... keep his airways clear... yes, right...'

Oliver was already lowering Jack to the floor and putting him into a haphazard recovery position.

'I think this is right,' he mumbled, moving Jack's arms and legs, Jack didn't resist and lay with his mouth ajar, his eyes rolling again.

'Oh God, oh God!' Kate clutched her hair with her free hand. 'Yes, it's 45 Oakwell Park, …okay… okay… they're going to stay on the phone 'til the ambulance gets here,' she said to Oliver, and automatically put her arm around Lucy, who had appeared beside her.

The next few minutes passed like agonising hours, Oliver continued to tap Jack's face and check his breathing, Lucy cried, the telephone responder murmured encouragement and assured her the ambulance was on its way, asking her if she had any idea what Jack might have taken.

Kate heard the sound of the sirens and ran to let them in, finding herself wondering what the neighbours would think and hating herself for being like her mother. She opened the door to two impossibly young but very calm and sturdy paramedics and led them up the stairs. the responder had rung off, but she clutched the phone like a comfort blanket. One of the paramedics got to work on Jack immediately, gently moving Oliver out of the way. Jack was now emitting low moans, though still immobile. Oliver got up and helped Kate answer the questions of the other paramedic. No, they didn't know what he'd taken. No, to their knowledge it hadn't happened before. They didn't know where he could have got it, but he had a new group of friends at college.

'I think it's ketamine,' the paramedic on the floor said. 'He'll be okay,' — this to Kate who had put her face in her hands — 'but we'd best take him in.'

So they'd loaded Jack's limp form onto a stretcher and carried him out to the ambulance. Oliver was going to stay home with Lucy whilst Kate travelled with Jack, she would call Oliver when she knew what was happening and he would join her at the hospital once he'd got hold of Jan to sit with Lucy (who of course objected and wailed that she wanted to come too).

Kate had to answer all the same questions to a doctor at the hospital and was now sitting by Jack's bedside. Jack, wired up to all kinds of gadgetry to monitor his vital signs, had remained unresponsive as the doctor examined him but he was breathing normally which was apparently a good sign. All they could do now was monitor him and wait. A kindly nurse had brought Kate a cup of tea and told her not to worry, things weren't as bad as they appeared.

Kate put her aching face in her hands. How had this happened? Their life had been so uneventful, busy perhaps and with its own kind of stress but free of *drama*, as her mother called it, for years. In fact, the last time there had been blue flashing lights outside their house was the night Annie had been arrested, almost thirteen years ago.

Nine

Things had got crazy after that first phone call, back in 2002. Kate could still remember how she replaced the receiver with a shaking hand, how she'd returned to Jack in the kitchen with that strange ringing in her ears, like they have in a film after a bomb blast. The house had felt eerily quiet, as though it were holding its breath. Then Jack was laughing and chattering about his trucks and the spell had been broken.

'Let's go outside and play!' he'd cried, so they had.

It was May, everything was beautiful in the manicured garden. Last year Oliver had built a playhouse in the far corner and painted it dark green. It was Jack's *commando hut,* and he would happily spend hours out there. Such a contented little boy. At not yet five he was tall for his age; his rich red hair was thick and incredibly curly. Kate knew one day soon they would have to cut it short to save him from being teased but for now it reached down his long neck to his collar bones, curling in ringlets around his freckled elfin face.

'I'm the goodie and you're the baddie!' Jack yelled over his shoulder, running to his playhouse. 'You have to get to base without me shooting you! Bam, bam,

bam!' He used his little fingers as a mock gun. Kate wouldn't buy him toy guns and had tried to dissuade him from playing such games, but he would often come home from school with some new, imaginative play which involved a shoot-out.

Kate had tried to relax and enjoy the fun, Jack rolling around on his belly, commando style, and laughing with glee when he *got* her again and again. But she found she was breathing high up in her chest, her mind kept wandering off as to what might happen next; how had she become so complacent, so relaxed? The idea of Jack being anywhere but with her seemed ludicrous, impossible. When exactly had that happened?

'Kate!' a woman's voice called out and Kate's breath caught in her throat; her heart seemed to stop. In one motion, she pulled Jack to her and whirled around to face the passage which ran down the side of the house, where a figure was standing.

'Sally!' Relief swept over her, and she released Jack, who rubbed the top of his arm and looked up at her crossly.

'You're not playing properly!' he reprimanded her, then, 'Auntie Sally! Maisy!' and he ran to greet the new arrivals. Maisy was Sally's two-year-old daughter and had been the first baby that Jack had met; he doted on her and glowed with pride when told what a good boy he was with her.

'What's up with you?' Sally asked Kate as she put Maisy on the grass and ruffled Jack's hair. 'You look like you've seen a ghost!'

Kate could hear her heart hammering away in her chest and wondered at her disproportionate reaction. *Was it disproportionate though? Would Annie just show up here?*

'Let's go back to the house,' she muttered.

In those days, they had a small plastic conservatory with French doors opening from the sitting room. Kate and Sally sat in high-backed wicker armchairs with faded yellow cushions whilst the children played on the grass in front of them, Jack zooming his trucks past Maisy as she cried out excitedly and clapped her hands.

'God, I can't believe it,' Sally breathed when Kate told her that Annie had called. 'I really thought she was gone for good. Or dead. Does Jack know?' She kicked off her sandals and folded her feet beneath her.

'Jack? No! We don't speak about Annie.' Kate felt a flutter of anxiety. 'When he first arrived it just upset him if we spoke about her or if she called, now he doesn't even think about her. I'm sure of it,' she added, which she was.

Just for a moment a shadow of scepticism passed over Sally's face, but she was too good a friend to question Kate's judgement.

'Well, she won't come here, will she?' she said instead. 'Isn't she still in trouble with the police? And she can't just take him, can she? You've got that residency thingy.'

'I honestly don't know what she'd do,' Kate breathed, shaking her head. 'She didn't even mention Jack when she called.'

'Bitch.'

'But that doesn't mean anything, Sal. That's how she is when she needs drugs, then the next minute he's the most important thing in her life again.'

'You definitely think she's still on drugs then?' Sally asked, half distracted by a yell from Maisy.

'Jack honey, could you just let her have it for a minute? There's a good boy.'

'Definitely,' Kate replied, without hesitation. 'I know her so well now, all she wanted was the money and nobody needs money that quickly. And I can just tell by the way she spoke… and because she didn't ask about Jack.' Kate started to pick at a stray piece of wicker, pulling it back until it finally snapped.

'Well then, you've nothing to worry about.' Sally heaved herself up and went out to pick up Maisy, wresting Jack's truck from her grip. 'Her life must be chaos, she's not going to get it together enough to worry about Jack, not now.'

'Yes. Maybe,' Kate said, unconvinced.

Sally took Maisy home shortly after that and Kate prepared the supper whilst Jack *helped*. Oliver had been with his parents for most of the day, doing some odd jobs that Jan couldn't manage. Kate found herself longing for his solid, stoic presence. What would happen if Annie showed up here? Would Jack remember her? What then? Would it set off all that awful clawing and crying for Mummy again? Yet Kate remained convinced that Jack was too young to question his parentage. He'd always known her as "Date" and this hadn't changed when he came to stay. Oliver had progressed from "Oi" to "Oyey" and now they were simply "Kate and Ollie". His class at school was full of children with stepparents and even foster parents; Jack's situation wasn't all that unusual. But Kate was troubled. Perhaps she was going to have to open up that old wound again, to prepare Jack for what might come next?

She told Oliver the news over supper, once Jack was in bed. As usual his calm, unwavering presence was far more satisfactory in her imagination than in reality. When it came to it, she found his composed, impassive response didn't allay her fears but instead irritated her.

'There's no point in worrying about it,' Oliver had said as he helped himself to extra potatoes. 'If she turns up here you tell her to hand herself in; she can't be part of Jack's life as a fugitive.'

'But what if she doesn't listen? What if she tries to take him away?' Kate found she had no appetite.

'Then we call the police,' Oliver said flatly. 'I'm sorry but it's the right thing to do; she got herself into this mess, she's not dragging us into it too.'

'But she probably just wants to see him, it must be breaking her heart, I know she loved him, I know she did…' Kate dragged her hands through her hair.

'But she doesn't want to see him, you said so yourself.' Oliver put his fork down and looked at her. 'I'm sorry Kate but you're blowing this out of all proportion. Nothing has actually changed. So Annie rang and asked for money, like she's done a million times before; we probably won't hear from her for another twelve months.'

***

But they did hear from her. The very next day, Annie called Kate's mobile while she and Jack were in the park. They'd been playing on the roundabout, Jack hanging on whilst Kate ran, making it spin as fast as she could to Jack's demands of 'Faster! Faster!' Kate heard the phone ring over the pounding of her shoes and relinquished her hold on the wheel. She looked down to see an unknown mobile number displayed on the screen as she fought to catch her breath and felt a whoosh of anxiety from her navel to her throat. She stepped away to answer the call. Jack yelled 'Hey!' but she put a hand up to silence him.

After some brief preliminaries, Annie asked to speak with Jack, no mention of yesterday's call. She sounded cool and confident, not at all like the Annie of yesterday. Kate took a deep breath and explained that it wasn't possible for Annie to just step back into Jack's life when there was no guarantee she could keep up a consistent presence. It wasn't fair on Jack. Annie should hand herself in to the police, Kate said, and then they could go from there. Annie hung up without replying.

Ten minutes later, as Kate and Jack walked home, the phone rang again. Kate flicked it off. When they were back at the house and Jack was happily ensconced in his commando hut Kate checked her messages to find the most poisonous diatribe from Annie—: Kate, she snarled, was a lying, conniving bitch. She'd stolen Jack and never intended to give him back. Why didn't she have children of her own? Aspersions were cast about Kate and Oliver's sex life, about their ability to have children, about Kate being an ice queen who wouldn't give birth to a child of her own. Kate listened with a pounding heart; her throat constricted. How dare Annie say such awful things after they'd done so much for her? If Annie had got her shit together Jack would be back with her by now. That had always been the plan. Hadn't it? When had it changed? When had having Jack around become so permanent, so *vital?*

The following days and weeks were a rollercoaster on which Kate tried and failed repeatedly to resume normal life. First there was another answerphone message, which must have been left at some point during the night. Annie was crying and apologising and thanking Kate for everything she'd done, no mention of speaking to or seeing Jack. Then there was a week of silence, which was almost worse.

Kate wrestled about whether to speak with Jack about Annie. Where would she even begin? She'd been so sure that he never thought of Annie, didn't remember her, but now she trawled articles well into the night about how much a four-year-old remembers. There was much ambiguity, but consensus seemed the more a parent spoke with and relived the memories of a young child, the richer and more detailed those memories would be. This left Kate feeling guilty and confused. They never spoke about Annie; there were no pictures of Annie in the house, and she certainly wasn't going to be re-enacting any of Jack's earliest memories. Did that make her a terrible parent? *No!* They'd stopped talking about Annie because Jack found it so distressing. It was the right thing to do at the time… and it had just stayed that way. How had this happened? Kate felt crazy.

Next a letter arrived, confirming Kate's fears that Annie still remembered the address. An untidy scrawl that looked like a child's writing, with Gs that looked more like Qs. The letter was heart-breaking, smudged in places where big, fat tears had obviously fallen on the crumpled page. Annie hated herself, she said, she'd tried so hard to get straight, had committed to herself that she wouldn't get in touch until she was clean, but had failed again and she missed them so much, Kate and

Jack. She had no one, nothing. Please could they just meet, please could she just see Jack once and then she would hand herself in? The letter almost broke Kate who was all but ready to call Annie on the number scribbled at the bottom of the letter, but Oliver put his foot down and she was glad to have the responsibility taken away.

'Kate are you mad?' he'd said, not even looking up from the cart he was fixing for Jack. 'There's absolutely no way you can take Jack to see her. No way. Get a grip.' And that was that.

The phone calls started again, alternating between vicious, unrelenting attacks, hysterical sobs, and most unnerving, quiet, flat pleas delivered in monotone. Then the unsettling silences stretching out for weeks. Kate spoke with the family solicitor, just to be sure, about what their rights were whilst having a residency order for Jack. This left her feeling like she was groping in the dark; Annie still had parental responsibility, what did that even mean in a situation like this? Once more Oliver came to her rescue.

'Kate, she's wanted by the police for God's sake. She can't just show up and start making decisions about him now,' he'd hissed; Jack was sitting at the kitchen table playing with his trucks.

'But what if the police don't want her any more, what if it's all been forgotten? What if social services get involved and give him back to her?' Kate vaguely knew it wasn't the time to be discussing Annie, but she was desperate, she reasoned that Jack was absorbed in his own games and didn't understand what they were talking about anyway.

'That's highly unlikely, not with what she was charged with.' Oliver came and stood next to her so he could speak in lowered tones. 'They don't just write off drug charges like that. But either way, Kate, we have to take this a step at a time. And we shouldn't be talking about it in front of Jack,' he added, ending the conversation.

That night, as Kate tucked him in, Jack asked, 'Who's in trouble with the police?'

Kate's breath caught for a moment before she replied smoothly, 'No one silly, that was just grown-up talk, not for you to worry about.' She pulled the duvet up to his elfin chin.

'*I'm* not in trouble with the police, am I?' he'd asked anxiously, his eyes wide.

'Of course not! The police aren't interested in little boys... unless you're a bank robber?!' Kate jiggled his little frame and tried to make a joke. He giggled.

That night Jack wet the bed and woke screaming and sobbing. Kate hated herself for letting her anxieties spill out and affect him. She tried doubly hard to *act normally* and not talk about Annie whilst Jack was around. A week later, Annie arrived.

Ten

She came just after ten p.m. It was early July and the sun had not long set. Being Sunday, they'd spent most of the day at Jan's house along with Karen and her three boys who were a year and more, older than Jack and whom Jack thought were brilliant. They'd kicked a ball around endlessly and cooled off in the paddling pool; Jack had folded into bed pink and happy, falling asleep before his head touched the pillow. Kate had an early start in the morning and was just about to head upstairs when the doorbell rang.

'Who the heck's that at this time of night?' Oliver pushed himself from the sofa to get the door. Kate, who'd been in the kitchen, met him in the hall.

'Don't answer it!' she hissed urgently. 'It'll be her! I know it will.' She went to the window at the kitchen sink and tried to get a view of the door, her heart hammering in her chest. Suddenly a hand slapped the glass, inches from her face and Annie loomed at the window. Kate cried out in alarm and stepped backwards, tripping over Oliver who had come up behind her.

'Kate! Open the door!' Annie's voice was an urgent staccato. Then she was gone from the window and the doorbell was ringing again.

'Annie, you need to leave,' Oliver was saying in his strong, level voice as he strode back into the hall. Kate followed him, clutching her throat and saying nothing. The letterbox opened.

'Fuck you, Oliver. Kate, please, just speak to me. Please Kate, open the door.'

'No Annie, you have to go.' Kate finally found her voice. 'Go or we'll call the police.'

'Call the police? You'd really do that? What the fuck did I ever do to you to make you hate me so much?'

Kate was in freefall. What *had* Annie done? Shouldn't she just speak with her? Try to reason with her?

'This isn't about you and Kate, Annie,' Oliver interjected, 'it's about Jack. He's in our care now and we're doing what's right for him. Leave now or I swear I'll call the police.' Oliver slapped the door with the flat of his hand, the noise making even Kate jump. It must have caused Annie to fall away for a moment because the letterbox snapped shut but a second later, she launched an attack on the door, kicking and hammering it with her fists.

'What's happening?' Kate turned at the sound of Jack's voice to find him standing halfway down the stairs in his Spiderman pyjamas, clutching his toy rabbit; his hair was all over the place as he rubbed an eye with his knuckles. 'Who's banging?'

'Oh Jack!' Kate cried, lurching towards him. 'It's fine honey, don't you worry, let's get you back to bed.' But Annie was at the letterbox again and she'd seen or heard Jack too.

'Jack! Jack! It's Mummy, Jack! It's Mummy. I love you! I love you, Jack!' She was straining her fingers pitifully through the letterbox as though she could somehow reach out and touch the little boy. Jack started crying, noisy, wordless sobs.

'Jack! Kate! Please, please! My baby… my baby!' Annie disappeared from view as Kate scooped Jack up and ran for the stairs.

'I won't let her take you, I won't let her!' Kate wailed, hugging the little boy close.

'For God's sake stop saying that, Kate! You're scaring him,' Oliver snapped.

'Please Ollie, just call the police!' Kate begged as she headed upstairs, but it sounded like Oliver was already doing it.

'Police please…' she heard him say as she sprinted into her and Oliver's room, which was at the back of the house and less likely to be penetrated by Annie's yells. She leant against the wall, clutching Jack to her. All seemed to be quiet. Had Annie heard Oliver phone the police and made a run for it? Jack was still sobbing, though saying nothing coherent and after a few more minutes he seemed to have cried himself to sleep. *Thank goodness he was so tired,* Kate thought, cradling the little boy's head and laying him on the bed. Oliver came into the room.

'They'll be here any minute,' he said quietly, moving over to the bed and tucking a tear-soaked tendril behind Jack's ear. Jack took a raggedy breath but didn't wake.

'Has she gone?' Kate asked, getting up and going out onto the landing. Silence. She went into the bathroom. By standing on the toilet, she could reach the window and look down; cricking her head to one side, she could just about see the front door. There was a crumpled-looking figure huddled on the doorstep. Kate could make out a pair of dirty trainers, a grey hoodie and a few stray red curls, nothing else. Kate wasn't sure if she imagined the low moans and muttering as Annie rocked back and forth, hugging her knees. The next moment, sirens were blaring, making Kate jump again and nearly displacing her from her precarious perch. She looked down quickly; Annie hadn't moved. Jack started wailing again. Someone was banging on the door.

Kate felt like her heart had stopped beating as she moved out onto the landing. Her mouth was dry, her ears were ringing. Oliver had scooped Jack up and was carrying him downstairs to the front door. *Was that really the best thing to do?* Kate's brain was too slow to keep up. Oliver was holding Jack to him with one arm and opening the door with the other. Kate moved in beside him and took Jack, who was wide awake now but just looking at her silently, huge owl eyes in his pale, tear-streaked face.

A police officer stood on the doorstep. Beyond him, a few yards away, another was standing behind Annie, his hands on her shoulders. She wasn't resisting; she looked such a feeble and pathetic sight that Kate began to cry.

'Jack,' Annie mewled feebly. Jack looked towards the sound of his name then turned to Kate and buried his face in her neck.

Oliver sounded a hundred miles away as he explained to the officer what had happened and that there was a warrant out for Annie's arrest. On hearing this, the officer turned away for a moment and ran a check of Annie's details on his radio. Annie had locked her eyes with Kate, not in anger, rather she looked beaten, dejected and utterly lost. The officer nodded to his companion who began the formal proceedings of making the arrest. Everything seemed to be happening in slow motion. Kate was acutely aware of everything around her; she could hear a dog barking down the street, the *snik* of the car door handle as it was opened by the arresting officer, Jack breathing in her ear.

'And what's your relationship to Annie?' the policeman was asking. Kate was looking past him, her eyes still locked onto Annie as the other officer put his hand on her head to guide her into the car. Was that her imagination or had Annie managed a sad little smile as she mouthed "I love you"?

'She's Jack's biological mother,' Oliver was saying.

'She's my little sister,' Kate said simultaneously as her tears flowed in earnest.

Eleven

The court case didn't happen for another three months, during which time Annie was kept in custody, on remand. She was too much of a flight risk they said, and besides, she had no fixed address to which she could be bailed.

Jack had nightmares and wet the bed for weeks. He would cry out, 'Mummy, Kate, Mummy,' his little body contorting in his sleep, waking up confused and frightened. Kate sought the help of a child psychologist and together, through games and pictures and asking questions they helped Jack make sense of his short history. Two months after that dreaded night, Jack was his usual sunny self; he slept through the night and didn't mention Mummy again, neither did Kate.

There was still no word from Annie. Kate was beside herself with guilt and worry. She wrote repeatedly, suggesting that Annie send a visitors' order, but Annie didn't respond. Kate continued to write, sending money and stamps and then finally, in the last week of September she received a letter.

Dear Kate

I'm sorry I haven't written before; I've been ill coming off the gear. And I didn't know what to say.

Thank you for the stamps and money, you've done so much already, you shouldn't do more.

The court case is scheduled for next Tuesday at Exeter Crown. Jack's birthday, can you believe it? It's unreal that he's going to be five. I miss him so much.

I've made such a mess of everything Kate. I'm sorry for all the things I said, you don't deserve them. You're the good one, I know that. Thank you for taking such good care of Jack. He's very lucky to have you.

Would you send some photographs? I'll understand if you don't.

Someone came round talking about 12-step meetings yesterday. I think I might try them.

Sorry doesn't seem enough any more. But sorry.

I love you

Annie xx

Jack had a birthday party arranged at the local indoor play park; guests weren't arriving until two. At ten thirty Kate was sitting, ashen-faced, in the gallery of Exeter Crown Court wondering how she was going to face the mothers of Jack's school friends when she felt like her heart was being wrung dry.

Annie was brought into the dock by a security officer. She was uncuffed and left alone in the plastic cubicle; she looked so young and vulnerable. Kate watched as Annie's eyes scanned the room, eventually finding Kate and giving a sad little smile. Annie looked well, she'd put on some weight and her hair was clean and bright. She was wearing a drab grey tracksuit which Kate assumed must be prison issue.

Annie pleaded guilty to all charges — possession with intent to supply and conspiracy to supply class A drugs. Her solicitor made a case of mitigating circumstances; Annie had a troubled background; she'd become addicted to drugs as a teenager and had struggled with mental health problems; she was vulnerable and had been taken advantage of by more serious criminals. She had a young son, (Kate's stomach flip-flopped). Furthermore, during her short time in prison Annie was co-operating fully with a drug treatment officer and was keen to attend 12-step meetings, her solicitor said. Annie was determined to use this time to make a fresh start.

She was sentenced to five years, half of which she would serve in custody.

'All rise.'

Kate stood, that strange ringing in her ears again. She looked down at Annie who was being cuffed ready to be led away, her pale face tilted up towards Kate; she looked dazed but dry-eyed. Kate was crying freely. Her brain seemed to have jammed. She was crushed for Annie, the thought of what might happen to her in prison, how alone and frightened she must feel. But another thought was lurking behind the horror and mingled with the tears of sadness were also tears of relief. Two and a half years. They had two and a half years of breathing space. Two and a half years to forget. Two and a half years of uninterrupted time with Jack.

A sound, half mumble, half groan brought Kate speeding back to the present; she jolted upright and realised she'd been nodding off.

'Mum?'

Jack was awake.

Part II
Annie

*"I understood myself only after
I destroyed myself. And only
in the process of fixing myself
did I know who I really was"*
    Sade Andria Zabal

One

The door closed and the lock clunked home, the sound of finality.

Annie stood just over the threshold, clutching her few belongings and smilingly uncertainly at the room's other occupant.

'Hi,' she managed, not moving.

The cell was not so different to the one she'd inhabited on remand. That had been in the South West of England, a holding prison until her sentence was determined, now she'd been moved much further up the country. This cell was long and narrow with two single beds rather than bunk beds, a space of less than three feet between them. Each had a headboard with built-in shelves for personal items. There was a desk and a chair, made in the same factory-pine colour as the beds, along with a stainless-steel washbasin, topped with a little polished stainless-steel mirror, and a stainless-steel toilet behind a privacy screen. A small, high, barred window punctuated the farthest wall.

'I saw yous in Eastward Park, innit?' her new roommate said. She'd been lying flat on the bed when the guard showed Annie to the cell but had pushed herself up on her elbows when Annie entered. Now she swivelled upright and put her bare feet on the floor. 'You comin' in den? I won't bite ya.' She had a deep chuckle that made Annie think of treacle and she relaxed a little. 'I'm Veronica,' she added, 'peeps calls me, Vern, doh.'

'Annie,' Annie replied with a tight little smile, moving into the room and putting her things on the unmade bed. The guard had made a hurried introduction, but it was reassuring that Vern wanted to properly introduce herself. Annie's first experience of cell life had been her new cellmate barking a list of dos and don'ts at her and she'd anticipated more of the same.

Vern watched as Annie put her spare clothes in her allocated drawer and began making her bed.

'You ain't got much stuff!' She chuckled again.

'No, they lost my luggage on the flight over, so annoying,' Annie quipped, and Vern let out a cackle of mirth. 'I only had the clothes I was arrested in,' Annie explained as she wrestled the thin pillow into the even thinner pillowcase. 'And I've had no visits.'

'No visits? Jeez. But you was in da Park in July, innit?' Vern began rolling a cigarette. 'You smoke, yeah?' She leant over to pass the pouch to Annie, who raised her eyebrows in surprise. 'Just a slim one mind!' Vern added jovially, but Annie knew she meant it. Smoking was an expensive luxury and people rarely gave tobacco away. It had been a standing joke when Annie was on remand to watch new inmates roll their cigarettes progressively thinner as the weeks passed. Annie was cautious about taking the tobacco, potentially becoming indebted to a stranger.

'I'm jus' being kind, innit?' Vern assured her. 'You looks like you could use it.'

Vern was a kind woman. She was a mother and a grandmother and the idea of three months without seeing her family appalled her. She was of Jamaican descent, her parents being some of the first settlers of the Windrush generation, and she had extended family living across Brixton and other parts of London. Despite being in her late teens during the riots of 1981, Vern had mostly been shielded from any kind of real criminality until her early thirties. She was part of a strong, churchgoing community with tight family ties. She had four children whom she'd raised with the help of her family, due to their mostly-absent father, and she worked part-time at the job centre. That was until the late nineties when she was first introduced to crack cocaine and spent the next fifteen years sliding deeper into addiction and its attendant criminality.

Annie accepted the tobacco pouch.

'Thanks,' she said, making a rare decision to trust on first sight and hoping she wouldn't regret it. 'I was worried we wouldn't be allowed to smoke, this being the rehab wing an' all.' She sat on the half-made bed to roll a cigarette.

'I think I might spontaneously combust if I had to give up smoking on top of everything else.'

Vern hooted again, 'Spontaneously combust? Get you wich yer fancy words!' Laughing, she clambered back onto her bed, leaning against the rickety headboard. 'Seriously doh,' she said, with a look concern, 'how come you've had no visits? Where's ya people?'

Annie surveyed her companion as she thought about her answer. Vern was in her early fifties but with her smooth, rich mahogany skin her age was indeterminable. Her hair, cropped tightly to her head, was the only feature that didn't appear soft and rounded. She had a kindly face, the laughter lines around her eyes being her only wrinkles. She was plump with an enormous bosom.

I bet she gives the most amazing cuddles, Annie found herself thinking.

'I didn't want to see anyone,' she heard herself say. 'My sister, Kate, kept asking. My da did too, bless him, but it just didn't feel right.' Annie took a long draw and exhaled slowly; she was still trying to make sense of her actions to herself, let alone explain them to a stranger.

'I just thought I should press pause. Change the tape. I don't know, Vern.' She got up and stretched, feeling the familiar scratchy sensations of anxiety in her stomach. She began tucking the sheet haphazardly under the mattress.

'I've reeled from one disaster to another for so long, I just didn't want it all to merge into one. People rushing to my rescue is so *same old, same old*. This time I'm going to get my shit together.'

Vern looked at her with kindly scepticism. Annie didn't feel she was being made fun of but at the same time Vern had a face which said she'd seen it all, many times, and knew the outcome. The knowing look threatened Annie's delicate tendrils of hope, which retracted like the tentacles of a sea creature.

'I don't know,' she said again, a little defensively, squinting against the cigarette smoke as she flipped up the flimsy mattress to tuck the sheet beneath. 'That probably sounds stupid; I expect you've heard it a thousand times before, but it's how I feel.'

'Sounds more like you was ashamed to see 'em to me.' Vern said, not unkindly, stubbing out her cigarette and hissing as it burnt her fingers.

'Maybe.' Annie had finished making the bed and sat on it, folding her legs beneath her. 'I'm just fed up with being the *fuck up*. I tried so hard to clean up last year but just couldn't do it. This is my chance now; I'm going to make the most of what's happened.'

'You been banged up before?' Vern asked, rolling onto her side to face Annie.

Annie mirrored her so that both women were lying facing each other, their legs curled up and their heads on their arms. Annie had the feeling she'd known this person her whole life.

'No,' she replied, 'I mean, I've been in police custody plenty of times and been nicked for possession, had the house turned over, stuff like that.' She paused as she remembered the broken doors and trashed furniture. 'They've never found anything or been able to make anything stick. Things just got crazy; I never meant to get in so deep.'

Annie rolled onto her back, the enormity of the situation a physical pain below her ribcage. 'I had... I have... a son.' Her voice cracked and she wondered again why she was telling a stranger all this. 'He was my world and I fucked it up.' She put her arm over her face and said no more. Vern didn't press her. The two women lay in silence for a long time.

Eventually Annie rolled over again. Vern was still lying in the same position but had noiselessly acquired a book, which she now lowered to observe Annie.

'I went on the run, over two years ago now,' Annie's voice was gravelly with emotion, but her eyes were dry. 'If I'd just faced up to things, I would probably have Jack back, but I gave him up, I let her take him thinking some miracle was going to happen, I was going to get clean and we were going to live happily ever after.'

Annie's mind started spinning and she felt far away from herself, as always seemed to happen when she thought about Jack. 'I just don't know what I was thinking,' she managed, bitterly.

'You was in da chaos,' Vern said knowingly. 'Don't be so harsh wiv yerself, innit. You was fire fightin, y'know? Reactin. And everyfin's blowin up in yer face. When it gets like that ya tinkin' gets real small, ya can't see the bigger picture, ya get me? Ya just reactin... Reactin yerself right into a big 'ole mess.'

Annie understood exactly what Vern meant. Her whole life had felt like she was being catapulted from one bad decision to another with no time to think and respond, just react and run. She felt like the ball in a pinball machine.

'What about you Vern?' she asked, keen to take the attention from herself. 'What are you in for?'

'Murder,' Vern said simply, putting her book down and propping her head up on her hand. Annie was trying to arrange her face into a look of mild curiosity. 'Ma fella, I stabbed him, innit. I'd taken nuff of his shit; he was a monster. I din't mean to kill him. Self-defence, y'know what I'm sayin? Judge dint 'ear dat. Anyways 'ere, I am.' Vern shrugged and turned her palm up.

The women talked easily as Vern told her story. Her *fella* had been a notorious crack dealer in South London. A decade ago, when he first stayed in her bed, she'd thought it an ingenious way of ensuring her drug supply never ran out. But this huge man — in stature, character and reputation, was not about to be anybody's free ticket. He dominated her totally, encouraging her not only to increase her use of crack but also plying her with benzos and barbiturates to keep her compliant. Her home became a crack den; her children stopped visiting and Vern found herself alone in a world of violence. Twice she'd taken the rap when the house was raided, as well as having numerous arrests for possession and anti-social behaviour. She was too terrified and too far gone to ask for help, even in prison, and each time returned home to continue the nightmare. In recent years she'd seen the boy-runners getting younger and more vulnerable and being sent out to rural towns and villages. She'd watched them get beaten for mistakes and taken beatings herself for intervening. During one such beating a kitchen knife came to hand and she inadvertently freed herself for good.

'So now I aim to ge' off dis shit for good, innit, spend the time I got lef' wiv ma family,' Vern said finally, reaching her hand across the narrow gap between the beds. Annie took it. 'I'm like you now, see? I've had enough, I aim to clean up proper dis time.'

Annie was filled with a rush of happiness, the tendrils of hope flaring once more. She felt so grateful for Vern and that things seemed, finally, to be going okay. The feeling was so new and unexpected it caught in her throat and made her eyes burn.

'Anyways,' Vern's mellow tones broke into her thoughts. 'Dinner!'

Two

The dining hall was a large, open space below two floors of cells. D wing, where Annie and Vern were housed, adjoined this block via a corridor which opened onto the hall through double doors. Several other doors led off the vast, echoey space, giving access to other parts of the prison. The hall was also used for *Association* and there were pool and ping-pong tables at the far end along with a number of small telephone cubicles and a huge pinboard displaying notices about activities and house rules. Four staircases led up to the galleried floors above and the serving hatch, with kitchens beyond, ran along one of the longer walls of the rectangular space.

Annie was used to prison routine by now, the chatter and clatter and more than occasional scuffle that broke out the moment doors were unlocked, and the women came together. If she were honest with herself, she'd not found the process of integration all that difficult. Annie was an adapter. When she was a child, she learnt the best way to get along was to work out what others expected of her and be that. She'd mastered the art very well, except with her mother. No matter how much Annie tried she never seemed able to please her mother. On rare occasions she would gain approval but when she repeated the behaviour would find it was no longer enough, she needed to do it better or more in order to meet requirements. Annie's entire working model came undone with Jacqui Harper, perhaps that's why the relationship damaged her so. Annie didn't fully understand this yet.

For now, and in most life situations, being able to adapt to her environment suited Annie very well. She was relaxed and easy going, as though she'd been here a thousand times before. It wasn't that she became a totally different person, but that she blended herself to best meet the needs of those around her. When quiet was expected, she was quiet, but mostly she would sing and dance and tell stories appropriate to her audience, always gaining approval and popularity. Everybody liked Annie.

It came as a real shock, therefore, that when she walked across the noisy dining hall somebody deliberately barged into her, causing her tray to tip and cascade potato and beans down her only set of civilian clothes before splattering on the floor.

'Watch yerself ging-er,' the woman spat before laughing to her companion and moving on.

'You be watchin' yaself, bumbaclot!' Vern appeared at Annie's side, sucking through her teeth and looking threateningly at the back of Annie's assailant.

Some of Vern's friends sitting at a nearby table, looked over.

'You okay der, Vern?' one of them asked, half rising. The woman who had shoved Annie, looked over and sneered as she sat at a far table but otherwise didn't react and after a few rumblings the women got back to the business of eating and chatting.

The guard who had shown Annie to her room earlier appeared with a dustpan and mop and passed them to Annie.

'Then go get yourself another plate of food,' she said kindly.

'God that's all I need on my first day, a gingerphobe.' Annie sighed, as she cleared up the remnants of her dinner.

They ate with Vern's friends, or her *sistren* as she called them with another rich chuckle. Annie relaxed, at least outwardly, and by the time they went back to their cells she'd won the approval of the little group and the incident was forgotten in jokes and laughter.

That night Annie lay awake as Vern snored gently in the bed opposite. She was thinking about the tall blonde woman who had barged into her and how she, Annie, had reacted. She'd frozen, she knew it and it left her feeling embarrassed and vulnerable. Once upon a time, Annie was thought of as someone who could handle herself; certainly as a teenager in the schoolyard, and during the sibling scuffles she'd had with Kate, she would be the one throwing punches, lairy and aggressive. But that was before she met Jack's father, her first introduction to real violence. Her mother had been violent, lashing out, pulling hair and striking her face, sometimes enough to bruise, but Jacqui's real weapon was emotional bullying. With Paul, Jack's father, Annie had known true terror.

In the early days, once or twice, she'd tried to fight back but this had made Paul's rage all the more terrible. Fleeing, too, made the beatings worse when he finally caught her, which he always did. So she'd learnt to freeze, protecting her face and body as best she could from his battering fists and feet and waiting for it to be over. Later, when Jack came along, the whole process was repeated — at first she tried to fight Paul off when he would rage at the tiny baby, then she tried to flee, the result being that Paul allowed her no money or access to the car or phone. So she resorted to putting her own body between the baby and Paul's white-hot rage and *numbing out,* as she called it, until it subsided. Some fundamental thing seemed to shift within her so that now when confronted by violence or aggression, Annie would freeze and numb out even without intending to, only coming back to herself a good while after the danger had passed. *What kind of stupid defence mechanism is that?* she grumbled inwardly to herself as she rolled over, trying to get comfortable on the thin mattress.

She spent the rest of the night lying awake with the enormity of her life situation. She wasn't really thinking, there wasn't a single loose thread to start unravelling the knotted tangle of bad memories, losses and regrets. Rather, a kind of blank buzzing filled her mind, and she had a feeling that something, like hot, black tar, was filling her insides from her navel to her throat. Occasionally her mind would open just enough to allow a thought or an image of Jack to surface, but she would immediately cringe away from it as though it were a hot flame which might ignite the dark, viscid substance which consumed her.

Three

'Tell me about when you first took drugs, Annie.'

It was the following day. The morning had passed with a hasty, pre-packed breakfast, a walk around the yard and her first 12-step meeting. Thankfully, Joni (Annie now had a name for the tall, blonde woman who had taken such an instant dislike to her) had kept her distance when they were in the communal spaces and wasn't housed on the rehab wing. Now Annie sat in a bright, airy office filled with pot plants and coloured cushions. The walls were adorned with paintings and inspirational quotes. *'Don't give up the day before the miracle happens!'* urged one particularly vibrant piece of artwork from the opposite wall.

Annie looked at Julie, her newly assigned recovery worker, and thought how best to answer the question. Julie was slight and willowy looking with very fine, very straight mousy brown hair. She wore no make-up and a plain, heavy linen shift dress, yet she seemed to emit a kind of glow that was both reassuring and uplifting.

'I heard something brilliant in the meeting today.' Annie spoke after a moment. 'It just made so much sense to me. This lady said, *"people kept telling me I had to stop taking drugs, that's all I ever heard — you take too many drugs — but nobody ever spoke to me about how I felt when I didn't take drugs".* Annie paused as she tried to recollect the exact words. 'She said, *"'it took me years to realise I couldn't stop taking drugs because I didn't know how to do life without them'.*' She looked searchingly at Julie, hoping she was making sense.

'Yes, go on,' the counsellor prompted. 'How does this relate to when *you* first took drugs?'

'Well, it got me thinking you see,' Annie replied, pausing again to gather her thoughts. 'I was always so scared when I was a child. I don't even think I knew how scared I was because I've always been scared, and I was so good at pretending that I wasn't.'

'Being scared all the time sounds like hard work, Annie.'

'God it was. It is!' Annie corrected herself, 'But I remember the first time I took something—actually, it was alcohol, and I suddenly felt like everything was okay, like I didn't have to try so hard any more, like I could be like everyone else without pretending. It felt amazing,' she finished, wondering whether that was the right thing to say.

'Do you think everybody feels that way, kind of invincible, when they drink alcohol, Annie?' Julie asked, smiling encouragingly.

'Well, yes,' Annie replied. 'that's the point, I guess. People, myself included, always seem to focus on what happens when we take drugs but *this*, this is about how I feel when I *don't* take drugs.' Annie swept her hair from her face and looked earnestly at the counsellor. 'I think I got in such a muddle because the only time I really felt okay was when I took drugs. I guess if someone feels okay when they don't take drugs, they don't need to take them all the time. Does that make sense?' she asked anxiously.

'Yes, that makes sense,' Julie said, nodding, 'but what matters most is what makes sense to you, Annie.'

'Oh, this does!' Annie replied enthusiastically, 'This really does. I'm learning that it's not just about stopping the drugs, I need to learn how to live without them. I don't think I've ever known how to do that.'

'That's interesting, Annie,' Julie said, making a little note on her pad. 'What makes you think you've never known how to live without drugs?'

Again, Annie paused. Her thoughts were such a jumble. She felt hopeful, excited even, for the first time in so long. The feeling had burgeoned yesterday, when she realised she had a true companion in Vern, but today, when she'd met the other women on the rehab wing and heard the story of someone who'd left prison last year; someone who'd lived like her, used drugs like her and was now living a productive life, back with her family, well now her hope was really sprouting wings and she felt a little groundless and unstable. She'd trained herself so well, for so long, not to look too closely at the reality of things, that it was hard to get her mind to play ball.

'Well,' she began slowly. 'I guess, when I think about it, I always felt like I didn't know what I was supposed to do. I looked at other people and they all seemed to be getting on with it, like they *knew*. My sister, Kate,' she went on, gaining confidence as she spoke, 'she always seemed so certain about things, like she just knew what was right and what was wrong, what she liked and what she didn't. But me? I just felt confused. Everybody who mattered seemed to want different things.' Annie began to feel muddled again.

'Do you mean when you were a young child Annie?' Julie asked, helping Annie to see where she was going. 'Who were the people who mattered?'

'Yes, when I was young,' Annie confirmed. 'From as young as I can remember. I always loved Da; he was always happy with me, always pleased to see me. We were always laughing and *having the craic*, as he called it. But Mum was always angry with him, always saying how useless he was, and she would get mad if anyone suggested otherwise. So to keep her happy it was best not to mention Da at all and even to pretend I didn't like him much either.'

'That sounds difficult.'

'Yes. Looking back, it was. I always felt guilty, like I was doing something wrong, but I wasn't sure what. I don't think Kate had that problem because she didn't like Da very much anyway.' Annie managed a laugh. 'I mean, don't get me wrong, I don't think it was easy for Kate either. My mum was always angry at both of us. But I don't know, it didn't seem to bother her so much.'

'How people appear on the outside isn't always a good reflection of how they are inside, Annie, that's an important lesson you'll learn whilst you're here.'

'Yes, I suppose.' Annie sighed, picking up one of the cushions and hugging it to herself. 'But Kate never seemed to upset Mum quite as much as I did. And she was definitely pleased when Da left for good. It was obvious. But it was the worst day of my life. Ha! All seven years of it!' Annie started to pull a loose thread on the cushion. Julie said nothing, leaving space for her to continue. 'It still feels like one of the worst days of my life,' Annie said finally. 'I felt utterly alone in that house with Kate and Mum being so *good riddance!* and me feeling like my world had fallen apart but being afraid to show it, because that would mean I was on the *wrong side*.' Annie felt herself being sucked back into those enormous childhood feelings and it felt dangerous, like quicksand; she was afraid she'd get pulled under for good.

Julie seemed to sense this and said, 'It's okay Annie, this is all in the past. You're safe here. It might not feel like it but shining some light on these early memories will help. Trust me when I say they're right there under the surface, festering, whether you're willing to acknowledge them or not. But you don't have to talk about anything you don't want to, not today,' she added kindly.

'No, no, I want to talk about it. I do feel safe,' Annie said, sitting up a little straighter again. 'It just felt so hard. I missed Da so much, but I wasn't allowed even to mention him, if I did then Mum would blow up, going on and on about all the awful things he'd ever done, how he couldn't love me because he wouldn't stop drinking. I never believed he didn't love me because he drank; I always seemed to know that he just couldn't stop drinking.' She paused, letting that idea sink in. 'Anyway, I had to keep all those feelings bottled up. I wet the bed, you know, right up until I was about ten! And I would sleepwalk all the time. Mum would get so cross: *there's something wrong with you!* she'd say, and I really believed there must be.' Annie's throat felt raw as she spoke. 'Every so often it would all burst out and I'd really let rip. I was just a little kid, seven or eight, but she'd go wild, telling me how I'd ruined her life, how ungrateful I was, how she'd thought about just leaving me with my drunken father and making a new life for herself. And I think the worst thing, the thing that really twisted me up, was that she'd tell me I was crazy. She'd tell me I hadn't seen things that I knew I had or that things hadn't happened when I knew they did. She really made me *feel* crazy, you know?'

Annie looked up at Julie and saw tears in the counsellor's eyes; it was the last thing she'd expected, and tears sprang into her own eyes.

'Oh!' she gasped in surprise, 'Oh! I haven't cried properly in so long! God, it's actually hurting my eyes!' She laughed it off and took a tissue.

'And what happened then, Annie, after your Da left?' Julie pressed her gently after a significant pause.

'Well, it just went on like that for a while I think,' Annie replied, wiping her eyes. 'Mum made us change our name to Harper, I didn't want to. I changed it back to O'Shea when I was fourteen; she's never forgiven me. But in the beginning, I didn't have a choice.' Annie rolled the damp tissue between her fingers. 'Then we moved in with Mum's new bloke when I was nine; it was going to be a new start for us, Mum said, but he wasn't really interested in us, and they argued all the time.'

'The arguing sounds difficult, Annie.'

'It was,' Annie said, leaning over and putting the shredded tissue in the bin. 'I remember when I was, like, ten, eleven? Just about to start secondary school. All we'd ever known was rowing. Jeff, Mum's second husband — oh yeah, she married him in the end —' Annie added hastily to her story, 'he would bang his fists on the table and crash about. Mum would take it out on us, say she'd been cursed. It's funny...' Annie paused thoughtfully. 'I don't remember me and Kate being together hardly at all. You'd think we'd look out for each other, wouldn't you? That it would push us closer together?' She looked up at Julie. 'But it didn't. I think it was those early messages from Mum; we were in different camps. We just didn't trust each other, even as kids.' Annie felt the sting of tears once more. 'Jeff moved out in the end, ha, out of his own house. My mum can be such a bitch,' she added with a glimmer of admiration. 'I barely saw Da, not for a few years. I would see him at Granny O'Shea's but that was difficult too because Granny O'Shea really didn't like Mum so she would bang on and on. I know she wasn't trying to make it difficult,' Annie added quickly. 'I love Granny O'Shea to bits, but she was on the wrong team too, so I'd always be treated like a deserter when I got home.' Annie paused; she was beginning to get that strange, faraway feeling she got when she touched anything too painful. 'Then *he* came,' she said. 'But I don't want to talk about that today. Please.'

'Of course, Annie. You've done so well,' Julie said, reaching over and touching Annie's hand. The unexpected gesture made Annie jump a little. 'I'm sorry Annie, I shouldn't have touched you without asking if it's okay,' Julie said, sitting back.

'Oh, no, no, it's nice!' Annie said, putting the cushion back and clasping her hands in her lap. 'I just feel a bit weird. Spacey…' she tried to explain.

'Don't worry, that's just a normal response of your psyche trying to protect itself from painful things. It'll get easier as we work with it.' Julie said, gently touching Annie's hand again. This time Annie didn't jump but found her fingers gripping Julie's briefly. Julie sat back after a moment.

'Now, I'd like us to do one last thing before you leave. There's no need to look so worried!' she added as Annie recoiled a little. 'Because we're talking about these difficult things it's a really good idea for you to have a safe place, somewhere in your mind you can go if it gets too much or as a kind of reset at the end of a session,' Julie explained. 'It's fascinating really that when we take our minds to somewhere that's comforting, our bodies respond accordingly, they produce *happy hormones* that bring us out of fight or flight and help us feel safe. It will really help you with this work. Can you think of a place like that Annie?'

Annie considered this. *God, I must have one happy place!* she thought, not without mirth. First, she thought of Granny O'Shea's garden, she used to love it there, but then she remembered all the difficult conversations and how horrible it was facing her mother after a visit and that memory was tainted. Then she thought about the little flat where she'd lived with her Da for a year when she was fourteen, but that memory quickly turned sour. She thought about the park where she used to take Jack and her mind jumped back in panic, *no, no, don't think about that!*

'When I was a little girl there was a wood near where we lived,' she began. 'Da would take me there before he left but after that it was just me. Kate didn't like it and Mum would never go anywhere that wasn't tarmacked.' As she spoke the memory became clearer. 'There was a little stream, and in the spring, there would be wild garlic and bluebells. It was a magical place. I used to pretend I lived in the woods, in a hollow tree!' Annie laughed as she remembered. 'I had such an imagination when I was a little kid.' She paused. 'Imaginary places were always safe and happy…'

'Keep with the woods Annie, tell me more about them. Were there sounds? Smells?'

'I remember birds singing. Sometimes a woodpecker. I can't remember a smell… Well, the garlic I suppose, and that warm damp smell of mulch and earth. The sound of old beech nuts and acorns crunching under my feet… the sound of the little stream… mossy rocks… light coming through the canopy of leaves, looking like rays of magic.' Annie found herself smiling and breathing calmly.

'That sounds like a very safe and happy place,' Julie said, smiling, 'I want you to work on that, okay? Between now and when we next meet? And practise going there before you go to sleep at night. Well done, Annie,' she finished, standing up.

'Thank you so much.' Annie replied, meaning it.

Four

The next few days were the best Annie could remember in a long time. She wasn't sure she could call herself happy, she still felt so frozen inside, as though everything were happening to someone else, and she was witnessing it through frosted glass. But there was much laughter and joviality, especially with Vern and the sistren, a number of whom were on the rehab wing. Annie found herself laughing so much her belly hurt. She was also being more honest than she'd ever been as she engaged in 12-step meetings and recovery groups.

She'd secured a job in the kitchen garden, a highly prized position but less so with the winter months approaching. Annie didn't care about the encroaching cold and had spent several glorious hours outdoors with her hands in the soil and clearing out the polytunnels ready to plant winter vegetables. She'd been kitted out with prison-issue shirts and jumpers but was often stripped down to her tee shirt as she laboured away, finding that when her body was most active her mind was most still.

On the weekend a number of the women had visits and Annie had her first really low day. Alone in her cell she tried, without success, to take herself to her safe place but found she couldn't keep the negativity from seeping in. Who did she think she was? She had no right to laugh or be happy, she was a horrible person. Not only had she made a complete mess of her own life, but she was also a terrible mother. *No! No!* Thoughts of Jack made her feel physically ill. She lay on her bed, gripping her sides. The thick, black tar had returned, spreading about her abdomen, burning as it went, blistering the tender place below her ribcage and constricting her chest, searing her throat like acid. There were no tears. Who was she kidding? She wasn't going to get her life together or see Jack again; she wasn't like those women who came in for the meetings. She wished so much that Vern was here, but Vern was on a visit with her eldest son and grandchildren.

Later in the morning the cell was unlocked to allow prisoners to shower or use the library. Annie pulled herself together enough to head down to the showers, which they shared with C wing. She kept her head down as she walked the corridor, the all too familiar feelings of fear and shame lapping at her insides, causing her to feel naked and dirty.

The shower block was an L-shaped room with a row of stainless-steel sinks and three toilet cubicles at the foot and a row of a dozen showers along the length. A long bench with hooks above ran opposite the showers and served as the changing area. The walls were a dirty, pale pink and the floor was made up of grubby beige ridged tiles with a channel cut through to carry excess water. Several of the mildewed, greying shower curtains were missing.

There was a little huddle of women by the sinks to Annie's right as she entered, none of whom she knew. Annie felt relief that she wouldn't have to make conversation as she moved ahead to the bench and undressed quietly. She had very little money but had managed to buy some cheap shampoo, which doubled up as shower gel, and some conditioner, without which her thick curly hair was completely unmanageable. Clutching her toiletries, she pulled back the flimsy shower curtain and hid herself in the cubicle, but before she could turn on the water, she heard a voice that made her insides shrivel.

'Oi! Ging-er, on yer own today then?' Joni grabbed the shower curtain and shook it, causing Annie to cringe away.

'Oi! I'm talkin' to ya!' The shower curtain was ripped back, and Joni stood there with three cronies, one of whom was the skinny girl from the canteen. Annie kicked herself inwardly for not recognising them.

'Joni please…' Annie began.

'Oh, Joni puh-leez.' Joni put on a ludicrously well-spoken voice as though mimicking Annie whilst her friends cackled.

'Please Joni, I just can't handle this today,' Annie said again, trying to cover her nakedness, which was making her feel doubly vulnerable.

'What ya covering yerself up for? Like we wanna see yer ginger minge!' Joni grimaced and made vomiting sounds. 'Ere, keep her there a minute,' she added to the others and disappeared out of sight. She returned moments later holding the plastic cup from her flask. Annie shrank away, fearing the boiling sugar water of which she'd heard nightmare stories.

'Here's a shower for ya!' Joni spat as she threw the liquid into Annie's face. 'Drink my piss, bitch!' she added, shrieking with laughter. Annie flung her arms up but not quickly enough and the hot liquid caught her full in the face, going up her nose and in her mouth. It had the undeniable stench of urine. The four women hooted gleefully as Annie slid down the wall, hugging her knees and feeling herself numb out, awaiting the inevitable assault.

'Everything all right in here?' A guard's voice came from the doorway of the shower block and Annie gave an involuntary moan.

'Yes miss, just finishing up!' Joni's skinny friend called, aiming a kick at Annie before the four women moved away to gather their things. As they passed Annie's cubicle on their way out, Joni reached in and grabbed Annie's shampoo.

'Say anything an' I'll fucking kill ya,' she said coldly. And they were gone.

Annie managed to haul herself upright and turn on the shower, splashing her face and gargling the clean water, then she slid back down the wall and let the feeble spray fall on her until she was shivering with cold. She stood and washed herself the best she could with her conditioner, dried and dressed then, avoiding the lunch queue, headed back to her cell.

'Hey, where was you a' lunch den?' Vern asked an hour or so later when she returned to the cell, glowing from her visit. Annie sat up and looked at her friend, she felt genuine pleasure at Vern's obvious happiness, it was the first positive feeling she'd had all day and it surprised her, like the sun coming out from behind the clouds and giving unexpected warmth.

'I haven't been feeling great today. Headache.' She lied easily as she stood up and stretched. 'Anyway, how was your visit?' Annie smiled; it felt like her face had been set in clay.

'Ah, it was so good. My boy? He's such a handsome ting, y'know!' Vern's face was like the sun shining and Annie felt herself thawing out. 'You look like shit, innit.' Vern added, looking concerned, 'You sure nutting else gwan?'

'I'm fine, honestly.' Annie turned her back to look in the mirror. Her hair was a catastrophe, her face looked drawn, and her eyes shadowed. She pulled a face and turned away. A familiar *shkid* made her look to the door to see a number of papers slide across the floor. Vern got there first.

'Canteen sheets,' she said, handing one to Annie. 'And you got mail!' she added, passing Annie an envelope, sliced open across the top. Annie took it, feeling her chest constrict. She could already see the small package contained photographs and sat jerkily at the small desk to empty the contents. Four photographs: Jack on a swing, Jack sitting on the floor with a collection of brightly coloured trucks, Jack pulling a small wooden cart, Jack peering out of a dark-green little hut, laughing. Annie's head whirled; Vern's voice sounded a long way off. Her heart didn't seem to be beating, just filling up painfully in her chest. She found she couldn't look at the images any longer and turned instead to the letter.

'Ah! So dis ya pickney den, yeah?' Vern was leaning over her shoulder, sliding the pictures towards her across the desk.

'Yes,' Annie managed. 'Yes, that's Jack. This is from Kate. She says she'd like to visit.'

'An' you gon let her dis time?' Vern asked. Annie could feel her eyes boring into her.

'Yes, yes I am,' she breathed.

That evening, Annie filled out her canteen sheet, requesting a new bottle of shampoo and a small pouch of tobacco. She also completed a visiting order, carefully entering Kate and Jack's full names. Kate hadn't specifically said she would bring Jack and it was a long way for him to travel, Annie reasoned. But Kate had sent the photos and Annie couldn't tolerate the thought that Kate would have brought him if only his name were on the VO.

That night she dreamt she was trapped in a glass tank which was slowly filling up with a murky liquid. At first, she thought it was piss but then realised it was heroin, cooked and ready to inject. She flailed about trying to keep from ingesting the shiny brown liquid, and as she struggled, she could see Jack being led away from her, the tall blonde woman holding his hand became interchangeably Joni then Kate.

Five

Annie was surprised at how quickly the week passed. Her days were mostly spent with the other women on D wing, in recovery groups and meetings.

It was incredible to her that she was not alone in her suffering, that other women had felt as she did, had made the same awful mistakes. Most importantly, when the women came in to share from outside the prison, Annie learnt that they were free from the grips of addiction and were building full and happy lives for themselves. As she listened and shared some of her own story, she began to gather some paltry crumbs of hope. When she wasn't in her groups she was in the garden where she found she could lose herself in the physical demands of the job. She'd seen Joni once in the dining hall but had been with Vern and the sistren and Joni didn't look up. On Thursday she had her weekly session with Julie but this week, without really knowing or understanding it, she was holding far too much inside herself to fully engage in the process.

'You seem far away today, Annie,' Julie said finally, around halfway through the session when they'd shared little more than small talk. 'Why do you think that is?'

Annie was silent for a while, pulling the strands of her favourite cushion. She knew she'd had difficulty relaying her week because she was avoiding any mention of the incident in the shower or the dreams and memories that the bullying had elicited; that meant cutting out great swathes of her waking and sleeping life. It interested her how one lie by omission could seep out and taint so much of everything else.

Then there were her desperate hopes and fears about seeing Jack on Saturday. She was trying so hard not to hope, to *let go*, as they were always talking about in the meetings, but she found she couldn't. She'd stuck Jack's pictures to the cell wall with toothpaste, as Vern had shown her, and even though it was too painful to fully look at them she knew they were there and could allow herself a glance as she entered and exited the room and got dressed in the morning.

What confused her most and felt impossible to articulate was the abject fear she experienced at the thought of seeing the little boy. Would he remember her? Call her Mummy? Would he be angry with her? What on earth would she say to him? He was two and a half years old when she'd last properly spoken to him, now he was five, at that age it was a lifetime of difference. She didn't know him, and she didn't know any five-year-old little boys on which she might base any assumptions about him. In fact, other than Jack, she hadn't properly known any children; she'd no idea how she should behave. These fears felt so shameful to her, that she was afraid of her own child rather than brimming over with excitement, that she couldn't begin to explain them to Julie or anyone.

'I'm just wondering what you're thinking about Annie.' Julie's voice broke into Annie's reverie.

'I was thinking about Jack,' Annie replied, then immediately wished she hadn't. She'd spoken to no one about Jack bar a few short sentences to Vern, who so graciously accepted that she was unwilling or unable to say more.

'Jack,' was all that Julie said, smiling and nodding as she leant forward to put her elbows on her knees and her chin in her hands.

Annie relaxed a little and smiled. 'I think my sister might bring him to see me on Saturday.' She hesitated. 'I was just thinking about that.'

'Wow, that's big stuff. How are you feeling about it?'

'Good!' Annie replied, a little too quickly. 'I mean, I'm really looking forward to seeing him…' Her voice trailed off.

'That's great, Annie,' Julie said, then leant back looking thoughtful. 'I think, if it were me, I might be feeling pretty anxious too.' She looked up to see that she'd caught Annie's attention. 'I mean, I don't want to put my feelings onto you, but I think if it were me, I'd be worrying what it will be like, not having seen him for so long.'

Annie felt herself sag in the chair, as though she'd been physically holding herself together.

'Is it normal, then, to feel like that?' she asked as Julie smiled and nodded. 'I've been feeling like I'm crazy.'

'You are not and never have been crazy Annie,' Julie said firmly.

'I do feel scared. I just don't know how I should be. I don't know him or what he likes or anything.' Annie began to feel that floaty, distant feeling she always had when she thought about Jack.

'Annie, you just need to be yourself. Children are attracted to authentic people, and trust me, they can spot the frauds a mile off. Just be your wonderful, funny and colourful self.' Julie smiled warmly.

Annie blanched. Far from feeling encouraged by these words, she felt in freefall again.

'But I am a fraud!' she cried desperately, chucking the cushion to one side and standing to pace the room. 'I have no idea who I am; how can I be myself when I don't know who that is!'

The rest of the session was patchy. Julie assured Annie that it was unlikely others saw her in the way she saw herself. She reminded Annie that, when she wasn't trying too hard, when she was singing and dancing and larking around, she was well liked by everyone. But when Annie heard this, she could only think of the little group of women who clearly didn't like her at all, and she became lost in her own private thoughts again. Finally, Julie assured her that how she felt was perfectly normal, and if she were brave enough to speak to other women, she would find that many of them had felt the same. Annie returned to her cell feeling marginally better than before.

Friday came and went in a flurry of activity; gardening in the morning then group in the afternoon, followed by the gym. D wing showered together after gym, for which Annie was thankful; she hadn't braved the shower block alone since last week's humiliation.

Then it was Saturday. In a way Annie was pleased that all she had to wear was her prison-issue tracksuit, the baked beans stain proving immovable from her own tee shirt. She'd washed her hair the day before and her cheeks were coloured from hours outside in the weak autumn sunshine but when she looked in the little mirror, Annie saw only fear and shame in her hollowed-out eyes. She'd had another nightmare last night, this time arriving in the dream to find she'd just taken heroin, the syringe still in her hand but no memory of using it, just the terrible realisation of what she'd done. Joni and her cronies laughed and blocked her way as Kate hurried Jack away, calling over her shoulder that she knew Annie could never come good. Annie had woken in a cold sweat in the early hours and lain awake ever since.

Visiting took place in a single-storey red-brick building on the far side of the exercise yard; a plastic-covered walkway linked it to the main prison block where Annie found herself being chivvied along with the other women who had their visits at ten. The room itself was large and open-plan. There were dozens of low tables with moulded plastic chairs attached by metal bars, like you find in some fast-food restaurants. There were two vending machines in the far corner selling hot drinks and snacks and at the opposite end of the room were the double doors from which the visitors would enter.

By the time Annie was seen to her table, a number of visits were already in progress, some with small children clambering about, the guards hovering to ensure nothing was being passed to an inmate and reminding the adults to sit back in their chairs and adhere to the required distancing. Annie found she couldn't breathe, at least her breath seemed to reach the hollow of her throat but no further; these women looked so relaxed with their children, as one would expect mothers to be. *I must relax and be myself,* she said to herself, forcing her breath a little deeper into her constricted chest.

Then Kate was walking towards her. There was a group in front of her so she could only see a bit of blonde hair and face, Jack was hidden from view. Annie's heart seemed to have almost stopped, emitting the occasional, huge thud. The knot of people had found their tables so that Kate was now clearly in view. She was carrying what looked like a bundle of clothes and she was alone. Annie stood up then sat down, not sure of the etiquette. She stood up again hoping to give Kate a quick hug but as she put her arms out a guard appeared from nowhere.

'No contact,' he said brusquely before melting back into the wall.

'Hi,' Kate said breathlessly, pushing the bundle across the table towards Annie. 'These are for you… they've been searched,' she added, more to the loitering guard over Annie's shoulder than to Annie.

'Thanks,' Annie managed, looking but not seeing. She was reeling from the emotional rollercoaster of acute anxiety, bitter disappointment and… was that relief? She couldn't get her head together at all.

'Shall I get us a coffee?' Kate was talking. 'They let me keep some coins!'

'Um… yes… sure, thanks.'

Annie leafed through the clothes whilst Kate was gone, more for something to do than anything else. She could feel the guard's eyes burning into her back. There was a pair of jeans, two long-sleeved tops and a roll-neck jumper.

'I wasn't sure what to bring.' Kate had returned with coffees and a couple of Mars bars. 'I thought it would start getting cold soon… and I guessed you didn't have any clothes when I saw you at court.'

'Thanks Kate, that was really thoughtful,' Annie said, meaning it and feeling wretched. Silence stretched out between them and then they both spoke at once.

'How long—'

'I'm sorry I didn't bring Jack, Annie.'

'It's okay,' Annie said, realising she meant that too. She felt flat, distant, drained by emotional output but at the same time, in some deep place, she realised she hadn't wanted to see Jack like this either, to put him through the stress of it all. 'I… I just put him on the VO in case, y'know, I would've hated him not to be able to come because I did it wrong. It's a very long way.'

'It's a very long way,' Kate said simultaneously, and they managed a little laugh.

'I'd hook pinkies and make a wish, but y'know,' Annie flicked her head in the direction of the guard behind her, 'Lurch here might have a coronary.'

'Annie!' Kate hissed, looking anxious but laughing all the same. 'It was awful getting in here,' she said after a moment, as Annie took a sip of her coffee and pulled a face. 'Everything searched. Mobile, keys and wallet taken. I felt like a criminal.'

Annie didn't know what to say this so said nothing, feeling soiled, feeling backfooted and uncomfortable that *good Kate* had put herself out in order to step into her world. They sat in silence sipping their drinks and looking at the other tables.

'Oliver and I are getting married!' Kate blurted out eventually as she made a grab for a Mars bar and opened it.

'Oh really?' Annie picked up the other bar. 'Congratulations. When's the big day?'

She couldn't get the packet open so went to use her teeth.

'Here,' Kate said, passing Annie her opened bar and taking Annie's, opening it easily. 'Not til next spring.' She took a bite, swallowed then said animatedly, 'But it's really exciting planning everything! Oliver proposed a few weeks ago so I've only just started looking at dresses and venues. I'm going to have three bridesmaids, I think, and Oliver's nephews are going to be pageboys! And Jack's...' Kate's voice trailed away awkwardly.

'Go on,' Annie said, 'Jack's what?' She knew she sounded moody but found she didn't care. She felt humiliated, rotten, inadequate next to Kate's glowing *ordinary life*.

'Jack's going to be ring bearer,' Kate finished lamely, putting down her half-eaten Mars bar and not meeting Annie's eyes. Annie finished hers and scrunched the wrapper into her empty paper cup.

'How is Jack?' she asked eventually.

Kate looked up with genuine sadness and concern in her eyes. Annie didn't want her sympathy; she didn't want to feel weak and vulnerable, so she bristled all the more.

'Jack's really well Annie,' Kate said, with a tight little smile. 'Did you get the photos I sent?' Without waiting for an answer, she rushed on. 'I've got loads more from his birthday party, I'll send them. He had such a great time. He loves the indoor play park and loads of his little school friends came. He's doing really well at school and we're going on holiday in December; we're taking him to Disney World in Florida! He doesn't know that yet, he just thinks we're going on holiday. We went to Spain last year but that's not the same at all...' All this came out in a great rush of words, tumbling over each other as Annie sat looking stony-faced.

'Sounds like you've been celebrating my incarceration pretty well,' she said caustically, looking around for a clock and wishing the visit would come to an end.

Kate looked like she'd been slapped. 'You did ask, Annie. I'm not trying to be insensitive—'

'Oh no, not at all,' Annie cut in. 'I just love hearing about your fabulous life and all the amazing things you're doing with *my* son whilst I'm stuck in here.'

Kate looked riled. 'And whose fault is that, Annie?' she hissed, keeping her voice down and looking nervously at the guard. 'I didn't put you in here. It took nearly four hours to get here today, I left at six o'clock this morning. I want to see you and support you. I brought you clothes.'

'But you didn't bring Jack,' Annie spat, feeling like a runaway train.

'No, I didn't bring Jack.' Kate looked at Annie with pure venom. 'You want to know why? Because you've fucked up his life enough already and you're not doing it any more, not if I have anything to do with it.' Kate was breathing hard.

'Oh Saint Kate,' Annie said slowly, in cold fury. 'Never got it wrong in her whole life and now she's going to take my son and make out she's doing it because it's the honourable thing to do.'

Kate looked stunned, her mouth slightly open, 'Would you listen to yourself?' she whispered furiously. 'Everything you put that little boy through in the first two years of his life. Violence, drug addicts, dirty needles, hardly bathing him, or feeding him, or giving him attention…'

'How fucking dare you!' Annie raged, standing up, 'That's absolute lies! Is that what you're telling everyone, telling Jack? You bitch, Kate!'

Annie was vaguely aware of the guard putting his hand on her shoulder.

'Sit down and calm down or this visit is over,' he said firmly.

Annie tried to shake him off irritably. 'I want this visit to be over anyway,' she spat at Kate. 'It wasn't even the visit I wanted.'

She saw one final look of hurt on Kate's face before she was marched out of the hall.

Later, in her cell, Annie went over the whole thing in her mind. Vern was being her usual tactful self and leaving her be. Once her initial rage had abated, Annie felt saturated in her own self-loathing. What had got into her? Kate had driven all that way to visit her. The clothes she'd so thoughtfully brought were on the desk beneath the photographs she'd sent, as requested. Why shouldn't Kate be happy with her life? And wasn't it brilliant that Jack's life was so full and happy too? And when she thought about it, deep down, hadn't she been relieved that Jack was absent, that they hadn't been reintroduced this way? So why had she hurled such abuse?

'Oh!' she couldn't help moaning out loud, the feelings of shame like a body blow. 'I really do just want what's best for Jack,' she moaned and knew it was true.

'True ting lil' sister,' Vern said, lowering her book a moment and looking at Annie, eyes full of compassion.

So why have I just burnt my bridges yet again Annie thought bitterly.

Six

The following day Annie knew she would have used heroin if it were at hand. The awareness terrified her, that after all she'd learnt, and the opportunity she'd been given, she would still reach out and flush her life down the toilet yet again.

Having talked it over with Vern she decided to write Kate a letter. She was very grateful, she said, that Kate was doing such a brilliant job of raising Jack and she knew that she, Annie, had made an utter hash of things. She would do her utmost to put it right. She wished Kate and Oliver every happiness and hoped they all had an amazing time in Florida. It cost her deeply to write it, for though she meant every word, she'd once more placed herself in the role of offender, the offensive and the miscreant, and Kate as the offended, the admirable and the innocent. Somewhere, nibbling away at her insides, was the idea that things weren't that simple; that Kate's motives were purely altruistic, and she gained nothing from the arrangement or the dynamic between the two women. But as Vern had reminded her, recovery was about keeping *her side of the street clean*, and she'd clearly made a right shitty mess of her side.

Having posted the letter, Annie still felt shaky, as though her few paltry crumbs of hope had been burned up in the heat of her outburst. She committed to redoubling her efforts in recovery, attending every 12-step meeting that was available to her, whether it was part of her compulsory timetable or not. She shared at every meeting and took phone numbers from the women who came in from outside the prison, halving her tobacco intake so that she had money to buy phone credits. With Julie's help, she examined the build-up to that damning visit with Kate. She realised that by denying her feelings and refusing to share them, she'd not only robbed herself of support from the other women, but had turned herself into a powder keg, ready to blow at the smallest spark. She committed to sharing, at least in a general way, about everything that was going on for her with at least one other human being.

It also helped that Annie had barely seen Joni at all. She heard on the grapevine that Joni had been sent to the block, an isolated wing devoid of privileges, following a series of rule breaks. Most of the information came by way of Louise, the skinny girl who usually followed Joni everywhere. In another unexpected turn of events, Louise had started working in the garden, a situation which had initially filled Annie with dread until it transpired that Louise on her own was a very different proposition to Louise as Joni's sidekick. She seemed eager to befriend Annie and to explain herself. She knew Joni *on the out*, she said, and it was an expectation that they should pal up in prison lest her life be made a misery later. Annie remained cautious but Louise was easy company and mostly it was a relief to discover there would be no further animosity, at least in the garden. Annie couldn't help thinking, and hoping, that she was in some way being rewarded for her efforts to do the right thing.

***

'Anything from Kate yet, Annie?'

It was a Thursday, almost six weeks since the awful row and Annie was in Julie's light and colourful office, sitting cross-legged on one of the low fabric chairs, hugging a cushion to herself.

'No, nothing.' she replied, then pressed her lips together in a tight, unhappy line. Whenever she spoke or thought about Kate, the same emotions would arise: shame, inadequacy, a feeling of being something rotten but mingled with a sense of injustice and frustration that she couldn't seem to redress the power balance between them.

'It's very early days Annie,' Julie said, as though reading Annie's thoughts. 'She might remain upset for a while.'

'I know,' Annie sighed, shifting her position because her foot had gone to sleep. 'I suppose I just worry that it suits her to stay sore forever. She has all the cards and I feel like I'm sat here with my begging bowl.'

'Now that's not strictly true, is it? You have a lot of rights as Jack's mother; we've talked about this.'

'I know we have,' Annie sighed again, 'but I'm really not prepared to go to the courts about it. No really,' she said more boldly as Julie made a rare attempt to interject. 'Growing up surrounded by warring adults was awful; it made me crazy. I'm not doing the same to Jack. If that's the only amends I can ever make to him then it will be something, that he's not put through that,' Annie said firmly. She had searched herself endlessly to understand why she resisted seeking legal help with Jack, she'd spoken with Vern long into the night and written page after page in her journal. The more she delved, the more she realised how much her need to win approval from the disparate adults in her life had damaged her as a child. She was not prepared to put Jack through it.

'What I really want is for Kate to *want* Jack to have a relationship with me,' Annie said earnestly, 'but if she stays mad at me and never gives me another opportunity to prove myself then I don't see how that's ever going to happen.'

'You know my thoughts on this, Annie,' Julie said, a little curtly. 'You don't have to instruct a solicitor to get some legal advice or just get some support behind you; I've given you the number for CAFCASS. I think you might be disappointed if you try to manipulate Kate into giving you what you want.'

'I don't want to manipulate her,' Annie replied, nettled. 'I just want her to give me a chance. I mean, what have I actually done to *her* that's so terrible? I had barely anything to do with her before Jack was born!'

'Annie, do you think that Kate might be resentful at you on *Jack's behalf*?' Julie asked carefully. 'I know this is a tricky area for you, but you realise that it's difficult for people to understand the behaviour of an addict and they become particularly fierce when children are involved. You have to remember, too, that Kate has her own history of feeling let down by your father and his addiction. All this will be shaping her thinking, whether she acknowledges it or not.'

'Ha!' Annie spat, her temper rising, the tortured creatures that were thoughts of her childhood and memories of Jack had escaped their hidden cages and were prowling the periphery of the room. 'Kate never suffered because of Da, she just hated him because Mum did. He never neglected us, beat us, or stole our pocket money like Mum and Kate said he did, he just couldn't stop drinking and he wasn't *good enough* for them.' Annie was breathing heavily. 'He loved us, he wanted to take care of us, he just couldn't!' Now she was crying. 'And I love Jack! I've only ever wanted what's best for him. She said... Kate said...' Annie paused to take a tissue and wipe her nose, 'Kate said I didn't feed him or change him or take care of him. It's fucking lies!'

'Tell me how it was then, Annie.'

Annie sat, ashen-faced, her eyes looking haunted; she'd stopped crying abruptly. 'I tried,' she said quietly. 'I tried to look after him.' The room was starting to spin, and she had a cotton wool feeling in her head. 'I would take him to the park and the indoor play area. Everybody loved him. I did feed him. I did change him. I would speak to him all the time; he started talking really young,' she said earnestly. Then she was remembering the phone calls when he first went to live with Kate. 'He loved me, I know he did. He would cry for me! *I want Mummy!* But I wasn't there for him. Oh!' Annie clutched her chest at the searing pain that shot through it. 'It would break my heart; it breaks my heart now. He must have been so scared!' She was sobbing now; her throat was so constricted that her laboured breath came in noisy groans. 'It was me. It was all me! I fucked it up. I didn't look after him, I couldn't look after him.' Annie rocked back and forth. 'He must have been so scared in that flat with all the people coming and going and me out of it all the time. Just toddling around on his own. I remember one time...' Annie shuddered, sniffing noisily. She suddenly felt cold and distant again. 'I remember one time he'd been out with Kate; she'd taken him to the park,' she said in a flat monotone. 'He was only about two years old. When they came back, he just cried and cried and clung to her, he didn't want her to go and leave him there.' Annie took a sharp intake of breath, it felt like she couldn't breathe. It was too much, she couldn't take it, she felt like she was going to vomit or pass out. Julie sat, motionless, letting Annie spend herself.

'When Kate finally left, I just stood in the kitchen, facing the sink. I felt wretched. I heard the door creak open and there was Jack, standing in the doorway looking at me, he looked at me like… like *he* was sorry for making such a fuss. Oh!' Annie groaned, curling up on herself, her face a mess of snot and tears. 'We looked at each other for the longest time and then he ran to me, and I swept him up, I said *I'm sorry, I'm sorry* over and over again. This was to a two-year-old little boy!' She looked beseechingly at Julie. 'Oh, what have I done? What have I done?' Annie sobbed and moaned the guttural sounds of a wounded animal, her whole body wracked with the force of it. Tears and pain from the depths of her being that had been locked away for so long ripped through her and as she cried, she wondered how she would ever heal, how she could ever forgive herself, live with herself.

Julie sat quietly, letting Annie rock, and groan and sob. It was like poison coming out of her, the darkest fears she'd kept hidden from herself, not daring to look, yet still they festered and rotted, their noxious fumes seeping into every part of her, fortifying her self-hatred and shame.

'Annie,' Julie said eventually when Annie had no tears left and simply rocked silently, hugging her knees. 'Annie, I have no wish to rescue you. This is an important process that you must go through in order to begin healing. It cannot be avoided; the only way is through.' Julie passed Annie the box of tissues, she looked up momentarily, like a beaten animal. 'But I'm going to give you some things to hold onto as you go down this road, okay?' Julie looked to Annie for a response and Annie nodded as she blew her nose and tried to gather herself. 'I'm going to ask you this and the answer is really important so don't brush it off, okay?'

Again, Annie nodded.

'Okay,' she said, sitting up a little straighter.

'Annie, if Jack were in your care now would you behave in the ways that you did in active addiction?'

'What? No, no, of course not... no,' Annie replied, wringing her hands in her lap.

'Really let that sink in Annie, it's important,' Julie said firmly. 'I hope that you're learning to understand addiction as a mental illness, an obsessive, compulsive mental illness. It leads us to behave in ways that we never otherwise would, like any other mental illness affects the sufferer. The important and fabulous news is that you can treat your addiction; what you learn here you can practise for the rest of your life and stay well, do you understand?'

'Yes,' Annie said quietly.

'But a really important aspect of that is understanding the ways that you behaved were a consequence of being very unwell. That's not shirking responsibility, quite the opposite, it means it is absolutely your responsibility to take all the necessary actions to stay well because you fully appreciate the depth to which you go when you're unwell. You can't change the past, Annie. But you can begin to make amends by the choices you make in the future.'

'Yes, I understand,' Annie said, more strongly. 'There's a part of me that thinks I should just fall apart; who am I not to? I should just crawl back under my rock and die.' Annie looked at Julie. 'But that's old thinking. That's not going to help Jack, that's not going to help anyone.'

'That's very true,' Julie said encouragingly. 'It won't be easy, but not running away, facing reality, one day at a time, you'll begin to build a new life for yourself, a productive and happy life that will benefit you, Jack and everyone.'

'That's what I want to do,' Annie said firmly. 'I want to start again. I want to make amends to Jack, to Kate, my Da… even my Mum.'

'That's good Annie. That's really good,' Julie said, smiling. 'Now I think we have a few minutes to visit your woods.'

***

Annie walked back to her cell feeling absolutely wrung out. D wing was a single storey block that had just ten double cells and four singles. There was an art room, a TV room and a laundry as well as two larger rooms where they held 12-step meetings, and a bunch of smaller offices for the recovery workers and guards. The corridor always seemed light and airy compared to other parts of the prison; the walls were covered in artwork and inspirational quotes and there was more light than usual because of the high window which ran the length of the south-facing block.

Annie felt ultra-sensitive, as though she'd been stripped of a layer of skin, and someone had been fiddling with the volume and contrast dials in her wiring. Everything looked brighter and in sharper focus, her trainers seemed to boom down the corridor and echo disproportionately, her skin seemed to prickle in response to the air. She felt raw.

The door of the cell was open as Annie approached, which was unusual as Vern worked on a Thursday afternoon when Annie saw Julie. She arrived in the doorway to see Vern packing things into a clear plastic sack.

'Hey,' Annie said, taking in the scene, 'wha gwan?' she mimicked her friend in a way that usually made Vern laugh. But Vern didn't laugh today.

'Mi flash out, Annie,' Vern said, looking at Annie with sad eyes as she paused in her packing.

'What do you mean? Where are you going?' Annie didn't move from the doorway; her heart was thumping in her chest; her hypersensitive system seemed to have jammed.

'Dey got me a bed dahn Holloway, innit? Closer for me peeps, Annie,' Vern said, putting down the book she'd been about to pack and moving towards Annie, her arms open, but Annie ducked away from her into the corridor, her face stunned, her heart frozen.

'You're leaving?' she managed breathlessly.

'What's going on here?' A passing guard stopped. 'O'Shea, aren't you supposed to be in the garden this afternoon?'

'Yes Miss,' Annie replied, her head whirling. 'I was just dropping off my folder; I've been with my recovery worker, Miss.'

'Well, get going then.' The guard stood back and ushered Annie in front of her.

'But Miss...' Annie felt like she was coming undone. 'Vern's... Vern's leaving, Miss.'

And suddenly she was crying. The guard raised her eyebrows.

'Please,' Annie went on. 'Please can I just stay here a while and say goodbye... please, Miss?'

The guard looked from Vern to Annie with a look of exaggerated confusion but then softened.

'Go on then. But not long. Tap on the office when you're done, and I'll let you through.' And she walked on.

'Annie...'

'I don't get it. Why aren't you finishing the programme? You've only been here a month longer than me. You can't have finished.'

'Dey got der ting dahn Holloway, innit,' Vern said, moving back into the cell.

'But not like this,' Annie said, gesturing around her as though that explained everything. 'Are they making you go? Can't you say no?'

'Nah, Annie, dey ain't makin' me go. I pu' in a request tahm ago, when I knew dey was shippin' me ou' dese sides.'

Annie started to cry again. 'You can't go,' she said, realising she sounded ridiculous. 'What am I going to do? We're a team. I thought we were going to be together the whole way.'

She cast her eyes down and more tears spilled out. Her bottom lip was stuck out and trembling like a toddler's; she was clasping her hands, her shoulders hunched. She felt stripped bare.

'Anneee,' Vern crooned, putting her arms around Annie's shrunken frame and enveloping her. 'You gon' be okay, ya get me? You's strong, gal, so strong!' She held Annie tightly to her breast and gently rocked her. 'You keep workin' your ting, ya get me? An' ya get Jack back where he belong, innit.'

Annie felt like she was falling, falling. She knew her response was disproportionate; she'd known Vern just eight weeks. But they felt like some of the most important weeks of her life, like she'd crawled into the cocoon of prison and was just emerging and unfurling her feeble wings. She'd thought she was going to learn to fly with Vern at her side. Vern, with whom she'd shared so much, let her guard down, got vulnerable. And now she was leaving. Annie allowed herself to be held as she cried; it felt like some hidden dam had broken. She cried for Jack, she cried for Kate, she cried for her childhood and for her Da. And she cried for the loss of her dear friend, Vern.

The women promised to seek permission to write, and Vern gave Annie contact details for her family in case they lost touch, but once this was done, a painful silence fell between them, and it seemed best for Annie to leave. She wondered how much more her fragile heart could take as she tapped for the guard to let her out to the garden.

Seven

Annie passed through the remainder of the day in a trance-like state. She barely acknowledged Louise or the other women as she worked, using the barrow to shift dozens of heavy sacks of compost from where they were stacked at the main gate to the polytunnels some distance away.

It began to rain at around three, a steady, relentless downpour but she didn't stop. She had no waterproofs, and pretty soon her prison-issue tracksuit was sodden. Her hair was plastered to her face, and she no longer knew or cared whether she was wet with rain, sweat or tears. At four thirty the rest of the women made their way back to the guard's office, but Annie found she couldn't stop. Somehow in her mind she felt if she could just get this job finished, get things in order, then she would feel more in order herself. On she went, back and forth, several times losing her grip on the barrow handles that were slippery from the rain. Just three more sacks.

'O'Shea, you need to come in now please.'

It was the guard who'd let her stay with Vern earlier.

'Please Miss, I just need to get this finished,' Annie said, struggling on with her load. She looked a pathetic sight, and the guard took pity on her.

'Annie, you have to come in now,' she said kindly. 'You're going to catch your death out here and I have to go to the dining hall. Come on. It will keep until tomorrow.'

'Right,' Annie said, dropping the barrow and gazing vacantly about her, as though she couldn't quite work out what she'd been doing anyway. She followed the guard meekly back to the dining hall.

'You'll make other friends, Annie,' the guard — Susan was her name — said in an upbeat tone as she marched along. 'You'll have a new cellmate tonight or tomorrow and I'm sure you get on with other women in here.'

'Yes. Kind of. Not like Vern,' Annie mumbled, feeling like an idiot child again. 'It's not just that Miss... it's been a tough day... having to face up to some stuff that I didn't want to, I guess. Knowing I could chat it through with Vern tonight was keeping me sane.'

'Use the groups, Annie, that's what they're for,' Susan said as she opened the gate and ushered Annie through. 'This can't be the first difficulty to come up since you've been here.'

'No,' Annie replied, knowing that was true; it felt as though she'd been excavating into the very foundations of her being since she started on the 12-step programme but that had felt empowering, freeing, even though parts were painful. Today she felt like she'd been popped like a balloon, all the buoyancy had left her, and she felt empty and shrivelled, diminished. 'I think maybe I was on a bit of a pink cloud Miss, everything felt like it was going my way... well, almost everything,' she added, thinking of Kate and Jack.

'It can't always be rosy y'know, Annie, you've got to learn to take the rough with the smooth,' Susan encouraged stoutly as she moved off to attend to her duties.

Annie felt bereft. The hall seemed far noisier than usual. The scraping of benches, general chatter, shouts and laughter were like an assault on her senses. She stood passively for a moment, allowing herself to be jostled by the women making their way to the dinner queue. She knew she couldn't eat a thing, but she wouldn't be allowed back to her wing until after dinner.

Eventually she noticed the sistren at a table close by, and though the sight of them made her gut twist in grief for Vern, a couple of the women beckoned to her, so she drifted over and perched on the end of a bench. It helped, a bit. They seemed as shocked as she that Vern had been transferred so quickly, with no advance notice, but they understood that was the way of things in here, they were in prison, after all. Annie allowed herself to be carried along by the conversation and left feeling marginally better.

It was Association after dinner, so Annie used the time to shower. She'd been to the shower block alone many times now and barely flinched if there were sudden shouts or tussles whilst she was in there. She'd worked with Julie to better understand what led her to dissociate and to train herself to stay present when she felt herself spinning off. Tonight, there was no space left inside her to consider an attack.

She got back to her cell before Association was over and sat on her bed with the door open until lock-up, her knees hugged to her chest, casting glances at Vern's empty, stripped-down bed.

It was the first time she'd slept alone since those crazy nights on the run, and even then, she was rarely alone, she was usually huddled in some squat, pooling her pennies with a handful of other desperate souls hoping to get a bag of gear or bottle of cider to keep the fears and the rattles at bay or else bedded down in a doorway with another rough sleeper, sharing the warmth. Other times it would be a hotel room with a stranger who had bought her attention for an hour or an evening and who had taken pity on her and allowed her to stay the night; most often she didn't stay though, preferring the street to the possibility that he may wake and demand more from her. No, it was rare she was alone despite those days being the loneliest of her life.

She felt so lonely now, it would be easy to get swallowed up by the darkness of her memories and allow the despair to take her. *I have to keep my shit together*. She glanced again at the empty bed, half wishing its new occupant had arrived tonight, so she didn't have to sleep alone with the anxious anticipation of who would be there next.

At seven thirty, the door was locked for the night. Annie wrote Vern a long letter though she didn't have permission to send it; she also wrote to Kate, this time berating herself for the harm she caused Jack, caused everyone. Julie had advised against this, but Annie felt she had to do something with the overflowing emotions of the day. Perhaps she wouldn't send that either.

She slept fitfully and dreamt that she was locked outside in the rain; she could see through a window which glowed with warm, golden light and there was Vern, Jack, and Kate. But when she tried to knock on the window her knuckles had no power, she couldn't get them to make contact with the glass enough to be heard. Then she noticed that the rain was actually washing her knuckles away, she stared in horror at her hands as her fingernails began to dissolve and when she grabbed her hair in fright it came out in great clumps. She tried to scream but made no sound as her teeth fell from her mouth. She woke before midnight and lay staring at Vern's bed, finally drifting off just an hour or so before the door was unlocked.

***

Annie passively followed the lines of women as they were taken to their various work placements. Yesterday's rain had finally stopped, though it was still barely light, and the dark clouds rumbled threateningly. It was cold and the wind picked up the fallen leaves then spat them out again. The gravel walkways between the polytunnels were full of potholes and these had become muddy puddles that loved to overturn a barrow or twist an ankle. Annie found a strange comfort in the harsh, gloomy conditions as she set to work.

Lunchtime came quickly and though she had no appetite she needed to change out of her muddy clothes before groups that afternoon. She loitered around the dining hall until she could be let back onto D wing, and as she walked down the corridor, she could see that her cell door was open. She felt a moment's trepidation but reminded herself that she wasn't the new girl this time. Last night she had committed to herself to be as warm and welcoming as Vern had been for her. With a little pang of grief, she shrugged her shoulders to dispel the anxiety, put on a smile and turned to face the open doorway.

Her first surprise was that the cell's new occupant hadn't taken Vern's old bed; rather, Annie's own possessions were piled there along with a heap of bedding, whilst her new cellmate was sitting on Annie's bed, her own items dotted across the headboard. These first impressions happened in the split second before Annie identified the occupant.

It was Joni.

'Annie, hi,' she was saying from a long way off, 'You don' mind do ya, I juss can' sleep on tha' side of the room so I took this bed. I was careful wiv yer stuff,' she added, as though this made all the difference. Annie just stared; her mind blank. She realised her mouth was open and closed it, then found she couldn't breathe and opened it again to take a gulp of air.

Joni had stood up. 'Listen, Annie, I don' want no trouble, alrigh'? Seriously.' She wiped her hands down the front of her tracksuit bottoms before holding one out. Annie could feel her head shaking, almost imperceptibly, *no*! It was dawning on her that she was behaving like the village idiot, but she was struggling to hold onto herself. A fuzzy thought came to her that at least watching herself losing it was an improvement on spinning off altogether, like she was tied to herself by the finest thread.

Joni was speaking again, 'You alrigh'?' she asked, frowning, and realising Annie was not going to take it, shoved her hands deep into her pockets. 'Listen, this is last chance saloon for me. I don't have no beef wiv you, Annie, I just wanna make a go of it, ya get me?'

Annie began to get herself together. Using techniques she'd practised with Julie, she began to reel herself back in, as though she were a kite. She felt the soles of her feet and the weight of her body holding her to the floor, she focused on her breath as it went in and out. She looked at the walls, *cream walls* she thought to herself, she looked at the flask on the desk behind Joni, *blue flask*. She worked her way around the room, bringing herself back, grounding herself, finally looking at Joni, *red tracksuit*.

'Sure,' she managed.

Joni was watching her cautiously, her brows knitted, as though Annie might suddenly start shrieking and waving her arms around or sprout another head or something. Annie took a deep breath and moved past her to make up the bed.

'It will actually be nice to sleep in Vern's old bed,' she surprised herself by saying and found she meant it. She used a sock to wipe the dust from the shelves on the headboard and added her few items before carefully peeling the photos of Jack from the wall at the end of Joni's bed and putting them in a little pile, ready to put on her wall at the end of the day.

'You don' 'av a CD player then?' Joni said, looking around.

'No, Vern had one, but she took it with her,' Annie replied as she pulled off her muddy top and pulled on the roll-neck Kate had brought her. 'I don't have enough money to buy one yet.'

'No bovver,' Joni replied easily, flicking on the little television and throwing herself back on the bed.

'Aren't you coming to group?' Annie asked as she hopped into a clean pair of joggers.

'Nah,' Joni replied, kicking her trainers off. 'Day's grace firs' day, innit. I ain't watched *Loose Women* for time!'

Annie caught a snatch of Kaye Adam's rich, earthy burr before she slid out of the cell for group and Joni was locked up until dinner.

Eight

The next week passed without any real incident and though Joni was outspoken and bullish, demanding her own way in the cell and being noisy and disruptive in groups, it seemed she was making a genuine effort to be amicable. She'd used her canteen money to buy a little stereo and when she wasn't relentlessly playing *The Eminem Show*, she was hogging the television and endlessly changing channels, but she seemed completely unaware that this might be considered antisocial, and in the grand scheme of things, Annie was hard-pressed to find anything concrete to complain about.

Yet Annie was a twisted knot of anxiety. She felt bullied and intimidated and added to her own discomfort by beating herself up, telling herself she should be more assertive and stand up for herself. Without any real transgression on Joni's part, she was left feeling confused as to why she felt so impotent. Time in the cell was spent walking on eggshells, constantly on high alert, holding her breath, her shoulders about her ears. At some level she sensed she'd tripped into playing an old script, but she felt powerless to break out of it.

On Thursday, a full week after Joni had arrived in the cell, Annie was sitting in Julie's office feeling frayed and distracted. Again, she'd lain awake most of the night, drifting into exhausted sleep only to wake with a jolt, hoping she hadn't grunted or breathed too loudly. She would hold her breath in the darkness, waiting for Joni to speak, whilst another voice berated her for being crazy: why didn't she just loosen up and go to sleep?

'You look tired, Annie,' Julie said, turning to face her having just finished inputting something on her computer. 'What's been happening for you this week?'

Annie gave a dry little laugh. Since their last, gut-wrenching session it felt that her whole world had been turned upside down, like a year had passed rather than seven days.

'I have a new cellmate,' she managed.

'Okay…' Julie replied, leadingly.

Annie paused. Where should she start? Vern's departure, feeling like she'd had pieces ripped from her in the parting, was pressing against her insides. But sharing the cell with Joni, the long nights lying awake, holding her breath and pretending to be asleep, had awoken demons that she'd kept hidden for a lifetime.

'Just start at the beginning, Annie,' Julie said helpfully.

'So, my new cellmate,' Annie started, not really knowing what she was going to say. 'She's... we've... we had some issues when I first arrived here... she didn't like me very much... and... even though she's being all right now, trying to be nice, even, well, I just can't keep a hold of myself; I keep spinning off and I'm on high alert the whole time.' Annie felt stupid, bumbling, unable to explain what she was making such a fuss about.

'That sounds hard Annie,' Julie said reassuringly, 'but don't forget it's really early days for you with this. Have you been using the techniques we've practised? What about the band?'

The band was a piece of elastic which Annie wore about her wrist which could *pling* against her flesh when she felt herself disappearing, the sharp sensation helping to bring her back to the present.

'I've tried everything,' she replied dully. 'I just can't keep it together.'

'Annie, it's only been a week,' Julie said firmly. 'Let's have a look at what's happening, and you can practise staying present with it here, with me, okay?'

'Okay,' Annie replied, taking the cushion and hugging it to her but sitting up a little straighter. She had confidence in Julie; she'd come so far in this room.

'So,' Julie spoke in her calm, reassuring voice, much deeper than one would expect from such a slight frame, 'tell me about when you notice you're losing yourself, tell me about what leads up to it.'

Annie thought about this. She didn't feel like she'd had a grip on herself all week, even in the garden or in her groups, it was like she was walking, talking, even laughing but she wasn't really there. But the nights were worse and so she started there.

'I'll get into bed,' she said, imagining the scene. 'Joni will still be awake, maybe watching TV, or reading. I'll face the wall and say to myself *just relax, just go to sleep.* I try all the things you've taught me, body scans, breathing techniques... but I just feel frozen, my mind feels frozen, my breath feels frozen, I'll get it together for a moment then trip back into it.' Annie took a deep breath, realising she'd been holding it.

'Then Joni will say goodnight. Sometimes I'll say goodnight back, other times I'll just pretend to be asleep and... I think that's what does it... pretending to be asleep, I start feeling afraid to move and even though I say to myself I'm being stupid, of course I can move, I just can't get myself together.'

'So, you're lying in bed. Keep breathing normally now, fully and deeply. What happens next? Can you ask yourself why you're frightened to move?'

'Because I don't want something bad to happen,' Annie said, focusing on her breath.

'What might happen, Annie?'

'I don't know. She might get angry with me; I might wake her up. I don't know. She might want to talk to me...'

Annie started to feel unduly agitated.

'Okay, Annie, we're going to leave Joni for a minute. I just want you to imagine that you're lying in bed. Still breathing for me, I want you to think about why you're scared; why don't you want to move?'

Annie kept breathing but could feel herself spinning off, because she already knew the answer, it had been lurking, unbidden, in the corners of her mind for days, pressing at the edges of her consciousness as she tried to go to sleep.

'Because it reminds me of when *he* came,' she heard herself say. 'Because he would come into my room at night, and I would pretend to be asleep... because I thought that might make him go away.'

'Are you able to say who came into your room, Annie?'

'*He* did.' Annie said, her eyes had been closed but now she opened them to look at Julie. 'My *stepdad.*'

'Your mother's new husband?'

'Him, yes, the next one."

Annie felt odd, half in the room, half out. It felt like bringing this memory into the present had brought her back to herself a little, like before she was a blank page, and now she was in watercolour.

'He moved in when I was thirteen. Mum'd been seeing him for a while I think, but he moved in then. Failed marriage number three,' Annie said bitterly. Julie just waited, giving her space to continue. 'He used to call himself my *stepdad*, he used to get off on it, I think.' Annie paused, unclear of where to go, she felt alternately cold and distant then flushed and claustrophobic.

'Keep breathing Annie,' Julie reminded her.

Annie *plinged* the elastic at her wrist. 'He used to come into my room at night.' She pushed the words out. 'At first, he just used to stand and stare at me. I could feel him staring, that's when I first pretended to be asleep.' Annie paused and took a shuddery breath. 'It was weird you know, because during the day I stood up to him. I hated him, you know, I would backchat him, refuse to do things he asked me, like housework and stuff, that's when Mum would say "*You do what your stepdad asks if you want to live under this roof!*" Annie imitated her mother's voice. '… And stuff like that. Like he'd just come in and had more rights than I did.'

'Where was Kate in all this, Annie?'

The question didn't surprise Annie; she'd asked it herself many times. Where *was* Kate?

'I just don't know. I mean, I don't remember.' She felt a little flutter of panic. 'She was fifteen by then, she had a waitressing job and friends. Kate used to work all the time, I mean, we both had holiday jobs, but Kate worked *every* hour God sent… she still does… her way of escaping, I guess.' This all tumbled out first, then, 'But why? Why was it only me? I mean, once I figured she might have been keeping quiet about it, but I used to watch really carefully… he was… just… different with Kate; it must have been something I was doing that made him like it, right?' she asked fearfully, wringing her hands.

'Of course it wasn't Annie,' Julie said calmly. 'If only one child is targeted it makes it far easier to deny, to do exactly what is happening now, isolate them and make them think it's somehow their fault. And, of course, two of you would be more believable should you tell.' Julie looked grim, then said, 'Annie, I'm sorry, I think I interrupted your flow.'

'No, no, it's fine.' Annie tried to catch the thread of her thoughts again. 'So, at first, he would just stare, and I would pretend to be asleep, that went on for ages. I would spit at him the next day that he was a weirdo, but he would just laugh and carry on as though nothing had happened. Then he started touching me…' Annie's breath caught as she gasped. 'He started touching me and I would just lie there really still, not breathing, and he would kneel… he would kneel down by the bed and put his hands under the covers… oh God!' Annie was really crying now. 'I'm so sorry, I just haven't spoken about this since… for so long…' She sobbed and rocked back and forth.

'Annie, I need you to come back to me now, okay, take a breath. Can you feel your feet on the floor? Good. Keep breathing. What can you see in this room, right now?'

Annie began naming objects and their colour or position; she felt her heart rate slowing. She took a deep, shuddery breath. 'I started wearing my clothes to bed,' she said, her voice sounded dull and far away, 'but he always got his hands underneath them... inside them. And I would just lie there! God I just lay there and let him!' A shiver ran through her. 'I still don't understand, I just don't understand it! In the day, at school, everywhere, I was a nightmare, shouting, fighting, but at night I would just lie there and let that creep touch me! What's wrong with me?' Without waiting for an answer, she ploughed on, 'It was around then that I started drinking... and smoking pot, every day, I used to kid myself that made it better, made it easier. Then, one night, this was... about a year after he came, and he'd been touching me all that time. Urgh!' She made the sound involuntarily and a shudder ran through her as though she were about to vomit. 'Licking me, kissing me...' She shook her head slightly trying to rid herself of the thought. '...This night he... he... had sex with me,' she said finally, and she was expressionless and still, a vacant look in her eyes.

'He raped you, Annie.' Julie's voice reached her.

She snapped back, her eyes finding Julie's.

'But he didn't, did he?' she said, in that same, flat voice. 'I let him. I didn't fight him off; I didn't scream. I just lay there and let him.'

Tears began to slide silently down her face. The protective shell around her most hidden secret, the one she'd buried in her deepest parts, had cracked open and her shame oozed out.

'Annie, listen to me. Look at me,' Julie said sharply as Annie stared at her hands. 'You were a child. This man had absolute power over you, you've just told me what it was like in your house and where the power lay. You were a child; you were at his mercy, and he abused you.'

'But I wasn't a virgin!' Annie wailed. 'I wasn't a virgin! I'd already had sex with boys, men really, much older than me. I was… I was a little slut.' She said this really quietly, looking at her hands again. 'That's what Mum said.'

'Annie that's a lie! So you weren't a virgin, join the queue of all the other fourteen-year-olds who could say that. This man touched you and had sex with you against your will; he was in a position of power, and he used that to abuse you. Many women, *many women,*' she stressed the words, angling her face to seek Annie's downcast one, 'don't fight back when they're raped. Are you saying they're all responsible too?'

'No,' Annie said quietly, then she looked pleadingly into Julie's eyes. 'But I told Mum,' she wept.

'I told Mum what he'd done, and she didn't help me! She was angry at *me*!' she wailed and began crying again in earnest. 'At first, she said I was lying. For days it was like that; she wouldn't even look at me, said I was trouble, just like Da. Then after days of misery, wandering the streets, drinking loads, coming home and just staying in my room…' Annie wiped her nose with the back of her hand and looked every bit that troubled teenager. 'No one talking to me, not Kate, not anyone… Mum came to me and said… she said…' For the first time Annie's face showed real anger. 'She said I'd *seduced him*. She said I was a little slut and I'd seduced her husband. I mean, how the *actual fuck* could she do that? God, I hate her!'

Annie threw the pillow aside and stood up, pacing the small room. Julie watched her but didn't intervene.

'She stayed with him,' Annie said dully. 'After all that, she stayed with him until he left her for another woman. I moved out that day. I went to live with Da.' Annie sat back down and sighed. 'But he was living in this pokey little flat, so I was sleeping on the sofa, going on fifteen, both of us drinking every day, me missing school. And I… I got really promiscuous then, you know. Mad how that happens isn't it?'

'It seems strange, but very common, that we seek out and re-enact the things that damaged us most as children. Although it's painful, it's strangely comfortable; this is the life we know, it feels safe, even though it's damaging, it fits our view of the world.'

'Yes, I guess that's what happened,' Annie said sadly. 'I was with Da less than a year. It was a nightmare really and we ended up at each other's throats, which was awful because I'd always put him on a pedestal; he was my *safe base*.' Annie was shredding a tissue as she spoke. 'I had nowhere to go; I couldn't go back to Mum's. I stayed with Granny O'Shea for a while but that didn't work because she had rules.' Annie managed a dry little laugh. 'I was so far gone by then the idea of going to school and being home by ten, well, I just couldn't manage it. So we fell out too.'

Annie could remember feeling utterly alone, she remembered the fear that would lap at her insides when she wasn't drunk or stoned and often when she was.

'I started using more and more to shut my head up. I stayed with this bloke or that.'

She put the shredded tissue in the bin and began again, more matter-of-factly.

'Then I moved to London. A little group of us went and stayed with this guy's brother. I had no money and one of the girls, Amber, was dancing in a strip club…' Annie sighed. 'I guess I'd learnt by then I was good for one thing: *fucking*. I'd slept with so many men by then I'd lost count, I thought I might as well get paid for it.' Another tissue was crumbling between her fingers as she spoke. 'So I started at the strip club. Pretty soon I was doing *extras*. It was just a tiny step, prostituting myself.'

Annie gazed out of the window, remembering times less than a decade before that felt like a lifetime ago. Back then she was still young enough to believe it was just a blip, that at some point she was going to grow up and get her life together. She sighed again. She felt a hundred years old.

'By the time I was eighteen, I was renting my own place back in Devon and earning more than I'd ever dreamed. I was caning vodka, ecstasy, speed. There would always be half-naked bodies strewn around the flat from the partying; everyone thought it was really cool that I was a hooker—that and the fact I always had money and drugs. When I think about it now, those were some of the best days of my life,' Annie said sadly and realised it was true. 'Yes, I was a hooker, but it was my money. I was independent; No one treated me that badly, 'cept maybe the odd weirdo, but generally people were kind, and I had enough money to do whatever I liked... which granted wasn't much.'

'I can imagine being independent and in charge of your own destiny felt good, Annie.' Julie spoke for the first time in a while, bringing Annie back to the room.

'Yes, it did, for a while.' Annie realised she was exhausted; she'd talked so much and remembered so much. Joni felt a long way off now. 'Then, just before I turned twenty, I met Paul.' Annie started biting her thumb nail. 'Everything changed then. It was mad. Of course we had sex before I even knew him, then he was only going to stay a night or two. He told me he was on the run; I thought it was cool. Huh.' Annie laughed and shook her head. 'What an idiot. When he first asked me to score heroin, I thought he was joking, I didn't even know you could get heroin in Devon, I was so naïve. It wasn't hard to find in the end. I loved it.' Annie stared out the window again, a faraway look in her eyes. 'It was what I'd always been looking for but hadn't realised. It made everything feel okay. It took me where I wanted to go, where I felt nothing. Then Paul started smashing up the flat if we couldn't score. He started demanding my money. I only stood up to him once. He broke my nose. Then sex work became a necessity not a freedom. Everything I earned went to Paul and that went on drugs. I don't remember any laughter, any fun times after that. I was totally trapped. I hated the sex work then; I would use drugs to work and the money I earned would get spent on more drugs just so I could work some more. Paul never let me use heroin more than two days on the trot. He said it was so I wouldn't get a habit but really it was just another way to control me, keep me begging for scraps.'

Annie stood up again and stretched; she felt toxic, like talking about all this was releasing the poison and she had to get it out of her system.

'I stopped using heroin when I found out I was pregnant. I stopped drinking too. A lot of people don't believe that, Kate doesn't,' she added bitterly. 'But I smoked loads of pot. I'm not proud of it. Paul was so violent. He threw me down a flight of stairs when I was seven months pregnant.' Annie sat back down, feeling spent. 'He hurt Jack too. Twisted his little nose when he was only a few weeks old. It was awful. I couldn't get away.' Annie felt too exhausted even to cry. 'Then finally, finally he got arrested.' Her face lit up a fraction at the memory of her good fortune. 'He had so many outstanding charges, he'll be away forever.'

'Probably not forever, Annie. Do you think he will ever come looking for you? Looking for Jack?'

'He won't,' Annie said. 'At least I'm as certain I can be that he won't. He has half a dozen other kids; some he's never seen. What a catch, eh?' Annie managed a sad little smile. 'I'm done now Julie, truly, I've nothing left.'

'Of course. You've done brilliantly. We've covered a lot of ground.'

***

Annie was so exhausted that night that she slept, just a little. It felt like she'd begun to exorcise her demons, and by shining a light on them, had taken away their power.

Day by day she used the grounding techniques Julie had taught her and little by little she reclaimed her nights. By the following Thursday she was able to share real progress with Julie and on the Friday morning she woke to find Joni up and brushing her teeth.

'God, you was proper snorin' last night!' Joni said through a mouthful of toothpaste.

Annie felt a rush of anxiety. 'Oh fuck, I'm so sorry, you should have woken me!'

'Don' be daft.' Joni spat into the sink. 'I was awake anyways, wouldn't've 'eard you uvverwise; I sleep frew anyfin' me!'

Annie smiled at the irony and went out to the garden feeling like a new woman.

Nine

The days seemed to blur into one. Annie worked in the garden as the weather got colder, they now had abundant crops of winter cabbages, parsnips and Brussels sprouts and mealtimes were taking on an unmistakably festive feel. Annie's weeks were punctuated by her visits to Julie where she continued her excavation work with determination. She attended every group and 12-step meeting available to her and used her phone credits to speak with the women she met at her meetings. Three weeks of sharing a cell with Joni had passed without incident and Annie slept more nights than she lay awake.

She'd come to a critical point in the programme where she was asked to offer restitution to the people she'd hurt. She wrote to Kate, her father and even her mother asking if they would be willing to visit her. She'd wrestled endlessly with the idea of making amends to her mother, now realising the depths of her own pain and resentment, but she acknowledged that she herself had harmed an innocent, in Jack, and wasn't she hoping for forgiveness and understanding? Then she must first be willing to offer these to her mother. For the first time in her life, she felt empowered rather than the victim of others.

She was shocked and relieved to finally receive a letter from Kate, agreeing to visit the following weekend. As yet she'd heard nothing from her mother but was surprised to find it didn't bother her too much. She'd just come off the phone to her Da. He sounded worryingly frail but assured her he was fine, *just a wee bit scuttered* and she was smiling happily to herself as she made her way back to the wing,

'Night Miss,' she sang buoyantly to Susan as she swung into the cell. Joni was still out and wouldn't return until the last moment, as was her way. Changing into another set of joggers she tied her hair back and went to the sink to brush her teeth. It was then that she noticed something in the toilet pan… photographs, *her* photographs, photographs of Jack. She whipped around to see several white blobs on the wall where the pictures had been. Letting out an involuntary moan she plunged her hand into the pan.

The picture on the surface was Jack with his trucks, it looked like it had been scrunched up before being thrown in the toilet and the water had caused the surface to wrinkle, with blotchy patches of discolouration. The second picture, of Jack in his green hut, was disappearing around the U-bend, and when she fished it out, was almost beyond recognition. The others were missing and must have been flushed. Annie felt winded.

What had happened? She was certain only Joni could have been in the cell but couldn't begin to think what had upset her. There'd been no argument, not even a cross word.

Annie lay the two remaining photos on the desk and used the edge of her palm to iron them out. There was no getting away from it, they were ruined. Perhaps Kate would send her more? But that didn't change the fact that Joni had suddenly turned vicious again, like the scorpion in the old fable. *And I'm the stupid frog,* Annie thought with a flutter of anxiety. She was standing at the desk, staring down at the photos but not really seeing them when Joni exploded into the cell.

Annie felt herself cringe but stood her ground. 'Joni, what—'

'Just don' even fuckin' talk to me Annie, alrigh'? I mean it, I ain't responsible for my actions if ya do.' Joni stormed past and threw herself onto the bed, rolling over to face the wall.

Annie stood for a moment, stunned, her ears ringing, before quietly stepping over to her own bed and switching off the light. She lay awake, her heart pounding, her thoughts whirring at the speed of a race commentator. She must have drifted off at some point because she woke to the scraping and clattering of the day's first risers. Joni lay immobile, still facing the wall. As Annie got up and dressed quietly, it felt horribly like those first days when Joni moved in, but she told herself this was different, *she* was different, she just needed to get out into the garden to clear her head. She glanced sadly at the ruined photos then left the cell the moment the door was unlocked. As she allowed herself to be jostled down the corridor with the other women she decided on her next course of action.

Louise seemed genuinely saddened that Annie's photos had been destroyed.
'I'd be gutted if it was me,' she said, passing Annie a mug of builder's tea. They were in the little hut which sat between two of the largest polytunnels. It was essentially a garden shed with big, Perspex windows on each side; a narrow Formica shelf held tea, coffee and a kettle, and several stained mugs hung from hooks above. A shelf opposite held stacks of paper, magazines and an array of coloured A4 binders and the floorspace was littered with garden tools. The women perched on compost sacks as they drank their tea.

'I *am* gutted,' Annie said, wrapping her cold hands around her mug, 'but I'm more worried about what's going to happen next. I mean what do I do if she turns all feral on me?' She bared her teeth and made a claw with her free hand, making Louise laugh for a moment before she looked serious again.

'Listen Annie, I'm gonna tell you something, okay?" Louise put down her tea and looked grave. 'But please don't say anything, it's a touchy subject.' She held Annie's gaze until she nodded.

'Joni's got this big custody battle going on wiv her kids.' She sighed. 'She's got three kids, right, and they've been split up and put in foster care. The youngest is only two. They're probably gonna be adopted out,' Louise said sadly, and Annie was surprised to feel a wave of compassion; this was a pain she could relate to. 'Joni had the first court hearing yesterday by video link. Seems like it didn't go so well,' Louise said sadly. 'I reckon she came back before dinner, saw them pictures and just flipped. She doesn' wanna fall out wiv you Annie, I know she don't, she told me she likes you!' She laughed at the turn of events.

Annie was temporarily distracted.

'She likes me?' she asked in astonishment.

'Ha, yeah, I know, mad innit? She is a bit mad though, y'know,' Louise added seriously. 'Listen, Annie, if I was you, I'd let this one slide, y'know, just give her some space, she's grievin'.'

Annie didn't even need to think about it.

The women returned to their work shortly afterwards, and as Annie headed back to the wing at lunchtime, she realised that the awful scratchy feeling she'd had all night had left her and instead she felt a warm and genuine connection to Joni which definitely hadn't been there before.

Joni was already in the cell; it looked like she'd opted to stay locked in rather than go to work, which was allowed on rare occasions. Annie had hoped to slip down to the shower block before lunch but instead went to the basin, rolled up her sleeves and began washing her hands and arms whilst Joni resolutely faced the wall.

'You okay?' Annie asked tentatively, keeping her eyes on the sink. Joni didn't respond. Annie dried herself and wiped up around the basin before changing into jeans and a jumper.

'Look.' Annie had the dubious feeling that she was trying to reason with the scorpion. 'Don't worry about the pictures, okay?'

No response.

'We all have bad days.'

She was wishing she'd kept quiet.

Joni had thrown herself upright.

'What the fuck would you know about it?' she asked fiercely.

'I don't know anything,' Annie said simply. 'I know it was a bad day for me. Those are the only photos I have of Jack, and I haven't seen him for nearly three years.' She said this without heat.

Joni said nothing. She stared at Annie for a moment then huffed and rolled back over to face the wall.

After lunch, Annie returned to the cell to collect her folder for group. Joni had stayed put but now she sat up and Annie could see she'd been crying; she felt a strange mixture of fear and concern, like one might experience when trying to free a trapped animal that had particularly sharp teeth.

'Hey,' Joni said.

'Hey,' Annie replied.

After this rather awkward beginning, neither said anything for a time. Annie went to her drawer and made a fuss of retrieving some papers which had fallen from her folder.

'What you said before,' Joni said, drawing her knees up to her chest, 'bout yer son…'

Annie turned to look at her, holding her folder to herself like a shield, saying nothing.

'I got kids,' Joni continued stiltedly. 'Bastards are takin' em off me.' She stood up suddenly making Annie jump and the ghost of a smile passed over Joni's face before it turned stormy again. 'They got no righ', no reason, my kids love the bones o' me!' she spat, retrieving her tobacco from her headboard, taking a pinch and flinging the pouch down. 'I only came on this wing for me kids. What's the fuckin' point now, eh?'

Annie wasn't sure if this was meant to be rhetorical, but she plunged in recklessly. 'There's every point Joni! I've had no contact with Jack at all, but I know I've got no chance if I'm using. And not only that, but *I* also want a life, for *me!* I'm tired of all that shit, I want better.'

'Yeah, well, it's all right for you,' Joni exhaled a long plume of smoke in Annie's direction. 'You got prospects, innit. I ain't got no prospects, I got fuck all.'

'Joni, I get it, I promise. I've been smashing the shit out of myself for years for losing Jack, I just didn't see the point any more. But I've been working my arse off in here and things are really changing for me!' Annie was surprised by her own enthusiasm. 'I don't mean out there,' she swung her arms out to emphasise her meaning, 'but in here.' She banged a fist against her chest. 'Everything's changed in here.' She felt herself lose momentum as Joni smirked at her.

'Yeah, alrigh', I get ya,' Joni said but her voice sounded mocking. Then she said, more seriously, 'It fuckin' hurts though, right?'

'Damn right it does.'

'I just can't handle that shit, you get me?'

Annie sighed. She really could understand, she remembered that feeling so well, not being able to grab a single loose strand with which to begin unravelling the mess.

'Of course I understand, Joni, I've been there. I *am* there... only... I don't know, something changed.'

'I knew you'd understand Annie. You're alrigh' y'know.'

Annie smiled, 'Are you coming to group?'

'Nah, I ain't up to all tha' shit today,' Joni said, throwing herself back down on her bed.

'It might help you know, to talk about it.'

'Oi, I said you was alrigh' Joni said, pulling the thin duvet about herself, 'I dint say you could start 'givin' opinions, start that shit an I migh' change me mind.' But she was laughing as she said it and Annie relaxed.

'Haha, sure thing!' Annie did a little mock salute and left the cell.

Ten

Groups ran all afternoon with just a ten-minute break between sessions. The second group was a 12-step meeting with women from the local community. These were Annie's favourite meetings; she loved to hear the stories, how the women used the programme and supported each other as they found work and housing and gained access to their children; they gave her such hope. She returned to the wing in high spirits, and for the first time, was actually looking forward to spending time with Joni.

The moment she entered the cell, Annie could smell heroin.

Joni was sitting on her bed, leaning against her headboard and smiling goofily at her as she stood frozen in the doorway.

'Come in then fer fuck's sake and push the door to!' Joni hissed.

Annie didn't move. A sense of panic threatened to overwhelm her as the cloying, sickly fumes ripped her mind back to darker times.

'Joni, what have you done?' she breathed, her heart thudding somewhere near her throat. Joni had heroin in the cell, in *her* cell; she had to get out. Should she charge down the corridor now, calling for help?

Suddenly Joni was upon her.

'I said ge' in for fuck's sake and close the door!' She put an arm around Annie and chivvied her into the room, sticking her head out to peer down the corridor before closing the door.

Annie stood immobile in the centre of the room, the village idiot again. 'Joni… I—'

'Want some?' Joni was asking, holding out what looked like a yogurt pot lid with a tiny black beetle of heroin leaving its skid marks across the surface.

'Go on, Annie, a little toot ain't gonna kill ya,' Joni said thrusting the foil lid and a rolled-up tube at Annie, whose heart was fluttering. She wanted to turn and bolt. She wanted to cry out. She wanted to take the tube and draw deeply on the golden elixir that would carry her off to a place with no edges.

It was as if she watched herself reaching out to take her reward for trying so hard, for feeling so much pain, for getting this far. She'd inhaled the fumes anyway; she may as well do it properly.

'I can't Joni.' She snapped her hands to her sides and took two big steps back, as far as the walls would allow her without fleeing down the corridor, which didn't seem the best course of action either. 'I'm sorry but you need to get that shit away from me.' Her head was getting clearer; she felt stronger.

She watched as Joni put the tube in her mouth and a lighter under the foil, drawing deeply as she crackled the beetle into nothing, holding her breath as the two women observed each other, then blowing the yellow smoke in Annie's direction.

'You gonna grass?' Joni asked, her voice choked up with the fumes.

'I'm not going to say anything,' Annie replied and meant it; she'd been turning it around in her head at lightning speed. 'I get it, you're hurting, you want to hurt yourself, story of my life,' Annie said clearly, 'but I can't let you fuck it up for me too. If you have any left it has to be gone by the time I get back from dinner. It has to Joni, or you're gonna have to kill me, I swear, because I can't have it in here.' Annie marvelled at her own boldness.

'That was the last of it,' Joni said, unfurling the tube, running the lighter beneath it and inhaling the last remnants, then scrunching the whole lot up in her fist. 'Gone, okay? *Okay*?' she repeated, for Annie had said nothing.

'Okay,' Annie finally managed, ducking out the door and heading for dinner.

She put her arm to her face and breathed deeply; did she smell of heroin? Was she going to get pulled in by a guard? Now the immediate danger had passed, her mind was reeling again. Had she made the right decision? What would the consequences be? Would Joni do this again?

She reasoned that Joni was having a really hard time, she understood this. How many times had she sabotaged herself, right when things might have turned around for her, just because she couldn't bear the difficult feelings? She wanted to give Joni a chance. And if she reported her what would the other women think? Would she find herself sent to Coventry, would there be a shower incident all over again? Surely it was better to try to brush the whole thing under the carpet if she could.

She sat with Louise at dinner, who seemed strangely distracted too. She didn't ask Annie how things had gone with Joni, so Annie didn't bring it up and the two women sat and ate in near silence. Association was always a noisy affair but on Friday nights the women would surpass themselves. Annie wasn't in the mood for the clatter and revelry, but she wasn't in a hurry to return to the cell either. She loitered around the TV room for half an hour, attempting to distract herself, before requesting she be let back on the wing.

Cell doors were left open during Association and Annie made her way down the corridor alone. It felt like her feet were set in concrete and she slowed her pace as she approached the cell. The door had been pushed closed again. Was it her imagination or could she smell heroin already? She took a deep breath as she took the last few paces and pushed open the door. The smell was unmistakable now, it seemed the air was thick with it, Annie had a panicky sensation that she was high just from the fumes.

Joni was on her bed, head and shoulders slumped over yet remarkably upright, as only seems to happen in a heroin gouch. Annie had seen people seemingly unconscious whilst standing up and holding a tin of beer. She took a shuddery breath and approached. The remnants of Joni's session were scattered around her, the bed littered with foil lids, criss-crossed with blackened lines. A hand-rolled cigarette looked to have fallen from Joni's sooty fingers and extinguished itself on the bed. Even as her heart pounded, Annie felt pity wash over her. How she knew this place of utter defeat, where all seems so lost that the only control one feels is the nature of one's own destruction. Self-sabotage, Annie was intimately acquainted with it.

And then she saw it. Tucked carelessly beneath Joni's inner thigh was a bag of heroin, so much heroin that it couldn't possibly be intended solely for Joni. Finally, Annie's mind snapped into action. What was she even thinking? She bolted from the cell only to collide with Susan who was making her way down the corridor, it must be time for lock-up.

'Miss!' was all Annie could manage, wild-eyed. 'Miss!' She waved her hands around in the direction of the cell realising she must look like a lunatic. Susan frowned and pushed past her into the room. With some sixth-sense alarm bell, Joni had come to and was in the process of leaping from the bed but there was no time. She had the drugs in her hand and the bed was littered with detritus.

'Harding!' was all Susan managed before Joni barged past her and out of the cell.

'Fuck you!' she yelled, wide awake now, as she shouldered Susan out of her way. 'And you!' she screeched maniacally at Annie, thrusting her into the wall before staggering along the corridor, trying to secrete the drugs on her person. The wind had been knocked from Annie as she crashed into the wall, but still she could see the futility of Joni's plight and it felt desperate and tragic. Susan had already raised the alarm and within moments, Joni was being restrained with significant force and led away. Annie felt a deep sadness. Was this really what Joni had wanted? Was this her way of making the world conform to her expectations, as Julie would explain it? Was she even aware that's what she was doing? Annie thought about the many times she'd burnt her own life to the ground and thought probably not. She found she was crying. She thought of Joni's children, the youngest just two years old, it made her think painfully of Jack at that age. She cried and cried, for Jack, for Joni, and for all the poor, innocent children.

Eleven

Early on Monday morning Annie was moved to one of the prized single cells and nothing could have described her relief, as she transferred her few belongings, that she wouldn't have to take pot-luck with a new cellmate. Finally discarding Jack's ruined photographs, she instead tacked to the wall drawings she'd created in the art room, smirking to herself at their childlike quality but revelling all the same in the feeling that this space was *hers*, probably for the first time in her life. She discovered that she enjoyed her own company, something she couldn't remember doing since she was very young.

Later in the week rumours abound that Joni had been bringing heroin into the prison through the garden and Annie was hauled in for questioning. The whole ordeal was horrible, but Annie was able to answer honestly that she knew nothing of it, another first. She didn't see Louise again after that and shed many more tears for the awful futility of it all. For once she was a survivor, forced to watch those around her being dragged under by the currents of entrenched behaviour and hopelessness.

Before she knew it, Saturday was upon her and Kate was making her way across the busy visiting room, looking pale and anxious. Annie found her heart was tender, so unlike her usual, defended self. Kate was probably fearing a scene.

'Hi.' Annie smiled as she stood to greet her.

'Hi.' Kate stopped a few feet away, no bundle of clothes today. 'Annie look,' Kate spoke again without preamble, 'I'm just going to say this now.' She closed her eyes briefly, as though steeling herself. 'If you shout at me or say anything horrid, I'm just going to get up and leave and I'm *never* coming back, do you understand?' Kate was breathless with the exertion of her ultimatum and Annie felt guilty for putting her through it.

'Of course, please let's just sit. I promise, I don't want to fall out.'

Kate didn't offer to get coffees this time and perched, rather than sat, on the metal-framed chair. For a moment there was silence.

'How are you?' Annie asked eventually.

'We're all fine,' Kate said. Then, after a time, 'How are you?'

'I'm good, Kate, thanks.'

More silence.

Annie took a breath. 'Look, I've made an utter balls-up of everything, Kate, and I want to start putting it right. I've treated you terribly, been angry at you when you've been trying to help me, wanted everything my own way, called you to bail me out over and over again.' She took another breath as Kate stared stonily at the floor. 'I've been a lousy sister," she said with conviction. 'Please, tell me if there's any way I can make it up to you.'

Kate said nothing for a time, then, rather defensively, 'Look, I'm sure this is all part of your programme or whatever, but you can't just fire all that at me and expect me to respond. I have no idea where to start.'

'No, no, I don't expect you to say anything at all!' Annie said fretfully. 'I mean, of course I want you to say something, but you can say it whenever. Go away, think about it, whatever. I just wanted to say this, to properly acknowledge it, you know.' Annie felt flustered. 'I mean, I hope this is different to all the other times I've just said sorry. I really mean it this time and… and if there's a way I can make it up to you…' Her voice trailed off uncertainly.

Kate studied the toe of her shiny, heeled boot and said, 'I just can't help thinking that you're only saying this so you can see Jack. I'm not sure you actually feel bad about how you've treated me. You made it perfectly clear last time that it wasn't really me you're interested in.' She looked up as she folded her arms.

Annie started to protest but caught herself. 'I understand,' she managed levelly. 'And I did say those horrible things, after you'd driven all this way. It was totally out of order, and I understand why you're pissed off. But I promise I'm saying these things to *you* and just for you.'

Kate said nothing for a minute then suddenly burst into tears, catching Annie completely off guard.

'You bitch, Annie!' She wept, searching for a tissue and realising she'd left her bag in a locker. 'I just want you to be okay, okay? I've always just wanted you to be okay!'

Annie felt herself bristle but took a breath and let the irritation wash over her; she wasn't even sure what caused her hackles to rise, poor Kate was breaking her heart. 'I know,' she said. 'I know. And you've always been there for me and I'm really grateful.'

Kate wiped her face with her sleeve and nodded tearfully.

They made small talk. Oliver was fine; the wedding plans were going well. Yes, they were really excited about Florida. Time passed quickly and when Annie looked there were just ten minutes of visiting time left. She braced herself.

'Kate, I'm so glad we did this,' she started, 'and this has truly been about you, about us. I just wanted to ask while you're here…' *why did she feel so treacherous?* 'I… of course I owe Jack a lifetime of amends…' She could sense Kate closing down but plunged on, 'but I hoped I could at least start… just… sending him letters, cards, stuff I make… Just as a way of being in his life. I think it's important,' she said a little more boldly, 'most people agree it's important for a child to know their mother.' *Too defensive!* Kate's face was frosty. 'I promise I don't want to barge in or expect anything, I just want to be in contact with him… please?'

'Sure. Whatever.' Kate stood up abruptly, making Annie jump. 'Look, I've got to go,' she was saying. Annie found she couldn't speak; her brain had jammed as she opened and closed her mouth and suddenly Kate was leaving.

'Take care,' Kate was saying as she leant in and brushed her jaw against Annie's before she turned on her heel and swiftly left the hall.

Twelve

'Well, Annie, how very far you've come.'

It was late February. Christmas had come and gone and been swept away and those who were watching noticed the light return by increments. Snowdrops and daffodils braved the frosts to decorate the edges of the polytunnels and veg patches where the awakened earth had been turned and seeded with the first crops of spring. Today was Annie's last meeting with Julie before she left the rehab wing to join the main prison.

'I'm very proud of you, Annie,' Julie said with a sincerity that made Annie's eyes well up. 'How does it feel, to hear that?'

'I think it's the first time I've ever heard it!' Annie said, reaching for a tissue. 'No, that's not true; Da used to say it when I rode my bike without stabilisers and stuff like that!' She laughed. 'It feels great.'

'How are you feeling about moving into the main prison?'

'I feel okay. I mean, I'm nervous, that whole *meeting a new cellmate* thing, especially after being on my own since December… but you know, I feel okay about it.'

'And have you asked anyone to be your sponsor yet?'

'Not yet, but I know who I'm going to ask: Sarah. She comes to all the meetings, and I already call her every week,' Annie replied enthusiastically.

Julie smiled. 'Well then, the fledging is leaving the nest. You know what you need to do. I have no doubt you'll continue your beautiful journey of recovery.' Annie glowed. 'And how are things with Kate?' Julie asked, resuming her air of professionalism.

'They're okay,' Annie answered honestly. *Okay* pretty much covered it. Kate had responded to all of Annie's letters and even made the long journey through awful January weather, bringing more clothes and some beautiful photos of Jack, one looking a little apprehensive with Mickey Mouse and Donald Duck and another holding an enormous chocolate ice cream, looking delighted and wearing a chocolatey grin. Kate assured her that Jack read her cards and letters, but she felt it best they didn't speak on the phone whilst Annie was in prison. Annie didn't want to argue with Kate, she wanted to do whatever was best for Jack and she felt she didn't have the right to rock the boat.

'She's very kind to me,' she added, 'and it's obvious she really cares. I don't want to fall out with her about Jack, not for us and not for Jack.'

'What does that mean, Annie? *Not for us and not for Jack?*'

'I mean, I promised Kate that I want a relationship with her, y'know, aside from Jack, and I really do… so I don't want to fall out with her about it—'

Julie interjected as Annie was about to continue, 'And do you think you're managing that, to keep those things separate?'

'Well, yes, that's what's happening, isn't it? That's what I'm doing,' Annie replied, feeling irritated and not understanding why.

'Really?' Julie asked carefully. 'Only… and I could be wrong, but it seems to me you're not happy with this arrangement at all, that although *Kate is kind*, what you're really hoping for, I would say absolutely hanging out for, is that Kate will stand aside and give you access to Jack.'

Julie leant forward to seek Annie's eyes, which were downcast.

'I could be wrong, Annie, but I wonder if you're still hoping that being nice enough to Kate and making enough effort in that relationship will lead her to want a relationship between you and Jack and I'm afraid I don't think that's going to happen. It seems to me that Kate really does see these things as very separate; she wants to have a relationship with you, but she's not prepared to include Jack in the deal,' Julie said with finality. 'I think you need to let go of any hope of *winning her over* in that respect.'

Annie searched herself. Is that really what she was doing? She definitely *did* want to have a relationship with Kate but that was with a Kate who would eventually let her see Jack. Did she want a relationship with someone who might block her at every turn? Or would she fight that person every inch of the way? And just like that she had her answer.

'Of course I want to have a relationship with Kate,' she said, 'but if she blocks me from seeing Jack then it will definitely change things between us.'

Julie nodded in agreement.

'But,' Annie went on, 'that doesn't mean I'll get into an all-out war with her about it, because I won't. I won't because I don't think that's the best thing for Jack,' she said simply, 'Jack's happy there, that's all I could want for him. He probably doesn't even remember me.' Razor blades seared her throat and tears sprang to her eyes, but she continued. 'I'm not surrounding him with warring adults, making him choose, he's not going to feel responsible for the happiness of the adults in his life, like I did.'

'You know I'm not going to direct you, Annie, I just wish you would seek advice. Jack is young, children are very resilient—'

'I wasn't,' Annie interjected. 'I'm sorry but I wasn't. And I don't think Kate was immune to it either, though it affected her differently. We're all the products of our upbringing, you know this, Julie.' Annie was surprised at her own boldness. 'So much of the way Kate behaves is about pleasing Mum, about being good enough for her. I felt like I tried and failed and couldn't bear the failure so learnt to blow it all up in my face instead and in a weird way that's saved me. But most importantly,' Annie felt high with insight and decisiveness, 'I think the reason Kate doesn't want me to have a relationship with Jack is because she sees that as a threat to *her* relationship with Jack, because we were brought up to believe in different camps, and if you wanted to be in *that camp* you were being traitorous to *this camp*, if you loved *this grown-up*, you were being disloyal to *that grown-up*. Because they were at war. So much resentment and hatred. I'm not doing that to Jack, if I don't join the dance then it can't happen.'

Julie said nothing for a moment, then, 'I'll say again, Annie, how very far you've come.'

Annie made her way back to her cell with a sense of calm that hadn't been there before. She didn't know how things would pan out with Kate; she sensed the possibility that she was being naïve to think they could start afresh and make up for all the wasted years, to get to know each other in roles other than victim and rescuer. But she wouldn't go to war with Kate, she wouldn't inflict upon Jack what had been inflicted on them and if that were the only way she could make amends for now, well then it seemed like a pretty good start.

She reached her cell with the intention of dropping her folder and heading out to the garden and found she had post, she scooped it up and took it with her. The first was a letter from Vern; the two women had been corresponding since early January. Annie smiled as she skimmed over Vern's elaborate scrawl then tucked it in her pocket for closer inspection later. The second envelope was written in a neat, rather jagged hand which Annie recognised at once. Her chest tightened and she trembled slightly as she relieved it of its contents, unfurling the letter she read:

Dear Annie

Thank you for your letter.

I'm pleased to hear that you're finally facing up to the consequences of your actions. Though I wish you every success I'm afraid, for now, I'll keep my distance. Let's face it Annie, it's hardly the first time you are 'stopping for keeps' so please allow me a little time to see how this works out for you.

This said, I really do wish the very best for you, as I always have. You were gifted with above average intelligence, and you've been given every opportunity to make a go of it, remember you are far more privileged than many, make use of what you've been given, and it will make everyone very happy!

Finally, Annie, I urge you to please be sensible when considering your next actions in relation to Jack. I've never known such a happy and contented little boy and I hope you will consider the impact on him should you decide to start throwing your weight around. I trust you'll think on this and do the right thing.

I'm well, thank you for asking. I have a recurring issue with my back and suffer terrible headaches but other than that, I can't complain.

Take care of yourself, Annie.

Love, Mum

Annie had stopped walking at the opening line and now she stood in the corridor, her mouth open and her heart pounding.

'Are you coming through then?' the guard shouted irritably.

'Yes, yes, sorry.' Annie jogged across the threshold and out into the garden, welcoming the icy blast on her face. She shoved the letter into her other pocket, not wishing to contaminate Vern's with it.

She could feel white-hot rage flaring from beneath her ribcage, across her chest and down her arms; there was a hot pulsing in her hands, despite the bitter cold. It felt as though her heart-led plans to protect Jack and do the right thing had been hijacked and poisoned by Jacqui's fear-driven toxicity. For the first time she realised that she hated the idea of Jack being anywhere near her mother, with her warped ideas of how the world worked. *And what about 'make the most of what you were given'? Ha!* She thought furiously as she stomped towards polytunnels. *That was always her way, when I did something right it was because I was born with potential and when I did something wrong it was because I screwed it up!*

It took three hours of shovelling earth and weeding out a new bed before Annie calmed down and got some perspective. Interestingly, the first thought to save her was *'we're all the products of our upbringing, you know this Julie'*. She laughed at her own audacity, but wasn't it true? She knew little about her mother's childhood but enough to realise that it had caused Jacqui tremendous pain. She, Annie, wanted forgiveness, understanding, space to learn and grow, so she needed to find it within herself to give her mother the same. In that respect, it was probably a good thing that there would be some distance between them. She went to dinner feeling wiser than she'd done in all her life.

Annie left prison twenty-two months later, in December 2004. During her time, and inspired by Julie, she began a foundation degree in counselling. She got herself a 12-step sponsor and continued to attend meetings, one day discovering that she was among those women whom she'd so admired when she was on the rehab wing. She continued to correspond with Vern and the two women wrote long, hilarious anecdotes about prison life. Every week she wrote to Jack. Over two years she received two cards, one with handprints in red and blue paint and another with a jagged drawing of a house and three stick people, both signed *love Jack*; she treasured these, like gold. She didn't hear from her mother again.

It felt to Annie as though time had behaved like a piece of elastic, stretching out unbearably then abruptly plinging away from her, so that suddenly she was planning her resettlement. She felt as though she'd spent her entire adult life in prison, arriving a chaotic and frightened child. She'd learnt so much about herself yet still knew nothing of living in the world as this new, grown-up version. But she had hope. Hope, determination and a 12-step meeting list in her pocket, and that would have to be enough.

Part III
The walls that divide us

Nothing hurts more than trying your
absolute best and still not being
good enough
r.h.

One

Kate stood at the sink looking out onto the dreary day. Nothing seemed to be stirring, no leaves being tossed on the wintery air, no birds on the wing or in the barren-looking hedge which framed the driveway, not even a passing car. It seemed incongruous to her, at a time when her life and her inner landscape felt like a kaleidoscope of change, that the world seemed so still, so indifferent.

It was Saturday and Annie had called that morning hoping to speak with Jack. No, Kate had said, Jack had swimming lessons on a Saturday morning, Oliver took him and a couple of friends and then they all went for a McDonald's afterwards. Annie then asked if she could call that afternoon, but Kate had explained they were going Christmas shopping, and anyway, it really was better if they all met in person first at the Christmas party as Kate had suggested just a few days ago, the day of Annie's release.

The weeks leading up to that fateful date had been almost unbearable. Kate had thought to collect Annie from prison and was wracked with guilt at the idea of her travelling all that way alone by public transport but, as her mother had warned, Annie would most certainly want to see Jack the moment she was free, and Kate wanted to delay that moment for as long as possible. At some level, she recognised that her behaviour was irrational, that she needed to accept that Annie was going to be around for the foreseeable future, but the reality was so unpleasant to her that she felt compelled to resist it, as one resists immersing oneself in cold water for as long as possible.

She had the unshakeable sense that everything she'd worked so hard to create was teetering on the edge of a precipice. Perhaps this was why it seemed that the world was holding its breath. Right up until Annie's release, everything had been on course, the way she'd imagined it should be, the way she had *willed* it to be.

Last year she'd had her fairy-tale wedding, with her bridesmaids and flowers and Jack winning every heart as he carefully delivered the rings on a red satin cushion. The service was followed by the most immaculate wedding breakfast in great white marquees on the lawns of Powderham Castle. The photos, now on stretched canvas, adorned the living room walls and looked truly magical. She'd also received a promotion to area manager last year, and by putting in some brutal hours, was expected make regional executive by next spring.

Oliver was being brilliant, not only ferrying Jack about and essentially being a single parent for two or three nights a week, but also transforming the house, knocking through walls and building an extension, digging out the garden and creating a decking area. Sometimes they argued about Kate's busy schedule and her grand designs for the house but when they stopped arguing and talked about it, Oliver always agreed; they were working hard and making sacrifices now for the life they both wanted. *Nothing good comes without struggle and sacrifice,* Kate would quote one of her mother's favourite sayings and Oliver would concede and the world would continue spinning on its axis.

But now it felt like everything could come crashing down; the ducks were carefully placed in line and Annie could come along and kick them asunder in one fell swoop.

'You have to be very clever now Kate,' her mother had said. 'You have the upper hand here. Annie is nothing if not impressionable and Jack will see things as *you* see them. You have to set the rules.' Jacqui made it sound so easy, so unemotional. 'Annie's just not a big deal in Jack's life. He has his life here with you,' she said firmly, then added, 'You don't want Annie going off getting solicitors, so you need to appear willing. But Jack has a full and busy life, Annie should want that as much as anyone. She will have to accept that she takes a back seat.' She'd shrugged, then added, 'And let's face it, Kate, how long do you think she'll keep her act together? She'll be back on the drugs in no time, if she isn't already; you can get that stuff in prison, you know.'

Jacqui had nodded knowingly. 'You won't have to play the game for long, just hold your line until she makes a mistake and then you've got her.'

Kate was appalled by the way her mother spoke about Annie but even more so because she found herself hoping she was right. She didn't allow herself to fully appreciate what *a mistake* would spell for Annie; she just wanted her life back to the way she'd planned it.

'She phoned as soon as she got to her accommodation,' Kate said glumly. 'They've put her in Exeter.' Whatever her mother said she couldn't see how it was going to be that easy to keep Annie at bay. Yet her mother had a way of making her feel stupid, to forget that she was a successful saleswoman who closed deals for a living. 'She wants to see Jack this weekend.'

'Well, she can't. It's inconvenient, tell her. She can't expect to come out of prison and immediately start making demands.'

Kate felt torn. It hadn't seemed as though Annie were making demands, more that she'd simply been excited to see Jack, and her, for that matter. Kate had felt awful stalling her, saying she wasn't yet sure of their plans, but she hadn't been ready to plunge into the icy water so soon. Annie had taken it well enough, simply asking if Kate could get back to her to let her know. Kate hadn't got back to her which was probably what instigated this morning's call.

'The best time for Jack to meet her,' Jacqui had said, 'is when there are lots of other people around. It will take the intensity out of it for the poor boy and make sure Annie doesn't have the opportunity to fill his head with nonsense.'

Kate nodded, that did make sense and her mother seemed genuinely concerned for Jack's welfare. Yet at times she had a vague suspicion that Jacqui's pessimism might not be the most helpful influence in her already fear-saturated mind. Occasionally she would glimpse an alternate reality where Annie wasn't so much of a threat, where everybody got on and Annie was the occasional visitor. But then she would picture scenes of Jack and Annie together, imagining how that could so easily landslide into something devastating to her status quo, then she would be back in her mother's corner: the only way to manage this was to not let it start in the first place. It was what was best for Jack; he didn't need all this added confusion in his life, especially as Annie would probably relapse anyway.

So they'd decided on the Christmas party next week as the ideal opportunity to introduce Annie. Most of Jack's school friends and their parents would be there, making it easier to diffuse any kind of *situation* should it arise.

Two

Annie stood outside Niebuhr House, the large white building which was to be her new home. She scuffed her trainer across the gravel as she smoked her cigarette, steeling herself to go inside. Being in prison had accustomed her to meeting new faces but she still felt nervous. *Once upon a time I would have used on this*, she thought, *just to take the edge off.* She picked up her bag and went into the foyer.

The building had once been an enormous house before it was converted into flats and then, more recently, commissioned to provide accommodation for women leaving prison. A large room downstairs had been converted into an office of sorts and there was a large communal kitchen and a lounge area where the weekly house meetings were held.

Annie's room was on the first floor. It was small and cosy, painted blue with blue-patterned curtains. There was a single bed next to a large sash window which flooded the room with wintery light and gave views to a small green and three enormous, skeletal trees. At the end of the bed was a chest of drawers whilst a simple kitchenette lined the opposite wall. Annie glowed.

She left her few belongings and headed into town. She'd been given a small discharge grant and wanted to buy a phone to call Kate. It felt strange, other-worldly, to be walking down a street full of people; it reminded her of when she'd had a difficult session with Julie, when she'd feel like she was walking around with a layer of skin missing and the volume turned up. It was going to take some getting used to. Once she'd bought her phone and a few essentials she headed back to the house. She felt a giddy joy as she let herself into her room, put her milk in the fridge and flicked on the kettle. *Mine,* she thought in elation, as she hugged herself and fell back on the bed.

But her sister sounded cool and offish when she called her. She was working away for the rest of the week, she said, and didn't know what their weekend plans were. She suggested a Christmas party, in a little over a week, as the best time to meet. Feeling as though she'd run headlong into a wall, Annie called her sponsor.

Sarah's story was quite different to Annie's; she hadn't used street drugs but was addicted to alcohol and prescription medication. She was a decade older than Annie, had no children and had held down a job for most of her adult life. That was until, driving her car one night and heavily under the influence of alcohol and benzos, she took a bend too quickly and ploughed into an oncoming car. There were no fatalities, but a child suffered *life-changing injuries* and Sarah was sentenced to five years in prison. It was the way Sarah shared about living with her guilt, how she used it to propel her recovery, to be the best possible version of herself, that had drawn Annie to her. Sarah had been abstinent for six years and exuded an aura of togetherness, wisdom and kindness that Annie wanted for herself, so she tried to follow Sarah's suggestions even when they were uncomfortable and counter to what she would like to do. One of Sarah's many sayings was, *'often the right thing to do is the hardest thing to do.'*

Today was no different. Annie was to give Kate plenty of space, Sarah said; Kate would be afraid of what Annie was going to do next, of course she sounded cool and distant. She suggested that Annie be patient and concentrate on the things she could do for herself; eat well, sleep well, go to meetings and let go of the things she couldn't control. It was hard to hear but felt intuitively right. Annie took a deep breath, said the serenity prayer, and after preparing herself something to eat in her little kitchen, set off to find her meeting.

***

'How are you finding Niebuhr House, Annie?'

It was the following day and Annie was meeting with her probation officer for the first time. The office was small and stale smelling, despite the building appearing modern and new. The light in the foyer beyond was flickering and caught Annie's gaze as it sporadically illuminated a curling poster which declared that abuse of staff would not be tolerated. Annie had heard some pretty grim reports about probation officers, that *they weren't really bothered*, that it was just a *tick-box exercise* and even that they are *just waiting to catch you out*, so Dawn was a pleasant surprise. A dark-haired, heavy browed, rather dowdy looking woman who seemed genuinely interested in Annie and as though she had all the time in the world.

'Oh, it's brilliant.' Annie dragged her gaze back and smiled happily. 'It's amazing to have my own space again, and to be able to cook for myself, and the view from my window is magical, three enormous oak trees that I can watch through the seasons.'

Dawn smiled. There was no getting away from it, Annie was very likeable, and her enthusiasm was refreshing. It was so much easier to work with people who wanted to engage.

'And you have a son, is that right?'

The question, coming with no preamble, was like a gut punch.

Annie was as surprised as Dawn when she began to cry. 'Yes, but I can't see him. I don't know when I'm going to see him.' She wiped her eyes with her sleeve, her tears stopping as quickly as they started. 'But I just need to be patient, it's early days and I need to prove myself.' She sat up a little straighter.

Dawn was frowning, looking over her paperwork, 'But I don't see any kind of injunction. You still have parental responsibility?' Dawn looked up, her impressive brow furrowed. 'Why can't you see him? What's stopping you?'

'Well...' Annie hesitated, feeling somehow conspiratorial, 'my sister Kate, he's lived with her since he was two and she... well she just wants to do the right thing. I completely understand it, of course, she doesn't want his life disrupted again, she probably thinks I'm going to relapse at any moment and be gone again.' Annie said all this very quickly. 'And that's no good for Jack,' she added.

Dawn was typing and scribbling. 'This,' she said, passing a scrap of paper to Annie, 'is the telephone number for CAFCASS, the children and family—'

'I know who they are,' Annie interjected, taking the paper but putting it on the desk, 'but I've decided to give Kate some space. I don't want to get into a battle with her over Jack. She just needs some time to see I'm no threat, to understand we can both be part of his life.'

Dawn folded her arms on the desk and leant towards Annie, her lank hair falling in curtains and hiding much of her broad face.

'Your sister has no right to stop you seeing your child, Annie,' she said, very slowly and deliberately. 'You're his mother. The reason the law often sides with the mother is because we know children do best with their mothers.'

Annie was torn. She'd had this conversation with Julie so many times. She hated to give the impression that she wasn't prepared to fight for Jack. She knew that Julie understood this but what about Dawn? What about the rest of the world? Society expects a mother to fight for her children like a lioness for her cubs. She often felt ashamed and unable to talk freely to the other women about her decisions regarding Jack because so many were engaged in court battles of their own.

'Every situation is different,' she heard herself saying. 'If Jack were younger, too young to understand what was going on, of course I'd go to court. I'd hate arguing with Kate, but I think in the long run it would be the best option. But Jack's seven. I was his age when Da left and I know the damage that it did to me, him wanting to see me and Mum saying what an arsehole he was, saying by wanting to see him I was being disloyal to her. It screwed me up.'

'And you think Kate will be saying those things to Jack?'

'I just don't know,' Annie said honestly. 'I would really like to think she wouldn't, I definitely don't think she'd be as awful about it as Mum was... but it's obvious she isn't *for* me at the moment. I need to prove myself to her, that's all. If I go and get professionals involved, she'll get defensive, we'll be fighting, and Jack will get dragged into our grown-up squabbles. I just want to take it slowly, so we don't have to fight. I want to do the right thing.' She smiled though she saw the cynicism written on Dawn's face.

They spoke a little about Annie's 12-step meetings and what else she could do with her time. Dawn was surprised that Annie wanted to find work and advised against taking on too much but, as usual, Sarah had different ideas. Annie had been drug-free and working a 12-step programme for two and a half years. She worked and studied in prison, why was she not able to work and do her degree in the community like anybody else? Dawn had smiled and given her blessing then said goodbye until the following week.

Three

Days passed in a blur of activity. Against what she felt were very bad odds, Annie found a job as a cleaner, and having tried repeatedly to call her Da to share the news, decided it was time to seek him out. On Friday afternoon she caught the bus to Cullompton, the nearby town where Kevin had lived, since he left her mother. She gazed out the window as she travelled and marvelled at how, even in the dead of winter, the Devon countryside bewitched her with its rolling hills and woodlands, a patchwork in every shade of brown and green.

Getting off the bus outside Kevin's flat, just as she had when she was fourteen years old, Annie had the odd sensation that she was watching herself, both her adult self and that damaged, angry girl about to set out on a terrible path and ricochet from one damning consequence to the next. It was an unsettling feeling. She reached her Da's door without noticing how she got there and wriggled her toes and shrugged her shoulders to get a grip of herself. She knocked.

There was no reply. Had she expected one? She knocked again then went round to peer through the grimy kitchen window. There was no *Withnail and I* scene at the kitchen sink. Her Da didn't eat so there was never much washing up. There were three or four empty bottles of cheap, strong white cider which made Annie gag as she remembered the taste. The cat was meowing, she could see its crusty, empty food bowl and overflowing litter tray. She imagined the stench and gagged again. No sign of movement. She was heading back to the front of the building thinking she might check the pub when she heard a yell from across the street.

'It's me darlin' Annie-girl!' Kevin was weaving across the road, narrowly missing an oncoming vehicle. Annie's breath caught in her throat as she saw him up close. In the five or so years since they'd last met, Kevin O'Shea looked to have shrivelled to less than half his size. His frame was bent as he staggered, his scarlet cheekbones were at odds with his grey, sunken face whilst purplish broken veins criss-crossed his nose and under the eyes which had once sparkled with mischief. His crumpled shirt hung slack over his once muscular torso.

'Where've you been Daddy?' was all she could manage as Annie caught his arm to keep him from toppling past her. 'Granny's been worried sick.'

'Oh, it's me darlin' wee Annie-girl,' Kevin continued in his sing-song voice as he tried to tweak her cheek but overshot and clouted her instead. 'Oh, I'm sorry... sorry,' he mumbled as he put his hand to his mouth, looking suddenly childlike.

'Come on, let's get you indoors,' Annie said with a little more authority, as she steered him the short distance to the front door. 'Key?' she asked, putting out her hand.

'Oh Annie-Panny!' Kevin staggered again as he broke free from her. 'Tis under the mat as it always is!' He almost keeled over as he reached down to lift the doormat.

'Here!' Annie lurched and beat him to it, trying to hold him upright at the same time. Eventually she got them both inside and deposited Kevin on the worn-out sofa, the same sofa she'd slept on for a year as a broken, teenaged girl. The curtains were still drawn so she pulled them back despite the fading winter light outside, it made the room feel less claustrophobic.

Kevin was gibbering nonsense in that same sing-song voice whilst she went to the little kitchen and put the kettle on.

'Cuppa tea, Da?' she called, opening the cupboard where the tea used to be housed, only to find it bare. She opened the next cupboard, again bare except for a mouldering tin of corned beef which looked as though it had been there since the Second World War. She went to the fridge. Empty.

'Da, you have to look after yourself!' she chastised him as she marched back into the lounge with the tin of corned beef. 'How long—' she stopped. Kevin had passed out on the sofa.

Annie took off his shoes and made him comfortable then headed to the local shop to buy groceries. As she wandered back up the little high street, she was struck again by memories of her fourteen-year-old self. Kevin had not been as far gone back then but between them they rarely got food in the cupboards and waking up to no milk or, indeed, no electricity, was a common occurrence. They rarely ran out of booze. *No wonder I was such a mess,* Annie thought sadly, *we're going to be okay now,* she whispered, hugging herself.

Annie spent most of the following two days with Kevin, trying to get him to eat and bullying him into taking walks with her. It felt like the battle was already lost. Kevin had to drink early to avoid the DTs, and understanding this predicament, Annie didn't try to stop him. But once Kevin started drinking it was very difficult to get him to stop and eventually, he would become irritated with her.

'Why don't ye feck off back where ye came from?' he snarled at her on Sunday afternoon as she'd tried to convince him to come to a meeting rather than to the pub. He was already slurring and staggering about.

Annie was mortified. But she knew that she couldn't control him; the only person she had any control over was herself and she had to get to a meeting each day and back to her accommodation each night.

She was already spending too much time in the booze-saturated, claustrophobic flat with only Kevin for company and if she didn't look after herself, she couldn't help anybody. Her agonising about what she should do was cut short by a phone call from her new boss: one of the full-time girls had broken her arm over the weekend, how would Annie feel about covering her hours for the next six weeks?

***

And now it was Saturday again, *the* Saturday of *the* Christmas party and for the first time in a long while Annie was reunited with that itchy, scratchy, burning feeling that seemed to spread from her navel to her throat, reminding her of rodents frantically scratching at the inside of a sack.

She was standing at the threshold of the indoor play park. In front of her was a small queue of *yummy mummies* in skinny jeans and knee boots with tinsel in their hair. Annie felt fidgety and uncomfortable; her hands and feet felt too big, and she couldn't work out what to do with them in order to look at ease. How could she have forgotten how to stand up? Her jumper felt itchy around her neck and for the first time she wished she'd worn something other than the jumper Kate had given her in prison, it had seemed like such a good idea when she put it on. She watched the laughing, pretty faces, the swishing of shiny, poker-straight hair and felt like a big-footed, bushy haired clown.

Eventually the little crowd made it past reception and into the play area and Annie slunk in behind them. There were around a dozen adults loitering about and sitting at the tables which lined the left corner of the room; to Annie they all looked beautiful and very grown-up and again she felt ungainly and awkward, like a big red teapot in a cupboard of dainty Doulton china. There were smaller children clinging to a parent or sitting on a lap whilst the older ones charged around, climbing up netting, through tunnels and diving into ball pools, their yells clashing spectacularly with the Christmassy music.

Annie scanned the room searching for a flash of red hair, it didn't take long. Her chest constricted and her breath caught in her throat as she saw Jack climbing through a set of bars directly opposite where she stood. She felt as though she'd fallen several feet and stopped with a sudden jolt, her heart in her mouth. Their eyes met as he straightened up and she managed a little wave and a smile, which faltered and died as Jack looked at her in horror and darted off towards a gaggle of grown-ups to his right. Annie watched, not breathing, as Jack found Kate, who bent down to hear him over the clamour and looked in the direction in which he was frantically pointing; her eyes met Annie's. She straightened up smiling, and taking Jack's hand, made her way over.

Annie found she was rooted to the spot, clutching her badly wrapped present and feeling as though she were being throttled by her roll-neck jumper. She longed to take it off, but she'd stupidly worn nothing underneath. She had a fleeting image of herself standing there in her greying bra, and felt the shame wash over her. *Stupid, stupid* she was saying to herself as Kate and Jack were upon her.

'Hi Annie!' Kate was saying, a little breathlessly. She leant in and administered an awkward, one-armed hug whilst still holding Jack's hand. Then she stood back, and Jack reversed into her, clutching both her hands at his shoulders as he looked up at Annie.

'Hey Jack,' Annie said as warmly as she could, smiling down at him.

'Hi Annie,' Jack replied, looking down and stamping his feet awkwardly.

Annie. It was as though someone had slipped a knife below her ribcage. What had she expected? That he would still call her Mummy after all this time? *Yes!* Said a tiny, wounded voice.

'Are you having a good party?' she said instead.

'We're having a great party, aren't we Jack?' Kate answered when Jack said nothing, still looking at his feet.

'Er... I have the secret Santa thing,' Annie said awkwardly, thrusting the package towards Kate, who had to shake off Jack's hand in order to take it.

They stood in silence for a moment, then, 'Can I go and play?'

Jack swung away from them but kept hold of one of Kate's hands, making it a game.

Kate hung on to him for a moment, taking his weight, then let go so he staggered back, laughing. 'Go on then,' she said, smiling broadly before looking back to Annie. 'Glad you made it,' she said, turning to put the present on a pile of others behind her. 'Have you got yourself a drink? There's no alcohol served down here I'm afraid.'

Annie just looked at her for a moment, backfooted. 'I don't drink alcohol, Kate,' she said eventually.

'Oh, okay,' Kate said, looking past Annie to the entrance. 'I wasn't sure if that was just a prison thing. Look, sorry, Sally's just arrived, I'll see you in a bit, okay?' She took Annie's upper arms and gave her another squeeze before moving past her, leaving Annie feeling dazed and horribly self-conscious. She realised she was dangerously close to spinning off all together and made her way back outside, giving Kate and Sally an awkward little wave as she headed for air.

She took great gulps, gathering herself. There was a brisk wind, and she felt the sting on her face and watched the leaves being whipped around the car park.

What had she expected? Perhaps she shouldn't have come alone. Sarah did suggest bringing someone, but Annie didn't feel she knew anyone from the meetings well enough yet. She'd thought about Granny O'Shea but her relationship with Kate was always strained, and Annie didn't want to do anything to ostracise herself further. No, she'd had to come alone, unarmed as it were, and of course it wasn't going to be easy. This was her way of making amends, of facing up to her consequences. She closed her eyes for a moment and let the sleety rain bring her home to herself then, saying a silent prayer, she headed back inside.

Jack was with two other boys who looked about his age. They were in the ball pool, gambolling around and aiming missiles at each other. Annie kicked off her shoes and trotted over. They all looked up as she yelled and attempted a wonky somersault into the fray; she righted herself, laughing and before they'd closed their mouths, she started launching balls at them. It wasn't long before all three were launching balls back and climbing over each other to reach her. She laughed maniacally, trying to cover her face as she shot upright, roaring like a giant, and leapt from the pool and towards the tunnels. The boys were in pursuit as she shimmied through the tight space as fast as her frame would allow, only to find Jack and one of his friends at the other end, firing balls at her. She rolled onto the floor laughing and grabbed an ankle.

'And what's your name?' she asked the little boy as he laughed, hopping on the spot.

'Joe!' he yelled. 'And that's Ali!' He pointed to the boy appearing from the tunnel. 'We like you!' Joe continued in his funny, shouty way, as the little squadron formed again. 'Chase us!'

And so, she did. God, she wished she could take off her jumper. She knew she must be red and sweaty; her hair was plastered to her head. Other than the odd lone dad she was the only grown-up climbing on the apparatus and running around like a lunatic, but she found she didn't care, let the *yummy mummies* look, she couldn't compete with them anyway.

Eventually they were all puffed out and Annie went off to buy them all a Fruit Shoot. When she returned Kate was at the table.

'Look at the state of you!' she said as Annie approached clutching her purchases. 'You look like you've been dragged through a hedge backwards,'

Kate was laughing amicably but Annie felt the subtle put-down.

'Hey ho,' she said lightly as she set the drinks on the table. 'We're having fun, aren't we?' she asked the boys.

'Yes!' Joe replied punching his fist into the air. *Bless darling Joe,* Annie thought.

'Jack, why don't you come over to our table? Maisy's here with Auntie Sally.' Kate stood up, holding out her hand.

Jack looked torn; his little mouth downturned slightly.

'No. No, stay and play!' Joe was yelling again as he jumped up. 'She's the wicked witch!' he pointed at Annie as he jumped up and down a few feet away.

'Can I stay and play?' Jack asked uncertainly.

Kate looked from him to Annie and Annie thought she looked cross.

'Yes, okay then,' Kate said, and she was gone.

'Yeeeah!' The three boys jostled together and ran backwards, taunting Annie to pursue them. Rolling up her sleeves and cackling like a witch, Annie gave chase.

Not long after this, when Annie's hair was pretty much stood on end and her sides hurt from screeching and cackling, Jack said quietly that he needed to use the bathroom, so they left Ali and Joe swinging on the monkey bars and set off for the toilets in the outer foyer. The main doors were open, and Annie was thankful for another icy blast of wind as they went into the hall.

'Here we are.' she motioned to Jack. 'I'll just wait here.' He nodded and disappeared. Annie leant against the wall. She'd kill for a cigarette, but it felt like the height of indiscretion to be out here smoking with Jack. She swallowed the impulse and waited. She looked at her watch and realised that nearly two hours had passed when she hadn't felt self-conscious or inadequate and Jack actually seemed to like her.

'Ready?' she said, daring to put out her hand as Jack came out of the bathroom.

But Jack stood rooted to the spot as the door swung closed behind him. He was biting on his lip and looking worried before he blurted out, 'I don't want to live with you.'

Annie was taken aback. *Where had that come from?* She retracted her hand and squatted down so that she was looking up at him slightly.

'I know that, sweetie!' she said ardently. He still looked troubled, so she tentatively took his fingers and gave his hand a little shake. 'I just want to get to know you, is that okay?'

Jack nodded cautiously. 'You won't take me away? Because I definitely want to live with Kate and Ollie and if anyone asks me that's what I'll say!'

Annie was mortified to think he'd been turning all this over in his little head.

'Jack, I promise you, okay? I don't want to take you away; I just want you to be happy.'

Just at that moment Sally came bursting through the double doors.

'Oh my God!' she shouted, then, 'Kate! He's here. They're here!' as Kate came hurtling through the doors after her.

'Oh Jack!' she exclaimed, grabbing the little boy and holding him to her, cradling his head into her body. 'What were you thinking, Annie!' she spat, taking Jack's shoulders and holding him away from her as if examining him for damage.

'It's all right Jacky, are you okay?'

Jack nodded.

'Where were you taking him?' she asked furiously of Annie, who realised her mouth was open. Her ears were ringing.

'I wasn't taking him anywhere!' She looked from Kate to Sally as though they'd gone completely insane. The next moment Joe and Ali had arrived looking breathless and frightened, stopping short when they saw Jack had been found.

'Kate, he needed to use the bathroom.' Annie was amazed that her voice sounded level and thought it must be shock. A woman, whom she assumed was Joe's mother, had joined the little crowd and took Joe's hand.

'Why didn't you come and get one of us?' Sally was asking huffily.

'Oh, this is ridiculous,' Annie said, feeling the edge of her temper. 'Because I'm quite capable of taking him thirty feet away to use the bathroom, Sally.'

Kate had crouched in front of Jack, speaking with him softly, now she stood up and looked stonily at Annie.

'Please don't take him out of my sight again without telling me first,' she said coldly. 'I would have thought that would be obvious,' she added as she stalked away, holding firmly to Jack's hand. The little group encircled them like a pack and Sally gave her one final, hateful glare as they went back through the double doors.

Annie realised she was trembling. She hadn't even said goodbye to Jack or asked if he was okay, but she couldn't bear to go back in there now. She could imagine what Kate's cronies would be saying, *'Taking him outside, what was she thinking!'; 'Probably trying to steal him away!'; 'She's a junkie, you just can't trust them!'*

She knew Sarah would tell her to be stricter with her thoughts, that she didn't know they were saying anything of the sort. *But I can hazard a pretty good guess,* Annie thought glumly, *and in front of Jack too.* Pretty soon he'd believe she *was* the wicked witch.

Realising she couldn't loiter any longer, she wandered out into the cold. She'd bought a return bus ticket but decided to walk, the movement and the bitter chill helping her to keep a handle on herself. It just felt too enormous to process; the joy of being with Jack, the laughing and joking and tussling had just felt so natural, so right. The pain of him calling her Annie but also a realisation that this was okay, so long as he was happy, so long as he could make sense of things. But what had just happened? What *was* that? Did Kate really believe she was going to steal him away? She'd been stupid to take Jack outside, she supposed, but it had all happened so quickly. Did she owe Kate an apology? Probably. Either way, she needed to talk it out with her and take responsibility for her side of the mix-up. But what troubled her most was how the whole scene must have affected Jack, and worse, he *already* worried that she was going to take him away. What had Kate been saying to him? She needed to talk the whole thing through with Sarah and then speak with Kate as soon as possible.

She arrived at Niebuhr House without remembering the journey and was just fishing her door key from her back pocket when her phone started ringing. Perhaps it was Kate, wanting to sort things out? But it was Granny O'Shea. Kevin had been rushed to hospital with a gastric bleed. He was in very bad shape, she said, could Annie come at once.

Four

Kate gently kissed the top of Jack's head and pulled the covers more tightly around his chin. Despite being pretty shell-shocked by the incident with Annie he seemed to have forgotten about it within moments of hurtling around the play area with Joe and Ali.

Kate had scolded him more forcefully than she ordinarily would, albeit at a whisper, as she'd crouched beside him in the foyer. She didn't want to scare him, but he had to realise the dangers of wandering off alone with Annie. What would have happened, she'd asked him, if Annie had put him in a car and driven off with him, too far away for him to get home? What if Annie told people Jack should live with her, that really, he *wanted* to live with her? How would he explain that he'd wandered off with her then? He'd cried and she'd felt awful and hugged him to her. Then they were off playing again and the whole thing was seemingly forgotten.

Annie had slunk off and Kate had stayed furious with her, easily fuelled by Sally and some of the other mothers who'd witnessed Kate's terror when she realised Jack was missing. *I mean, what was Annie thinking,* Kate had raged to herself, *taking Jack out of my sight the very first opportunity she got? Of course I freaked out, anybody would!* She thought these things as she bathed Jack, put him into his pyjamas and tucked him into bed, trying not to let her irritation spill out onto the little boy. But now, as she switched off the light and tiptoed from the room, she was tormented by the look on Annie's face as the little group of adults and children had marched away and left her in the foyer. She really did look distraught, and if Kate were honest with herself, she didn't think Annie had deliberately tried to cause trouble. *But what an idiotic thing to do!*

She'd tried to speak with Oliver about it when they got home but he'd refused to engage in the character assassination that Sally so enjoyed, and which made Kate feel so much better. Did she really believe Annie would steal Jack away? Oliver had asked. Had Annie given any indication that this was her intention? She'd seemed very accepting of the current situation, he'd pointed out, and if Kate really were concerned that Annie was going to do a runner then why was she letting her loose in big social gatherings like today?

This just left Kate feeling irritated and defensive. Did she really believe Annie was capable of running off with Jack? If Annie were on drugs the answer was easy: — yes, she was absolutely capable. But Annie as she was today? She just couldn't be sure. Certainly, in the heat of the moment it had seemed very real, but Kate was frustrated with herself that she'd panicked so easily. Because she had definitely frightened Jack; in the same way, as Oliver was always pointing out, as when she felt the need to ask Jack just once more what he would say if someone asked him who he wanted to live with.

So was today her fault? *No!* How could any of this be *her* fault? She'd taken in a neglected, damaged little boy and given him a full and wonderful life, she was doing the right thing. Annie had made her choice; she chose drugs over Jack and now she just wanted to swan in and expect everyone to dance to her tune. Kate could hear her mother's voice during a phone conversation just a couple of days ago.

'It's crucial that you get this right, Kate,' Jacqui had said for what felt like the hundredth time. 'Jack is at a very impressionable age. You can't give Annie the opportunity to start getting in his head.'

'I know, Mum,' Kate had replied wearily.

'You don't need to take that tone with me,' Jacqui snapped. 'I don't think you understand the seriousness of what's happening here. The courts will be on Annie's side if she applies for access rights and then where will you be? With Jack spending every weekend with her? You'll have no control of the situation then. She'll be filling his head with all kinds of nonsense and the next minute you'll have a custody battle on your hands.'

'I can't stop Annie from seeing him Mum, how am I supposed to do that?'

'Aren't you listening to me, Kate? That's why you have to be clever!' Jacqui had barked. 'Jack isn't old enough to understand but *you? You* know, Kate! Annie gave up any rights she had to that little boy when she chose to keep taking drugs. You need to let him know that.'

'No,' Kate had replied flatly. 'I'm not filling his head with poison, it's... it's not fair.' She'd felt dangerously close to criticising her mother.

'Well, you do it your way then, Kate,' Jacqui had said, and Kate could hear her lighting a cigarette, 'but you're playing a very dangerous game.'

Is that what I'm afraid of, Kate asked herself, *she's not going to physically steal him away but she's going to turn him against me?* She had a fleeting image of Jack and Annie today, so alike with their elfin faces and russet hair. Had she really believed Annie had taken him or was she just desperate to get Jack from her clutches? She looked at her watch; it was only eight o'clock, but she felt exhausted. Oliver was downstairs watching sport on the television and wouldn't be great company, not that she much felt like company anyway. She went downstairs with the intention of making a hot chocolate and bidding him goodnight.

As she passed the hallway phone it began to trill, making her jump. She felt a whoosh of anxiety, it was bound to be Annie and she just hadn't the energy to deal with it. She thought about letting it go to answerphone, but the noise might wake Jack and then he would hear

Annie blurting out whatever she had to say to the machine.

'Hello?' she said curtly, hearing her defensive tone but feeling it was the only way.

'Kate, it's Annie—'

'Yes, I thought it would be,' she said, more coldly still and hearing Annie falter.

'Look... I'm sorry about today, I want to talk about it properly. I was stupid... thoughtless—'

'Yep.'

'Kate, please listen! It's Da. He's ill. He's... he's probably dying.'

Kate said nothing, her thoughts seemed to have jammed.

'Kate? Are you there? Kate, will you come to the hospital? Would you bring Jack, he's asking to see you both?'

Kate's brain swung back into gear.

'Jack?' she asked, astonished. 'Why would I bring Jack? He doesn't even know him.'

'He knew him when he was little, Kate,' Annie said quietly. 'Please. It will probably be the last chance.'

'I'm not taking Jack to hospital in the middle of the night to see an old man he won't even remember,' Kate said with finality. There was a pause and she heard Annie make a blowing noise as she exhaled. It irritated her.

'Will *you* come then, please?' Annie was asking.

But Kate's hackles were up, she felt cornered and defensive. 'No, I'm sorry Annie. I don't know him either; he isn't part of my life and never has been really.'

'Kate, please—'

'Look, haven't you caused enough trouble for one day?' Kate fired back hotly then slammed the phone down without waiting for an answer and unplugged it at the wall.

'Who was that?' Oliver called.

'No one, just Annie, it was nothing,' Kate heard herself saying. The last thing she needed was to have to explain herself to Mr Reasonable. She moved like a sleepwalker into the kitchen, flicked on the kettle and sat down at the table.

She couldn't get the image from her mind of her father on her wedding day: wrinkled, shrunken, toothless, his suit hanging from his shrivelled frame. *Why would I want to see him looking like that?* She thought crossly. And once again her mother's voice was in her head, *'He made his choice, Kate, and he chose the booze. He loved his booze more than any of us.'*

Kate was not quite nine years old when her mother finally kicked Kevin out for good. She could still remember everything about that day, right down to the weather. It was very hot, a hot summer's day. She thought it strange that school holidays always seemed to be hot when she was a child but now Jack was at school it always seemed to rain in late July and August.

She wondered if it had something to do with how a child perceives things, but her other childhood memories weren't particularly sunny, just the opposite. But on this day the sun was shining, and she was happy. She felt so *glad* that her Da was finally leaving, that her mother really seemed to mean it this time, and secretly known to Kate, already had another man who visited, who seemed to like her mother very much, not like her silly, stinking Da.

Kate could still remember that her feelings troubled her. Shouldn't she be sad that her Da was leaving? Shouldn't she be crying like he was as he pulled her drunkenly to him, smelling horribly of whiskey and cigarettes? Or like Annie, sobbing inconsolably on her bed, like one of those movie actresses in the black-and-white films, refusing to speak to anyone?

But to Kate it was plain: her Da made her mother unhappy, he never did what he promised, he never took them out like he said he would; he disappeared for days at a time and when he returned, all they did was argue. What had he ever done for Kate? She had plenty of friends and she saw how their fathers behaved, they were nothing like her Da, in fact she often felt embarrassed when people mentioned her Da, they all knew he was a hopeless drunk. If he left for good, they would all be much happier. Kate could remember feeling angry that Annie didn't see that. She also remembered feeling confused and even jealous that

Annie was getting some kind of satisfaction and happiness out of this man who gave Kate worse than nothing.

As she sat at the kitchen table, the kettle long since boiled and forgotten, she sensed those same feelings now. What was this mysterious, magical relationship that Annie shared with their father that was somehow denied to her? What was it that he gave Annie that made her run off and abandon Kate when they were teenagers? He'd always appeared to Kate like a dirty drunk who did nothing but let them down. Even after he'd left, he would call the house drunk, slurring his words and crying. He couldn't even stay sober for one phone call. Was that love? Kate certainly didn't think so.

Her mother was domineering, opinionated, even bullying but she was always there: she was never drunk, she put food on the table and clothes on their backs. Yes, she would shout and be mean, but Kate truly believed it was because her mother wanted what was best for them. She wanted them to have good lives, with good things and that meant discipline and hard work. Why couldn't Annie ever see that? Was it because, even then, she was just a drunk like Kevin? Was she going to meet the same grisly end?

The end. Was he really dying? she wondered idly as she doodled on one of Jack's colouring books. How did she even feel about that? Did it make her happy, like the day her mother had kicked him out? No, she didn't feel like that. She felt sad for him, especially when she pictured him at her wedding, but then she felt angry. *He* was the one doing it to himself, no one else. *He* was the one who'd robbed her of a father, robbed Jack of a grandfather, not her. And now she was supposed to feel guilty for keeping Jack away.

She could hear Granny O'Shea now, '*Oh, that Katherine, just like her mudder that one.*' *Well, she can fuck off.* Kate thought savagely. Where was Granny O'Shea when Kevin would come home drunk in the middle of the night, waking them all up when they had school the next day? Where was she at Kate's eighth birthday party when he came crashing in, practically landing in the birthday cake, knocking over chairs and scaring her friends? Kate could feel the shame, as though it were yesterday. Where was Granny O'Shea, when he promised her mother for the umpteenth time, he would quit drinking tomorrow only to stumble in the next day saying he'd lost another job? *That's not love,* Kate thought grimly, standing up, abandoning the idea of a hot drink and heading upstairs.

And it was she, Kate, who always had to hold it all together. Had to listen to her mother, try to be the good girl so as not to add to Jacqui's worries. It was she who always had to do the right thing. It was she who had to grow up and take responsibility whilst Annie was just a little girl, disappearing down the woods every five minutes, singing songs and telling stories, then, later, going all dark and weird, backchatting everyone and getting into trouble at school. All that nonsense about Frank, just to give her an excuse to run off to their Da, to do exactly what she wanted, as usual. Not Kate, she had to be the responsible one, the *good* one. And now she was supposed to feel guilty. Well, she wouldn't, and more to the point, she would protect Jack at all costs, from her Da, from Annie, from anyone.

Five

Annie glanced over at Granny O'Shea. The old woman looked exhausted, like she'd aged twenty years since yesterday, but nobody could have looked as old or as ill as her Da. The doctor had mercifully put him in a private room, and he lay, looking as small as a child with tubes appearing to come from everywhere.

The hospital was within walking distance for Annie, and she had run there through the sleet and sludge, her lungs on fire in the freezing air. Granny O'Shea had met her in the car park, and they rushed to the ward together. The nurses had been like angels, taking the distraught women to a side room and explaining that, although they'd administered medication to treat the gastric bleed, Kevin had also contracted sepsis, perhaps from one of his many sores or potentially related to the bleed itself. Kevin had been diagnosed with cirrhosis two years prior but had refused treatment or to seek help for his drinking. He'd been admitted to hospital six times in eighteen months for alcohol-related illnesses and injuries. Annie was aghast, she'd had no idea. It turned out that Kevin had sworn Granny O'Shea to secrecy whilst Annie was in prison.

Kevin had been given a massive dose of antibiotics and the following hours would be crucial. Even as the kindly looking nurse spoke it was clear to Annie that they were acting more out of duty than any real belief that Kevin would survive. He was currently being kept alive by a ventilator, but it would eventually be down to Granny O'Shea, Kevin's next of kin, to decide what should happen next. The old lady had crumpled like a bit of old newspaper.

Annie called Kate when they first arrived at the hospital. At that point Kevin had been conscious and relatively lucid. He'd clutched at Annie's hand and tried to speak, encumbered by the breathing tube, his eyes rolling. He wanted to see Kate and Jack; he was adamant. He'd made lots of mistakes, he said, 'Explain for me Annie-girl, explain,' he said. Then he'd waved her off urgently and she'd staggered from the room leaving her broken heart behind her.

In her heartbreak she'd forgotten the fiasco at the play park and was caught off guard when Kate was so cross with her. She did her best to persuade her sister to come, but when she came off the phone, she felt she'd done a poor job. Should she call back? But Kate had been so cold and unyielding, and Annie feared she would simply widen the great chasm between them.

By the time she returned to Kevin's room, his condition had worsened. He looked at her with wild eyes and she wasn't sure he even remembered where she'd been.

'They'll be here soon, Daddy, just you rest,' she managed, and this seemed to soothe him. Granny O'Shea had looked at her searchingly and Annie shook her head. The old woman looked sour, and Annie wished she'd lied to her too.

'That girl!' Granny O'Shea barked furiously when Annie had motioned her from the little room. 'Just like ye mudder! Just the same, tinks she's better than the rest of us!'

'Granny, please, keep your voice down.'

Annie looked nervously through the glass. Kevin hadn't moved.

'Well! You'd tink Kevin was Adolf Hitler himself the way that child goes on. He's a lot of tings, my Kevin, but he has a heart of gold. A heart of gold, not like that witch he married—'

Annie felt like she was fourteen again, desperate for support, for comfort, but finding only bitterness and blame at every turn.

'Granny!' she cut into the old woman's rant in a way she never would have. 'Granny,' she said more calmly. 'I know you're scared. I am too. But this isn't helping or changing anything. Kate has her own version of events and it's just as true as yours or mine.' Annie surprised herself as she quoted one of those lightbulb moments from Julie's therapy room.

'No, it's true,' she went on as Granny O'Shea made a face. 'Why should my version or your version, be more right than hers? I want her to come; I want Jack to see his Granda… one last time…' Tears sprang to her eyes. 'And I want it for Da. But I understand why Kate doesn't want to bring him.'

'She could come herself!'

'Yes, she could,' Annie said simply, 'but we can't make her. Now let's go and be with him.'

And so they sat. Annie was awash with memories; going out with Kevin when he had his delivery round, sitting on his lap and pretending to drive, she could only have been five or six, yet she remembered it clearly. She could recall him creeping in late at night, waking the house up and how he would wink at her whilst she stood on the landing and her mother yelled at everyone. She remembered them playing in the woods, him teaching her the names of the trees, ferns and flowers. She could remember watching him ride a horse on a neighbouring farm, how it was mad and wild and tried to buck him off, but he sat there barely moving until the animal calmed down and walked quietly for him. She remembered deciding there and then that she would ride that well one day.

And she remembered the day he told her he was leaving, how he'd told her it would all be okay and promised she would still see him every day. She remembered how she knew, even at the tender age of seven, that this was a lie and beyond his ability to control. What she remembered most, as she watched him wasting away, kept alive by the pump and whir of the ventilator, was that this man had never judged her, never made her feel that she wasn't good enough or that she had to try harder to earn his love or approval. He was always pleased to see her, always overjoyed with anything she did, even if it were being naughty; he always made her know she was loved, that she was enough. She went over to the bed and stroked his thin hair.

'Annie-girl,' he mumbled. 'And where's Katy and wee Jack?'

He remembered. She'd thought he was out of his mind with the infection. It was difficult to hear him over the sound of the machine and Annie had to put her face right up close to his. A tear splashed from her eyes onto his cheek, and she carefully stroked it away, smoothing her thumb over the broken veins and papery skin, her heart breaking.

'They'll be here soon, Da, don't worry, just rest.'

'She's right to be angry, Annie, so she is. I did wrong by you girls, ye ma too. I've not been a good man, Annie-girl.' He suddenly seemed so lucid.

Annie longed to put him right. She couldn't bear the thought that he would slip away, his last thoughts being of what an awful person he was, just like she used to believe of herself. She longed to impart on him every lesson, every wise word that she, herself, had been blessed with. Many times in prison, she'd imagined speaking with him about these things, that perhaps he would go to a meeting and the lights would come on as they had for her and they would recover and grow together, make up for so much lost time. But Kevin seemed to have used all his strength with his final utterance.

A while later a nurse came in and said that it didn't look good, Kevin's organs were shutting down and it was unlikely he would survive off the ventilator. An hour after this, when Kevin still hadn't regained consciousness other than to moan and writhe and roll his eyes, Granny O'Shea, ashen and frail-looking, said that nature should be allowed its course.

It was nearly midnight. Annie daren't call Kate again but she sent a text, thinking if by some miracle she got it, well, then she was meant to get it. Kate didn't reply or arrive and in the early hours of Sunday morning Kevin O'Shea breathed his last, shallow breath.

Six

Mary O'Shea was a strong and courageous woman. Belfast-born, she'd grown up and married Daniel O'Shea in an atmosphere of animosity and segregation, when it felt that terrible violence could break out at any moment, and it often did. Kevin, an only child, was nearly ten years old when Daniel joined the throng of hopefuls seeking work in the rapidly growing construction industries of London. It meant starting from nothing, leaving with just a few possessions and a week's rent money but, as Mary liked to remind her granddaughters, that was the way of life back then, living on nothing but hard work and determination.

In the late sixties, Daniel was diagnosed with asbestosis and the family moved to Devon for the cleaner air. Just two years later, not yet fifty, Daniel died of mesothelioma, long before companies were paying compensation for asbestos-related cancers. Kevin, then in his early twenties and already drinking heavily, never came to terms with his father's death and was unable to offer Mary any kind of support. Presently he was to meet and fall in love with Jacqui Harper and Mary watched, aghast, whilst her son's confidence seemed to fade and rust like old metal as, year by year, Jacqui and her parents convinced him he was less than useless. As Kevin's drinking worsened and Jacqui's resentment reached boundless proportions, Mary became increasingly protective of her once bright, sensitive and talented boy, apportioning all blame on Jacqui, her ever-growing expectations and never-ending criticism. She conveniently forgot that Kevin was showing every sign of alcoholism long before he met Jacqui Harper.

***

The weeks following Kevin's death were like a baptism of fire for Annie and though her own grief felt like barbed wire around her heart, she was forced to hold herself together in order to care for Granny O'Shea. The old lady, seemed to have aged a lifetime, the sprightly and agile gait which once belied her seventy-nine years was now a shuffle and her eyes, usually so full of light and mischief, were vacant and lifeless.

To Annie's surprise, Dawn, in her cool efficiency, proved to be an enormous help when it came to making funeral arrangements and managing Kevin's affairs, for which Granny O'Shea showed little interest. As it turned out, Kevin hadn't been as disorganised as he appeared and amongst his stacks of paperwork Annie had found a will, leaving ten thousand pounds each to Kate and Annie and a further five thousand to Jack.

How her father had managed to save this money was beyond her, and it broke Annie's heart a little more to think of him doing the best he could whilst hating himself for not being able to quit drinking. She was reminded of something a woman said in one of her earliest meetings: '*If you'd asked me to cut off my arms and give them to my children, I would have done it willingly, but I still couldn't stop drinking for them.*' Once again, she was filled with a rush of gratitude for her recovery and a deep sadness that she wasn't able to share it with Kevin. They'd run out of time. The tragedy of it threatened to wash her away when she dwelt on it too long.

The funeral was a simple affair at the crematorium with a buffet afterwards laid on by Kevin's local pub, free of charge. Kevin had always been well liked so Annie didn't have to worry that she and Granny O'Shea would be giving him a lonely send-off, the little room was filled with people who loved and appreciated him, and Annie found that after ten minutes of welcoming guests she stopped looking out for her other family members.

Two of Kevin's drinking buddies read a poem and gave the eulogy; Annie had no desire to put herself in the spotlight, and anyway, these men knew her Da better than she did, so robbed had they been of the deep and meaningful relationship that seemed certain in her early childhood.

Over the coming weeks it would feel to Annie as though she were suddenly the parent to Granny O'Shea, the old lady seemed so lost and fragile. Visiting every day after work, Annie often found Mary still in her dressing gown, having eaten nothing.

'S'not right to bury yer own child, Annie,' was her constant refrain as she shuffled around, obedient as a frightened child. The two women shared a quiet Christmas together, which seemed fitting and not unpleasant, whilst Annie had arranged to meet with Kate and Jack on the beach at Exmouth in early January.

It was the second visit they'd shared since the awful scenes at the play park, and just like the previous occasion, Jack seemed sullen and cross with her whilst Kate barely spoke at all. Annie had stood slightly apart from them watching as they skimmed stones across the shallow waves, wanting to join in but feeling every bit the intruder. Towards the end of the visit, Annie had noticed Jack's lace had come undone and beckoned to him to let her tie it, as she was kneeling in front of him a wave came in and Annie got soaked whilst Jack got wet feet. Annie had stood laughing and cried, 'Oops! My fault,' then cringed as though scalded when Jack replied coldly, 'I know; it's *all* your fault'.

When she spoke with Dawn about these awful scenes, which left her feeling like she'd been dragged through broken glass, the response was always the same: get a solicitor or at least seek legal advice, demand her rights, see Jack on his own, away from Kate. But whenever Annie thought about this, she would remember visiting her Da as a child, the grilling she received before and after, the poison her mother would spout about what an awful person Kevin was and how he didn't love her anyway. No court in the world could control that.

Of course she couldn't be sure that Kate would be like her mother; in fact, she believed that Kate was an altogether kinder, more gentle person than Jacqui but something told her intuitively that Kate couldn't help but play out the script which had been written for them as children and she was already beginning to sense the possessive fear in Kate that was so prevalent in Jacqui. No, she wasn't prepared to have Jack's head twisted in the way that theirs had been. But as the clocks sprang forward and the frantic whisperings of spring were in the air, Annie felt at times as though her yearning heart might burst wide open.

Seven

For Kate those first few months were some of the hardest in her life. At first, she compared them to the weeks before Annie was arrested but soon realised this was far, far worse. For although those times were frightening and chaotic, she'd always sensed that she had the upper hand; Annie was unpredictable, yes, but she was on a course of self-destruction where she must surely end up in prison or dead. Today's Annie was a different story, and despite her mother's cynicism, seemed to be going from strength to strength. She was working and studying and had even moved into a little cottage by the quayside, using some of her inheritance to pay her rent in advance. This had been particularly unsettling for Kate who'd been as sure as her mother that a swoop of that size, especially so soon after losing Kevin, was sure to set Annie off on a bender from which there would be no return. Kate had once more experienced that awful sense of guilt which accompanied her disappointment that Annie was doing okay.

It wasn't that she didn't want Annie to be okay, she wasn't such an awful person as that! But it seemed inevitable that an Annie who was doing okay could only be a threat to the life Kate had worked so hard to create. Jack was such an integral part of that life; the whole thing was nonsensical without Jack. And it was obvious to anyone who knew them that Jack was best off where he was, with the only family he remembered. Annie could never add to that, only take away. Even if Annie stayed on the straight and narrow—and it was still very early days, her presence only complicated things for Jack, gave him worries he didn't need. Kate had witnessed this during the two visits since Christmas.

Annie had hoped for many more visits, but Kate followed her mother's advice and carefully stretched out the time between each, not denying Annie but changing plans at the last minute or calling off when Jack had a bit of a cold. Kate felt guilty at first, but when she saw how unhappy the visits left Jack, she was convinced she was doing the right thing. He was withdrawn and visibly frightened of Annie, clinging to Kate like a five-year-old. On the way home he cried and asked why he had to see her at all. It had broken Kate's heart and she promised that it wouldn't be very often. After that she'd cancelled on Annie twice, and in fairness, they did have other things to do. Jack was always being invited to play-dates and birthday parties and wasn't it more important that he enjoy those things than go and spend an awkward, frightening hour with someone he hardly knew?

And yet Kate was troubled. She felt as though a whole area of her mind was unsafe to tread. She was haunted by the look on Annie's face at the end of a visit or when Jack called her Annie or, worse, one of those brief moments when the two really seemed to connect and she would witness the fear-tinged rage within herself. Then she would become angry and defensive, why should *she* be the one to feel guilty all the time? Annie had made her own bed, her own choices. She'd chosen drugs. So she would hide the cards that came through the post, ignore the phone calls and delay any plans as often as she could reasonably manage.

But as Annie was rebuilding her life piece by piece, Kate felt as though the ground were sliding beneath her, like the early rumblings of a great tectonic shift. For although she couldn't yet comprehend it, Kate was experiencing a deep threat to her own identity. She was the good one, the responsible one, the achiever; if Annie became those things, then where was Kate's place in it all?

***

As the weeks and months passed, Kate threw herself into the one safe area of her life where she felt strong, able and admired, where goals were clearly defined, and accolades were tangible. By the end of March, she'd made regional manager and in early April she was rewarded with a significant pay rise and a swanky new company car. It had meant some major sacrifices on her part and on Oliver's. She was now away from home for three nights every week. She loathed missing so many of Jack's activities but reasoned that they could afford to do so many things because of her salary. She was always there at the weekends, and come the summer, they would be going on another amazing holiday because her earnings allowed it.

Oliver was less reasonable. Kate suspected he was also getting pressure from Jan, but the older woman never said anything in front of Kate. Jan was a housewife, Kate once again reasoned, their worlds were light years apart. But she couldn't reason away the stony silences that were building between Oliver and herself, the nights he spent in the spare room after yet another row, him sullen, she defensive and unyielding. Lately even the weight of her salary didn't sway him; they could live on less money, he said, they could take fewer holidays, Jack would be happier if he just saw her more, he said. *All from Jan*, Kate suspected.

'Oliver, we've been through this a thousand times.' she was saying crossly one Sunday morning. Jack was on a play-date at Joe's house, and they had one of their rare opportunities alone, which inevitably led to a row. 'Our system's always worked; I don't understand why it's a problem now. I earn the money, you keep house.'

They were having a sort out in the garage, which was resembling the storeroom of Toys "R" Us after a minor explosion. Kate was trying to extract a small bicycle whose pedal was lodged under another pile of junk.

'Kate, it was never like this,' Oliver replied levelly as he leant over and gave the bike a good yank, freeing it, 'Rubbish?' he asked, tossing it onto the *chuck* heap. 'You're away more than you're home nowadays, that was never in our plan.'

'*Our plan.* You say that like we had an exact idea of how things were going to pan out. We could never have known that.' Kate delved into the mass of objects once more. 'What we do know is that I'm always going to earn more than you, therefore my work has to be the priority, I can't just pick and choose, Oliver!' She threw a mangled basketball hoop on the *chuck* pile. 'If you want me to keep my job I have to go where it takes me. Or are you going to be the breadwinner now?' She knew that she reminded him of her greater earning capacity to belittle him, but she needed to take charge of the conversation; her work life simply wasn't up for negotiation.

'Kate, why can't you see that this is getting out of control?' Oliver stood up, wiping his brow. 'You can't just go on working more and more and expecting everyone else to pick up the slack!'

'Everyone else?' *Here it is,* she thought. 'You mean your mother? What's she been saying? Has she been complaining? I pay her good money to look after Jack.'

'*You* pay her?'

'Yes, *I* pay her, let's not beat around the bush, Oliver. I work to support this family, to give us a good life, to give Jack a better life than he ever had with Annie, than he ever *could* have with Annie and if your mother doesn't like it, she should tell me to my face instead of taking *my* money and complaining behind my back.'

Kate turned and began rifling through another pile of toys.

'God you're a bitch sometimes, Kate,' Oliver said to her back.

She swung round, '*I'm* a bitch? *I'm* the one trying to keep this family together! Can't you see that? Can't you see what's happening in front of your face, Oliver?' And suddenly she was crying. 'She's going to try to take him! Annie will try to take Jack and we have to show him, show *everyone* that what we have is far better than anything she could ever provide!'

Oliver looked at her, stunned. 'You can't honestly believe that?'

'Of course I believe it. It's the truth. Why else do you think I'm working every hour God sends? I'm just trying to do the right thing, to hold it all together. As always, it's me having to hold it all together!'

'Kate, I just don't think that's true.' Oliver shook his head sadly. 'I don't think it's true that the best thing for Jack is more money, more stuff…' he motioned his hand across the detritus to make his point, 'but I also don't think that's the reason you're working so much. No, listen! I think you work so much because it feels safe, because it gives you something to focus on, something to have control over but don't you see, Kate, it's tearing us apart!' He pulled his hands through his hair, the picture of frustration.

'What kind of bollocks is that?' Kate said furiously, but then she sagged. 'You don't understand, Ollie…' she shook her head sadly, '…I work, because it feels like it's the *only* thing I can do to make a difference. It feels like it's falling apart. She's going to take him and there's nothing I can do about it. I just can't bear it; I can't bear the thought of losing him. Don't you see, I have to do something? I can't just do nothing at all!'

Oliver pulled her to him and held her as she sobbed into his chest. He kissed the top of her head.

'I know you're doing what you think's best, Kate, but please hear me that it isn't.' Then he tentatively delivered what was on his mind: 'Why don't we have a baby of our own?'

Kate immediately pushed away from him. 'I can't believe you'd suggest that now!' she said, astounded, 'Haven't you been listening to me? This is about Jack. Having a baby will just push him further away. And anyway, how on earth could we afford for me to stop working?'

Oliver appeared to swallow down his retort. 'Whatever,' he said moodily and returned to the task at hand.

They were still working in stony silence when Joe's mum delivered Jack home. Oliver had taken most of the rubbish to the recycling centre and there were just some odd bits on the drive as Jack ran towards them. 'Yeah! I remember this,' he said gleefully as he sat astride a little rocking horse that was too good to discard. 'I must have been titchy!' he exclaimed as he rocked, his knees up around his ears. 'What are we going to do with it? We mustn't throw it away!'

'Well, we won't be giving it to your little brother or sister,' Oliver said moodily as he stomped past to put some of the remaining things back in the garage.

Kate snarled at him to shut up.

'What do you mean, a little brother or sister?' Jack asked excitedly, jumping from the rocker and charging towards them.

'Nothing,' Kate replied, taking his hand and casting Oliver a furious look. 'Ollie's just being stupid.'

'But I want a brother or sister!' Jack whined, pulling on her arm. 'Please? All my friends have brothers and sisters. Please Kate?'

'Would you really want that?' Kate asked, surprised. 'You'd have to share everything all the time.'

'I don't care! I want to share!' Jack said, bouncing up and down. 'Please Kate, I want a brother or sister more than anything in the world!'

Oliver was smirking at her and Kate felt like she'd been slapped. Was it really this easy? Was this how she kept her life intact? Of course, she'd always planned to have a child at some point, it just never seemed the right time but now, as she looked down into Jack's eager, glowing face, she realised she'd found the way to keep her family together.

Eight

Annie opened her front door and stepped into the cool of the cottage. It was the middle of the summer holidays and Exeter quayside was bustling with families enjoying the afternoon sun. Annie loved living on the quay, it had its own little subculture of dog walkers, meanders and office workers looking to escape the urbanity of the city. Every day as she headed to college, she would chat with the water taxi man and the manager of the pizzeria, revelling in the feeling of the little community waking up to another day. But on days like today the yells of small children and the happy scenes on the pedalos felt like a physical pain to her already shredded heart.

It had been six weeks since she'd seen Jack. Kate hadn't explicitly told her she couldn't see him, but they were always so busy, she said, or they had to change plans at the last minute because something important had come up or, as happened last time, Jack was unwell. Each time Annie would suffer the torment of feeling that she should be doing something more, she should be fighting harder, making Kate listen. Each time she would hear the same advice, Sarah would remind her that she couldn't *make* Kate do anything, that in the big scheme of things it was still early days, whilst Dawn, with increasing frustration, would tell her she should be speaking with a solicitor and forcing Kate to comply. The idea of involving professionals and properly going to war with Kate, filled her with horror, but surely she had to do something? It had been nine months since she left prison and things were getting worse not better.

She went into her little kitchen to make a jug of squash. The cottage really was tiny, with a front room just large enough for one small sofa and a TV cabinet. The stairs opened directly onto the bedroom with a disproportionately large bathroom leading off that. She had no garden but a little bench outside her front door surrounded by potted plants and hanging baskets was still more than she'd ever dreamed of possessing. Annie took the jug outside and placed it on the bench beside her as she dialled Kate's number. It rang so long that she was expecting the answerphone and was caught off guard when Kate answered with a curt hello.

'Kate, hi,' she said, gathering herself; things had become so awkward between them. 'I just wanted to check we're definitely on for this weekend?' She felt tense, apologetic and she imagined Kate bristling.

'Yes, we're on, why wouldn't we be?'

'…Well… it's just… look Kate, I really don't want to fall out again but it's just hard when you change plans at the last minute.'

Annie wondered why she was throwing a grenade now when things were going smoothly and asked herself for the umpteenth time if it were not all in her imagination, that she simply expected too much.

'Listen, Annie...' And now she'd upset Kate again. 'I realise in your world the only person you have to think about is yourself,' Kate sounded so furious so quickly, 'but we actually have other things going on. I don't think you realise the hours I work, and Jack has a very full and happy life, as he should at his age.'

Annie thought she sounded just like Jacqui.

'Jack was ill last week, are you blaming me for that too?'

'No,' Annie said meekly, wishing she'd said nothing. 'So, I'll see you on Saturday then.'

'You will. And Annie...' Kate's voice sounded softer, gentler. 'There's something you should know.' She paused, as if steeling herself. 'Jack has started calling me Mum.'

Annie felt nothing for a moment; it was as though Kate had said something in Chinese, then, with no particular thought in her mind she was hit with a wave of grief so titanic that it threatened to wash her from the bench.

'Annie?' Kate was speaking. 'Did you hear what I said?'

'Yes, I heard you,' Annie managed to respond, her mind blank, her ears ringing, her heart thudding painfully.

'I'm sorry,' Kate said, sounding more defensive than apologetic, 'but I thought it was best to warn you before Saturday.'

'Yes, sure, of course. What... er... what do you think brought that on?' Annie felt dazed, her brain seemed to have shut down.

'Come on Annie, I have parented him for most of his life, it's hardly surprising.'

'No, I suppose,' Annie said dully. 'It's just the timing. I hope his little head isn't too battered by all this.'

'By all what?' Kate sounded cross again.

'Well... me.'

'Why does everything have to be about you? God, Annie!'

Annie wished Kate wouldn't get so angry. She thought this made perfect sense; she wasn't trying to be difficult; she was genuinely concerned about how Jack was making sense of his current situation.

'If there's any other reason for it then it's probably because I'm pregnant, he's old enough to realise the new baby will call me Mum so he wants to as well.'

Tears burst into Annie's eyes though she wasn't even sure why.

'Pregnant?' she heard herself say.

'Yes,' Kate snapped. 'There's no need to sound so shocked, it was always in the plan. You could even congratulate me.'

'Congratulations.' Annie said quietly, then she was sobbing, taking herself by surprise. 'Please, Kate, please!'

'Please what? What are you crying about now for goodness' sake?'

'You have to give me something more, Kate, please! I just want to know him, be a small part of his life, that's all!'

'I don't understand what you're talking about, Annie. How can you know him? You've missed most of his life, you're not going to know him in five minutes.'

'Kate, it's been nine months and I've seen him a handful of times and always with you breathing down our necks—'

'I'm sorry? Breathing down your neck?' Kate fumed. 'I'm there because he's scared of you, Annie!'

'And whose fault is that?'

'Whose fault? I can't believe you'd even ask that. It's your fault, Annie, *yours*!'

'It's all my fault,' Annie said quietly, remembering Jack's recent accusation.

'What? I can't hear you,'

'Nothing.' Annie pulled herself together. 'I just think it would help if you were a bit more enthusiastic about Jack and me seeing each other,' she said carefully. 'I think if he knew you were okay with it then he'd relax a bit.'

'I'm sorry but I'm not influencing him one way or the other,' Kate replied, matter-of-factly. 'You don't have to comfort him, Annie, when he's bawling his eyes out after seeing you, begging me not to make him do it again. You have no idea what it's like.'

Annie felt like an icy knife had pierced her heart. 'But Kate, you could help him, you could tell him that it's okay, I'm not going to do anything awful to him or try to take him away.'

'I'm sorry but I'm not going to lie to him. No, let me finish!' Kate fumed as Annie tried to interject. 'That would be a lie. I've no idea *what* you're going to do next. This might seem like a very long time to you Annie but for the rest of us who went through years of hell with you it really isn't very long at all. You've proven nothing; you've only been out of jail five minutes. You might have conveniently forgotten everything you did, how you neglected Jack, but I'm afraid the rest of us haven't. I'm not going to lie to him by pretending you're the fairy fucking godmother!' Kate took a breath then, but before Annie could say anything she went on. 'I don't ask anything of you, Annie but please just remember I'm pregnant now, I don't need you stressing me out, neither does Jack. Could you please just think of other people for a change!'

Annie said nothing for several moments, then, 'Of course. I'll... I'll see you Saturday then.'

She barely made it into the house before she curled into a ball and wailed like an animal. The pain, the grief, felt more than she could bear. Was she just being selfish? Was she bad for Jack? Should she just back off and let him grow up in peace? The thought of walking away made her physically retch, it felt like something large and metallic was lodged in her throat obstructing her breath. Images of Jack as a baby and a small toddler swam before her eyes, she remembered the day in the kitchen when he'd looked sadly at her, like a little old man, and the shame and regret threatened to choke her, the remorse and loss like a physical pain.

Staggering to her feet, she retrieved her telephone and dialled Sarah's number. For several minutes all she could do was cry and Sarah patiently waited for her to speak.

'I have to do something!' Annie wailed when she could form coherent words. 'I can't just let him slip away from me like this.'

'Annie, I can't begin to understand the pain you're feeling and I'm not going to pretend to,' Sarah said kindly, 'but I'm at a loss to see what you can do to change this situation.'

'I can go to court, I can fight! I should have done that in the first place.'

'You could,' Sarah said simply, 'but you've explained to me very clearly why you think that might be damaging to Jack. Have you changed your mind about that?'

Annie drew a raggedy breath and pulled herself together.

'No,' she said clearly.

'What do you think would reasonably happen if you involved a solicitor now?'

'I think Kate would fight me all the way, drag up every awful thing I've ever done and add some more to boot, and Jack will be stuck in the middle of it,' Annie said blandly.

'And do you think, once that has happened, you'll be any further forward?' Sarah asked gently.

'I might be! Like Dawn says, if I can get to see him on his own every other weekend or something then he'll eventually get to know me, get to know I don't want to ruin his life. But if I do nothing all he'll ever know is what she tells him about me.'

'I don't think either of those things are true, Annie. You've explained to me how your mum used to be when you visited your dad and you've told me there's a good chance Kate will be the same. Do you think Jack will listen to you over her or do you think he'll resent you even more?' Before Annie answered she went on. 'And it's not true to think this situation will go on forever; he's going to grow up, have a mind of his own, Kate can't stop that. One day he'll want to hear your side of the story, but I think, right now, you want to bypass all the difficult stuff and get to that. I just don't think it's going to happen Annie; I think you're kidding yourself that if you just do *something,* you can repair all the damage but it's just not like that.'

'Then how come other people see their kids? Go to court or whatever? If it works for them then why not me?' Annie asked, clutching at straws.

'It doesn't work out for everyone, Annie. Every situation is different and you're choosing to look at situations where it all worked out. Many don't. Look at your own childhood.'

Annie took a breath. Sarah was right, she couldn't push forward without hurting Jack. She had to let go.

'Remember the programme, Annie. You let go and have faith with everything else, why not with Jack? You have to trust these principles with Jack as much as anywhere.'

And so, Annie relented. She took a deep breath and chose to trust that things would all work out in the end, believing that she was doing the selfless thing, doing what was best for Jack and not perpetuating the damage inflicted on herself and Kate.

Nine

Lucy arrived eight days before Christmas, three weeks early and by Caesarean section. Kate was working in London when she was taken ill with terrible headaches and blurred vision. She was advised to go straight to hospital and was diagnosed with advanced preeclampsia. Oliver and Jack arrived just as Kate came out of theatre. Despite the urgent delivery, both mother and baby were well. Kate's blood pressure took a couple of days to return to normal but on the fourth day, both were fit enough to return home. Jack was beside himself with excitement and couldn't wait to hold the baby girl. More photos were taken of these and other touching moments, which would eventually be stretched on canvas to adorn the walls alongside those of the wedding.

Despite Lucy's unexpected arrival, they had a wonderful Christmas, just the four of them at Kate's request, with Jan and Oliver's sisters visiting on Boxing Day with gifts, cuddles, and coos. Oliver was attentive and doting in a way he had never quite managed before, and for a time, Kate felt secure in herself and her place in the world.

The light returned by fractions and in the chill winds of early March the first frothy white flowers of the blackthorn appeared, always a welcome sign to Kate that spring really would return. By late March, the weather was balmy, and the hedge was green, Kate could break up the day with trips to the park and had recovered enough from her C-section to join a Buggyfit class, pushing Lucy along in front of her as she jogged with other new mums. Oliver had been saintlike, doing more than his share of the night feeds and chores around the house. Jack was besotted and Annie, with unexpected grace and tact, seemed to have backed off to allow the family to adjust. Despite all of this, Kate felt an increasing unease. She longed to return to work and found domestic life both boring and anxiety-inducing: there was always something else to do and none of the satisfaction of a job well done. As time went on she also worried that her bond with Lucy was not as it should be. Lucy seemed to cry all the time and she couldn't help but compare her to what she knew of Jack around that age, he'd always seemed such a quiet and serene little baby whenever she saw him. There was also the problem of breastfeeding. Kate had given up within days of returning from hospital, on the suggestion of the health visitor. Lucy simply wasn't latching on properly; Kate was getting really sore, and the baby wasn't getting enough to eat. Better to move on to formula, the health visitor said, and Kate had been relieved that the decision had been taken away from her. Yet she saw the disapproving looks from Jan and had to endure endless suggestions from Karen, Fay and Deborah. Though she knew it was ridiculous she couldn't help blaming Lucy for somehow causing her failure.

Her mother was possibly her worst critic as Kate tried not only to gain her approval but to demonstrate, in some small way, just how a loving mother should behave. She longed to be everything Jacqui wasn't: warm, attentive, adoring. Yet she found she was increasingly irritated by Lucy and her crying, the way she took Kate's attention from Jack, and more recently, how she kept her from her work. Jacqui seemed to point out her every failure and Kate lost confidence, resenting Lucy for being a *difficult baby*. Despite arranging nine months of maternity leave, Kate returned after six, negotiating local work with her employers for six months and arranging childcare with Jan, the latter requiring far greater negotiating skills.

***

Annie had spent another quiet Christmas with Granny O'Shea as the old lady continued to wither over the year following Kevin's death. Annie was reminded of the photographs that Joni had flushed down the toilet; Mary seemed to bubble and crack, her discoloured skin appeared to blur at the edges and Annie felt powerless to save her. At times she felt overwhelmed by remorse, cursing her inability to help the old lady, to encourage her to eat and take care of herself, somehow linking Mary's survival with her own ability to heal from the loss of her Da. Time and again Sarah would help her to detangle her inner life, and invariably the cause of despair traced back to Jack and her utter powerlessness in that relationship.

She aced her degree and accepted a position with the local drug and alcohol project. She loved her little cottage and made firm friends in her meetings. She was planning a little holiday in the summer. Aside from her worries about Granny O'Shea, her life was happier than she could ever have imagined but, as she sobbed to Sarah, one squally March day, she would give it all up if she could just know Jack a little.

She'd now been out of prison for sixteen months and could count on her fingers her visits with Jack. The circumstances surrounding each occasion left her feeling confused and ashamed. Kate continued to change arrangements at the last minute, cancel and postpone but always seemed to have a good reason. During the latter part of the pregnancy and once Lucy had arrived, Annie felt she'd even less right than before to start making demands or complaining. At times she was tormented by the idea of an eight-year-old Jack trying to work out his place in the world once he discovered Kate was pregnant. She could imagine him lying in bed worrying, then getting up in the morning and tentatively calling Kate, 'Mum'. Despite being desperate to see him, Annie didn't want to do anything more to upset him or increase his feeling of otherness.

Spring turned to summer and summer to autumn. Annie spent many hours outdoors walking the banks of the Exe, all the way to the estuary to gaze out over Topsham and Exmouth. Eventually she bought a little car and drove up to Dartmoor and to the woods on Haldon Hill; as Jack seemed to slip through her fingers like mist, she sought solace in the bluebells, the campions and foxgloves and before she knew it, the leaves were turning to the colour of his hair and beech nuts were crunching beneath her feet.

***

Jack turned nine in early October and Annie braved the discomfort of another *yummy mummy* party. Once again, she felt like the carthorse in the show pony class, standing on the fringes and smiling awkwardly. Oliver was there and he was nice; Sally threw her icy looks and walked past with her nose in the air; Jack had no time for her at all as he hurtled about the apparatus with Ali and Joe, the latter managing to give Annie a covert little wave.

But it was Kate's avoidance of her hopeful gaze that really crushed Annie that day. What had happened between them? How had they arrived at this bitter stalemate? And how could she ever make it better if they never spent any time together?

Now Kate was walking towards her carrying Lucy. The toddler was squirming to get down and finally Kate relented, allowing her to scuttle off, crab-like in the other direction. She really was very agile for her age. Kate looked exasperated and yelled for Oliver to take over.

'Hi,' she said to Annie with a smile that didn't reach her troubled eyes. 'Glad you could make it.' She swept her long blonde hair from her face. She'd definitely made *yummy mummy* status, her high-waisted skinny jeans surely being a size ten, her hair, nails and shoes immaculate.

Annie didn't feel as scruffy as she once would have, in her ripped jeans and oversized tweed jacket, she knew she was never going to be a *hair, nails and shoes* kind of girl.

'You look fabulous,' she said, meaning it but thinking it looked like awfully hard work.

'Thanks,' Kate said, loosening up a little. 'I'm sorry about Jack, he doesn't want to know any of us at the moment. He's a Power Ranger apparently.' She rolled her eyes.

'No problem.' Annie smiled. 'It's just good to watch him enjoying himself… that's all I've ever wanted.' She watched Kate retract a little and inwardly kicked herself. 'Look, Kate, why don't you and I do something, just the two of us? I dunno, go to the pictures or something?' she said without having planned it.

Kate looked at her blankly for a moment, then, 'I'm sorry Annie, I'm just so busy at the moment. I've been promoted to a national position with work, it means three nights away from home again, so I want to spend every spare minute with Oliver and the children.'

There was something about the way she said *the children* that made Annie's skin crawl. It also annoyed her that Kate could make spending three nights a week away from home sound self-sacrificial. She took a breath.

'Sure,' she managed. 'Well at least come to Granny's sometime, she really isn't doing great, and she would love to meet Lucy.'

'Huh, I doubt that but yes, sure, we'll sort it out. Speaking of Lucy…' she let the sentence hang and looked over her shoulder. Annie took the hint and waved her off with a tight little smile.

Ten

Kate, Jack and Lucy finally made it to Granny O'Shea's on Christmas Eve. Jack had only met Mary a couple of times since he lived with Kate and seemed scared of this frail, shrunken stranger. Annie had to concede there was something slightly sinister about Granny O'Shea's gnarled appearance now that her face lacked its old sparkle. It made her sad to remember Mary when she and Kate were children, always laughing and joking around so that even Kate had enjoyed herself when Jacqui wasn't looking. Now the old lady was mostly silent or quietly muttering to herself. She showed them around the garden but there was nothing much to see in the dead of winter and Annie was concerned about the cold, uneven ground under her Mary's poorly balanced frame.

Lucy was the star of the show and once they were all settled inside the little girl toddled about distributing presents. Annie was enchanted, aware of the bittersweet twisting of her gut as she remembered Jack at that age.

Jack was greedily ripping wrappings from a small pile of gifts, barely looking at each as he moved onto the next, his eyes finally lighting on a remote-controlled car which would zoom up walls and across ceilings and which had been on his extensive wish list.

'Yeah!' he cried enthusiastically as he set about relieving it of its packaging and Annie felt a rush of gratitude to Kate for sharing the list with her.

'You look just like your Granda, Jack O'Shea,' Mary had said clearly and unexpectedly, surprising them all.

Jack said nothing for a moment, appearing to be engrossed in his new toy, then he looked up and said, just as clearly, 'My name isn't O'Shea, it's Harper-Jones, like Mum.'

He looked at Granny O'Shea defiantly for a moment then seemed to lose his nerve and shimmied his bottom across the floor to lean up against Kate's legs where she sat on the sofa.

'Ha!' Mary had barked, appearing more like her old self. 'Ye can call yeself what ye fancy but ye be an O'Shea to ye bones, just look at ye! Ye'd haf te chop off ye loaf for starters!' she cackled, and Jack looked mortified.

'Granny don't be mean,' Annie cut in as her mind whirred. 'Jack can call himself whatever he likes... although I think I'd have to sign something to make it official?' She looked searchingly at Kate, who didn't quite meet her eyes.

'Let's not do this now.' Kate sounded defensive.

'But I want to help,' Annie said, thrown, looking from Kate to Jack. 'If you really want to change your name of course I'll help you do that.' Then to Kate, 'Why would you think this was a problem?' She felt nettled and tried to keep her voice level.

Once again Kate's temper seemed to flare at lightning speed.

'Whatever,' she said, gathering up wrapping paper. 'Let's talk about it another time. I think we'd better go now; Lucy will throw a tantrum if she gets overtired and you really don't want to see that. I think we've upset Granny enough.'

Annie was confused; it was almost as if Kate *wanted* there to be a problem. She let out a sigh without meaning to.

'Sure,' she said as she got up to help Mary to her feet. They made their way to the door and once again Annie felt heartsore. How had things got so fractious and bitter? As she leant in to say goodbye, she found herself saying again, 'Maybe you and I should do something, Kate? We could go for a walk, or even look at the sales if you like?' She heard the pleading tone in her voice and immediately regretted it.

'Yes, maybe.' Kate sounded non-committal as she brushed her jaw against Annie's. 'I go back to work next week so I'll have to look at my diary. Say goodbye Jack!' she yelled as Jack went to disappear down the path to their car, he about-turned and stomped towards them with his hands in his pockets.

'Bye,' he said, kissing Mary on the cheek and bumping himself awkwardly against Annie.

Annie took his shoulders and looked full into his sludgy gold-green eyes.

'Jack,' she said as he went to look away, 'whatever you need to do to feel like you belong is okay with me, I need you to hear that.' It felt like an absurd thing to say to one so young, but she needed to say it and she believed he was old enough to understand. 'I just want the best for you Jack, whatever that is.' He looked at her for a fraction of a moment and for the first time Annie felt a connection, like a spark when two live wires touch. And then it was gone.

'Come on, before Lucy starts yelling,' Kate cut in, shifting the car seat to her other hand and reaching for Jack's. Granny O'Shea had shuffled back inside but Annie watched until the car disappeared around the bend. She waved though no one was looking.

Back in the cottage, Granny O'Shea had already resumed her seat. Annie piled more logs on the fire, put a blanket over the old lady's legs and made her a cup of tea. They sat silently watching the flames for some time before Mary spoke.

'Ye be wasting yer time with that one, Annie,' she said as she looked at the fire.

'With Jack?' Annie asked, shocked that Mary would say such a thing.

'Not the wean!' Mary exclaimed, coughing. 'Wit ye sister, Kate. I see ye fawning all over her. 'Twas the same when ye were wee dolls, always following her about so ye were, but she never did like ye, Annie, e'en back then. Cruel to ye she was.'

Annie let the old lady's words wash over her, she was used to hearing Mary's take on her childhood, on Jacqui and even Jacqui's parents, whom Annie had never known, she didn't take it too seriously.

'Ye mudder built walls round the pair of ye from the moment ye could walk and talk,' Mary was saying. 'Divide and conquer, that was her way, turned ye agin each udder, so she did. Like she tried to turn Kevin agin me. Ha! She could have sooner turned the tide.' She coughed again, seeming incredibly frail. 'Ye had walls around ye back then, Annie, and now Kate's built a whole new set a walls to keep ye 'way from Jack. She can't let ye in, Annie, not wit her and Jack on the one side and you on the udder.'

Eleven

The following years were hard ones for Kate. Time seemed to behave like a runaway horse and though she was incredibly organised, she was often rushing from one activity to the next without time to pause or reflect. Her work life was very demanding but when she was honest with herself, she looked forward most of all to the three nights a week she spent away from home, in hotel rooms with a TV, bathroom and king-sized bed all to herself.

Not that she had to share her bed at home too often. She and Oliver were experiencing an all-time low and their activity packed lives meant that they could play-act normality, whizzing from swimming club to birthday parties to football training without really needing to speak to each other at all and when they did it was always pragmatic — whose turn was it to drop the kids to Jan; could Oliver step up when Kate was stuck in traffic; had anyone paid the cleaner? They'd learnt so well to dance around each other, avoiding intimacy and eye contact, that it had begun to feel normal, and busyness was their friend. At night when the children were in their beds they might attempt to connect, each lonely and in need, but finding that they repelled each other like two magnets facing north.

Kate was also confused about Annie, who'd suggested twice more that they meet. Kate had felt guilty and then angry, that Annie could still make her feel like the wrongdoer. But there was also a sadness about the whole thing, a grief for the sister she could have had. Oliver was so close to his sisters, and they were close to each other, holidaying together and looking after each other's children. She'd never had that closeness with Annie. At times she wondered whether she should take up the offer of meeting but then she would worry that Annie had some kind of ulterior motive, and she was just being naïve, certainly Jacqui thought this to be the case.

'She's never wanted to be friends with you before Kate, why would she be any different now?' Jacqui had asked. 'That girl has only ever been interested in herself.' Kate had quietly wondered whether Jacqui's nose was put out of joint because Annie had made no attempt to contact their mother at all. But she wasn't willing to take the risk of Annie making a fool of her and Jacqui saying *I told you so*.

Lucy was growing into a cheerful and confident little girl. She was playful and happy, singing and dancing and chattering away to her toys. Everybody loved her and at any party she was the centre of attention. Kate wanted to delight in her the way that Jan and Oliver's sisters did, but she was often appalled to find herself irritated. In quiet moments she acknowledged what needled her most was that Lucy reminded her of Annie, especially when they were children. Annie was always singing and dancing and making up stories, never was she serious and responsible like Kate had to be.

Kate knew it was absurd to resent Lucy for being a happy child, yet she just couldn't help herself; she found she avoided her responsibilities with Lucy in favour of spending time with Jack. But the little girl seemed happiest when Kate was around, laughing and whooping with glee just at the sight of her, right up until Tuesday evenings when Kate would leave for her early start in London the next day and Lucy would scream and wail inconsolably, often making herself sick with exhaustion. Kate would feel guilty and resented the little girl for vilifying her when she was working to create a good life for them all. It felt so unfair to bear the weight of Oliver's disapproval as she fought to get out the door, and it did nothing to improve relations between them.

The only thing that brought her any joy in that house was her relationship with Jack. The two of them had an extraordinary bond and she loved it most when it was just the two of them on an adventure, off to football practice or running some errand or another, playing the car stereo loud and singing along, going for a sneaky McDonald's or sharing ice cream straight from the tub. Even the journeys to meet Annie were an occasion when she could get him all to herself.

***

Annie continued working for the drugs project; she still lived on the quay and visited Mary most days. She took a postgraduate diploma and dated a little, went to her meetings and spent time with her friends. Mostly she enjoyed trudging the Devon hills or shorelines and finding her solace in nature. Her heart ached for Jack. It was hard to watch other women, through her work or in the meetings, getting clean and sober and having regular access to, if not custody of, their children. Time and again she would spin off into self-doubt, fearing she should have done it differently, tried more, pushed harder. Often, during these times of torment, she would get back in the fight with Kate and gradually their relationship eroded until there seemed little hope of repair.

There had been a subtle shift in Jack following that first Christmas at Mary's. Visits were still hard to come by, but it seemed to Annie that Jack was more relaxed around her, even playing football, or pool, or whatever the occasion allowed. He was more likely to laugh at her antics and they had little conversations about school, his friends and things he got up to in his spare time.

When Jack was twelve, he got a mobile phone, and with a little encouragement, gave Annie the number. This meant they could stay in touch without having to go through Kate. It was a fragile thread, not only threatened by Kate's disapproval but also by Jack's trepidation, Annie sensed he was as likely to dart off as a startled fawn. But in the summer before Jack's fourteenth birthday, nearly seven years after Annie left prison, it seemed that the tide might finally be turning.

Having exchanged some text messages one day, when Jack seemed unusually chatty, Annie felt inspired to suggest she pick him up sometime and they go off and do something together, just the two of them; to her astonishment Jack said yes. Annie called Sarah. She called Granny O'Shea. It seemed the day had come, just like Sarah had promised, that Jack was making his own mind up about things. Later that day she received another message. *Hi Annie, I'm sorry but I've changed my mind. I don't want to meet with you on our own, I like it the way it is. Thanks anyway. J*

Despair quickly turned to fury. Kate must have said or done something to make this happen. Kate had ruined it all through her own selfishness! A hatred like she'd never known burned at her insides and left her trembling. Somewhere, a long way off, a still small voice whispered that she should take a breath, calm down, that she didn't know Kate had done any such thing but her whole body seemed to pulsate to the rhythm of her pounding heart as every lame excuse and broken promise caught like tinder and spread her rage like a bushfire. Shaking, she dialled her sister's number.

Kate's *hello* bristled with defensiveness and Annie cut her off before the word was fully spoken.

'You evil bitch,' she spat in cold fury.

'Don't speak to me like that, Annie, and I have no idea what you're talking about,' Kate replied coolly, her voice dripping with condescension.

To Annie she sounded more like Jacqui by the day. 'Don't give me that,' she snarled, her voice shaking with the effort of speaking at all. 'What the fuck did you say to Jack? You're twisting his head up, Kate, you must be able to see that?'

'*I'm* twisting his head up? Ha! Nothing's ever your fault is it, Annie?' Kate's voice began to lose some of its composure. 'You're never going to accept the consequences of your own actions, your own *choices*.'

This sounded so much like Jacqui that Annie wanted to reach down the phone and throttle her.

'No, Kate,' she managed. 'Jack going to live with you was the consequence of my actions. Repairing the damage, earning his trust, and yours, proving myself for a year, two or even three, that would be the consequence of my actions. But it's been *seven fucking years* Kate and you still haven't given an inch—'

'Rubbish!' Kate cut her off. 'Fuck me Annie, you've got to be the most selfish person I've ever met!

Who's the one who drops plans and rearranges things and drives all over the place to meet you? Who's the one who has to explain to Jack why we can't go to the football match or the party or the beach with Ollie and Lu because we're going to see you? Who's the one who has to console him afterwards because he hates it that you're his mum?' This last she spat with venom and her aim was true.

Annie was winded, confused; was she just being selfish? Was she still ruining Jack's life all these years on?

'But he's been so much better lately,' she managed haltingly. 'I think he's enjoyed the last few times we met... and he definitely wanted us to do something together.'

'God you're such an idiot,' Kate said with disdain. 'He just doesn't want to upset you. He's a polite boy, he's been brought up to be polite and kind. He told me the only reason he said that was because he didn't want to make you feel bad. God, Annie, what did you expect him to say? He's thirteen.'

Annie felt like she was falling. Was this true? Was Jack just trying to be kind? After everything she'd sacrificed to try to protect him, did he still feel responsible for her happiness? She felt crushed.

'I can't do this any more, Kate,' she said quietly.

'What?' Kate barked. 'Speak up, I can't hear you.'

'This just isn't right,' Annie said a little louder. 'Jack's fourteen in a minute. I can't go on colluding with you that this is a normal way for us to have a relationship, with you chaperoning us everywhere. It's just not right.'

Annie was coming to these conclusions as quickly as she was saying them.

'You've done nothing to help us have a relationship, nothing to help Jack come to terms with the reality of the situation—no, let me finish!' It felt imperative that she get this out before Kate hijacked her thoughts again. 'I can't make you see it my way; I can't make you want a relationship between us, but I can't do it your way any more, either. If what you say is true then Jack already thinks he's got to pretend, to try to please me. I had to accept a long time ago that the only amends I might make is by not fucking his head up like mine was—'

'Oh, how very noble of you!' Kate finally interjected. 'You've no idea what's best for Jack, Annie, I do. I know he just wants to be a normal boy, growing up in a normal family. He's never asked about you, never speaks about you. I'm sorry if that hurts you but you're just not important in his life, you just complicate it.'

Annie was quiet for a moment then said, 'I wish you could see that all I've wanted is for him to have a normal, happy life with you. I've just wanted to know him. Kate, and for him to know me. I can't go on like this. If it means sacrificing this weird non-relationship we have now, then that's what I'll have to do. If anything, it's more damaging than healing anyway. Goodbye.' And she hung up.

Another evening was spent wailing like an animal caught in a snare. She called Sarah and then carefully texted Jack telling him that he need never worry about keeping her happy, that was not his responsibility. She told him that she didn't want to make his life more difficult but at the same time, if he wanted it, she would fight to see more of him, but only if he wanted it. Whatever he wanted was okay with her. Later that evening she received a single line message: *I want to live with Mum and Dad.* She wept some more but didn't bother to address this spectacular miscommunication, she'd spent the past seven years trying to do that.

***

Annie saw Jack twice more over the following four years. Once a random, rather awkward meeting in the street and once at Granny O'Shea's funeral. The old lady lived much longer than Annie had expected but was rarely happy following Kevin's death. Though it was a wrench to lose her it was also a mercy and Annie grieved little compared with her other losses.

On the whole, Annie was happy. She moved into the hills above Tiverton, to a dilapidated old bungalow she bought with her inheritance from Granny O'Shea. She loved her job and hoped she made a difference; she attended her meetings and tried to be the best version of herself. But she missed Jack every day and grieved every milestone, birthday and special event like a missing limb. There were nights when she would rip herself open, searching for the answers, tormented that she'd made the wrong decisions, that she should have done things differently, but she saw no way back in. She'd made it clear to Jack that she would be there in whatever way he wanted; it seemed he didn't want her in his life and the path she'd chosen meant that she must honour his wishes.

Part IV
The Ties that Bind

At that moment just before the dawn

when everything falls apart...

Frank Turner

One

'Mum?' Jack's voice sounded ragged and fearful.

Kate leapt up from the chair where she'd slumped, her reminiscing sliding into troubled dreams.

'Oh Jack!' she sobbed, taking his face in her hands; he looked deathly pale and bewildered. 'You scared the shit out of me!' She gripped his face, kissed his forehead, stroked his cheek, all as though checking he were really alive. Jack looked at her but said nothing, he seemed in shock.

'You're in hospital,' Kate said rather unnecessarily as she finally relinquished her hold and stepped back. 'Do you remember anything?'

'No, nothing.' Jack finally spoke, looking away shiftily. 'How long have I been here?'

Kate looked at her watch, 'Just over an hour.' *God, it felt so much longer!* 'Oliver will be here soon; he's had to get Jan to sit Lucy. You've really screwed up, you know that?'

Now that the immediate danger had passed, her anger bubbled to the surface.

'Where did you get the ketamine? Yes, I know it was ketamine,' she added as Jack looked at her for the briefest moment before turning away again.

'I don't know what you're talking about,' he said huffily, attempting a return to his surly self but still looking scared and bewildered. 'I had some kind of fit or something.'

'That could well be true,' a woman said as she slipped inside the privacy curtain, 'but the doctors may want to keep you in for further tests if that's the case.'

Kate felt as though the floor had dropped several feet, leaving her insides behind. The woman was Annie.

'But we tested the little packet given to the paramedics,' she was saying. 'It contained traces of ketamine and that would definitely be the easiest explanation for your symptoms.' Annie smiled, a trace of laughter in her eyes.

Kate wondered for a moment if she were still asleep. Her brain seemed to have jammed; she realised her mouth was open and closed it. Annie looked older and younger somehow, her thick red hair was gripped neatly at the back of her head with tendrils curling around her face, a pair of thick-rimmed glasses perched on her freckled nose and her skin seemed to glow with good health. Her simple white blouse and navy trousers were unlike anything Kate could ever remember her wearing.

'Hi Jack,' Annie was saying, smiling again. 'Kate.' And she smiled at Kate too.

Kate thought she saw a smugness there and noticed how Annie's eyes scanned her face, taking in the bruises, now faded to yellowish-green, but still very evident. Annie looked at her quizzically, opened her mouth as though to ask then seemed to decide against it.

'You look tired, Kate, has someone offered you a coffee?'

Kate's brain ground into gear.

'What are you doing here, Annie?' she managed, hearing the accusatory tone in her voice but not caring.

'I work here,' Annie replied simply. 'With the addiction services team.' She waved an identity badge which she wore on a lanyard about her neck. 'I wouldn't usually be here this late, but we've had a bit of a full-on day!'

Kate wished she'd stop being so smiley.

'I help triage any drug-related cases and make the necessary referrals. I think we can pull these back now you're awake,' she added as she opened the curtains. 'It wouldn't be appropriate for me to work with you, Jack,' she said when she was done, coming to stand at the head of the bed. Kate felt a powerful impulse to attack her.

'But I just wanted to come and say hi and give you my number, in case you don't have it any more.'

A burning rage spread across Kate's chest and into her throat as she watched Annie pull out a business card and pass it to Jack, who was reaching out his hand to take it. Kate fought a mad urge to lean in and grab it, to rip it into tiny pieces. *Trust Annie to show up at exactly the wrong moment and start interfering.* Kate chewed her lip and wondered how she might intervene, but Annie appeared to be leaving anyway.

'I'll see you around,' she was saying. 'Oh, hi Oliver.'

Kate nearly cricked her neck as she looked around to see Oliver walking down the ward towards them, holding tight to Lucy's hand. Kate raised her eyebrows and held her palms aloft.

'Mum couldn't come, she's got Eddie's lot staying,' Oliver said in explanation. 'Wow, hi Annie. You're looking well,' he added, and Kate could have thumped him. 'Er... how come you're here?'

'She works here,' Kate cut in before Annie had a chance to speak. 'You were just leaving, weren't you?' she couldn't help but add.

Annie smiled, light amusement dancing in her eyes again and Kate felt a renewed urge to attack. Then, to her horror, Lucy was walking past her and standing boldly in front of Annie.

'Hi, I'm Lucy,' she said and stuck out her hand. 'Who are you? You have pretty hair; it's like my brother's.'

Kate watched as Annie laughed and flashed another of those film-star smiles.

'Hello Lucy,' she said, shaking the little girl's hand. She paused for a fraction of a moment to look over at Kate, who looked quickly away, then said, 'I'm your mum's sister, Lucy, your auntie. We've met before but that was when you were very young.'

Lucy looked from Annie to Kate, her mouth a perfect O.

'My auntie? But—'

'Lucy, are you going to speak to your brother or not? He's the one in hospital after all,' Kate said crossly, and Lucy jumped.

'But—' Kate gave her a warning look, and after making a face, Lucy seemed to decide it best to let the subject drop. 'Jack, you scared us!' she chided, stepping closer to the bed.

'Probably not as much as he scared himself,' Annie said softly.

'Jack had a funny turn, Lulu, that's all,' Kate cut in, flashing a warning look at Annie. 'He's fine now. I would imagine we can take him home, can't we Annie?'

'Oh, you'll have to check with the nurses, but I'd imagine you can pretty soon. I'll go and find someone for you.'

'Mum's had enough of hospitals,' Lucy was saying. 'She was in here a few days ago!'

Kate could have throttled her. 'That's enough Lucy!' she barked. 'You were going to find us a nurse weren't you, Annie?' Annie looked at her with brows knitted in exaggerated concern but when Kate wasn't forthcoming, the expression melted away as quickly as it had arrived.

God she's such an actress, Kate fumed.

'It was very good to see you again, Lucy. I expect Jack's pleased to have you to look after him,' Annie was saying as Lucy glowed. 'Jack, you have my number, you're very welcome to call about anything at all. No pressure though.'

Jack nodded and Kate bristled.

'Kate, Oliver.' Annie dipped her head and turned away. Kate found herself following.

'Annie,' she called, and Annie turned before she reached the desk. 'I'm sure I don't have to tell you that this is a really tricky time.' Kate tried to keep her voice level, 'Jack's been going through… a… strange phase, he's met up with a bad crowd at school that's all.'

Annie was nodding with that stupid, vapid smile.

'It's a sensitive time. I'm asking you to back off a bit please, he doesn't need the past being dragged up now.' *That made perfect sense, surely Annie would see that.*

'Kate, all I've done is give him my number,' Annie was saying in her most reasonable tone. 'I'm not going to call or show up or anything else. But if he calls, I'll speak to him, I really can't see how that could make things worse… it might even help.'

'You never change, do you? Why can't you just leave us alone?'

Annie looked as though she'd been slapped and finally Kate felt a little better. She turned on her heel and stalked off.

***

It was another two hours before the family finally left the hospital. Lucy had fallen asleep, and Oliver carried her out to the car. She looked soft and vulnerable, and Kate's earlier resentment abated as she tucked her into bed and kissed her gently goodnight.

Jack said almost nothing the entire evening. Kate burned to grill him about Annie, to ask why he'd taken the business card but somehow, she managed to keep her thoughts to herself. *He probably just felt awkward and didn't know what else to do,* she reasoned as she poured a large glass of wine and went to join Oliver in the front room, *and he'll just contact her to spite me if he thinks I have a problem with it.*

'Penny for them,' Oliver was saying.

'Annie,' she said grimly, sitting beside him on the sofa. He put his arm about her shoulder and the unexpectedness of it was like balm to her frayed nerves, she was so appreciative of the little signs of affection he displayed lately. 'I just can't believe her, can you?' She took a sip of wine and put the glass on the coffee table so she could snuggle into him.

'I thought she looked unbelievably well,' Oliver replied. 'I'd never have believed she could turn her life around so much. You've got to give her some credit.'

Kate pulled away abruptly and turned to face him, 'How can you say that?' she fumed. 'She hasn't changed at all! The first thing she did was give Jack her number, trying to weasel her way back in. I told her she should leave us alone.' She took another slug of wine.

'What I meant was she's no longer a homeless, criminal, drug addict, Kate, I think we can both agree on that,' Oliver said in his calm, unreactive way. 'Who would have thought she'd be working at the hospital. Even your mum would be impressed,' he smirked and took a swig of beer.

Kate could feel her temper getting out of hand, 'And just think about that a minute, will you? Annie, working at the hospital,' she spat. 'What if she looks up our records? What if she knows about the termination? I don't want her knowing our business, she could use it against us!'

'Kate! Calm down, you're being paranoid. Annie works in a completely different department. Is that what all this is about…' Oliver's voice softened. 'The termination?' He tried to put his arm back around her, but she wriggled away.

'Of course it isn't, I only just thought about it this moment,' Kate said in exasperation. 'It's about Jack. She's going to start causing trouble again.'

'I don't see how she can do that,' Oliver said simply. 'She might even be able to help. She must be pretty high up in her department by now. Didn't she get that job soon after she left prison?'

Kate felt ready to erupt; was he deliberately trying to goad her?

'No, Oliver, she was a cleaner when she got out of prison and if the only qualification you need to work with drug addicts is being a drug addict well then, yes, she's probably really good at it—'

'But she got a degree, didn't she? More than one…'

'What the fuck are you getting at Oliver? What is this, sainthood for Annie? This is the woman who tried to ruin our lives, who *did* ruin Jack's life—'

'Huh, hardly—'

Kate leapt to her feet and stared at him.

'Are you deliberately trying to wind me up?' she fumed. 'Jack could have died tonight, choked on his own vomit or something, I'm worried senseless and you suddenly become Annie's biggest fan?'

'Kate, you're being ridiculous,' Oliver said evenly.

'How can you possibly forgive her for what she did to Jack? Have you forgotten how she neglected him? How she turned our lives upside down?'

'Kate, that was fifteen years ago!'

'Thirteen. It was *thirteen* years ago. And if we'd let her, she would have taken Jack away and continued ruining his life! She chose drugs Oliver. She had her chance, and *she chose drugs*.'

'But Kate, Annie's been out of prison for more than ten years; she hasn't caused any trouble and I think she genuinely wants the best for Jack—'

'How the fuck do you know that? She could still be taking drugs for all we know—'

'Oh, come on Kate, she wouldn't have that job, she wouldn't look that good—'

Kate slapped him, hard across the face. 'How could you?' she fumed, in a voice like ice. 'After everything that's happened, how could you take her side?'

Oliver looked at her, stunned. It was not the first time she'd lashed out at him, but it was the first time since he'd confessed, in a counselling session, just how much it belittled and humiliated him.

'I don't even know who you are any more,' he said in a flat voice as he got up from the sofa and walked out.

Kate stood rooted to the spot, her breath coming in great gasps, her chest painfully constricted. What had come over her? She'd promised herself, promised Oliver that she would never do that again. She felt as though she were going mad, coming undone. How could Annie show up now? She looked at her watch; it was still before midnight. It seemed like a hundred years ago she'd been dancing around the kitchen with Lucy having convinced herself that everything was going to be all right.

Two

Annie meandered down the long driveway which led to her bungalow and eventually to the farm beyond. The dogs ran ahead, leaping in and out of the hedges, flushing out the first pheasants of the season. There'd been hardly any rain this autumn and the ground was still hard and dusty, there was no sun, but the clouds were high and white and there was very little breeze. She paused at a metal gate and looked down the valley. The views really were spectacular up here with the Exe Valley to the north, the Blackdown Hills to the east and the Culm Valley to the southeast. In the four years Annie had lived here, whatever the season, the vistas never failed to calm her mind and cause her heart to swell.

But today her heart was heavy. Seeing Jack in hospital the previous day had rocked her to her foundations. He didn't know her, didn't trust her and she felt powerless to help him. The magnitude of their lost relationship crashed in upon her more forcefully than it had done in years. Of course she still had her bad days, the days when she couldn't accept what had happened, when she raged at herself, at Kate, at the unfairness of it all, but those days were few and far between now. She'd learnt to accept that Jack was happy where he was, and she was grateful that he was well loved and well cared for. Earlier that week she'd sent his 18th birthday card with a light heart, trusting that he knew where she was if he ever wanted or needed her. That seemed like foolishness now.

Was she concerned that he'd landed himself in hospital with a ketamine overdose? Of course she was, but her job gave her a more measured perspective than some might have; she'd seen many cases over the years, so many young people experimented with drugs. Even landing himself in hospital wasn't all that unusual, it might have given him such a fright that he would leave well alone in the future. No, that wasn't what unsettled her most.

Try as she might, she couldn't shake off the impression that something wasn't right and though she couldn't quite put her finger on it, she'd come to trust her intuition. Perhaps Jack's overdose hadn't been mere experimentation but a sign of something deeper and more significant within the family? Even the fact that she'd had to introduce herself to Lucy, her own niece, revealed some stark flaws which she herself had normalised, even colluded with.

And then there was Kate herself. Lucy had said she'd been in hospital, and by the bruising, Annie guessed a car accident or a fall, but her injuries weren't the most troubling part. Kate had been so hostile and prickly, still, after all this time. Annie had been taken aback. Kate seemed exhausted to the point of collapse and her irritation at both Oliver and Lucy came off her like a heat haze.

No, it was not the happy home that Annie had allowed herself to imagine, had even envied at times, and now she felt careless and irresponsible. She should have done a better job of keeping tabs on Jack and what was happening in his home. But then what could she have done? *He didn't want you*, she reminded herself as she called the dogs and headed for home. *He was taught not to want you*, she corrected herself. Had she abandoned him? The jagged thought ripped through her. Had she failed him all over again?

Two weeks later Jack called.

Three

It was another fortnight before Jack met Annie. She suggested he come out to the bungalow, the animals always provided light relief and it meant they could walk and talk, rather than eyeballing each other over a table in a café somewhere, getting pranged on too-strong coffee.

It had rained the previous week and the ground was beginning to get muddy. Annie worried that Jack's designer trainers might not be up to the job, but he didn't complain as they sploshed through puddles and Devon-red mud.

The whole thing had a surreal quality to Annie, as though she were watching herself in a movie. Here she was, walking side by side with Jack, *her* Jack who now towered above her and talked with the voice of a man. He seemed gentle, thoughtful and sensitive, and though she suspected it was at least part wishful thinking, he reminded her of herself.

'So why does Mum hate you so much?' he asked as he threw a stick for Gus, one of Annie's scruffy lurchers.

'Wow, ask the easy questions first, why don't you!' Annie laughed.

'Sorry, you don't have to tell me anything, no one else does,'

Annie could hear the resentment in his voice and realised there was a tightrope to be walked.

'Jack, I want to answer your questions and I promise I'll always tell you the truth,' she said, stopping so she could look up into his face, so like her own, 'but I'm not going to get drawn into whatever's going on between you and Kate. The fact is she took care of you when I couldn't, and I know she'll be doing the very best she can because that's what Kate does. And remember that Kate and I each have a *truth,* and neither is truer than the other, does that make sense?'

'I think so,' Jack replied slowly.

Annie walked on as she asked, 'Has Kate not told you why she doesn't want me around?' She couldn't bring herself to use the word *hate*, and aside from in her darkest moments, she didn't believe Kate hated her.

'She doesn't tell me anything. I mean, I remember when I was young, she used to say I had to tell people I wanted to live with her or else you'd take me away. And I know she thought it was a big waste of time meeting up with you when we did but… well, I thought that too… sorry.' He looked at her sheepishly through his thick lashes and Annie marvelled at his sincerity. 'You know she's never properly told me why I went to live with them in the first place. I used to ask when I was young, and she'd say she'd tell me when I was older. I've stopped asking, she's always too busy or stressed out about something. But whatever she says, I know she doesn't want me to have anything to do with you.'

'What do you mean, *whatever she says*?' Annie called the dogs, and they crossed the road at the end of the drive, passing through a gate and into a field. The small town of Tiverton was dusted across the valley below, as though someone had applied it with an icing shaker.

'Well, like, she told me to call you to say thanks for my birthday card.' Jack scooped up another stick and threw it.

'Really?' Annie was taken aback by this information.

'Yeah, but then she almost had a meltdown when she saw me take your phone number. I still had it, by the way.' He smiled sheepishly again, and this time Annie saw Kevin all over his freckled face. 'So it's like all these mixed messages, she says one thing, or rather she says nothing, but the way she acts it's just so obvious, it's like I've always known, you know, that it's not okay to be in contact with you. Like even though she said it was up to me whether I saw you, well, I just knew it wasn't okay, do you know what I mean?'

Annie took a deep, painful breath, 'I do know Jack, I guess I've always known.' Annie's heart was beating too fast, and she felt dizzy with the weight of her past decisions.

'Oh Jack, I hope I've done the right thing by you, I tried to explain this when you were younger, I never wanted to put you in a of tug of war between us and you just seemed so happy there, I was sure you didn't want me making your life more difficult, that's the only reason I didn't go to court.'

'Hey, no, I'm glad you didn't go to court!' Jack said earnestly. 'And I'm happy there, don't get me wrong, I just want to know the truth, that's all.'

'Of course you do, and you deserve the truth, my version of it at least. I'm just sorry you've had to wait so long to get it.'

So Annie talked to him, she told him everything she could, not glossing over the uncomfortable bits but not giving him unnecessary, gory details either. She tried to give him a fair picture of her terrible mistakes and failures but also of the good times. She thought of Kevin as she spoke, she tried to explain that a failure to get clean doesn't signify a lack of love for one's children. She explained why Kate might think this way and how difficult it was for them as the children of an alcoholic father and embittered mother. She told him about their upbringing, how they'd been taught to take sides, to mistrust one another and compete with one another; she tried to give Kate a fair representation and explain how things had got the way they had, without casting blame, she hoped she'd achieved that.

She was taken aback by Jack's openness and depth, they laughed as they shared stories of their acute self-consciousness and social awkwardness and Jack unbuttoned about how pressured he felt to perform, how he feared letting people down but at the same time resented Kate and Jacqui for telling him he must try harder. To Annie it sounded all too familiar.

'Of course this is just my perspective,' she said, as they turned for home. 'And my life hasn't been a shining example of getting things right first time! But I found those messages about life having to be hard, about having to try harder, do more, I found all that really damaging.' Annie hoped she wasn't being contrary, 'I've learnt that the only thing I have to do, really, is look after my mental health. Yes, I have a good brain but that can also make me pretty neurotic!' she laughed easily. 'I was so knotted up when I was young, and my *good brain* was usually my worst enemy. Being told that I wasn't trying hard enough just made it worse.' She thought back to those awful teenage years. 'I suppose some people need a stick and some need a carrot. The stick just made me self-destruct.' She hoped she was making sense. 'I do wonder, if someone had been there to explain these things, whether it would have been different, but the people around me measured success by outward appearances, by performance, and I was so twisted up inside there was no way I was going to perform. I suppose...' she hesitated, not wishing to speak out of turn. 'I suppose the *push harder* model has worked for Kate so why would she question it? She's only telling you what she believes to be true, what she believes is best for you...' She paused to call the dogs from a stubble field. 'I heard something useful once; when someone's telling you what to do, first see if they're following their own advice, if they are, how's that method working out for them? Do they have the life you want? Do they have the life *they* want? If the answer's yes then go ahead and follow their advice but if it isn't, well...'

At that moment the heavens opened, and the rain came down in sheets. Shrieking and laughing, they hotfooted it up the drive, splashing through puddles and crashing into each other, taking shelter in the nearest building they came to. Their hair was plastered to their faces, and they were panting and laughing as the dogs shook off the excess rainwater and splattered them further in the process.

'Well, look at the doppelgangers!' a man's voice remarked jovially.

'Oh, hey Joel,' Annie smiled, still catching her breath as she scraped her hair back from her face. 'This is my son, Jack.' Her heart did a double thud at the word, it felt so right and so alien at the same time. 'Jack, this is Joel, he rents my workshop for his smithy.' She looked at Jack and could see why Joel made his comment, there was no getting away from it, Jack was her image, and if Kevin were here, there would be no mistaking the family resemblance. Annie never met her grandfather, Daniel, but knew he also had the red hair, freckles and sludgy hazel eyes; she also knew that having red hair and green eyes in four generations was a rarity and it felt like a magical connection between them. She wondered how Kate had tolerated such a likeness.

'The rain's stopped.' Annie stuck her head out of the workshop. 'Let's go and dry off indoors. Joel, would you like a cuppa?'

'Nah, I'm off home now, thanks Annie, I'll leave you to it.' Joel's dark eyes twinkled as he gave her a knowing look. He'd rented the workshop for almost four years, and in that time, they'd become good friends and occasional lovers. Annie welcomed his calm, uncomplicated aura which seemed to have no demands or expectations, such a natural contrast to her rather heady, flighty personality. They joked that whilst she was air and fire, he was earth and water and the clay they made could withstand anything. They'd often talked into the night about the most difficult area of her life; he knew how long she'd waited for this day.

Jack stayed another hour or so, chatting easily as he fussed the dogs and gazed about the place. *It probably seems like a zoo compared to Kate's house,* Annie found herself thinking, though she was long past being self-critical for her very different way of doing things. Eventually Jack said he had to go and seemed genuinely sad to leave. She waved until his noisy Golf disappeared around a bend then returned to the bungalow, throwing a log into the wood burner and slumping back on the sofa. The dogs were sprawled out in front of the heat, but when she sat, they jumped up beside her, sensing her need for comfort. Meg lay over her lap, as was her way, whilst Gus sat as close as he could, leaning into her as she scratched his ears.

There was just too much to process, her heart felt too big for her chest. She felt both empty and full, as though she were in shock and this day hadn't really happened. She had an image of Jack's face as they sprinted through the rain, laughing like maniacs. She knew she wasn't imagining it, they just fitted together. They knew each other without ever having known each other, they understood each other and had their own rhythm. They were cut from the same cloth, O'Shea cloth.

Four

The world turned. Winter came and left, Lucy turned ten and the blackthorn cried its snow-like tears as Jack melted away from her like the early March frosts. Annie became a regular guest at the dinner table, only as a topic of conversation but still, she was there. Lucy seemed so enamoured by that first meeting that Kate could only assume she'd sensed a weakness and was deliberately goading her. For weeks it had been *'Auntie Annie this,'* and *'Auntie Annie that,'* and *'could Auntie Annie come to my birthday party?'*, *'let's invite Auntie Annie for Christmas!'*

Jack had initially kept his visits to Annie quiet though Kate, loathing herself, had eavesdropped outside his bedroom door one afternoon and heard him arranging to meet. Weeks later, in his fierce and defended way, he announced he would be spending Christmas Eve and New Year's Day with Annie. Kate felt like she was handling a wild horse in open country, he would blow and stamp his feet and throw his weight around but if she responded with any force at all he might gallop off into the sunset, never to be seen again. So she kept quiet, doing her best to hide her disapproval but fearing he sensed it all the same and respected her less for it.

She felt utterly alone in her agony. She'd lost all confidence in Oliver since the night of the fight and he, in turn, seemed more remote than ever, sleeping in the spare room and leaving for the Midlands on Sundays without even saying goodbye, often not returning until after she'd left for London. It meant that Lucy was practically living at Jan's, and it felt to Kate that her family was disintegrating before her eyes. It seemed so unfair when she worked so hard, trying her best to do the right thing for a family that was falling apart.

The very last person she could unbutton to was Jacqui; in fact, she'd been keeping her mother at arm's length for several months now. She hated admitting it to herself but the idea that her life seemed to be crumbling whilst Annie's was coming together was abhorrent to her; she had to keep her mother off the scene until things were back under control. Jack would surely come through this *phase* and Annie would no longer be flavour of the month. But a month had passed, and then another, and Kate felt trapped in this travesty of a Groundhog Day, with little hope of resolution.

Then, one cold, sunny day she and Lucy bumped into Annie in Exeter high street. They stopped and chatted for some time whilst Kate felt she might develop an ulcer if Lucy gave one more theatrical laugh at some stupid thing Annie was saying. Just as she was thinking it must be a reasonable time to say goodbye, Lucy somehow got on the subject of her riding lessons and Annie was inviting her to *the bungalow* to meet her horse.

'I think you'd love it there, Lucy,' Annie was saying. 'I have dogs, a goat, chickens and two little donkeys.'

Kate had visions of the pied piper or the witch from Hansel and Gretel.

'I don't think that's a good idea, Annie, I—'

'Oh please, Mum, please!' Lucy had pleaded, her voice rising threateningly. Kate loathed a scene in the high street.

'Don't you dare start that, Lucy, you'll do as you're told,' she said in urgent undertones. 'I'm sorry Annie…' She made to turn away.

'You're so unfair!' Lucy shouted, full force, 'What's the big problem anyway?'

'Lucy,' Annie was saying gently in that fake voice, 'I shouldn't have invited you without checking with your mum first; it's my fault.'

'Thank you, Annie,' Kate said curtly, putting out her hand to lead Lucy away.

'No! I won't go. Why can't I go to Auntie Annie's? You're only going to dump me on Nanny anyway.'

Kate felt herself redden. *Trust Lucy to pull the guilt card.* She felt trapped, cornered.

In the end it was arranged for Lucy to visit one day during the school holidays, and though Annie offered to come and collect her, Kate said that she would drop Lucy off; she just couldn't bear the idea of having Annie in the house and playing happy families, perhaps making small talk with Jan or having Oliver smarm all over her again when he and Kate were barely talking.

***

And so it was that Kate was bumping up the long drive a week later, cursing the potholes and questioning her sanity. She didn't know what she'd expected of Annie's choice of home but this driveway, the remoteness and the *abnormality* of it all certainly fitted. *Why couldn't Annie live in a normal street like a normal person?*

As it happened, she was reluctantly impressed by Annie's home. It was relatively small, but the views were substantial, if you liked that kind of thing. The main living area faced south and had wide sliding doors which let in a lot of light and made the most of the panoramic views. Annie had met them on the doorstep and led them through to the lounge but now she offered to show them around and Kate found herself agreeing. Was she deliberately tormenting herself, or was she convinced, on closer inspection, that Annie's life would reveal itself as the sham it was?

After the impressive start, the rest of the property wasn't much to speak of. There were two bedrooms, smallish and not very well lit, they seemed impersonal, and Kate couldn't even work out which was Annie's. She allowed herself a moment of smug satisfaction, this could never compete with her interior-design skills and her beautiful, open-plan home. The kitchen was a small, square room with an old-fashioned Rayburn and cheap aluminium sink; most of the grubby-looking floor was taken up by a scrubbed wooden table and four clunky, mismatched chairs. A small window overlooked a yard area at the side of the property. Then there was a pretty standard bathroom, a utility room and a wet room, all overrun with boots and coats for human, dog and horse. Kate was glad she'd stayed to look around, this was not a home she envied, albeit the epitome of *the good life*.

Finally, Annie took them through a door which Kate had assumed was a cupboard, but which led up a steep, enclosed stairway and opened into a huge room which must have comprised the entire area of the bungalow. The roof was pitched which impinged on the floorspace, but integral cupboards and cubby holes lined the walls to make the best use of space. On the far side, and hidden from their approach on the driveway, was a double dormer-style window, reaching almost from floor to ceiling and looking out over the hills and valleys. The few items of furniture were large and rustic-looking; a huge bed covered in a patchwork quilt and assortment of blankets, an ancient rocking chair overlaid with a sheepskin and a full-length, free-standing mirror. There was no doubt that this was an incredible room or that this was Annie's bedroom, decorated as it was with tartan and lace and dotted with oddities like feathers, little stacks of stones and dried flowers.

'Hmmm, not really my style,' Kate commented as she picked up a weird stone ornament. 'Great views though,' she added, hearing the edge in her voice and seeking to disguise it.

'I think it's a-maz-ing!' Lucy cried, whirling around in the centre of the room below a weird Celtic symbol hanging from the ceiling.

'It's a Triskele,' Annie said in answer to Kate's disparaging, quizzical look. 'My friend, Joel, made it. Shall we go outside?' She had that maddening laughter in her eyes again.

Lucy led the way, practically skipping down the stairs and Kate was reminded just how much the little girl reminded her of Annie, wrapped up in daydreams, fairy tales and castles in the air; of course she would love it here.

They left through the utility room and went out into the yard, here there was some kind of workshop made of wood and corrugated metal, the big wooden doors in a sturdy frame appeared to be all that held the structure upright. They were open at the moment and a loud, tinny banging came from within. As they drew level, Kate saw a dark-haired man in overalls pounding a large hammer against an anvil; he desisted when he saw them and waved. Kate thought he had a distinctly pikey look about him.

'That's Joel, he rents the workshop.'

Annie had caught Kate's distasteful look and she regretted it immediately, was she really turning into her mother, as Oliver so often threw at her?

'And this,' Annie was saying as they walked across the small yard, 'is Shiloh.' She made clucking noises as they approached the stable, which looked far sturdier and better maintained than the workshop. Kate saw the movement of enormous hindquarters in the shadows before a bright bay head appeared over the stable door. She couldn't deny it, this was a beautiful horse, his coat gleaming like a conker, his glossy black forelock left long, partially obscuring his bright, long-lashed eyes. Kate put out a hand to stroke him and he nodded his head appreciatively. Lucy was awestruck.

'Would you like to ride him?' Annie was asking.

'Who?' Kate asked, surprised. 'He's too big for Lucy and I haven't ridden in years.'

'Both of you!' Annie replied, unbolting the door, 'Honestly, he's safer than riding the number 10 bus.' She'd slipped a headcollar over Shiloh's pretty face and was leading him into the yard. Kate sprang back out of the way and took Lucy's hand.

'Seriously, Annie, we can't ride him, Lucy hasn't been having lessons that long.' Kate's heart was pounding, she felt disproportionately afraid.

'Oh, please, Mum.' Lucy was now whining. 'I've never seen you ride, and *I* want to ride him!'

'I promise you, Kate, he's like an armchair, I wouldn't suggest it otherwise.'

Kate stepped forward and stroked Shiloh's muscled neck; his clipped winter coat seemed to gleam. He was a beautiful thing. Should she? Could she?

Twenty minutes later, Annie had helped her into the saddle and Shiloh was walking quietly towards the paddock, Annie at his head and Lucy trundling along beside her, barely able to contain her excitement.

'Don't jump around Lucy!' Kate said urgently. 'You'll startle him.' She collected up the reins a bit tighter, but Shiloh really did seem to be taking care of her. Within a few minutes Kate was walking him around the edge of the paddock on her own. The ground was quite churned up at the bottom and she worried he might trip but she gave him his head and Shiloh picked his way carefully towards home. Kate felt incredible, exhilarated, freer than she had done in years and she patted him enthusiastically.

'Push him on up the hill Kate!' Annie was calling from the gate.

'I can't!' she called back, feeling herself tense.

'Of course you can! Go on, he's got a lovely canter, like a rocking horse!'

Kate feebly nudged with her heels not expecting a response, but it was as though the big horse had heard his mistress and was determined to show Kate what a gentleman he was, bypassing trot, and breaking easily into a gentle lope which carried her up the hill. Her heart felt as though it were about to burst and the wind whipping her eyes was not the only cause of her tears.

'That was brilliant Mum!' Lucy exclaimed as Shiloh brought her gently to a standstill by the gate.

'You still ride really well,' Annie was saying, taking the horse's head and smiling up at her with genuine warmth. Kate felt confused and more tears leaked inadvertently from her eyes. She clambered down and the two women walked at Shiloh's head as he carried Lucy quietly around the paddock.

'Remember when Da used to take us riding up at the farm?' Annie asked.

'God, you can't remember that, Annie? Surely you were only about four!' Kate picked her way around the divots, her designer boots getting plastered in mud. 'I remember going to the riding school, when Mum was with Jeff, that's when we learnt to ride really.'

'Oh no,' Annie replied, smiling lopsidedly at her. 'I learnt to ride with Da because that's when the magic happened. Watching him ride made me fall in love with horses and I knew I would always want them in my life.'

Kate looked at her and felt that strange mix of grief and envy, what was this magic Annie spoke of? What had Annie seen in their father that seemed so out of her grasp?

They put Shiloh away and Kate said goodbye; Annie would drop Lucy home that evening. For the first time in many years the two women hugged, albeit briefly, and as they parted Annie kept hold of Kate's shoulders and looked into her eyes. For the briefest moment Kate felt a connection, a spark of something sincere but then the intensity felt too much, that feeling that Annie might see something hidden there, and she looked away. She felt oddly bereft as she drove home, it was as though the fight had gone from her but had left an aching void in its place. Something had passed between them in the presence of that horse, something innocent and honest, something of earliest childhood, before the battle had begun. Kate felt it and it changed her; perhaps this is what Annie called *the magic*.

Five

Many things changed for Annie over the following years. Lucy became a regular visitor, sometimes stopping for the day but, after a time, staying for a weekend or a few days in the school holidays. Annie had always sensed a tension between the little girl and Kate but as Lucy approached her teens it was obvious that the friction was reaching fire-starting proportions. Lucy seemed angry and disappointed with Kate as a mother which made Annie sad, knowing as she did how hard Kate tried to create the perfect life for her family.

Annie herself found Lucy engaging, she was bright, happy and often theatrical, singing and dancing and telling stories to the animals when there was no one else to listen. She was flighty and a dreamer but had more resilience and less of the intensity which Annie found in herself and Jack. She felt this boded well for Lucy, that Lucy was hardier for it, but she could see how her colourful characteristics might jar with Kate because they were so much like her own.

Kate and Annie developed a rather tight-lipped but cordial ceasefire. Kate didn't return to the bungalow, though Annie invited her several times, but she seemed tolerant, even grateful that Lucy was spending so much time there and it certainly helped with childcare issues. Annie had heard through Lucy that Oliver was spending increasing time in the Midlands and Jan seemed to be busy with her family's ever-increasing brood. From what Annie could tell, Kate's work also kept her away from home for several nights each month and she could understand why Lucy began to feel like a latchkey kid, despite knowing how this idea would appal Kate.

Jack now spent extended periods away from home and this was another cause of Lucy's loneliness. Soon after his first visit to the bungalow, Jack had explained to Lucy that he was not her brother but her cousin. Lucy was just ten at the time and took the news stoically enough, but it drove a further wedge between her and her mother, whom she felt had deceived her without cause. Annie was pleased that Jack had confided in Lucy, seeing it as a healthy sign that he was embracing his identity, but was dismayed at the growing rift between Kate and her daughter.

She and Jack had spent many beautiful times together since that first meeting on a rainy November afternoon. They would sit by the fire well into the night and share intense discussions about politics, philosophy and spirituality, Annie continued to marvel at his depth and sensitivity. They roamed across the fields in springtime, Annie teaching him the names of the trees and the wildflowers just as Kevin had taught her and she saw her Da in the dimples of Jack's easy smile, in the way his freckles merged when he caught the sun and in his long, fluid gait as he ran with the dogs. They camped in the woods in the summertime, shrieking and splashing in the deeper stretches of river, its waters resolutely icy even on the hottest days. They lay looking up at the canopy as Jack wrestled with his inner world, how disappointed people left him, how dissatisfying he found the human experience, how hollow. They watched the leaves turn amber then auburn, the colour of their hair, then they watched them fade to brown and trampled them under their feet.

Annie tried in every way she knew to reach him, to identify with his longings and his disappointments and to impart on him the hard-won lessons which had led her to freedom but no matter how cleverly she phrased it, how honestly she shared the torment of addiction, or the joy of recovery, it were as though he was committed to a course from which she was unable to steer him. She'd often wondered whether, had she been given the right information at the right time, she would have travelled quite so far down the road to self-destruction and in some ways, Jack was giving her the answer.

Still, she would tell herself, Jack was not nearly as far gone as she had been, she was gone beyond recall by his age whereas Jack seemed to peak and trough; he would disappear for months at a time only to emerge remorseful and in desperate need of love and forgiveness, and more than anything, empathy. Each time Annie would reach into the depths of herself and offer him all she had to give. She wouldn't give him money for drugs, and she wouldn't allow drugs in her house and at times he would rage at her, shouting and smashing anything he could get his hands on. He would throw at her every hateful thing he could think of, how it was her fault he suffered as he did, that she'd ruined his life by making him live with Kate, that she was ruining his life now. The words would pierce her like rusty blades, ripping and sawing at the tender flesh of her heart. Sometimes he would drive off into the night, at others he would rant until he was spent then dissolve sobbing into her arms and allow her to put him to bed like a small child. Then he would disappear again, and her heart would be ripped out once more. She would speak with Sarah, her anchor, she would share at her meetings, and she would speak with Joel, so steadfast and unaffected, but nothing could reliably ease the pain of watching her son, so recently returned to her, tormented by the demons which had taken so much from them already.

***

It was during the darkest of these times, the long winter following Jack's twentieth birthday, that Annie reached out to Jacqui for the first time since she'd been in prison.

It seemed amazing to her that fourteen years could pass without some kind of resolution, when every other area of her life, even her relationship with Kate, was at least partially healed. But Jacqui had asked Annie to give her time and had so far given no sign that she was ready to talk. In the meantime, Annie had embarked on the long journey of forgiveness and healing which she could undertake without having contact with Jacqui. She needed to fully accept and forgive herself for the many mistakes she'd made in order to move forward, and in the process, she was able to forgive Jacqui who, like her, had simply been doing the best she could with the tools she had for the job.

But it was through Annie's relationship with Jack, the torment of repeatedly trying and failing to reach him, to be hated and needed and abused and loved, that she began to appreciate what it may have been like for her mother. If she, with all her personal and professional experience, found the journey excruciating then what must it have been like for Jacqui, with her desperate need to control and her unyielding expectations?

So, as the first snowdrops scattered the verges, bowing their heads in reverence to the pale January sun and the early lambs took their first shaky steps, Annie, filled as usual with the hopeful stirrings of spring, decided it was time to take her own shaky steps towards her mother. It was harder than she'd expected, churning up those old feelings of abandonment and rejection, but she fastened her heart on her love for Jack, on herself as the imperfect mother and in the spirit of shared experience she picked up the phone. To her astonishment and trepidation Jacqui agreed to visit.

Six

The following Saturday found them taking the footpath to Warnicombe. The ground was hard and uneven, and to Annie, Jacqui looked as out of place as Joan Collins might in her shiny new Hunter wellies and impeccably clean wax jacket.

'I'm a country girl you know, Annie,' she'd insisted when Annie suggested they sit by the fire or drive the few miles into town. Now she was picking her way delicately over a particularly rutted part of the track. 'I used to come up here as a girl,' she said, pausing to look down the hill to the little clusters of houses and businesses which made up Tiverton town. 'That's Canal Hill over there isn't it? Your father had a bedsit there when first we met.'

'I know,' Annie said, coming to stand beside her. 'He pointed it out to me one day when we were in his delivery van.'

Jacqui tutted and walked on. 'How could you possibly remember that far back?'

Annie didn't want to debate it so said nothing, she knew she had unusually clear memories of being with her Da as a small child, but she didn't need to press the point, she had other things to discuss. She took a deep breath.

'Mum—' she began, but Jacqui cut her off.

'Have you seen Jack recently?' the question sounded genuine and without accusation.

'No,' Annie said sadly. 'I haven't seen him since the first week of January. He stayed with me for a few days; he wasn't in great shape.' It seemed so strange to be having this conversation with her mother.

'Yes, it was the same at Christmas, he just drifted in and out, rude to everybody.' Jacqui stopped to light a cigarette. 'Too much O'Shea in him; I should have known the moment he popped out with red hair that there was going to be trouble.'

Annie couldn't have helped her sharp intake of breath, but she caught herself in time. She was determined to let Jacqui have her opinions, that was her right, after all.

'Jack can't help his DNA Mum, any more than the rest of us. We're sensitive, us O'Sheas, we need... a very careful kind of handling.' She tried to make the comment light, not as though she were criticising Kate or Jacqui.

'Oh, don't be ridiculous, Annie. Kate has spoiled that boy rotten, even you must see it. That's been the trouble from the start; I warned her not to treat him with kid gloves, whatever his start was in life.'

Again, Annie recoiled from Jacqui's bluntness, but she let the irritation wash over her. After all, Jack did have a terrible start in life, she didn't need to defend her corner.

Instead, she said, 'I'm sure Kate has always done her best,' and she meant it. Then, before Jacqui could say anything else she went on. 'Mum, I want to acknowledge how difficult it must have been for you. I never stopped to think what it was like for you being married to Da, trying to bring up two girls and me always disobeying you and taking his side. Then later, when things got really bad, I told myself you didn't care about me anyway, so I wasn't affecting you...'

Jacqui turned sharply to look at her as she said this, and Annie felt the first sting of tears.

'I'm sorry Mum, I never considered you or your feelings; I would like to make it up to you if I can.'

For a moment Jacqui said nothing, it seemed whatever she'd been expecting, it wasn't this. It was also clear that she found such a display of honesty deeply uncomfortable. She dropped her cigarette and ground it awkwardly with her welly boot.

'Thank you for saying that, Annie,' she said stiltedly. 'I've only ever wanted the best for you.'

They walked on in a heavy silence, Jacqui leading the way whilst Annie lingered behind, wondering if she should say something more. Eventually they reached the level tarmac of Warnicombe Lane, and they walked side by side whilst the dogs trotted ahead, stopping every so often to bury a nose in the hedgerow. The silence was becoming unbearable, and Annie wrestled with the need to say something, anything, to relieve the tension.

Then Jacqui broke the silence.

'I got a lot of things wrong too, Annie,' she said, looking resolutely ahead.

Annie didn't know what to say to this and panicked as a second silence loomed. Hating herself she was about to smooth over Jacqui's words with a trite *not at all,* or *you did your best*, when Jacqui spoke again.

'I've hated your father for longer than I ever loved him,' she said baldly, sounding more like herself, 'for everything he took from me, for everything he took from my parents and for everything he took from you girls.'

A younger Annie would have interjected, would have been compelled to fight her Da's corner but she was determined to at least try to see things from Jacqui's perspective. She took a deep breath and said nothing.

'You have no idea what I went through trying to protect you from his drunkenness, his absences, his infidelities. I couldn't talk to my parents about it because they blamed me for ruining my life; I had to pretend that everything was just as I would want it. Then my mother died.' Jacqui stopped and took her cigarettes from her pocket, pausing before taking one from the pack. 'I was so young; I had no life skills and even if I had they wouldn't have helped with your father. I tried so hard to turn things around, to make a good life for you; I always put you first. Even marrying Jeff was an attempt to give you girls a better start in life. And you hated me for it.'

She put a cigarette in her mouth and lit it. 'You were just a child, I know that, Annie, you couldn't have known how much your hatred hurt me, every time you sided with Kevin, refused to apply yourself at school, threw all that talent out the window just to spite me, spewing your hate at me at every opportunity. By the time all that business happened with Frank, I'd concluded you'd do anything just to hurt me. You were too much O'Shea, drinking and swearing and sleeping around...'

Annie's heart felt like it was beating in her throat, constricting her airway.

'So I didn't believe you and I drove you out of the house. I know that. I've never forgiven myself for it.'

Annie had stopped walking; Jacqui noticed a moment or so afterwards and stopped to look around.

'You mean you believe me now?' Annie asked in a voice unlike her own.

'I realised the truth within a year of you leaving. I found... things... that's why I kicked him out. I was going to call the police, but I had no idea of the effect that would have on you.'

Annie digested this. 'But I never knew. I thought he left you for another woman, I *saw* him with another woman.'

'Yes, well, that was Frank, wasn't it?' Jacqui walked on and Annie trotted a few paces to keep up.

'But why didn't you tell me? All these years...'

'Oh Annie, have you forgotten what you were like back then?' Jacqui said in her usual, impatient tone. 'You wouldn't have listened to me! Your fury at me knew no bounds. I thought the best thing I could do was to keep out of your way and pretty soon you were too far gone to talk about it anyway.'

Annie said nothing. She sensed that Jacqui was telling herself a story, one that didn't feature her injured pride or her shame at her terrible error of judgement, one that made the whole thing easier to live with. But she had acknowledged she'd made a mistake, she'd said, *I've never forgiven myself*, and Annie believed her, that was enough. She was also struck, hard, by the realisation that she'd never appreciated what her mother had done for her, that in Jacqui's mind she was just trying to protect Annie from Kevin, that Jacqui was young and overwhelmed and alone.

'I forgive you, Mum,' she heard herself saying. 'I was awful as a teenager, I know I was, I think I can understand how it must have been for you.'

Jacqui seemed to bristle a little and a fleeting shadow of hardness darkened her face but then she relaxed and smiled.

'And I forgive you, Annie. And I'm so very happy that you've made something of your life, that you seem to be happy at last.'

Jacqui wasn't a hugger, but the two women had an awkward, brief embrace in the road as the dogs charged back towards them, wondering what they were missing.

'Have you heard from Kate?' Annie asked as they moved on, reminded of her sister by Jacqui's perfunctory hugging style.

'Not for nearly a fortnight,' Jacqui sighed. 'We used to speak every day.'

Annie heard the disappointment in her voice and felt sad for her.

'But she's so busy, of course, she has a very demanding job. Oliver's off mooning around whilst Kate works a sixty-hour week *and* takes care of Lucy. Jack's no help any more, even if he's around.'

'Yes, poor Kate,' Annie said, meaning it. 'She works so hard to get it right, if only she would let up on herself a bit.'

'What a stupid thing to say, Annie!' Jacqui snapped with a disconcertingly swift return to form. 'Kate's a grafter, she knows nothing comes from nothing; a good life comes from hard work and sacrifice.'

'Do you think she has a good life then?' Annie asked, not wishing to sound contrary.

'She has a worthwhile life,' Jacqui said, as though this settled it. 'Everything she's done has been for those children.'

'Ah yes, the *noble* addiction.' The words were out before Annie could stop them.

'Noble addiction? What are you talking about?'

'Workaholism,' Annie said, wondering if she shouldn't be back-pedalling. 'It can rob children of as many hours with their parents as drug addiction and leave them feeling just as abandoned or unloved but, because society values hard workers, the work addict gets praise and recognition for their dysfunction, which just feeds the belief that their only worth is their work.'

'What a lot of nonsense,' Jacqui said dismissively. 'I hope you're not filling Jack and Lucy's heads with such claptrap? After everything Kate's done for them!'

Annie decided it was time to relent.

'I'm sorry. Of course, that's just my opinion and I would never say anything like that to Jack or Lucy, I'm one hundred per cent supportive of Kate.'

'I should think so too.'

The afternoon was a little spikey after that. Annie concluded that too much had been said for it to be anything other than a little turbulent and didn't try too hard to smooth things over. They ate lunch at the Flying Pickle and wandered up the high street, Jacqui stopping every so often to reminisce outside a shop or public house. By the time they'd walked back to the bungalow it was beginning to get dark and Jacqui said a swift goodbye.

Annie felt like a rotary blade had sunk its teeth into the earth of her being and stirred the deepest contents of her soul, but the rocks there were too large to break. For a brief moment she'd felt closer to her mother than she had in her whole life and yet, now the moment had passed, there was a deep sense of dissatisfaction to it all. The beauty of the moment had been real, but it was as though a drop of purest oil had been added to water, it was utterly present yet unable to penetrate. For a time, Annie wandered listlessly about the place, turning on lamps and lighting candles, as a great sadness began to seep through her. She was sad for Jacqui, all that anger, blame and regret. She was sad that her mother was so shut down, seemingly unreachable save for that briefest of cracks in her veneer today. And she was sad for herself, the deepest, oldest sadness of a child longing for its mother. For the first time in many years, Annie felt lonely. She was hit with a wave of grief for Granny O'Shea, for her Da and even for Kate, for the relationship of which they'd been robbed. She knelt by the fire and felt five years old.

For what felt like the first time, she remembered a yearning, a child's confusion about why this woman whom she loved and needed didn't like her or want her around. She touched the depths of her sadness and remembered the moment she closed her heart to this person who seemed so out of reach. In that instant it felt like the rocks, so huge and impenetrable, imploded to dust, a great wave of pain and exhaustion swept through her as she wept.

Seven

Kate stood at the sink, her hands in water gone tepid, staring out the window but not seeing. The blackthorn was in full leaf and fledgling sparrows were dive-bombing the hedge, squabbling and chattering like maniacs, but the scene was lost on Kate. Trance-like, she pulled the plug and dried her hands. It was Sunday. Lucy was out with her friends somewhere and Oliver was upstairs doing goodness knows what.

Where was Jack? It was Easter in just over a week; she hadn't seen him since Christmas and that had been another disaster, another row. Whatever she did seemed to rub him up the wrong way. If she tried to be kind and show concern, she was *smarming over him* and if she challenged him on his behaviour or what he was doing with his life he would rear up like a snake and strike in the most lethal places: she'd ruined his life, he wished he didn't live with her, once he even said she should have left him to die as a baby. Her heart was so broken she felt it would never mend but she dared not show weakness lest he really go in for the kill. So she mastered the art of appearing supremely unconcerned, as she had with so many areas of her life, but each time she emptied her purse to him she hoped that this time he might be grateful, this time he might love her for it.

Perhaps he was at Annie's again. Even that had turned from red-hot, searing pain to a cold, dull ache. So he chose Annie. Perhaps she would be the one to help him, to reach him, to bring home the joyful, sunny boy whom Kate had adored for his constant smile and easy nature. Kate didn't care how it happened any more, she just wanted him back in his right mind.

She wandered into the lounge to stare out of the bi-folding doors to the immaculate garden beyond. They had a gardener now and it was all clean borders and pruned shrubs, the way she'd desired it, but for a moment she longed for the leaf-strewn untidiness of Annie's bungalow. Kate had only visited twice in two years, and she hadn't gone in. She remembered cantering Shiloh around the paddock, the big horse's gait carrying her easily; for a moment, she imagined how it would feel to canter off to a distant horizon with no hedges and no borders.

She'd thought about visiting Annie on several occasions since that day but couldn't bring herself to do it. Her brief time there had felt so groundless, so unsafe, she'd felt childlike and free but that hadn't felt comfortable at all. No, despite these fleeting yearnings for escape, she knew she liked borders, she needed neat edges and structure. She knew, instinctively, that none of these were compatible with Annie's life and so Annie and all she represented felt dangerous. A vast horizon felt unsafe, she needed boundaries with hard lines. Soft hurt, it was better to be hard, to be strong. Don't look, don't stop, don't feel. She couldn't turn back even if she wanted to, she'd come too far.

She heard the front door slam. She'd told Lucy a thousand times to be careful, that the wind would catch it with all the windows open.

'Lucy?' she yelled, striding out to the hall.

'No, it's me.' Jack was already in the kitchen, rifling through the fridge. 'God, is there ever anything decent to eat in this place?'

Kate looked at him. His hair was so long now that he wore the fringe tied back in a ponytail at the top of his head. There was a shadow of stubble around his jaw and upper lip and his usually pale skin was almost translucent, despite all the hot weather they'd been having. There were dark rings under his eyes.

'If you get out of the way I'll make you a sandwich,' she said, hearing a slight tremor in her voice and hating it.

'Don't bother, I'll get something when I'm out.' Jack grunted, taking one of Oliver's beers instead. 'Have you got any money?'

'Oh, Jack, you only just got here.' *Don't plead, be strong.* 'Why don't you hang around for a bit? Lucy would love to see you. She misses you. And if you get out of those clothes, I can wash them; you smell like hundred-year-old socks!' She tried for the banter they used to share.

'Better than smelling like a whore's handbag,' he spat, making her flinch. 'What is that smell anyway?'

'Don't speak to me like that Jack; if you're going to speak like that you can just turn right back around and leave.'

'One minute you're telling me to stay, next you're telling me to leave. Make your fucking mind up. I don't want to stay anyway; I just came to see if you'd help me out, but of course you won't so I might as well leave again.'

He was manipulating her, and she knew it, but she couldn't seem to help herself.

'Look, just hang on a minute and I'll get you some cash. But I'd like you to stay and see Lucy please, it's a two-way street, Jack.'

'Don't start lecturing me about being there for Lucy,' he said, draining his beer and going to the fridge for another. 'I practically brought her up when she was a baby; you were never here.'

'Oh, Jack, not this ridiculous rubbish again! You were eight years old when Lucy was born, not old enough to look after yourself, let alone a baby.'

'Listen, I was the one who was with Lucy all the time, looking after her, playing with her, calming her down when she was freaking out. That's the fucking truth! Ask her. Just because you weren't here to see it, doesn't mean it didn't happen.'

'You make it sound like I was out partying or taking drugs, Jack. I was *working,* paying the mortgage, buying your clothes and your Xboxes and your holidays. 'You've never complained about any of that!' She felt her temper rising dangerously, she didn't want to lose control. 'You've no idea the life you'd have had if I hadn't worked, because you're spoilt! Grandma's right, I've spoiled you rotten and this is the thanks I get. God, you would have a meltdown if you didn't have the right pair of trainers to go to school in! You're behaving like a brat.'

'I never asked you to take me in.' He played his trump card. 'And I don't, as I recall, remember *ever* asking you to buy me trainers; it was your guilty conscience that made you do that.'

She slapped him then, hard, across the face. For a terrifying moment she thought he was going to hit her back, he clenched his fists and his whole body seemed to quiver.

'After everything I've done for you!' Her voice was shaking over her raggedy breath. 'Everything I've sacrificed for you, my own marriage, my own child, my own fucking sister, everything took a back seat for *you* and you're just a spoilt, selfish drug addict. You're an O'Shea to your core. Now fuck off out of here. Now. Go. If you want any money, you can ask Annie!'

He looked at her with pure hatred then, his eyes narrow slits, his jaw set. This monster had nothing of the Jack she loved so well. She watched him fix his eyes on her bag, sitting on the worktop by the microwave.

'Don't you dare!' she snarled, starting towards him. But he had crossed the kitchen in two long strides, snatched up the bag and bolted.

'Jack! I'll call the police! Jack!' She ran after him, grabbing air as he swung open the front door. She caught his jacket as he stepped outside.

'Jack!' she said again, attempting to pull him back but he'd emptied her wallet of cash and now he slammed her bag back at her, almost toppling her, before he strode to his car, abandoned across the driveway, and hurtled away.

Half the bag's contents had spilled out in the tussle, and she crouched to retrieve a lipstick, notepad and packet of mints, covertly checking that none of the neighbours were looking, then scurried inside where she sat at the kitchen table and sobbed. Her throat felt raw from shrieking Jack's name; she'd broken a nail to the quick when she grabbed his jacket, but nothing hurt so much as her heart. How had it come to this?

Her mind taunted her with full-colour memories of the road trips they took, of sneaky visits to McDonald's when they were supposed to be going grocery shopping and secret afternoon trips to the cinema, just the two of them, when Oliver had sent them to B&Q for some DIY emergency. He was fourteen, fifteen, sixteen then and they'd seemed the best of friends, yet today he accused her of never having been there. How could he remember it like that? It was so unfair. She cried until she was spent, and her face was slick with tears and snot. As she stood to get some kitchen roll to mop herself up, she heard Oliver creaking down the stairs.

He seemed to take so much more stuff with him nowadays. True, he was away most of the week but how much did he need for goodness' sake? Right now, there were three suitcases lining the hall by the front door and he was heaving another bag down the stairs.

'What on earth do you need all this stuff for Oliver?' she asked, then blew her nose again noisily. He looked at her with distaste and she bristled. 'Oh, I'm so sorry if I look unpleasant,' she snapped. 'I've just been mugged by our son but don't worry about it, you just look after yourself as usual.' She turned to go back into the kitchen.

'Kate,' he said in that irritatingly level tone that he used when he wanted to drive her up the wall.

'What?' she almost shrieked, wheeling around to face him.

'I'm leaving.'

'I know you're fucking leaving, that's what you do every Sunday night isn't it? Leave me with this mess.' She waited for him to calmly state that she, too, would be leaving on Tuesday, she had her retort ready.

'No,' he said, looking at her steadily. 'I'm leaving for good. I've got most of my stuff, I've been taking it a bit at a time over the last few weeks. There's some bigger stuff I'll need to come back for but if you'll agree on a time, I'm happy to leave my key today.'

Kate's head swam and for a moment she thought she was going to faint, she lurched sideways and grabbed the worktop for support.

'What do you mean, leaving?' Her voice cracked on the last word, her raw, constricted throat refusing to play ball. 'Where… where are you going?'

'I'm going to Mum's tonight; she's expecting me,' he looked away when he said this. 'Then I'm moving up to Birmingham tomorrow. I'll need to talk to you seriously at some point about Lucy. She can come up at weekends; it's only two hours by train.'

Kate just looked at him, she had the information, but her brain refused to process it, to join the dots. Oliver was leaving her; he was talking about Lucy *visiting*. Two or three cogs moved at once, 'Where… when… how long has your mum known?' She'd been convinced they were discussing her, and she'd been right.

'Just a few days,' Oliver was saying. 'She's not happy about it; you know her, til death us do part and all—'

'Exactly!' Kate's voice cracked again, 'Exactly. You can't leave now Oliver, I'm sorry…' She sounded like she was telling him he couldn't go to the pub tonight; it all felt so surreal.

'I'm leaving tonight, Kate; it's all planned. I have to be in the Midlands by tomorrow lunchtime.'

'Oh, you've really thought it all out, haven't you?' Kate's voice was high and squeaky as she forced the words out. 'And where exactly is Lucy going to visit, some bedsit in Birmingham?'

'No,' Oliver replied with maddening calm. 'A house, a nice house in a nice area.'

'How can you afford that? Have you won the lottery and not told us? Wait a minute... oh my God, there's someone else, isn't there?'

Oliver looked shifty for a moment then met her eye defiantly.

'Yes Kate, there's someone else. There's been someone else for almost three years.' He ignored Kate's sharp intake of breath and looked at her pitilessly as she clutched her chest. 'I've tried to make it work; I've wanted to make it work. I've gone along with all your plans, done everything you've asked of me; I even went to your fucking counselling—'

It was the swearing that snapped Kate's mind back into gear, Oliver never swore.

'Oh, my God! Were you fucking someone else whilst we were having counselling?'

She quickly did the maths.

'Yes! Yes, if it's been three years. You bastard! I hate you!' She charged at him, but he put his arms out and caught her shoulders.

'I swear it Kate, if you hit me, I won't be responsible for my actions,' he said coldly, and she went limp in his grasp. 'You've done this to yourself, you haven't invested in our relationship for twenty years… no you haven't!' he shouted as she made to deny it.

Oliver, shouting and swearing. Oliver leaving. Kate sank to the floor, sobbing, all the fight gone out of her.

'How could you do this to me?' she wept. 'All I've ever done has been for this family…' She retched then, was she going to throw up? Still, he looked at her, with that cold, hard, slightly repulsed glare. 'Oliver, please…'

'No, Kate.'

'Who is she? What's her name? Is she younger than me?'

'Oh, stop it, you're embarrassing yourself.' He seemed so cold.

'Tell me! I have a right to know!'

He was walking away; she couldn't bear it.

'Oliver you can't do this!' she shrieked. 'I fucking made you! I've supported you our whole life—'

'Supported me?' He strode back to stand over her, 'Supported me how? Supported me emotionally? Supported me with the kids? With my family? My job?

You're never here! I'm just a fucking accessory to you, a convenience. I've tried Kate, I swear it…' He stepped away now and looked close to tears himself, pulling his hands through his hair. 'I just don't love you any more, I'm sorry.'

Somehow those words hurt the most; when had she last considered whether she was in love with Oliver? And now he was leaving, picking up a case and opening the front door.

'Wait!' She clambered to her feet. 'What about Lucy? It's the Easter holidays next week and I have to be in London on Wednesday morning.'

For a moment he looked at her in disbelief then he shook his head and sneered, 'You'll have to work it out then, won't you?'

He made two more trips to the car and back whilst Kate stood mutely watching, her mind filled with blank buzzing, her ears ringing. Then he was gone.

***

Trance-like, she climbed the stairs, walked across the hall and into their bedroom, her bedroom really, in recent years, Oliver spent so much time in the spare room. She couldn't remember the last time they'd made love, less than a handful of times since the termination. She'd never really got over that, given herself time to grieve. Had Oliver been having an affair back then? She worked out the timings in her head… yes, he must have been. Fury rose up in her like lava, no wonder he'd been so adamant he didn't want to keep the baby. The whole time he had another life in Birmingham. God, she'd been so stupid. There were times, if she were honest, that she'd wondered whether there might be someone else, but she'd squashed the idea down, it was too huge to contemplate, too inconvenient. Like so many other things, she'd chosen not to think about it or look too closely. And now he'd left her.

She still couldn't comprehend it. A broken marriage, *divorce*, it just didn't fit. Her whole life had been about doing things properly, doing them the way her mother had failed to do and now the whole thing was coming undone. She was out of tears. She gazed around the room. It had everything she'd wanted, faded now and unappreciated, it felt empty and fake.

She walked down the hall to Jack's room, the door was closed. She knew he'd be furious to think she was in there, but she turned the handle and looked in. It smelt stale, like something rotting, *like my life,* she found herself thinking. She stepped inside and sat on the bed, picking up a pillow and putting it to her face, the scent both beautiful and revolting to her. He still had a wedding photo on the windowsill, Oliver looking strong and handsome, she glowing with happiness, her hand closed tightly around a six-year-old Jack's, who was smiling stoutly at the camera, his face alight with pride. When did it go so wrong?

She padded out to the hall and closed the door. She cast a brief look into Lucy's room, now it was painted magenta pink, at Lucy's request, and the walls were covered with mirrors, posters and silk flowers but Kate could remember as though it were yesterday, the pale lemon walls and floral curtains, a Moses basket on the floor and Annie writhing on the bed. She watched herself scoop Jack into her arms and hold him to her, feeling the rightness of it, the inevitability. She'd let herself believe this superstitious nonsense.

She took a deep breath and squared her shoulders; it was no good moping about. She needed to arrange childcare for Lucy and there was no way she was going to ask Jan after she and Oliver had been plotting against her. She couldn't bear the idea of telling her mother just yet and who knew, Oliver might come to his senses before long. She went downstairs and phoned Annie.

Eight

Annie was worried about Kate; she'd never seen her looking so tired or strung out. She invited her for supper or even just a cuppa, but Kate had refused. Finally, she suggested they walk down to the paddock to see Shiloh, at which point Kate's eyes had cleared for a moment but immediately clouded again and she made her excuses to leave. Annie had watched her disappear down the drive with a heavy heart. Now she and Lucy were in the kitchen, Lucy on the floor with Meg and Gus, getting covered in dried mud and dog hair, whilst Annie scrubbed the potatoes she'd just pulled from the garden.

'Your mum looks tired, Lucy, do you think she's okay?' Annie asked tactfully.

'Yeah, she's fine,' Lucy replied unconcerned. 'She's always like that. Stressed. Ah, I love this song!' She leapt to her feet and turned up the volume on the radio, and Meg scurried to her bed in alarm.

'Dance with me!' Lucy cried, putting her hands on Annie's hips and rocking her from side to side. Annie dried her hands, laughing.

'What about your dad?' Annie had to shout over the music as she held her hand aloft for Lucy to swirl beneath. 'Is he helping much?'

'Dad's got to work away,' Lucy said, doing a little shimmy. 'That's what Mum's all stressed out about.'

'You should be kinder to her, Lucy,' Annie said seriously, standing still for a moment. 'She tries really hard for you.'

'Yeah, well, she's never kind to me,' Lucy replied, taking Annie's hands, trying to get her dancing again then, seeing the look on Annie's face she relented. 'I know, I know, I'm only joking!'

'Come on,' Annie said, turning the radio down as Lucy pulled a face. 'We need to bring the donkeys in, Joel's going to trim their feet.' She went to the utility room and pulled on a pair of boots, Lucy in her wake.

'Joel's going to trim their feet?' Lucy asked, pulling on her wellies.

'Yes, Joel's a farrier as well as a blacksmith,' Annie explained as they crossed the yard. 'Jack and Jill don't wear shoes, but they still need their feet taken care of.'

'Jack and Jill?' Lucy jogged to keep up.

'The donkeys,'

'Yes... but... you have a donkey called Jack?' Lucy had stopped walking, a smirk appearing on her face.

'But you knew that, surely?'

Lucy was giggling. 'A donkey called Jack!'

'Yes, yes, I know,' Annie replied drily as she opened the gate. 'I didn't name them, they're rescues. Come on then.' She held the gate open for Lucy to come through.

'You have a donkey called Jack, that's hilarious!' Lucy crowed in delight as they walked down the paddock.

'I can't believe you didn't know that, Lucy,' Annie said, then clucked her tongue and shook a bucket to get the donkeys' attention.

'Oh, no, I would have remembered that,' Lucy said, really laughing now.

'Come on Jack! Jack!' she called, then doubled up in laughter all over again. Annie couldn't help smiling. 'Jack, hello Jack!' Lucy was saying as the little donkey came towards her. 'Hello Jack, aren't you pretty? What big ears you have, Jack!'

Jack nodded his head appreciatively, his big ears flopping back and forth until Lucy was in such a fit of giggles she could barely breathe. It was no good, Annie started laughing too. Jack continued to nod his head, his big ears flapping, delighted by the attention he was getting, then all of a sudden, he let out an enormous braying hee-haw. Lucy was beside herself; she fell to the ground, clutching her sides. Struggling to speak she managed, 'Sorry, Jack, what was that? I don't understand you!' Tears were streaming down her face as the little donkey looked at her perplexedly. Annie was doubled over, her insides aching from suppressed laughter.

'That,' Lucy finally managed to say as she struggled to her feet and picked up the overturned bucket, 'is the funniest thing I've ever heard.' It took several minutes more before they were able to stop laughing long enough to put headcollars on Jack and Jill and lead them back to the yard, occasionally dissolving into another a fit of giggles.

That night Joel came for supper and after Annie had cleared away the dishes they sat and played Uno, a favourite of Lucy's. Joel kept winning and Lucy insisted on playing until she won a round. Eventually, when Lucy could no longer hide her yawns, Annie insisted she go to bed.

'Oh, but I haven't won yet,' Lucy whined. 'One more game. Pleeease.' She made a begging gesture with her hands and pulled a funny face to make Annie laugh.

'Nope,' Annie said firmly, getting up from the table. 'If you want to ride in the morning then you need to get a good night's sleep; come on, off to bed.'

'We can play again tomorrow, Lulu,' Joel said, also standing up. 'You're at a meeting tomorrow night, right?' he added to Annie as he scooped up the remaining cards to put them away.

Annie smiled, touched that he'd remembered and was offering childcare, something she hadn't even considered, 'It's not a problem to miss this week—' she started to say but he cut her off.

'Not at all. You go; we'll be okay, won't we Lu?'

'Of course,' Lucy said, stifling a yawn. 'Is that an AA meeting?'

'It is,' Annie replied, pouring a glass of water. 'Come on, I'll bring this in for you.'

'Would you get drunk if you stopped going to meetings, Annie?' Lucy asked as she dropped her clothes on the floor and pulled her nightie over her head.

'Maybe not straight away,' Annie replied, picking the clothes up and throwing them on the chair. 'I'd probably go mad first,' she added, only half joking.

'But why?' Lucy climbed into bed.

'Well, for lots of reasons I suppose.' Annie put the water on the bedside table. 'Firstly, because it would mean I'd stopped caring about the new people coming to the meetings, who need people like me, who've been around a while, to help them stay sober, just like I did.' Annie leant over and tucked the covers in a little tighter. 'And it would mean that I was avoiding being around people who know me, who I have to be honest with about how I'm really feeling. I used to drink and take drugs to manage my emotions and now I have to do that in a different way, going to meetings is a big part of how I take care of my mental health.'

'But why? I mean, aren't you okay now? When did you last take drugs?'

'Fifteen years ago, this July.' Annie smiled at Lucy's shocked expression. 'But going to meetings and having a programme are how I've managed that, not just managed to stay clean but hopefully managed to become a nicer human being too. I don't believe people kill themselves with drugs and alcohol for the fun of it, they do it because they find living so difficult. Take the drugs away and they still find living difficult, that's why I need a 12-step programme. You can take the booze out of a fruitcake, but you're still left with a fruitcake.'

Lucy laughed at this then became serious almost at once. 'Is that why Jack finds life difficult?'

Annie's chest tightened painfully. 'Yes, that could be why Jack finds life difficult,' she managed.

'And do you think he'll start going to meetings like you and be happy again?'

'I hope so Lucy, I really do.' Annie feared she might cry so switched off the light. 'Now get some sleep, I'll see you in the morning.'

Joel had tidied the kitchen and was leaning against the sink. He had his boots on ready to leave, *always so undemanding and uncomplicated*, Annie sighed inwardly; he understood how she needed her space and would let him know if she felt otherwise. Annie went to him and folded into his strong arms, burying her face in his chest.

'You're so good with her,' he said, stroking her hair. 'Makes me wonder why you haven't had more kids.'

'Yes, I do think that sometimes, especially after days like today.'

'Why haven't you, do you think?' He pushed her gently away so he could look at her face.

Annie looked up at him with a sad smile. 'Jack,' she said simply. 'I had no right to have more children when we didn't have a relationship, and now, we do... well... now I think maybe he needs me more than ever.'

Nine

It was Saturday morning. Kate had stumbled into bed after midnight having been stuck in a tailback on the M25 for almost three hours. An hour from home she'd begun to worry that Jack might be there and what kind of mood he might be in. She rehearsed how she'd handle it so many times that she was trembling with anticipation when she pulled onto the drive, which was empty, as was the cold, dark house. Relief crashed against disappointment as she moved about, switching on lights, checking everything was in its place. No one had been here since she left on Tuesday. Lucy wasn't due back until the following Friday and as she poured a large glass of wine and took it to bed, she thought she'd never felt so lonely.

There was a brief moment of relief the next morning before the enormity of her situation crashed in on her. Oliver had left her, he really had, and with him Kate had lost Jan's childcare services because there was no way around it, she couldn't bear the idea of asking Jan for help now. What was she going to do? Perhaps she could ask her mother? It wasn't unheard of for Jacqui to have the children, but it would mean admitting that her marriage had failed, and she didn't think she could bear that either.

Saying it out loud somehow made it more real. She hoped that if she stuffed it down for long enough it might not have happened, or Oliver would get to Birmingham and realise he'd made a terrible mistake. Not once did she consider whether she was still happy in the marriage, whether it was what she wanted; she knew to her core that she needed this marriage to work, there just wasn't another way. But Oliver had left her.

She threw back the covers and swung her legs out of bed, trying to muster her usual determination to *pull her socks up and get on with it* as Jacqui would say, but the fight just wasn't there. Her body felt heavy, weighed down by fear and uncertainty; her mind was sluggish, without a single idea of what she should do next. *If in doubt, start with the washing up.* She smiled. This was something Jack had come out with during one of his *good* phases recently, apparently something Annie had said to him.

Where on earth was Jack? What was she going to do? Her heart gave a little flutter of panic as she headed downstairs in her pyjamas. Looking at the clock she was amazed to see it was already gone ten. Is this what would become of her in a house with no children, would she just go to pieces?

She threw last night's wine down the sink, she'd fallen asleep before drinking it, and put the glass in the dishwasher. *Does that count as washing up?* she thought, wryly. As she stood upright, she caught sight of someone crossing the driveway before they were hidden by the blackthorn tree. The doorbell rang. Who on earth was it on a Saturday morning? Could she open the door in her pyjamas? The doorbell rang again.

'Okay, I'm coming!' she yelled, crossing the hall and opening the door a crack. A policewoman was showing her badge and Kate opened the door a little wider.

'Mrs O'Shea?' the woman asked whilst the young policeman beside her smiled uncertainly.

Kate's first, stupid thought was that her Da had got into some kind of trouble.

'No,' she said irritably, starting to close the door. 'I'm Kate Harper-Jones, sorry.'

'Sorry, Mrs... Mrs Harper-Jones, could we have a moment?'

By this time Kate's clogged-up brain had remembered that Kevin died many years ago.

'Is this about Annie?' she asked crossly. 'My sister is Annie O'Shea.' Then she had a horrible thought. 'Is everything okay? My daughter, Lucy is staying there.' Her heart started pounding uncomfortably.

'Mrs Harper-Jones... Kate... is it okay if we come in?' This from the policeman.

Kate's head started spinning. Whatever this was, it was serious. Her whole body was trembling, she couldn't remember the last time she'd eaten anything.

'Yes, yes, of course, come in,' she heard herself saying in a strange voice, her mind racing. 'What's this about?' she managed as she led them into the lounge and perched on the edge of the sofa, wringing her hands in her lap.

The male officer stood back but the policewoman came and sat on the oversized footstool and leant in to look at Kate. Every second felt like an eternity as Kate searched her face for a sign of what was to come. 'Kate… can I call you Kate?' she asked.

Kate nodded mutely, her heart crashing against her collarbone.

'Kate, my name's Cathy.'

Just get on with it! Kate wanted to scream.

'We had a call this morning from a janitor who works on the quayside. Kate, I need to ask if you recognise any of these.' As if from nowhere she produced a clear bag containing several items: a faded green wallet with a white keyring attached, etched with the words *Just for Today,* a mobile phone with a cracked screen, a thick silver ring large enough to fit a man's thumb and a set of keys — a car key and several others. Without looking she knew that one of those keys would fit her front door and that the keyring, faded and old, would have a photo of a rollercoaster at Disneyworld,

Florida, a family with their hands in the air, laughing in delight, a dark-haired man, a blonde woman and a little boy with hair the colour of autumn bracken.

Kate found she couldn't breathe, her trembling hand floated above the objects.

'Jack,' she whispered. Her heart was doing something peculiar, beating ten times its usual speed then seeming to stop for several seconds. 'But what's happened?' Her mouth was dry, she could barely form the words. The policeman had taken a couple of steps closer. The walls were closing in.

'Kate, the janitor found Jack in the public toilets this morning,' the policewoman was saying from somewhere far away. 'We can't know for certain yet, but it appears Jack suffered a fatal drug overdose,'

The room swam. *No, no, no!* Kate was wailing in her head, then she realised the wailing was filling the room. The policewoman had leant forward and taken her hands, but she instinctively pulled away.

'No,' she said loudly and clearly as she stood up, swayed and sat back down again. 'I mean...' she felt faint, sick, crazy, like her mind was locked in a distant room whilst her body was moving and talking. 'Where did you find these things, could they—'

'They were found with him, Kate,'

This couldn't be, this couldn't be. Kate found she was shaking her head from side to side. She picked up the wallet and turned it over in her hands.

'Can I ask what relation Jack was to you, Kate?' the policeman was now asking.

'He's my son.' *Was.* Kate thought she was going to vomit and tried to push herself to her feet once more.

'Ah, so O'Shea's your maiden name?' he was asking.

'Yes… No…' Dreamlike she stood, teetering, the room swimming. 'But Jack's name isn't O'Shea, it's Harper-Jones, like me.' She was turning the wallet over in her hands; without thinking about it, she put it to her face, breathed it in, she wobbled dangerously again, and the policewoman leapt up and took her elbow.

'Right.' The policeman made a note. 'Because it says O'Shea on his driving licence; that's where we found this address.'

Kate looked at him dully, then her trembling hands were opening the wallet. There, sure enough was Jack's photo licence, she slipped it out of the plastic cover and looked at it. The photo was taken when he was seventeen. His hair was short, and his eyes looked bright even in this little black-and-white print. Kate looked at the name. Jack O'Shea. She stared at it blankly for several seconds, feeling nothing at all, she didn't have the capacity to feel anything more. This, then, was the final blow. The final rejection. She could hear the policewoman talking to her.

'Kate? We'll need to know for certain, for the coroner, I'm sorry.' And she looked it. 'And someone will need to come and formally identify the body.'

Kate swayed violently again, and the policewoman steered her back to the sofa.

'Kate, we're going to have to go back to the station; is there someone you can call before we leave?' The policeman was returning with a steaming mug. Vaguely Kate noticed an irritation that he'd gone into her kitchen without permission. She said nothing.

'Kate?'

'Yes! Yes!' she said crossly, feeling beleaguered all of a sudden. Who could she call? She was all alone. The tears came then. Great gasping sobs; she found she couldn't breathe and let out a strangled groan, clutching her throat and retching.

'I don't know what to do! I don't know what to do…' She had slid from the chair and was on all fours, not understanding how she'd got there or what she should do next. She felt the policewoman taking her shoulders and half lifting her back into the chair before looking with concern at her partner.

'I'll get your telephone, shall I Kate? Can you think of someone? A friend or neighbour?'

A friend. But Sally was in Majorca with her family. Memories of shared family holidays when Jack and Maisy were small stabbed at her mercilessly. She meekly took the phone from the officer and dialled Jan's number. She found she could barely speak let alone form the words she needed to say.

'Please come, the police are here, please come,' was all she could manage. Then with the desperate, clawing ache of a child needing its mother, she called Jacqui.

Jan arrived first and the police left shortly afterwards. Kate watched dazedly as Jan confirmed that somebody would be there to identify the body tomorrow, probably her son, she said, taking a card. As usual Kate marvelled at the little woman's strength and stoicism. Jan, now white-haired and leathery, reminded her of Granny O'Shea.

Jacqui arrived at lunchtime and insisted that Kate went to bed. Kate allowed herself to be chivvied upstairs and undressed like a little child. She didn't want Jacqui to leave her but found she couldn't ask her to stay. She nodded meekly when Jacqui said she would be up later and lay staring at the wall, thinking nothing for what felt like hours. She could hear Jan and Jacqui downstairs and tried to make out what they were saying. She heard a man's voice and for a crazy moment imagined it was Jack, her heart leaping painfully into her throat before she realised it was Oliver. Without thinking she threw herself out of bed and careened across the landing; he met her at the top of the stairs, and she fell into his arms. Her legs gave way, and they staggered a little as he held her up. She cried and cried, unable to think or form words, the pain making her incoherent. He held her, saying nothing for a long time, then, when she'd spent herself, he asked in his quiet, level way, 'Where's Lucy, Kate?'

Lucy. She'd forgotten about Lucy.

'She's staying at Annie's.' Kate peeled herself from Oliver's tee shirt, her face wet with snot and tears. She suddenly felt angry and defensive but in an exhausted, muted kind of way. For a moment it had been as though Oliver hadn't left her, but now she remembered, and recoiled from him.

'I had to work.' She pushed past him, stumbling downstairs and into the kitchen.

Jan and Jacqui were sat at the table talking quietly, they looked around when Kate entered. Both women's faces were strained, their eyes puffy from tears. Jacqui's mascara had run. She got up and opened her arms as Kate moved towards her like a sleepwalker.

'Mummy,' Kate sobbed, needing something, anything. Jacqui's arms felt like balm around her.

'I'm going to call Annie; we need to get Lucy home,' Oliver was saying over the little beeps of the telephone.

'No!' Kate wheeled around, suddenly furious. 'Get away from it! You're not part of this family any more. You left, remember?' She snatched the phone which was already ringing. It rang and rang... *trust Annie not to have an answerphone,* Kate was thinking savagely, just as the call was answered. It was Lucy, she sounded breathless and overexcited.

'Lucy, it's Mum,' Kate cut across her sing-song voice. 'I need you to come home... please.' It took everything to keep from breaking down.

'Hey, Mum... what? No! I don't want to.' Lucy's voice changed immediately to a whine and Kate's rage flared.

'Lucy, I mean it. Something's happened. I can come and collect you or Annie can drop you off, but I need you here *now*!' She nearly dropped the phone from her trembling hand, she didn't think she could hold it together a moment longer. *Why couldn't Lucy just do as she was asked for once?*

'But why?' she was whining. 'What's happened? I want to stay here!'

Something inside Kate snapped.

'Stay there then!' she shrieked. 'Stay there forever you spoiled little witch! I don't care anyway!'

She'd been gripping the worktop but now she slid to the floor; Oliver was trying to take the phone, but she wouldn't relinquish it.

'Get off! Get off me!' she screamed, flailing her arms.

'Hello? Hello? Kate?' Annie's voice was coming from the phone. It was too much.

'You!' she shrieked, her voice cracking, 'You! This is your fault! Ever since you came back around! You were supposed to help him!'

'Kate? Kate are you okay? What's happened?'

She could hear Annie's bewildered tone and she wanted to reach down the phone and attack her; she wanted to hurt her, make her pay, make her suffer. 'You killed him! You've killed him. I hate you! It's all your fault!'

Finally, Oliver wrested the phone from her. She had no strength left, she curled in a ball by the kitchen cabinets, sobbing, refusing to be consoled, she could never be consoled. Nothing could ever be okay again.

Ten

When Annie looked back over the coming weeks and months, she wouldn't remember how she managed the drive to Kate's. Fixing her concern on Lucy, she somehow navigated the roads without a single thought entering her head. The girl sat silently in the passenger seat, trembling like a whippet and leapt from the car without a backward glance the moment Annie pulled up, leaving Annie to drop her few belongings on the doorstep and nod mutely to an ashen-faced, awkward-looking Oliver, who'd opened the door.

'I'm sorry Annie, Kate—'

'It's okay.' Annie headed him off; she didn't need him to explain that she wasn't welcome.

Without the safe delivery of Lucy as her objective Annie soon went to pieces, the torturous, razor-wired reality tearing relentlessly through her tender heart until she was no longer safe to drive. She swerved off the road at Bickleigh Mill and abandoned the car, stumbling blindly along the track towards the woodland and river. She didn't stop until she reached the shadowy canopy of trees where she sank down onto the dark, peaty earth, her head spinning, her heart too big for her chest, crashing against her ribs and obstructing her windpipe.

No, no, no. This couldn't be, this couldn't be. She clutched her knees to her chest and rocked back and forth. Reality felt too big, like her heart, expanding outwards from inside her, threatening to suffocate her, to obliterate her. She leapt up and crashed on toward the river; without thinking about what she was doing, she slid down the bank and waded out to the deeper, faster water. The river was still high from recent rains and the icy currents threatened to drag her under, but she needed something, anything to pierce her, to cut through, before she lost herself forever. The freezing water cut into her flesh like razor blades as it rushed past her thighs. She had no sense of time, just the burning cold.

Jack. Jack was... no, no, no! Her head swam. Birds were calling overhead; the sky was big, huge, disorienting. *Jack. Her Jack. Her baby boy.* She allowed the water to sweep her feet from beneath her and pull her under, *ice, fire, red, black.* Gasping, she struggled to stand and waded to the shore, trembling violently. *Jack was gone.* Jack was gone and she couldn't escape the thought any longer. It was her fault. She'd left him, abandoned him, somehow convincing herself she was doing the best for him. She'd failed him. *No, no, it wasn't like that! I was trying to do the best for him! Do the right thing, to protect him... but now... No...* even saying the word in her mind made the blackness creep into the corners of her vision as she struggled to hold on to her consciousness. *He was dead... and you couldn't get more messed up than that.* She'd done it all wrong and now it was too late. Kate was right, it was all her fault. She heard the words of an eight-year-old little boy: 'I know it's all your fault.'

I'm sorry Jack, I'm sorry! I was trying to make it right. I failed you. I failed you. The pain in her chest was unbearable; was she having a heart attack? How was her heart even beating?

She limped back across the field to the woods, the April sun unable to penetrate her frozen flesh. Her whole body burned. She felt acutely awake. The woods were full of bluebells and wild garlic and the ferns were the freshest, brightest green. She felt her soul had been skinned and the sounds and colours assaulted her. Never again would she walk in the woods with her beautiful autumn child. Finally, the tears came.

She drove home on the lanes, not trusting herself to navigate the main roads. Twice she pulled over, unable to drive, shaking violently from cold and grief. By the time she got back to the bungalow it was dusk. There was a light on in the kitchen. Joel must have let himself in. Relief swept over her, surprising her, as she realised she'd cut herself off from anyone who could help her, even the dogs who now ran to greet her and cover her in kisses, Meg barking crossly and giving her little nips, telling her off for worrying them with her unexplained absence.

Joel wrapped her in blankets and lit a fire, despite the warm evening. He'd been worried, he said, when there was no sign of anyone all afternoon and Annie wasn't answering her phone. He'd put the animals away and fed them but couldn't leave until he knew she was okay. Good, strong, gentle Joel. How she'd taken him for granted. He asked no questions until finally, tucked on the sofa with the dogs protecting her with their warm, lithe bodies she managed to say, 'Jack. Jack, he—' before looking at Joel helplessly and letting out a mewling, strangled wail which told him all he needed to know. He held her then, gently moving the dogs just enough to slip in beside her. He held her in his strong, unwavering grip saying nothing, asking nothing. They sat in silence for the longest time, the only noise the crackling of the fire as it burned low. Presently Joel steered her upstairs and put her to bed before taking a seat in the rocking chair where he sat vigil all night, and the next night and the next.

***

Weeks passed. Annie took care of herself the way she'd been taught. She went to a meeting every day, sometimes two, she journaled, she prayed, she meditated; she spoke endlessly with Sarah. She ricocheted, sometimes several times a day, from guilt and regret so painful that she wanted to peel off her skin, to relative tranquillity and acceptance that she'd done the very best she could, that torturing herself would help no one, then to more crushing guilt that she could possibly feel anything like okay ever again. The weather got warmer. She rode, she walked, she threw herself into work, into helping the people she could. She wept, she raged at whatever god there was; she prayed some more.

She worried about Kate and Lucy. She called the house several times, but nobody answered, and she hated the idea of being an unwanted nuisance, it reminded her too painfully of times gone by. She sent texts to both Kate and Lucy but heard nothing; it compacted her grief, her huge sense of loss, everything was ashes now. Eventually she called Jacqui to find out when and where the funeral would be held. Her mother was polite but terse, and she remained that way at the funeral a fortnight later. Annie understood and wasn't embittered by it.

The service was small and held at Exeter Crematorium, Kate was ensconced by Oliver's family and the families of Jack's childhood friends. Glued to her sides were Jacqui and Lucy; these were her pack, her tribe, just as they had been taught as children, there could be no mixing or even glancing at the enemy. Annie let it all wash over her, the deepest, densest sadness of a family still divided.

She longed to reach out to Lucy, to hold her, to speak with her, to support her. And Kate. For a short time, it had seemed that reconciliation was possible, by increments, yes, but a glimmer of hope no less. Now it seemed that hope had been snuffed out with Jack's golden light and Annie grieved the loss of her family all over again. Where was *her* tribe? She'd lost them all, her Da, her Granny and now her only son. Here she was alone, the last O'Shea.

Annie took a great shuddering breath and leant into Joel. This was her family now, Joel, Sarah and her other friends from the meetings who had all met Jack during the few times he'd attended. They wanted to be here with her today, supporting her. She was lucky and she knew it. She would heal, somehow, and she knew this too. She could choose to feel the loneliness, the apartness, that awful shame which washed over her as Kate openly ignored her and Oliver, Jacqui and Lucy looked awkwardly the other way, or she could choose to feel the love, the connectedness, the gratitude for this life, this second chance she'd been given, one which had been denied to her beautiful, enigmatic child.

Eleven

Kate was silent on the way home. The huge Mercedes limousine had delivered them to the funeral and back to the Devon Hotel for a small and sombre wake, but now she, Lucy, Jan and Jacqui were squashed into Oliver's Mini Cooper. She'd always thought it was the most ridiculous choice of vehicle. She felt utterly bereft. She couldn't remember the last time she'd eaten and this morning, when she'd applied make-up for the first time in six weeks, it took all her skill to disguise the blue-black rings beneath her eyes against her chalk-white face.

At least the funeral was over, and she could go back to bed; she didn't think she could bear to be around another person for a moment longer. It had taken weeks for the toxicology reports to tell them what the police already had, that Jack overdosed on heroin, deduced by the syringe still in his arm when he died. Kate hadn't bothered getting up to go to the inquest, there was nothing there which could help her.

Oliver kept casting covert glances in her direction. Someone, she thought her mother, reached forward and squeezed her shoulder. She cringed away from eyes and hands, pressing herself against the passenger-side door wishing she could dissolve into it, just disappear. Lucy needed her, she knew it but try as she might, she couldn't muster the old *get up and go* which had got her out of bed for the last decade. She was empty.

For the first time in her work history, she'd signed off sick indefinitely. Usually, she'd be going stir crazy by now but the heavy sedatives the doctor had prescribed kept her docile, now she barely had the motivation to drag herself to the bathroom. Today had been the first day she'd washed and dressed since she and Jan had identified Jack's body. *No, don't think about that.*

She glanced in the rear-view mirror. Lucy, sitting between her grandmothers, met her eyes then immediately looked down. Was she failing her, pushing her away? Probably. They had rowed again that morning. Lucy had wanted to call Annie, had even suggested that they all sit together. Kate had been furious.

'If you speak to that woman, if you even look at her, you will be a traitor to this family, do you understand me? *Do you understand?*' she'd shrieked, only just resisting the urge to take Lucy and shake her. She knew she sounded like her mother; at some level she suspected her behaviour was irrational, but she had to make Lucy understand. Annie was poisonous, dangerous, just like her Da had been. Jacqui had done the difficult thing, protecting them from Kevin, even if it cost her Annie's love. Kate was prepared to do the same; one day Lucy would realise, she would realise and thank her.

They were home. Kate found, now they were here, she didn't want to get out of the car. This wasn't home any more. Burned into her mind, like open sores, were the memories of the last time she saw Jack. Tussling with him, right here where she stood, as he thrust her handbag at her with hate in his eyes. The accusations he'd thrown at her, the lies… did he really believe those things? Did he die believing them? That she hadn't loved him, that she'd let him down? She swayed dangerously and felt someone grip her elbow. It was Oliver. She pulled away from him, stumbling towards the door and fumbled with her keys.

No, she couldn't bear to be in this house. Everything reminded her of Jack. This house was built on love for Jack. Her life was built on love for Jack. She had no tears left. She moved like a sleepwalker into the kitchen—no, she didn't want to be here, she turned to leave, to go upstairs but Oliver was in her path.

'What are you still doing here?' she spat, going instead to the fridge. 'Don't you have some whore waiting for you in Birmingham?' She stalked across the kitchen clutching a bottle of wine.

'Kate!' this from Jan. 'Just mind yourself in front of Lucy.'

So they were all going to gang up on her now, were they? She said nothing as she filled her glass.

'Why would I bother to make the effort now, Jan, I know you think I'm a terrible mother,' she said wearily, intending to go upstairs and leave them to it. Lucy was standing uncertainly in the doorway, blocking her path. Kate felt a momentary pang of guilt as she looked at her daughter's pale, tear-streaked face but she had nothing to give her.

'I'm sorry, Lulu, I have to go and lie down,' she managed.

'Well, that's just not good enough!'

Jan again; what did she want from her?

'Lucy needs you, Kate, don't you, love?' Lucy nodded feebly, looking six years old. 'We're your family Kate, we're all here for you, you don't need to do this alone.'

Kate wheeled around to stare at Jan. She looked from the little woman to her mother, to Oliver. She'd never felt more misunderstood or lonely and now they wanted more from her.

'No Jan,' she said in a calm, flat voice. 'You may be here for Oliver, you may be here for Lucy, you were here for Jack…' Her voice cracked slightly. 'But you've never been here for me, not really. You don't agree with me or my way of doing things. I've worked my arse off to provide for my family then turned myself inside out so I can be here every weekend, go to every parents' evening, every event, every holiday. I've driven through the night and the early hours. I've had to go through things... things you don't even know about and just keep going but it's never been good enough for you, because I don't do things your way...' Kate found her voice was rising. Lucy had gone to sit at the table, next to Oliver, he'd put his hand on her shoulder protectively and it made Kate want to attack him.

'And you,' she snarled. 'How you can be here pretending to your daughter that everything's okay, that you've just been working away—'

'No Kate.' Oliver cut her off. 'It was you who told her that; I would have told her the truth but then... this happened—'

'*This* happened? *This*? Is that what you call it Oliver? You deserted us, you left us. This family has been falling apart for years and is it surprising when you've been having an affair for three fucking years!' She slugged the rest of her wine down in one.

'Right, that's it, come on Lucy,' her mother now, striding across the room and putting her hand out to take Lucy's, to rescue her from the scene. It was too much for Kate.

'How can you do that?' She was crying now, bewildered, shaking her head. 'The arguments we saw as kids, all we knew was fighting, you and Da, you and Jeff, you and Annie. All screaming and rowing and hating each other and now you behave like you have to protect my child from me? *Me?* Come here, Lucy. I said *come here!*' she added forcefully, because Lucy was hesitating. 'Don't start behaving like some timid little wallflower!' Kate felt like she was going crazy. Why were they doing this to her? 'You were screaming in my face yesterday! You've been screaming in my face since the day you were born; why are you acting like this now? Lucy!'

But Lucy ignored her, instead she stood and buried her face in Oliver's chest. Kate felt something snap. The room was spinning, there was fire in her lungs, her whole body was buzzing; was she having a nervous breakdown? 'Why are you doing this to me?' She tore at her hair, sobbing, sliding down the kitchen cabinet to the floor. From the corner of her eye, she saw Oliver leave the room with Lucy; she heard Jan muttering something to her mother; she found she didn't care.

Then Jacqui was trying to lift her. 'Come on, up you get, up to bed.'

'That's all I wanted to do but Jan told me off.' She sounded like a child, felt like a child. She allowed Jacqui to steer her upstairs and put her to bed, opening her mouth so Jacqui could pop two Mogadon on her tongue before rolling over and waiting for the mixture of wine and sedative to take her away to dreamless sleep.

***

She woke up in the dark, the usual panic closing in, having fallen unconscious rather than fallen asleep. She clambered out of bed, still woozy, and padded out onto the landing. Silence. She had no idea of the time. She opened the door to the spare room, empty. She moved across to Lucy's room, also empty. She began to panic. Where was everybody? Had they left her? Was she still dreaming? She stumbled down the stairs, her heart thumping unevenly, and staggered into the kitchen. The room was in darkness save the light above the cooker. Was that someone at the table?

'Hello?'

'Kate?' It was her mother. 'Are you okay, darling?'

'Why are you sitting in the dark?' Kate asked crossly, flicking the light on. 'Where is everyone? What time is it?' She glanced at the clock: just after midnight. Panic began to bubble up inside her. 'Where's Lucy?' She turned for the living room.

'Kate? Kate, come in here and have a hot drink.' Her mother got up from the table, her face creased, as though she'd been sleeping with her head on her arms. 'Come on lovey, let me take care of you now.' She was moving forwards with her arms open, and Kate instinctively took a step back.

'Where's Lucy?' she asked again, her heart drumming a rhythm of its own.

'Now Kate, don't go overreacting again…' Her mother was acting strangely, as though she were frightened of her; why was everyone behaving as though she were a ticking bomb?

'Where's Oliver?' Kate asked breathlessly. 'Has he taken her? Has he taken Lucy?'

'Of course he hasn't, Kate. This is Oliver, he wouldn't do that.'

'Mum, have you been listening? Oliver's been cheating on me for three years! Has he taken her? When did they leave? Oh my God!'

'Kate calm down! He's taken her to Annie's! He's taken her to Annie's, and he's gone back to Birmingham. We all talked about it, and we thought… we thought it was best all round… for everyone.'

It was the strangest sight to watch her mother quail before her; Kate wondered if the fire she felt spreading through her body was actually visible.

'He took her to Annie's?' Her voice was icy. 'Are you fucking kidding me? Get out of my way!' She pushed her mother aside, nearly unbalancing the older woman, snatched her keys from the worktop and stormed to the front door. Her mother tried to stop her, reminding her harrowingly of her last moments with Jack.

'Get out of my way, Mum, or I swear I will make you!' Kate was trembling all over.

'Kate, you shouldn't drive,' Jacqui said but stepped away from the door. 'You're really not safe to drive.' But Kate was gone.

It started raining on the way to Annie's. There was very little traffic on the road, but Kate was aware, as the lights came towards her, that her vision was impaired; more than once she swerved towards the hedge, her tyre mounting the bank. She had no idea what she was going to do when she arrived, when she set off her mind was consumed by white-hot fury, at Oliver, Annie, her mother, everyone, but now that had dissipated, she was left with an empty, blank buzzing, like her system had overloaded and left her with nothing but white noise. She had the windscreen wipers on full blast and the monotonous pace was like an anchor, a meditation. She bumped along the drive and pulled up.

A light was still on in the kitchen. She had no plan, just to get Lucy home where she belonged. She left the engine running and went to hammer on the door. There was no porch and the rain gathering in the guttering was coming down in great sheets. Her hair was plastered to her face, in her eyes and mouth. She brushed it aside and banged again. She realised she was wearing her pyjamas, they clung to her otherwise naked body and she suddenly felt exposed and vulnerable. What was she doing here? She couldn't remember. Panic assailed her, the door opened, and she swayed, her heart hammering, her vision blurring. That was the last thing she remembered.

Twelve

'Kate? It's okay lovely, you're safe now.'

Someone was stroking her cheek. She was warm, hot, it felt like a tremendous weight was pressing down on her. She opened her eyes with a start. She was in bed; Annie's bed, in Annie's room, she knew by that obscure mobile hanging from the ceiling. The weight was what felt like a thousand blankets piled upon her. Fragments of memories fell like ashes, and she tried to sit up.

'No, no, stay where you are, honey. You've got yourself freezing cold and you bumped your head when you fell.' Annie again. Kate looked around her, there was nobody else in the room.

'Where's Lucy?' she asked, trying to sit up again but finding her strength had left with her fury.

'She's fast asleep; it's the middle of the night,' Annie said gently, tucking a lock of Kate's hair behind her ear. Kate wished she wouldn't. Memories were coming back thick and fast.

'My car, I left the engine running—'

'It's okay, Joel switched it off. You've got nothing to worry about, just rest, okay?'

Kate's heart was hammering again but her body felt like lead; the contrasting sensations felt unbearable, as though things were crawling all over her, but she was unable to shake them off. She took a deep, shuddery breath and looked about her again. Her mind felt as heavy as her body; was there something wrong with her? Perhaps it was the medication.

Finally, she said, 'How did you do it, Annie?' She watched Annie stiffen, thinking it was another assault so added, 'I mean *this*. How did you get from where you were to *this*? I honestly thought you were going to die. We all did.'

A part of her resisted, fearing she made herself vulnerable by admitting that *this* was something that interested her, but mostly she felt nothing, just a vague, flat sort of curiosity coupled with a strange desire to hurt herself, to rub salt into her own wounds. Annie was observing her, was that a pitying look? She bristled. 'Oh, don't worry about it.'

'Sorry, Kate, I was just thinking, that's all, I mean so much has happened…' Annie looked around the room as though searching for the answer. 'I suppose the first thing I had to do was stop,' she said simply.

This seemed like such an inadequate answer and Kate suspected that Annie was being deliberately evasive. 'Stop? You mean stop taking drugs?'

Annie gave a little laugh, 'Well yes, there was that. But mostly I mean just stop. I had to stop running, stop the momentum, stop all the strategies, all the ways I was running away and turn towards what I was running from. I had to be brave enough to feel.'

Kate just looked at her. None of this made sense and yet it made complete sense.

'I don't think I'd have done that if I hadn't burned my life to the ground,' Annie added with a sigh. 'If my particular flavour of running away had been less dramatic, less devastating, perhaps I'd have spent my whole life running but I had nowhere left to run. I'd destroyed it all. And, Kate, no one is sorrier about that than me but I've tried, I try to make amends. Jack—'

'I don't want to talk about Jack.' Kate cut her off and she meant it, she couldn't bear it. Not here, not now, with Annie. 'I think I'd like to go to sleep now.'

A shadow of sadness passed over Annie's face, but she didn't object. She stood.

'I've left you a jug of water. Kate?'

Kate nodded and Annie left.

***

Kate was surprised, when she woke much later, that she'd slept at all. It hadn't been her intention. She'd hoped that Annie would leave her so she could lie awake and wait for a more appropriate time to take Lucy and go. At some point in the night a dog — she thought it was Meg — had pushed its way into the room and was now lying at the end of the bed. She made a little beckoning sound and it scrambled up the covers for a scratch. There was no noise, no neighbours slamming car doors or passing buses. Fear lapped at her insides; she couldn't seem to form a single, coherent thought. Her mind felt like a washing machine of terrible ideas tumbling about.

She lurched upright, causing Meg to leap away, and crossed the room to pull back the curtains. It was fully daylight and for an instant there was a gap. For the briefest moment she looked out over the hills and there was nothing but green and blue and space, there was no fear, no sense of impending doom, before her life crowded in upon her once more. Her mother would be worried. She needed to get home. She needed to get Lucy home. She needed to get out of this place.

They were in the kitchen when Kate came downstairs and said they really must be leaving. Nobody tried to stop her. Even Lucy seemed calm and quiet, on the agreement that she could call Annie later. Kate found she couldn't quite look at Annie, there was just too much; too much to think about, too much to process, too much anger, too much blame, too much confusion. It was better not to look; whatever Annie said, some things were better off left alone.

She put their things in the boot of the car then called for Lucy to join her, so she didn't have to make any kind of goodbyes. She watched Lucy give Annie a brief hug before she ran to the car.

Kate looked at her as she buckled up. 'I'm sorry Lulu,' she said, meaning it to the depths of her being. 'I've got so many things wrong. It's going to be different now, I promise.'

Lucy burst into tears, and they hugged. Kate couldn't help hoping that Annie was watching.

'Come on, let's get home.'

Annie watched from the doorstep as Kate and Lucy spoke briefly in the car and then hugged. She felt a powerful mix of joy and longing as a part of her died. She would not have this, this was not for her, the unique, diamond-hard bond between mother and child. As Kate turned the car and pulled away and Lucy gave the smallest wave. Annie suspected, with a deep sadness, that she would not see or hear from either of them again and as the car disappeared from view, she opened her heart and let them go with love. Silent tears cascaded down her face, she did nothing to stop them as grief layered upon grief washed through her.

She looked about her, searching for solace in the beauty of her surroundings. There was nothing much here to catch her eye. One of the things which had drawn her to the bungalow was its seeming drabness from this approach, disguising its true beauty and potential when plumbed a little deeper. There was nothing to see here;

the long, pitted drive, the hedge, the rather untidy front garden, the corner of the chicken coop.

She turned to go inside but, as she did so, a movement caught the corner of her eye. It was a robin, pecking around the dirt in front of the chicken house, probably finding some spilled seed in the dust. Annie loved the robins with their cheeky, confident ways and she stopped to watch him at his work. They had a nest in the stable last year, and she wondered if perhaps this was one of the same family. She made a quiet clucking noise hoping to get its attention but not scare it away. The little bird hopped about to face her, and Annie's breath caught in her throat; his breast, usually the bright, fiery orange of the end-of-day sun, was the deep, rich auburn of autumn bracken.

'Jack,' she whispered, and the bird took flight.

Epilogue

Annie gave Shiloh his head and the big horse lengthened his stride to a gallop, carrying her effortlessly across the platinum-blonde stubble field. She drew him to a halt and paused to look down the hill. Gus and Meg were several yards behind them, older now and not so keen to race her home. Her heart swelled as her eyes drank up the valley. It was autumn, her favourite season; the hum of change was in the air, but it was not the heightened quiver of springtime, this was a mellower murmur: deeper, richer, denoted by the colours of amber, auburn and gold. She saw Jack in all of these.

Today would have been his twenty-fifth birthday. The years had worn the jagged edges of her grief as smooth as an Exe River pebble and though there were days when she couldn't accept, when she raged at the gods and blamed herself, mostly she was grateful for the brief but precious time they had shared, like a drop of purest gold. And she was grateful that his suffering was short.

'You burned too brightly for this world, my love,' she said to the hills then turned Shiloh for home.

The phone was ringing as she entered the bungalow and she ran through the kitchen with her boots on, cursing herself for leaving a trail of mud.

'Hello?'

'Annie? It's Kate. Annie?' For Annie had been silent for a heartbeat.

'Kate! Wow, hi.' Annie was thrown. She hadn't seen her sister since the morning after Jack's funeral and even the unexpected birthday and Christmas cards had dried up after a year or two. 'How... how are you?'

'I'm okay.' Kate's voice sounded soft, tentative, but warm. 'Today's difficult of course but it gets easier... somehow,'

Annie knew what she meant. It did get easier but alongside that was a strange kind of guilt that losing one's child could *ever* get easier.

'I know what you mean,' she said. 'I can't believe he would have been twenty-five today,'

'No.'

There was a long silence.

'How are you?' Kate said finally.

'Oh, you know, the same. A few more animals,'

More silence, then, 'I never said thank you.'

'Thank you for what?'

'That night, the night you looked after me when I came looking for Lucy.'

Again, Annie was thrown.

'Oh Kate. Crikey, what else would I do. How many times did you look after me—'

'Did I?'

'Did you what?'

'Did I look after you? Was I ever good to you?'

'Oh Kate, how can you ask that? Do you think I'd forget? You were always there for me... for Jack,'

'Not when you were younger... and not in the end.'

'Kate, where's all this coming from? We were kids before, kids who were taught to mistrust each other.'

'Do you believe that?'

'I do.'

'So, it's all Mum's fault then?'

'I didn't say that.'

'Well, no one else taught us... maybe Granny O'Shea.'

'Kate, everyone was just doing their best, Mum, Granny, they were doing the best they could with the tools they had for the job.'

'How can you be so okay about it?'

'I've done a lot of letting go...and I know I've made more than my fair share of mistakes.'

'Do you ever speak to Mum?'

'Sometimes.'

'She got married again.'

'I know.'

'I don't like him.'

'Oh.'

More silence.

'I left my job. Nearly three years ago now,'

Annie knew this; Lucy had told her in one of her rare text messages.

'Wow, that's great,' she said, then immediately regretted it. 'I mean, not great, but... what do you think about it?'

But Kate was laughing. 'It is great. It was killing me. It took a long time to let go of it. I went back part-time but it started creeping back in again. Like a drug I suppose. I started getting some counselling and it just became clear, you know, I had to stop. I had to stop running.'

Annie smiled to herself at Kate's reference to their last conversation, so many years before. *The seeds we sow,* she thought to herself. 'That's great Kate, I'm really happy for you.'

'We're organising a party for Lucy's eighteenth.'

Annie knew this also.

'I know Lucy would like you to be there; she wouldn't tell me that of course, she's thinks I'd do my nut... but... well, I'd like you to come... if you'd like to? I mean, no pressure of course, you might not want to—'

'I'd love to.'

Kate continued as though she hadn't heard. 'I realise it might be awkward but, well, Mum will be there, Lucy, of course, and her beau, Oliver's even coming with his wife... they have a little girl now... Lucy's sister... But—'

'Kate, I'd love to come,' Annie said again, a little louder.

'Oh. Oh good. Well, I'll let you know, okay? You can bring Joel... if you like.'

'Okay.'

'Good. That's good. And... maybe I could come and see you sometime, bring Lucy, she'd love to see Shiloh... if you still have him.'

'I do.'

'Well then, that settles it. I mean, we'll see you sometime.'

'I'd like that very much.'

'Goodbye then.'

'Bye Kate.'

Annie clutched the phone to her chest. All was quiet but for the tinny pounding of Joel's hammer somewhere far off, it seemed to match her heartbeat. Her throat was burning. Two big, fat tears had squeezed themselves painfully from the corners of her eyes. She wondered if this call had been as monumental for Kate as it had been for her. What had actually been said? Nothing really. And yet everything had changed, the world had shifted on its axis.

She looked up at the wall, to a photo of Jack., It was one of her favourites which she'd taken in the woods during a summer when he was tanned and happy, flecks of golden light shining in his sludge-green eyes. 'Did you do that?' She smiled up at him.

She had no idea how things would go; she'd learnt a long time ago not to let expectation get the better of her. What could it possibly take to heal the great chasm in her family? So much water had passed under an already shaky bridge. She thought of the years they'd hardened themselves to each other as teenagers, perhaps Kate had been thinking of these times too. She thought of the years as Jack grew up, the bitterness and mistrust. She thought of Jack's death, the blame, the hatred. Was there any coming back from that? And yet all of this, the pain, the fear, the loss, was theirs. Children, women, mothers, mourners, their suffering had been mutual, their journey was shared. Perhaps their shared suffering would prove to be the very thread that could draw them together and help them heal. Perhaps, after all, these would be the ties that bind.